"[A] TAUT THRILLER . . .
ANOTHER HOME RUN FOR CAROL GOODMAN . . .

The Seduction of Water combines folk tales and gothic horror with a thoroughly modern story. . . . Though this is the kind of book you'll stay up late reading, don't go so fast you miss the beautiful lyrical writing."
—*Burlington Free Press*

"The new novel more than redeems the promise of the first with a many-layered, subtle piece of fiction. . . . The reader steps into the story almost as one would step into a conversation with a good friend."
—*The Denver Post*

"Goodman's crisp, graceful writing keeps the reader engaged through the zigzagging plot. Lively and funny, Iris makes for a likable narrator. Throughout, the reader experiences pleasurable tension between wanting to find out what happens next and trying to savor the descriptions of place and people. . . . Fashioning one story from many, Goodman gives readers both an entertaining mystery and an intriguing glimpse into why we turn to stories in the first place."
—*The Boston Globe*

"Gripping . . . Entrancing . . . A completely involving mystery cleverly tied in with several fairy tales."
—*Booklist*

Please turn the page for more reviews . . .

"VERY INTRIGUING AND SATISFYING."
—*Charleston Post & Courier*

"Alluring . . . [An] atmospheric page-turner . . . Combining dark fairy-tale themes with a modern tale of suspense, Goodman succeeds in crafting another captivating mystery."
— *Pages* magazine

"With this exciting second book . . . Goodman establishes herself as a writer to watch in the field of literary thrillers."
— *Library Journal* (starred review)

"Mystery, folklore, a thoroughly modern romance, a strong sense of place, and a winning combination of erudition and accessibility make this second novel a treat."
— *Publishers Weekly*

"Goodman successfully plays along with the fairy-tale formula but translates it so successfully that the world she creates—and the people who inhabit it—are entirely believable."
— *Book Street USA*

BY CAROL GOODMAN

The Lake of Dead Languages

The Seduction of Water

CAROL GOODMAN

BALLANTINE BOOKS
NEW YORK

For my daughter, Maggie—
true princess of Tirra Glynn

Acknowledgments

I owe many thanks to my extraordinary agent, Loretta Barrett, whose faith and hard work have made writing this possible, and to my amazing editor, Linda Marrow, whose insight and humor have made writing it a pleasure. Thanks too to Nick Mullendore at Loretta Barrett Books for always explaining everything and to all the people at Ballantine who have made a home for me there: Gina Centrello, Kim Hovey, Gilly Hailparn, and Kathleen Spinelli.

I'm lucky to have a circle of friends and family willing to read and comment on first drafts. Thanks to Barbara Barak, Laurie Bower, Gary Feinberg, Emily Frank, Wendy Rossi Gold, Marge Goodman, Robert Goodman, Lisa Levine-Bernstein, Mindy Ohringer, Scott Silverman, Nora Slonimsky, and Sondra Browning Witt.

Thanks to Mary Louise Morgan for showing me St. Vincent's Home for Boys and to Ed Bernstein for rescuing the manuscript.

Most of all, thanks to my husband, Lee Slonimsky, for his constant encouragement, inspiration, and love. You are my muse.

The Seduction of Water

PART I

The Broken Pearl

Chapter One

My favorite story when I was small, the one I begged for night after night, was "The Selkie."

"That old story," my mother would say. She'd say it in exactly the same tone of voice as when my father complimented her dress. *Oh, this old thing,* she'd say, her pale green eyes giving away her pleasure. "Wouldn't you rather something new?" And she'd hold up a shiny book my aunt Sophie, my father's sister, had bought for me. *The Bobbsey Twins* or, when I was older, *Nancy Drew.* American stories with an improving message and plucky, intrepid heroines.

"No, I want your story," I would say. It was her story because she knew it by heart, had heard it from her mother, who had heard it from hers . . . a line of mothers and daughters that I imagined like the images I had seen when I stood by her side in front of the mirrors in the lobby.

"Well, if it will help you sleep . . ."

And I would nod, burrowing deeper into the blankets. It was one of the few requests I stuck to, perhaps because my mother's initial hesitation came to be part of the ritual—part of the telling. A game we played because I knew she liked that I wanted her story, not some store-bought one. Even when she was dressed to go out and she had only come up to say a quick good night she would sit down on the edge of my bed and shrug her coat off her shoulders so that its black fur collar settled down around her waist and I would nestle into its dark, perfumed plush, and she, getting ready to tell her story, would touch the long strands of pearls at her neck, the beads making a soft clicking sound, and close her eyes. I imagined that she closed her eyes because the story was somewhere inside her, on an invisible scroll unfurling behind her eyelids from which she read night after night, every word the same as the night before.

"In a time before the rivers were drowned by the sea, in a land between the sun and the moon . . ."

Here she would open her eyes and touch the knobs of my headboard, which had been carved into the shapes of a crescent moon and a sun by Joseph, the hotel gardener, to replace its original broken knobs. We used the bedding and furniture too worn-out for guest use—blankets with hems coming unstitched, dressers with rattling drawers, and tables with ring marks where careless city ladies had put down hot teacups without a saucer. The rooms we lived in were leftovers themselves, the attic rooms where the maids lived before the new servants' quarters were built in the North Wing. It's where my mother had stayed when she'd come to the hotel to work as a maid. Even after she'd married my father, the hotel manager, she told him she liked being up high. From the attic rooms you had the best view of the river flowing south toward New York City and then to the sea.

"In this land, where our people came from, the fishermen told a story about a man who fell in love with one of the seal women, selkies the people called them, seals that once a year could shed their skin and become women . . ."

"So were they women pretending to be seals or seals pretending to be women?"

This interruption my mother would take in stride because I always asked the same question and she had incorporated the answer into the story.

". . . and no one ever knew which they had been first, seal or woman, which is part of their mystery. When you looked into the seal's eyes you could see the human being looking out, but when you heard the woman singing you could hear the sound of the sea in her voice."

Still unsatisfied as to whether the selkies were mainly seal or human, I would indicate to my mother that I was ready for her to go on by burrowing deeper into the covers and closing my eyes. I knew my mother had some-place to be and the story could detain her only so long. If she didn't think I was falling asleep, I risked losing the story altogether.

". . . and so it happened that on that one day a farmer went down to the sea . . ."

"Did he go to collect seashells for his garden paths?" I would ask. "The way Joseph said they did in France." Joseph had worked at all the finest ho-tels in Europe after the war. On his right forearm, just visible when he rolled up the cuffs of his faded blue workshirts, were faint numbers, the same color as the shirts he wore.

"Yes, a path of seashells sounds nice," she would say, smiling. She liked it when I thought up new details for her stories. "He wanted the path to his house to glow in the moonlight like broken pearls. That's what he was thinking about when he looked up and saw, sunning herself on a rock, a girl with skin like crushed pearls and hair as dark as coal."

Black hair. Like my mother. Like me. Recently, I found my mother's old book of Irish folktales that contained "The Selkie." The selkie in it is blond. My mother must have decided to make the heroine of her story dark-haired like us.

"The dark-haired girl with pearl skin sang like something you might hear in a dream, sweeter than anything you'd hear in a theater or Carnegie Hall even . . ." Here, if I peeked, I'd see that my mother, her eyes still closed, wore the expression of someone listening to music. She'd be quiet for a moment and for once I wouldn't fill the silence with a question be-cause, I thought, if I listened carefully enough I would hear what she heard too. All I did hear, though, were the muffled footsteps and hushed whispers of the night maids and the groan of the old elevator taking late diners back up to their rooms. If there was singing it would be one of the retired music teachers who rented attic rooms for the summer. As soon as my mother opened her eyes I'd snap mine shut.

". . . and so the farmer fell in love with the dark-haired girl and de-cided he wanted her for a wife, but when he tried to get closer to the rock where she sat, she heard him and dived into the water. The farmer stood on the shore watching for the girl, sure that she couldn't stay in the water for long. Then he saw, out beyond the breakers, a sleek dark head appear. But she wasn't a girl anymore, she was a—"

"Seal!" I would say, forgetting in my excitement to make my voice sound sleepy.

"Yes. The farmer stood for a long time looking at the ocean thinking over what he had seen, or what he thought he had seen, but at last he remembered he had cows to milk and chickens to feed and so he turned his back to the ocean and went on home."

"But he couldn't forget the dark-haired girl and her beautiful voice."

"No. He couldn't. Could you?"

My mother always asked me the same question, but no matter how many times she asked it, I was always unprepared. Not that I doubted that I too, like the farmer, would have been smitten by the dark-haired singer; but there was something in the way my mother asked the question that made me think I should answer differently, that I should have been able to resist the selkie's song. After all, look what happened to that poor farmer . . .

He was so lovesick for the selkie girl that he was unable to sleep and the sound of the ocean, which he'd heard since the day he was born, began to grate on his nerves. It seemed there was always sand in his bed no matter how many times he'd shake out his sheets and even with all the windows open he'd feel as if he were suffocating inside his cottage.

(I could always hear, in this part of the story, an edge in my mother's voice. When I was little I thought it had to do with the sand in the sheets. My mother had been a hotel maid, after all, and she would often tell me how rude it was when guests left cracker crumbs or *worse* in their beds. But later I guessed the edge in her voice had more to do with her own trouble sleeping.)

Things went on like this until the farmer began to neglect his fields. His cows went unmilked and his hens wandered into his neighbors' yards looking for food. In desperation, he sought out the help of an old wise woman who lived in a cottage on a cliff above the sea. The minute she laid eyes on the farmer she knew by his shrunken pupils and the way his ribs stood out under his threadbare shirt like the hull of a staved-in boat, and how his hair was tangled like a mass of seaweed, what his problem was.

"How long has it been since you saw the selkie?" she asked him, sitting him down by the fire and giving him a cup of bitter-tasting tea.

"It'll be a year tomorrow," he told her, "to the day. I remember because it was the first day of spring."

The old woman smiled. "As if you needed that to remember," she scolded, but she didn't tell him to forget the selkie. Instead she told him to finish his tea, which would make him sleep through the night. "Then tomorrow, go back to the rock where you saw her. You must swim out to the rock, being careful she doesn't hear you. By her side you'll see a rolled-up skin that you must snatch away from her. Once you have her skin she'll have no choice but to follow you home."

"And she'll stay and be my wife?"

"She'll stay and be your wife."

"And bear my children?"

"She will bear your children."

"And she might, one day, grow to love me?"

The old woman shrugged, but whether to say she didn't know or that he asked too much, the farmer never knew. Already the tea was dragging his eyelids down and making his arms and legs heavy. He staggered from the old woman's hut and only made it home because it was all downhill from where she lived to his front door. He didn't even bother finding his bed but fell asleep on a rug in front of the fire.

When he awoke he saw by the angle of the light coming through the window that he'd nearly overslept the day—he felt as if he'd been asleep for a year—but then he heard above the roar of the ocean a voice singing. Her voice.

He ran toward the sea, remembering at the last minute to creep quietly down to the edge and slip into the water making as little noise as possible. Fortunately, the slap of the waves of the encroaching tide masked his clumsy thrashing in the water as he approached the rock. He saw the dark-haired girl and there beside her a bundle—her skin—sleek and shiny in the light of the setting sun, like a coal burning slowly from within. As soon as he laid his hand on the skin the dark-haired girl turned and gave him a look that froze his blood. Her eyes, fringed by coal-dark lashes, were the pale green of sea foam. He opened his mouth and swallowed so much sea-water he would have sunk to the bottom of the ocean right then if he hadn't clutched the skin to his chest. It acted like a life preserver; it was that buoyant. He turned and swam back to shore trying to forget the look the girl had given him. She'd change her mind about him, he thought, once she got used to him.

It was harder getting to shore than he'd figured. A sudden wind had risen that whipped the waves into a frenzy. Although the skin kept him afloat it also seemed to be pulling him out to sea. The current that wrapped around his legs seemed to have muscle to it, like a giant eel squeezing the life breath out of him. By the time he dragged himself out onto the sand, he was too weak to stand. He'd imagined himself holding the skin up before the girl like a proud conqueror, but instead he clutched the soft fur to his face like a baby mouthing his blanket for comfort. The skin still felt warm to the touch—as if it had absorbed the sun into its very fiber. When he looked up he saw the dark-haired girl sitting a few feet above him where the sand rose to a crest above the shoreline. Her knees were drawn up to her chest and her long hair fell around her legs like a curtain to hide her nakedness. Her sea-green eyes watched him impassively. Waiting to see if I'm drowned or not, he thought. When she saw that he wasn't dead, she got up and walked away from the ocean toward his house. It was he, after all, who followed her home.

At this point in the story my mother would pause to see if I was asleep yet. I had to gauge my reaction carefully. If I seemed too awake she'd decide the story wasn't working and tell me sternly to go to sleep. If she believed I was almost asleep she'd slip out without a word, turning the light off and closing the door behind her. Then I'd be left in the dark with the unfinished story churning in my brain, keeping me awake just as the selkie's song had kept the farmer awake. It was that feeling you get when you put down an unfinished sandwich and you forget where you've put it; you keep hungering for that last bite. I would be alone in the dark, the sounds of the hotel slowly winding down like a music box playing out. I knew my mother shared that same horror of sleeplessness and if I asked, in just the right sleepy voice, for just a little more she would sigh and pull the fur-trimmed coat a little tighter around her arms, as if she were cold, and go on . . .

For a time things seemed all right with the farmer and his selkie bride. She bore him five children: a girl first, and then four sons, all with dark hair and pale green eyes. She learned to cook and clean and tend the farmer's animals and garden. Everything she touched became beautiful. She hung shells and pieces of sea glass in the windows in such a way that they made music when the wind blew. Her voice could calm a mare in foal and coax the sheep to stand still for shearing.

The only thing she couldn't learn to do was to knit or tat lace or mend the fishing nets. No matter how hard the village women tried to teach her she couldn't make a single knot. She couldn't even learn to braid her daughter's hair or tie the ribbon on her own dress. In fact, the women noticed that when she came into the knitting circle they all dropped their stitches and the sweaters they were working on unraveled at the hems. Soon the women made up errands to send her on to keep her out of the circle and since the knitting circle was the time the women shared their stories and gossip she was, in the course of things, excluded.

She didn't seem to mind.

She could be heard singing to herself over her chores. Her singing was so beautiful that strangers would stand on the road to listen to her. Sometimes, though, the songs would grow so sad that people in the village would find themselves weeping for no reason and they would be unable to sleep at night. This was especially true on two days of the year: the vernal and the autumnal equinox. On those days her song—and it seemed indeed to be one song, which she started at the break of day and left off only when the sun had sunk into the sea—was so achingly sad no one was able to get any work done at all. Porridge was burned, fishing nets were lost, thumbs were hammered, cheese spoiled, ink spilled, and sweaters unraveled into heaps of greasy wool.

After a few years of this the villagers asked the farmer to prohibit his wife from singing on those days.

"I might as well ask the earth not to turn," he told them. "For spring not to follow winter and winter not to follow fall."

This is the answer he gave year after year, but when their oldest child was ten years old, he grew tired of the looks the women gave him and the things the men said behind his back about not knowing how to control his womenfolk.

"It's for your own good," he told his wife. "Your singing only makes you sadder. And then you don't sleep. Think about the children. Do you want them infected with your sadness?"

The look she gave him then was the same look she gave him from the rock that day he took her skin from her. He hadn't seen that look from her since and when he did it was as if his mouth filled up with seawater and he felt himself sinking. But she did as he said and never said a word. On that first day of spring she stayed inside the house and never so much as opened her mouth. She took the chimes from the windows and closed the flue in the chimney so she couldn't hear the wind whistling through it. She scolded her daughter for chanting a rhyme while skipping rope. She'd never scolded her for anything before.

The day after the equinox the farmer thought that things would go back to normal, but they didn't. She went about her chores like a thing made of stone. She made the porridge, but she burned it. The animals shied away at her touch. When she looked at her children it was as if she were looking through clear water.

Things went on like this through the summer. The farmer hoped at first that she would change, but when she didn't he hardened his heart against her. It was the girl who followed her mother when she left the house at night. She'd find her mother curled in a ball between the cows in the barn or wedged between the rocks on the shore, trying to find a place where she could cheat the sleeplessness that seemed to be always upon her now. As the nights grew cooler she saw her mother shivering in her thin night-dress out in the open and she thought that if things went on like this her mother would freeze to death.

It was a night in September—the night before the autumnal equinox—that the temperature, as if in anticipation of the planet's tilt away from the sun, dropped so low that the girl could see her mother's breath turn into ice on the rocks around her. The heavy mist from the sea was turning to crystals in her mother's hair, so heavy that she could hear the strands chiming in the cold sea breeze. If she didn't do something her mother would be frozen solid by the morning.

She ran back to the house and opened the blanket chest but the farmer had already heaped the extra quilts on his sons' beds. Her hands scraped against the bottom of the trunk, scrabbling over the rough wood until her fingers bled from the splinters. She dug her nails into the wood just to feel the pain and then, to her surprise, the bottom pried loose and her hands sunk into something warm and silky soft.

She thought it was something alive.

Even when she lifted the heavy fur up and saw that it was an animal skin she still couldn't believe it was a dead thing. The skin pulsed with warmth and glowed like a burning coal. She held it to her cheek and smelled the ocean in it. She heard the ocean in it trapped in each bristling hair, the way a shell holds the sound of the ocean deep in its whorls.

She wrapped the fur around her shoulders and ran to where her mother lay between the rocks above the beach. Instead of weighing her down, the shawl of fur seemed to float on the wind behind her back and buoy up her steps.

When she found her mother she thought she was too late, that her mother had already frozen to death. A fog was rolling in from the sea and as it touched her mother's skin it froze in a fine skein of ice so that her mother seemed to be caught in a net strung out of crystal beads. But then she noticed that her mother's breath was crystallizing too and she knew her mother was still alive. She lay the fur over her mother and crawled in under it, wedging herself between her mother and the rocks. Instantly she felt her mother's skin grow warm; the net of ice melted and soaked into the soft, heavy fur.

The mother and daughter slept together on the beach beneath the cloak of fur, but even as they slept, the girl could feel her mother's fingers in her hair, stroking away her fear.

I sometimes fell asleep at this point too. There was a corner of my blanket that had unraveled and then matted back together like a piece of

wool that's been felted. After my mother had gone, I liked to tuck this under my cheek and pretend it was the selkie's skin or the fur collar of my
mother's coat, the one she wore if she was going someplace special: a party
the local college was throwing for her, dinner with her editor across the
river in Rhinebeck, or a reading in the city. These things still happened
even though it had been years since she'd published her last book and the
books she had written—the two of them—sold fewer and fewer copies until
finally they went out of print.

Still my mother had her fans. She'd written two books in a trilogy
about a fantasy world called Tirra Glynn. The first book, written five years
before I was born, was called *The Broken Pearl*. The second book, written
while she was pregnant with me (she always told me that she'd conceived
both me and the idea for that book at the same time and that we both took
exactly nine months to bring forth), was called *The Net of Tears*. No one
ever knew what the third book would have been called because it never appeared. I remember that it was around the time of my sixth birthday that
my first-grade teacher asked me if I ever saw my mother writing. When I re-
layed that conversation to my mother she had me pulled out of the public
school and put into a private school in Poughkeepsie. Two years later I was
put back into the public school. Sales from my mother's books had dropped
precipitously. Who wanted to read the first two books in a trilogy if there
wasn't going to be a third book?

Also the hotel had fallen on hard times. It was the 1960s and Americans had discovered air travel and Europe. One by one the big hotels to the
south and west of us went out of business. If it hadn't been for a core of
faithful clientele—the families whose grandparents had stayed at the Hotel
Equinox and the painters who came to paint the view—we would have
closed as well. Who wanted to drive three hours to a resort to swim in an
ice-cold lake? The Hotel Equinox, perched on a ledge above the Hudson,
was too out-of-the-way and too old-fashioned and then, when my mother
left, just too sad.

She left for good when I was ten. She'd been invited to sit on a panel
of women science fiction and fantasy writers at a two-day conference at

NYU. She was supposed to leave for the city in the morning, but because she couldn't sleep she asked Joseph to drive her across the river to catch the night train. I heard her arguing with my father in the hall outside my room. "But where will you stay?" he asked. "Your reservation isn't until tomorrow."

"They're bound to have a room for the night," she told him, her voice light with laughter. I imagined her putting a hand on his forehead and stroking his hair back, something she always did to allay my fears. "You worry too much, Ben. I'll be fine."

Then she came into my room to kiss me good night and I pressed my face into the dark plushy fur of her coat collar. Her coat was buttoned to her throat and she didn't undo it or let it settle down around her waist as she usually did when she was going to tell me a story.

"Tell me the selkie story," I asked. She pressed her hand against my forehead, as if checking for fever, and brushed my hair away from my face, combing the tangles out with her fingers. I waited to hear her reply, *That old thing?* But instead she said, "Not tonight." She told me to close my eyes and go to sleep and when I had kept my eyes closed for several minutes I heard the clicking of the pearls around her neck falling against the buttons of her coat as she leaned forward and kissed me good night. And then she was gone.

When she got to New York she did not check into the Algonquin where her editor had made reservations for her even though we found out later that they did have rooms available for that night. My mother never went there at all. Instead she checked into the Dreamland Hotel—a run-down hotel in Coney Island near the site of the old Dreamland amusement park. It was the last weekend in September 1973, the weekend that the Dreamland burned to the ground. It was weeks before we knew for sure what had happened to my mother because she hadn't registered under her married name, Kay Greenfeder, or her pen name, K. R. LaFleur, or even her maiden name, Katherine Morrissey. She, and the man she was with, were registered under the names Mr. and Mrs. John McGlynn. The investigating officer who saw the registration guessed who it was because his wife was a fan of my mother's who had read that she was missing and she recognized the name McGlynn because my mother had named her fantasy world Tirra Glynn.

He'd come all the way from the city to show my father a charm bracelet, which my father identified as the gift he and I had given her for Christmas the previous year. They met in the library and I hid in the courtyard outside the library windows and listened to what was said. My father asked him if they had identified the man she was with, but the officer said they hadn't found the man's body. That my mother had died alone.

For years after I could only fall asleep listening to the story of the selkie girl. I would ask my aunt Sophie, who took care of me after my mother left, to tell me the story.

"That old thing?" she would say, using the same words my mother had, but meaning something else entirely, "That morbid story?" She said *morbid* the way she said *dirty* when I was little and tried to eat a treat that had fallen to the floor or a pastry left on the rim of a saucer by one of the hotel guests. Morbid thoughts were what I had when I wasn't attending to my chores or going to bed promptly so she could attend to hers. Morbid was what my mother had been before she went away. But like my mother, my aunt could be convinced to tell me the story if she thought it would put me to sleep. I would fold the felted nap of the blanket against my cheek and imagine it was the fur collar of my mother's coat and I would imagine my mother's hands stroking my hair, just as the selkie's daughter could feel her mother's hands in her hair even as she slept. My aunt could tell the story word for word because, as I knew by then, it was the first chapter in my mother's book, *The Broken Pearl*, but if I squeezed my eyes tight enough I still heard the story in my mother's voice.

"**In the morning,** when the selkie's daughter awoke she was alone on the beach. She'd heard her mother's voice in her sleep thanking her for returning her skin. 'Now I can go back to the sea where I belong and where I have five selkie children, just as I have five human children on the land, whom you must watch over now. You mustn't weep for me but instead, whenever you miss me, come stand at the water's edge and listen for my voice in the surf. And on the first day of spring each year, and the last day of summer, you'll see me as you know me now, a woman in a woman's skin.'

"The girl went back to her father's house, determined to keep her promise to her mother even though every step she took away from the sea felt heavy, as if her feet were caught in a net that was dragging her out with the ebb tide. Even her hair, which had frozen in the night, seemed to drag her down. But still she went home and lit the stove and made the porridge and when her brothers awoke she explained to them that although their mother was gone, she would take care of them now, and that twice a year she would take them to see their mother again.

"It wasn't until later, when she still felt the weight of ice in her hair, that she looked in the mirror and saw her mother's parting gift. She remembered her mother's hands stroking her hair through the night. Her mother—who couldn't knit a stitch, or tat lace, or even tie a knot—had woven a wreath of sea foam frozen into bright stone: caught in its net, a single green tear the color of the sea."

My aunt would turn out the light, then, and straighten the covers and smooth my hair away from my face. I'd feel her dry lips brush my forehead and then I'd be alone in the dark, listening to the sounds of the old hotel settling. On a windy night the beams and floorboards would crack and pop like logs in a bonfire and I'd imagine that the hotel was on fire. But on a still night, if I listened closely enough, I thought I could just make out the sound of the river far below us. I would think about my mother following the river south that last night and I would imagine that the ocean at the end of the river had called to her—that she hadn't died in the fire at the Dreamland Hotel, but that instead she'd gone back to her other family under the sea—that it was only fair that they have their time with her now. I only had to wait and she would come back to me when their time was up.

Chapter Two

WRITING ASSIGNMENT #3

Write about your favorite fairy tale from your childhood. Retell the story, but also say who told you the story and what you thought about it then. What did you learn from the story? What did it tell you about the world you lived in?

I always try to model the writing assignments that I give to my students. So I wrote the piece about the selkie girl for my remedial composition students at Grace College. I thought it was pretty decent. The best thing I had written for a while.

I share the piece with my students when I give them the assignment. Of all the places I teach, Grace is where I'm most comfortable sharing personal material. Many of them are recent immigrants to this country. Some have been referred through Grace's prison work-release program. It's not just that their limited proficiency in English makes them less intimidating or that they are unlikely, given their unfamiliarity with the American university system, to treat me, an untenured, part-time adjunct, with less respect. In fact, sometimes their naïveté leads to embarrassing questions, such as, why don't I have an office? Or why isn't my mailbox alphabetized with the rest of my colleagues? No, if I'm willing to share more of my personal experiences with my students at Grace it's because it's part of my directive from the administration.

"You might be the most literate person they meet all day," my dean told me at the fifteen-minute interview at which I was hired. "Or at least, the most literate person willing to take the time to talk to them about something other than how to make little Ashley's lunch or how much starch to put in the Brooks Brothers button-downs. Engage them. Talk about where they come from—then have them write about things they care about."

Of course I was thrilled to receive such a humanitarian, caring dictate from the dean of English. It wasn't until I realized that my students' final essays would be graded by a panel of tenured professors—and that nine out of ten would fail—that I began to question this charitable approach to teaching.

"I thought I was doing so well in your class," Amelie, a twenty-nine-year-old nanny from Jamaica who was trying to earn enough money to bring her own children to New York, said to me. She held up a bluebook dripping with red ink, a huge D scrawled across the top page.

I learned quickly that I was doing my students a disservice by not making them write every class, and not correcting every run-on sentence and fragment. Even then, half of them would fail to pass through the reading committee's gauntlet. Sometimes, I wondered if my own written work would survive their firing line.

Still, I try to find assignments that will interest them. I liked the fairy-tale idea because of its multicultural value, because the language of fairy tales is usually simple, and because I've always loved fairy tales. I chose them for my dissertation topic. I was raised on them. My mother could always be lured away from her desk by a request for a story. Later, when I was old enough to read her books, I realized that she had woven fairy tales into them. Maybe she was still looking for new fairy tales to incorporate into the third book that she never finished. It would have been good research—reading to me from the Grimms or Andersen. I learned early with my mother that if something could be connected to her writing she'd be more likely to go along with it. A walk to the falls would be welcome if I presented it as a quest to an enchanted locale. She must have started it—this idea that the woods around the hotel were inhabited by spirits of wood and water, that each spring and tree had its resident naiad—but I became adept at finding and identifying the nooks and crannies where magic hid. Where cobwebs grew over the violets in spring were fairy tents, the crevices in rocks embroidered with velvety moss were fairy quilts. My mother had named each rock and spring: Half Moon, Castle, Evening Star, Sunset, and Two Moons. Later Joseph built gazebos—or *chuppas* as he called them—on these spots, following my mother's ideas for their design. Sometimes I think that if she had spent less time pouring her creative energies into her surroundings and more time writing maybe she would have finished that third book.

"So your mother was a writer too?" asks Mr. Nagamora, an elderly Japanese man who works as a tailor in a local dry-cleaning store. "So you follow in her footsteps?" I didn't remember telling this class that I was a writer. Maybe they thought all English teachers were closet novelists.

"Well, my mother wrote fantasy novels," I tell Mr. Nagamora. "I tend to write more realistic fiction."

"Can we read your books in class?" Mrs. Rivera, who rides the Long Island Rail Road in every night after caring for three children in Great Neck, asks.

This is why I promised myself I wouldn't tell my students that I was a writer.

Because if there's anything harder than explaining why I'm not a real professor, not Dr. Greenfeder, but Iris Greenfeder ABD (and then explaining what "all but dissertation" means), it's explaining that there are no books. Some magazines, I am always quick to point out, hating my own fawning wish to impress this group of recent immigrants and paroled prisoners, but no, not ones you could actually find on a newsstand. And truthfully, even if they could find the little magazines and pale saddle-bound literary journals that have published my poems and stories, I'm not sure I'd want my students to read them. Just imagine Mr. Nagamora reading the one about the teenage girl who follows a rock band around the country and ends up marrying a rodeo clown in Arizona. Or what would Mrs. Rivera make of the clitoral imagery in some of my early poetry?

In fact, "The Selkie's Daughter" (as I called it) is the first thing I've written in years that I'm not embarrassed to have my students read. Mrs. Rivera is interested in the fact that I grew up in a hotel where my mother worked as a maid. She worked at one of the big resorts in Cancún and says the ladies were just like the guests I described—always wanting something extra, always ruining the furniture with some carelessness. Amelie, who is taking my class over after failing it in the fall, asks how I felt being raised by my paternal aunt and it comes out that her children are with her husband's sister in Jamaica and she worries that they are being "poisoned against me by that woman." Mr. Nagamora is interested in the use of seashells for garden paths. They all end up relating the stories they were told as children and they are so involved in writing that we are the last class to leave the building. Hudson Street is unusually deserted and, as I turn west toward the river and home, I feel for the first time in a long time that I'm actually looking forward to reading what my students have written.

Emboldened by my success, I decide to give the same assignment to my students at The Art School. They are already working on mythic archetype collages for their Assemblage class. I tell them they can hand in photographs of their artwork if they use the same fairy tale in both (they're always hocking me to give them extra credit for art projects). I show them a slide of Helen Chadwick's *Loop My Loop* in which blond hair is intertwined with pig gut and a still from Disney's *Cinderella* and invite them to consider the way fairy-tale images change meaning depending on who the teller is.

I read them a quote from the art critic John Berger that I underlined many years ago in my copy of Marina Warner's *From the Beast to the Blonde*: "If you remember listening to stories as a child, you will remember the pleasure of hearing a story many times, and you will remember that while you were listening you became three people. There is an incredible fusion: you become the storyteller, the protagonist, and you remember yourself listening to the story . . ."

Natalie Baehr, a third-year jewelry design student whose blue hair is held up by Hello Kitty barrettes, points out that the ugly stepsisters in Disney's *Cinderella* were a redhead and brunette in contrast to Cinderella's

Marilyn Monroe blonde. "Like how your mother changed the heroine in the selkie story from a blonde to a brunette, thus subverting the dominant cultural icon to foster self-esteem in her female offspring."

Is that what my mother had been up to, I wonder, half hypnotized by the dangling plastic cats in Natalie's hair, subverting the dominant cultural icon? I think about the way my mother would sit at her desk, abstracted, for hours, not writing, just looking out the window and watching the light change over the Hudson Valley.

"Or the selkie's refusal to knit," Gretchen Lu, a textile design major, says. "An obvious subversion of traditional gender roling."

Gender roling? I imagine the way Gretchen might spell such a phrase and see myself circling it in red and writing *word?* in the margin. I wouldn't subtract a point for it though. Not in this class. I'd have to at Grace because such a word would never get past the reading committee, but here at The Art School I allowed my students some liberty with the English language. They're more visual than verbal, as they are fond of pointing out. *Picta non verba* would be the school's motto if it had one.

The main thing is that my students are excited by the assignment. Gretchen wants to do "The Little Mermaid." She already has an idea for an installation piece with torn fishnet stockings and dead fish (I can only hope she means plastic dead fish). Mark Silverstein, one of the Fashion Tekkies as they are somewhat disparagingly referred to, has an idea for a display window for "The Emperor's New Clothes": naked mannequins holding placards with the names of famous designers. I remind them there does need to be a written component to the assignment, and leave them chatting happily at the entrance to Dean & Deluca on University. I walk south and then, just as I'm passing in front of Washington Square Park, a light snow begins to fall. It's not that unusual for it to snow the third week of March, but it feels like a sign of something. Of what, I'm not sure.

The next morning, taking the train north along the river, I see that the ice has melted from the edges of the river and the willows that line the water have taken on that yellow glow they get just before budding. As usual, by this time of the week, I am fresh out of ideas. I doubt that the dozen men in this morning's class—inmates of the Rip Van Winkle Correctional Facility—will be as enthusiastic about fairy tales as were my students at The Art School. Even though the prison class is supposed to follow the same curriculum as the Grace class (so that work-release students can transfer easily from one to the other) I've had to whittle down my Rip Van Winkle syllabus to reading assignments that will (a) interest my students, and (b) not cause a riot. Although I've never caused a riot, the guards did have to intervene once in a scuffle that broke out over the question of whether or not Billy Budd was Captain Vere's "girlfriend." I'm not sure if I even want to use the phrase *fairy tale* in this particular class.

When the conductor calls the stop before the prison's I'm halfway through my second cup of Dunkin' Donuts coffee and still more than half asleep because I stayed up late the night before with Jack. Maybe, I think, I could call them "bedtime stories" or "folktales." I wonder if either term means something else in prison slang.

When I step off the train into a light drizzle blowing off the river I am still undecided. It's only a short walk from the train station to the prison gates—which is one of the reasons I took this job when the dean at Grace asked if I would teach the prison extension class.

I also thought it might give me something to write about.

So far, though, there has been nothing in my students' lives I feel equipped to write about. If anything, the weekly experience of teaching grammar and literature to these men has made me feel acutely the hubris of ever trying to even imagine any other person's experience, let alone reproduce it in writing.

As I sign in at the main desk and wait for my escort I am dwelling not on what I'll do in class today but on the depressing fact that the more I teach writing the less I seem able to write. I had once thought that teaching was a good backup field for a writer—that's why I embarked on the Ph.D.— but now it's just one more thing in my life that lingers incomplete.

The officer (not guard, I was told during hostage training orientation) arrives and hands me my picture ID, which I slip over my head. IRIS GREENFEDER, ADJUNCT LECTURER P/T, it says. Iris Greenfeder, ABD, it should say. Iris Greenfeder, all but . . . the story of my life, a series of all buts: all but published, all but a teacher, all but married. Lately it seems the buts are winning out over the alls. What *all* is left after so many diminishing *buts*? A bagel eaten down to its hole, my aunt Sophie would say.

The officer stops at the entrance to the courtyard to exchange a cryptic series of hand gestures with the officers in the towers. I look away, as if caught eavesdropping on a private conversation. The grass lawn, bisected by crisscrossing cement paths, slopes steeply down to the river, but the brick wall with its spiraling crown of concertina wire is just high enough to obscure all but the thinnest strip of river water. I've often wondered if the prison's architect planned it that way, teasing the prisoners with that suggestive glimpse of freedom.

My escort has cleared our passage across the open space and we proceed, single file with him leading. The rain, which was a drizzle when I got off the train, is heavier now and I'd like to take my umbrella out of my book bag, but then, remembering the officers stationed in the towers and their proximity to automatic weaponry, think better of it.

My classroom is located in a low building abutting the prison wall. My students are there already. My escort waits until I take attendance and we learn that one of my students is in solitary and one has been paroled. When I've finished taking attendance, the officer leaves. It unnerved me when I first started teaching at Van Wink (as the inmates call it) that the officer left. I had expected when I accepted the job that there would be a guard present in the classroom at all times. Now what bothers me more is knowing the officer is standing just outside the open door within earshot of my lesson. The consciousness of that unseen listener comes to me at odd moments during the class.

As I shuffle papers from my bag the men in front of me shift from full slouch to a slightly more vertical posture. It's less disrespect than the confinement of their desks that makes them assume this posture. The desks in the classroom are the old-fashioned, grade school kind. If my men sat upright their knees would ram into the underside of the kidney-shaped writing surface. Simon Smith is so big he can only sit in the desk sideways. I've asked the warden if we could have different seating but the desks are nailed to the floor. The only movable piece of furniture in the room is the lightweight plastic chair behind my desk (also screwed tight to the floor) where

I've been warned to keep it whenever I dragged it around the desk so I could sit closer to my students. Now I just sit on the edge of the desk instead.

Emilio Lara, my oldest student this term, asks if there's anything he can pass out for me. He's my courtly one, always offering some gracious gesture within the limits of his confinement. I think if it were allowed he'd carry my heavy book bag, he'd walk me across the courtyard, he'd open all the doors for me. And then keep on going through them. He claims to be "in" for counterfeiting, but I mistrust the romantic crimes these guys invent for me, while being charmed that they bother to come up with alternatives to the likelier murder, rape, and drug dealing.

Take Aidan, for instance. He says he's here for gun smuggling for the IRA.

"Me too," Simon Smith, my three-hundred-pounder from the South Bronx, said the first time Aidan volunteered this information. "Kiss me, I'm Irish."

Today Aidan's blue-green eyes skittishly avoid me. Is there a paper due that I've forgotten about? I don't think so. I usually have these guys write in class. I figure they don't have the most conducive environment for homework (although they do, out of all my students, have the most time on their hands). Something else must be up with Aidan. He's got that kind of coloring—white skin, black hair, dark lashes fringing pale eyes—that my aunt Sophie called black Irish. (For years I thought she meant there were black people in Ireland.) Usually the effect is striking, but today his milk-white skin is so pale he looks as if he's about to melt into the chipped and peeling plaster. Those heavy black lashes are drifting down. He'll be asleep before we're halfway through the next grammar lesson. So that's what makes me decide. Later I'll claim it was also because my only other choice for how to spend that rainy morning in prison was my lecture on the perils of dangling participles. But I know it was really because I wanted to wake up Aidan.

"Aidan," I say, "have you ever heard the legend of the selkie girl?"

I'm gratified to see a little blood stir behind Aidan's pallor.

"Silky girl?" Simon Smith asks. "Knew a dancer named Silky once."

Emilio Lara makes a shushing sound and bares his teeth, revealing one gold tooth, but he says nothing. Courtliness has its limits and Simon is truly big.

"The selkie girl is an Irish legend," I tell Simon, "a folktale. That's what we're going to do today."

"You're going to read us a fairy tale?" Simon asks.

There's a general rustling of limbs in the classroom and the bumping of knees into wood. I think I even hear, from outside in the hall, an incredulous sigh. Now I'm in for it, I think, but then I see that the men are settling in, their attention more focused than I've seen it for weeks. Their bodies seem to lean forward and I think that if their desks weren't screwed into the floor they would inch their chairs closer. And even though they can't move, I get the feeling I've become the center point in a circle. They could be children waiting for a story. And then I realize. They are the perfect audience for my story.

Chapter Three

Ultimately, though, my students aren't audience enough. By the time I board the train at Rip Van Winkle I am thinking that the piece might be possibly publishable. I carry this phrase back into the city, along with the rain that follows me down from the mountains, across the Tappan Zee and into the brackish tides at Inwood Park, down to the docks of Hoboken and Chelsea Piers: a cool infusion that will swell out of Manhattan harbor, past the Narrows and the beaches of Coney Island, and finally into the Atlantic Ocean.

Possibly publishable, I sing to myself for the next few days as it continues to rain. I go up to the main library at 42nd Street one evening at dusk to check to see which of the obscure literary magazines that have published my work in the past are still in print. Most are not, but I'm not discouraged. I walk back home through Bryant Park where the raindrops have spun crystal nets around the bare branches of the London plane trees. The streetlights on Eighth Avenue are reflected on the wet pavement. The sound of traffic is not so much muffled by the rain as transformed into something more liquid. Cars sluice through the inch or two of water pooling in the gutters. Horns sound far away, as if carried over a long stretch of water. Usually when it rains in the city you smell either the sea or the mountains. Tonight I seem to smell both. A heady mix of pine and salt, snowmelt and decay.

The raindrops on my umbrella ping out my new favorite song: *possibly publishable*. Henry James's *summer afternoon* can eat grass; *possibly publishable* is the most beautiful phrase in the English language. It doesn't matter if those other magazines have gone out of print; I know whom I'll send it to: Phoebe Nix at *Caffeine*. When I met her at an open poetry night at the Cornelia Street Café a few weeks ago she told me she liked the poem I read. *Have you thought about writing more about your mother?* she asked. I shrugged and told her I hated that idea of relying on a parent's fame—or in my mother's case: once-fame-now-near-obscurity. I told her I'd spent most of my life trying to recover from my mother's writing block. People usually laugh when I say that, but Phoebe had looked dead serious. Since she also looked about nineteen I attributed her reaction to a lack of maturity.

Later, when I was standing upstairs in the restaurant with Jack, she handed me her business card, which identified her as editor in chief of *Caffeine*—the new literary magazine I'd seen in bookstores and cafés around town.

"Do you know whose daughter she is?" Jack asked out on the street.

"No, is she somebody famous?"

"Vera Nix," he said, a poet who was as famous for her suicide as her poetry.

"Shit," I said and told Jack about the *getting over my mother's writing block* comment.

"It's like you have a radar," Jack said, shaking his head, with something almost like admiration, "that picks up possible success and steers you the hell away from it."

Still, I sent her some poems. From one writer's daughter to another, even though mine hadn't killed herself. Not exactly. She wrote me a nice note, declining the poems, but encouraging me to submit again.

I put Phoebe Nix's note in my "submit again" box—my father's old humidor, which I kept on my desk. Whenever I opened it the odor of Cuban cigars wafted out and for just a moment it was as if my father were in the room. Or had just left the room. It was how I'd find him in the hotel when I was little—by following the smell of his cigars from the lobby to the Grill, back into the kitchens, up the back staircase to the linen closets, to his office on the second floor. I had this fear that if I opened the box too often the smell of cigars would someday dissipate and so I opened it sparingly.

I thought of my "submit again" notes as having the same kind of expiration date. My experience—over twenty years of submitting to literary journals—told me that once I snagged a line of encouragement from an editor I had about three tries. If they didn't take anything in three submissions they'd probably give up. The glow of promise would fade. My SASE would return with no encouraging scribble, merely a poorly Xeroxed rejection slip. Like a magic amulet given in a fairy tale, the notes possessed a finite power and must be used wisely.

By the time I reach the steps to my building I've resolved to cash in Phoebe Nix's note—I can almost smell Cuban tobacco on the damp wind blowing east from the river. I close my eyes, one hand on the wrought-iron railing as I climb the steep steps, to concentrate on that scent and trip over someone sitting on the top step. I draw back, expecting one of the neighborhood street people sheltering from the rain, but then relax when I realize it's someone I know. My relief quickly fades when I realize where I know him from. It's Aidan Barry.

"I didn't mean to scare you, Professor Greenfeder," he says, rising to his feet. "I wanted to give you this."

He's holding something wrapped in a blue-and-white Blockbuster Video bag. It doesn't look like a gun, but I back away from him and nearly trip backward down the steps. He reaches forward quickly and catches my arm to keep me from falling and I gasp. I look up and down the street to see if anyone is out, but even in clear weather my corner of Jane, right next to the West Side Highway and the river, is not well populated. Now in the rain, there are only the headlights of cars on the highway. It's Friday. Not one of Jack's nights to come over.

Aidan drops his hand from my arm, looks down and shakes his head. I notice that drops of water glisten in his dark hair. "I guess I shouldn't have come over here, but I was working on Varick Street and I saw from your address on that story you gave us that you lived close . . ."

"What do you mean working on Varick Street? Aren't you . . . I mean aren't you . . . in prison?"

Aidan laughs. "I was put on work release last month, Prof. I'm up for parole. I'm supposed to transfer into your class at Grace next week. I thought they told you that stuff."

I shake my head. I bet they tell tenured faculty at Grace when their prisoner-students are released. Or maybe the tenured faculty never teach the prison classes. "Did you say you saw my address on the essay I gave you?"

He draws a sheaf of folded paper from the Blockbuster bag and hands me the Xeroxed copy of "The Selkie's Daughter" I gave my classes. In the upper-left-hand corner is my address, phone number, and e-mail: my standard form for magazine submissions. I hadn't even noticed I'd left it on the first page when I copied the piece for my classes. I've given my home address to all my students, including a dozen inmates of the Rip Van Winkle Correctional Facility.

"Shit," I say, shaking the paper at Aidan. "Tell me my phone number isn't scrawled on the men's bathroom at Van Wink."

Aidan smiles and shakes his head. Drops of water roll from his hair and dampen the collar of his denim jacket. A drop hits me and rolls down the back of my neck making me shiver. "Hey, don't worry," he says, "Emilio noticed you'd left your address on the essays and we asked the guard for some Wite-Out. The guys in that class like you. They won't give your address out or anything. I guess I shouldn't have kept it—just, that story you read about your mother reminded me of this book of fairy tales I had growing up and I thought I'd try to find it so I could write my essay on it." Aidan is still holding out the blue-and-white plastic bag. I take it from him and look inside the bag. There's a book and another sheaf of folded paper.

"You're delivering your paper to me? I said I'd give you time to write in class next week."

Aidan shrugs, and then shivers. The denim jacket he's wearing is too light for the March night and it's soaked. In normal circumstances I'd invite him in, but even though I've gotten over my initial shock at seeing one of my prisoners out loose on the street, I'm not ready to invite him up to my apartment. "I had some time on the train," he tells me, and then, looking at his watch, says, "Actually, I've got to go or I'll miss my train back up. I'm staying at a detention house near the prison. They don't like it when you're late. I didn't think you'd be out so late. Big date, huh?"

I think of the hour I've just spent in the Periodicals Room at the library and I hate to disappoint Aidan. When was the last time I was out on a big date? Would you even say that the Wednesday, Saturday, and Sunday nights I spend with Jack are dates at all? "Yeah," I tell Aidan, "a big date."

Aidan pulls the collar of his jacket up and shoves his hands in his pockets. "So where is the lucky guy? You didn't have a fight or something?"

"I was hoping to get some writing done," I say, looking into Aidan's blue-green eyes. It's the first time I've seen him outside of the sickly glow of fluorescent prison lighting. Even streetlight is better. I notice that his long dark lashes are glistening with rain and even the T-shirt under his jacket is wet. He looks like he's shown up on my doorstep from the river rather than just Varick Street. "Now I guess I'll try to read some papers." I take out the folded pages from the bag Aidan has given me. They're handwritten I see. Inside the plastic bag is a smaller brown paper bag with the name BOOKS OF WONDER printed on it, a children's bookstore on 18th Street.

"Hey, I love this store," I tell Aidan.

"Yeah, I tried five stores before I found one that carried the same book I remembered."

I slip the book out from its paper covering and see that it's an old edition of Irish fairy tales. The binding is pale green cloth embossed with golden lettering, the letters springing from the sinuous hair of a woman sitting on a rock. The same hair billows out below her, ensnaring the figure of a man swimming in the waves beside the rock.

"Aidan, this is beautiful, it must have cost a lot, I can't accept this."

"Sure you can, Prof. Where would I keep it? What do you think my fellow parolees would make of me reading fairy tales?"

I look at the book and notice that the woman is naked. The man swimming in the ocean is also naked; the selkie's hair twines between his legs and wraps snakelike around his arms. I feel myself blushing and hope that Aidan doesn't notice in the dull gleam of the streetlights.

"Well, I'll keep it for you for now. But when you find some other place to stay . . ."

"Sure," he says, moving down the steps, his back still to the street. "In a month or two I'll be able to take my own place—if I can find a steady job. I hope you like the book . . . and my paper. I worked really hard on it. I hadn't thought about those stories in years."

Aidan's got one foot off the sidewalk into the cobblestone street when he turns back to me, casually, as if he's just remembered something. There's something in the deliberate casualness of the tilt of his head that makes me think he's going to ask for money, a place to stay, some favor . . . "So tell me," he says, "if your mother was Irish and your father was Jewish, what were you brought up as?"

I'm surprised by the question mostly because he is the only one of all who've read the piece so far to ask it.

"As nothing," I say. "No religion. You're only Jewish if your mother's Jewish, and my mother had given up Catholicism . . ." I pause, trying to think why it was again that my mother had rejected the church, but like so much else about my mother, I have no direct evidence, only a puzzling silence. Once, when I was about six, I found, in among my mother's costume jewelry, a slim gold disc embossed with the face of a beautiful woman holding a rose. Something about the woman's face drew me in a way that the glittery beads didn't and I put it on. It was a few days before my mother noticed it on me.

"Give me that," she told me, yanking it from my neck, "before your father or aunt sees it."

The chain bruised my neck when she tore it from me, but worse than that was the look in my mother's face. I'd never seen her look like that and I couldn't imagine what had made her so angry. "She never minded before when I wore her beads," I sobbed to my father while he put ice on my neck.

"Yes, but this was different. It was a saint's medal—something Catholics wear—and your mother promised me that except for being christened she wouldn't raise you as a Catholic. Not that I had any objections, but maybe she thought it would offend me or Sophie."

"She had me baptized," I tell Aidan, anxious to offer him something besides the bare lack of religion in my life.

"Oh well, she wouldn't want you to end up in limbo, would she? Even the most lapsed Catholic mother wouldn't want that."

"Yeah, but she waited until I was three. Apparently she wasn't in such a rush to save my immortal soul."

"Three!" There. Finally I've shocked this good Catholic boy. This good Catholic convict, I remind myself. For some reason it fails to satisfy me; instead I feel vaguely embarrassed, whether for me or my mother, I'm not sure. "She waited to take me to the same church in Brooklyn where she'd been baptized—St. Mary Star of the Sea?"

Aidan shakes his head. "I grew up in Inwood and most of my relatives live in Woodlawn. I don't know Brooklyn."

"When the priest saw me walking down the aisle to my own baptism he had a fit."

Aidan chuckles. "I bet."

I smile, warming to the story.

" 'What were you thinking waiting this long?' the priest said to her. 'She's here now,' my mother told him, 'do you want to baptize her or not?' "

"And he did?"

"One more saved soul."

"Your mother sounds like something," he says. "My mother would never stand up to a priest that way, she was that afraid of them. Now my gran . . . but I talk about her in my paper. You'll see." Aidan crosses his arms across his chest and rubs them, obviously chilled. "Well . . . ," he says.

I still have no intention of inviting him up—I'm not an idiot—but for a second I think we're both aware that if the situation were different this would be the moment when I would. I picture my apartment—I have the corner apartment on the top floor, which includes a hexagonal tower facing the river—like an empty boat drifting over our heads. He'd like the view. It's the view he'd have from the prison if not for that wall.

"I'd better catch that train," he says.

"Yes," I say, relieved. I think. "I'll see you next Thursday."

"Monday," he corrects me before turning away, "Remember, I'm in your class at Grace now."

I nod, but he's already turned around. It's on the tip of my tongue to tell him that he's really too advanced for that class. He should go into the next level of composition class—I could easily recommend him for it—but I say nothing. I don't teach the next level.

I watch him walk east on Jane and then turn north on Washington. I think of my father standing in the back drive of the hotel, seeing important guests and dignitaries off in their taxis. He'd always stand and wait until the taxi rounded the bend and disappeared behind the wall of pines that guarded the back of the hotel. When I asked him why he did that, if it was to be polite, he laughed at me. "No," he told me, "I just like to make sure they're really gone."

Chapter Four

Aidan's fairy tale, as I might have guessed, is an enchanted-prince story. He might have chosen from dozens, all with the same basic plot. A young man of royal lineage and sterling qualities is trapped in a loathsome disguise: a toad, a bear, a beast. *An ex-con.* The princess must see through this surface ugliness to the prince inside to save him and restore him to his true nature and his birthright—prince of all the realm. "Beauty and the Beast" or "The Frog Prince" would do the job, but instead he's picked "Tam Lin," a Celtic story of a prince kidnapped by fairies, redeemed by true love.

I toss his essay onto the unread stack on my desk. The paper, damp and rumpled, glows in the faint light that filters in from the street. I haven't turned my desk lamp on yet. And although I'd planned to retrieve Phoebe Nix's note from the "submit again" box, I do nothing for a few minutes but look out the window.

My apartment is the corner apartment on the fifth floor. It's only one room, but it's in the hexagonal tower at the corner of Jane and West. I've got three windows, each facing a different direction. My desk is under the middle window of the tower corner. Sometimes I think I'd get more writing done with a worse view, but it's the view that's kept me in this one-room apartment all these years—well, the view and rent control. I look southwest down a long expanse of river into the harbor toward a misty region that I think of as the beginning of the ocean. It's always been my dream to live within sight of the sea and I'm beginning to suspect that this is as close as I'll ever get.

Tonight though, in the dark and the rain, the ocean seems far away. I can just make out the oily gleam of the river, rolling dark and heavy like some sea creature carrying the lights of New Jersey on its broad back. The air that seeps under my window smells like stone, like water from a deep well. I notice that the wind, coming from the northwest, is driving the rain in, dampening the pages of my students' papers. I get up to close the window and my fingers brush against the soft wood of my father's old humidor. Not yet, I think. I'll read a few papers first, I bargain with myself, before opening the box. I turn on my lamp, but decide to leave the window open for now, and pick up Aidan's paper.

TAM LIN

This was a story my gran told me. She was always saying that if we were bad, if we didn't mind the nuns at school or learn our catechism, the fairies would come and take us away. She said the fairies were fallen angels who weren't bad enough to be devils but not good enough to stay angels. They liked to steal children so they wouldn't be lonely, but they could only take you if you'd done something bad. I thought that must have been what happened to my brother Sean who'd died when he was four and I was two but when I asked Ma what Sean had done to be taken she slapped me. It was the only time she ever hit me. Now Dad . . . but that's another story.

Anyway. My gran still told these stories about being stolen by the fairies and one was about a boy named Tam Lin. My gran said this Tam Lin was a good boy mostly except he didn't always mind his parents or the nuns at school and sometimes went out exploring in the woods when he should've been at school. One day he was out in the woods hunting and he got so tired that he laid himself down under a tree and fell to sleep.

I liked to imagine that part. Falling asleep under a tree. I liked to go into Inwood Park, way back where nobody went. A park ranger once told me that the trees in Inwood Park are the only trees on Manhattan Island that have never been cut. A virgin forest he called it, which seemed kind of funny for a city park where people did all sorts of things that weren't exactly virgin like. Anyway. I always thought it would be an adventure to stay all night in the park, but I'd have been afraid to fall asleep there.

This Tam Lin fellow, though, one day he was in the woods and he found this old well. He was thirsty so he drank from the well and then he fell asleep. When he woke up he was surrounded by fairies. The queen of the fairies was this old lady who was beautiful but kind of scary looking because her hair was white and she was dressed all in green. She told Tam Lin that the well belonged to the fairies and because he had drunk from it he belonged to the fairies now. She said he should be happy because now he'd get to live forever like the fairies. She gave him a white horse and a green suit (because that's what fairies wear) and made him go with her.

This part scared me because Gran was always saying that if Dad didn't stop drinking and hitting us the Social Services lady would come and take us away to a home. Our Social Services lady was very thin and tall and wore her hair pulled back so tight her skin looked shiny—like a balloon right before it pops. I thought she looked a little like the fairy queen would look and I guessed Tam Lin would've rather stayed with his folks than go with her even if he would get to live forever.

And then there's always a catch they don't tell you about first. Like when you buy cereal for the prize inside and then find out you've got to save like ten box tops and send away money to get the prize, which is just some piece of crap plastic anyway. You see, these fairies had to pay a price for getting to live forever. Every seven years, on Halloween, they had to sacrifice a human being. On the next Halloween, Tam Lin was out riding with the fairies and they passed the well where he'd fallen asleep. He was surprised because he hadn't seen it since he was kidnapped by the fairies and he knew then that he was back in the mortal world. He was just thinking that he'd make a break for it and head for home when one of the other riders got the same idea and broke from the pack. Right away all the fairies fell on the boy in a heap and when they were done all that was left was a pile of bones picked clean.

So you can bet Tam Lin was pretty scared and decided not to try getting away until he had a plan.

Four more Halloweens went by and Tam Lin couldn't think of anything. He saw that the fairy queen was getting tired of him and he knew he'd be the next to go if he didn't come up with something. Then, on the sixth Halloween, he kind of straggled behind the other riders and when he passed the well he saw a girl standing there. She looked like she'd just seen a ghost, which you could say she had. A whole troop of them.

Tam Lin got off his horse and went over to the girl. On his way he saw a rose and picked it for her—figuring she'd be less afraid if he gave her a present. He pricked his finger on the thorns, though, and cried out. He was pretty embarrassed that the girl saw him hurt himself, but then she got out her handkerchief and wrapped it around Tam Lin's hand and made a fuss over him. You see, that's how she knew he wasn't really a fairy. Because he bled.

"Come with me," the girl said, when she'd stopped his bleeding.

But Tam Lin heard the fairy horses returning and knew the fairy queen would kill both of them.

"I can't," he told her, "but if you come back here next Halloween maybe you can save me." Then he told her to bring holy water from the church and dirt from her garden. "When you see me ride past you must pull me from my horse and hold me tight no matter what happens. Then I'll be free of the fairies and we can get married. But if you don't save me, the fairies will kill me because it'll be seven years I've been with them."

The girl looked doubtful, but she said she'd wait for Tam Lin and be at the well next Halloween and then Tam Lin had to go.

I always thought that last year must have been the worst for Tam Lin, wondering whether the girl would come back or had she found someone else or would she be too afraid to keep her promise and knowing if she didn't he'd be eaten alive by the fairies. It's like when you're almost up for parole and you don't want to screw it up but you kind of relax because you start thinking about being home and that's when you screw up.

Of course I didn't know anything about parole back then, but I do now, which I guess is another reason I thought about this story.

Because things worked out for Tam Lin. The girl—Margaret I think her name was—was there at the well and when she saw Tam Lin she pulled him from his horse and held him so tight he half thought she'd choke him. The fairy queen was furious when she saw Tam Lin and the girl.

"Let him go," she said, "and I'll give you all the silver in the world."

"No," the girl said. "I'll hold on to my Tam Lin."

"Oh," says the fairy queen, "that's Tam Lin you're holding, is it?"

And when the girl looked she saw she was holding a huge snake—or it was holding her! Still she didn't let go.

"Let go," said the fairy queen, "and I'll give you all the gold in the world."

"No," the girl said. "I'll hold on to my Tam Lin."

"Oh," says the fairy queen, "that's Tam Lin you're holding, is it?"

And the snake turned into a lion who roared right in Margaret's face. Still she didn't let go.

The fairy queen was so mad then that she tore her white hair from her head and screamed, "I'll teach you!" and she turned Tam Lin into a burning brand that singed the girl's skin. Still she held on till she could smell her own skin burning. Then she took out the bottle of holy water she'd brought and sprinkled it in the well and she threw the burning brand in after and there, instead of the burning brand, was Tam Lin, naked, I'm sorry to have to tell you, because the clothes had burned right off him.

So Margaret pulled him out of the well and gave him her cloak. She sprinkled the dirt from her garden in a circle around them and even though the fairy queen screamed and raged there wasn't a thing she could do. Tam Lin and Margaret went back to her castle (she turned out to be princess) and . . . well, you can imagine the rest.

I think you can figure out too why I picked this story. I've been here at Rip Van Winkle for seven years—I was twenty-two when I was convicted—and now I'm up for parole. I didn't think I'd ever get out of here, but now that I'm going to be free I can't help thinking about what it'll be like outside.

I think that sometimes when you get used to a bad thing—like being in prison or getting kidnapped by the fairies—it's better to live with that bad thing than trying to change it. Because what if you get a chance to change things and you mess up? What if it's your last chance?

I mean, right now, I feel like I'd do just about anything to keep from coming back here, but I see these guys, they get out and then they're back on the street in their old neighborhood and they can't get a decent job because who's going to take a chance on an ex-con? So they fall in with their old crowd and whatever got them in here in the first place—drugs or guns or stealing cars—and pretty soon they're back in. And that's it for them. That's what their life's gonna be like from then on. In and out of prison like a revolving door. So I wonder. What's the point?

But then thinking about Tam Lin has made me feel better. Because Margaret believed in him. She held on to him even when he looked like a snake or a lion. Even when he burned her. She held on tight. So I think maybe someone will believe in me even though I'm an ex-con. Maybe someone will take a chance on me. What do you think, Miss Greenfeder?

I drop Aidan's paper to the desk as if it were the burning brand in the story, only there's no well here to douse it. The direct question—my own name—has startled me out of the lulling familiarity of the fairy tale. It's as if the knight on the cover of the Celtic fairy-tale collection Aidan gave me had turned to me from the green-and-gold cover and winked. I feel as if I am being watched, exposed in this circle of lamplight.

I reach across my desk and switch off the mica-shaded lamp and close the window. Something about Aidan's story has chilled me. It's not a story that my mother ever told me, but it reminds me of my mother's novels. Her books are full of shape-shifters, animals who shed their skins to live among people and beasts whose true human natures are cloaked by false pelts: women who turn into seals and men who sprout wings on their backs. Over the years I've tracked down most of the fairy-tale origins of her creatures. It's the subject of my dissertation: "Skin Deep: Strategies of Dis-clothe-sure and Con-seal-ment in the Fantasy Fiction of K. R. LaFleur." The creatures who are cursed to shed their skins again and again, never finding their true skin, are clearly derived from the Irish selkie legend. The men cursed to live as swanlike birds are drawn from a combination of sources including The Mabinogion and Hans Christian Andersen's story "The Wild Swans." I've never connected the shape-shifters in her stories, though, to the story of Tam Lin who changes shape three times before he escapes his enchantment.

I should be grateful and excited for this clue Aidan Barry has given me, but still I'm unnerved by his appearance at my apartment. Surely he'd know that his sudden appearance on my doorstep would startle me. It's definitely inappropriate—aggressive, even. And yet, when I think of how he looked, chilled and wet, waiting for me in the rain, I can't help but think how vulnerable he seemed. And afraid. The way he describes the perils of parole have truly touched me. It's as if he's afraid of his own nature, which he can't trust not to revert to some primitive throwback. He's like Tam Lin, asking for someone to hold on to him so he won't turn back into a beast, or worse, an inanimate thing that burns.

But what can I do for him, what does he expect from me?

Again I have that sense of being watched even though I have turned out the light. I reach up to draw the shade over the window to the left of my desk, but first I scan the street below. From this window, I can see the sidewalk and a narrow strip of the cobblestone gutter lit up by the street lamp on the south side of Jane. A shadow stretches over the sidewalk, but whatever casts that shadow is too close to this side of the street for me to see. I can't even tell if it's a shadow cast by a person or by something inanimate, a pile of garbage on the north side of the street, some discarded piece of furniture perhaps. I listen for footsteps, but all I can hear is rain and traffic from the West Side Highway and, faintly in the distance, the Hudson flowing toward the sea.

Chapter Five

I send "The Selkie's Daughter" to *Caffeine* and within a week I get a call from Phoebe Nix saying that not only does she want to publish it, but she wants to put it in her Mother's Day issue. The few times I've gotten a story accepted I've had to wait months—sometimes years—to actually see it in print. Twice the journals that have accepted my work have gone out of business before my piece could appear. Now Phoebe is saying that my essay will be on sale by May 1, just three weeks from today.

"I think it's very exciting that you've decided to explore these issues about your mother," Phoebe says. "Perhaps you'll want to do a *follow-up piece*?" Phoebe Nix's voice lilts upward on the words *follow-up piece* in a way that produces a flutter in my throat, something rising inside me like joy. *Follow-up piece* just might become the next chorus in the song I've been singing, edging out *possibly publishable* as my favorite phrase.

"Well, I have been thinking of something else along those lines," I lie.

"Maybe you could write more about what it was like to grow up in a hotel—that must have been interesting. After my parents died I practically grew up in hotels . . . I was trying to remember if I was ever at your parents' hotel . . ."

"My parents didn't own the Hotel Equinox—" I start to correct her, but she interrupts me.

"And you said your mother's maiden name was Morrissey? That name is certainly familiar. I think my mother might have mentioned it in her journals. Maybe our mothers knew each other?"

Although I think it's extremely unlikely that my mother knew the great poet Vera Nix I make a sort of noncommittal murmur.

"Anyway," Phoebe says, "why don't we have lunch when the galleys for 'The Selkie's Daughter' come in? Did I tell you how much I love the title?"

I'm so happy that I break our no-calls-during-the-day rule and phone Jack. He's so pleased for me he diverges from our Wednesday-Saturday-Sunday routine and asks me out to dinner that very night—a Tuesday. We agree to meet in Washington Square Park, midway between my apartment and Jack's loft on the Lower East Side. Walking through the West Village I'm not sure what I feel giddier about: Phoebe Nix's response to my story, the warmth my good news kindled in Jack's voice, or the way the unseasonably warm weather has coaxed the trees into bloom all down Bleecker Street.

When I get to the park I remember that it's only been a few weeks since I walked back from my class at The Art School and stopped to watch the snow falling through the arch. I remember thinking that the snow was a sign of something, but not being sure of what. Now I know. The snow foretold this good fortune, this early-spring evening and the way the last sun hits the slow drift of white petals so that they seem suspended in midair. The park is full of NYU girls in midriff-baring tops and boys skateboarding in circles around them. A crowd has formed around a pair of street dancers and the air is sweet with the smell of the white-blossoming trees and marijuana. What a magical transformation! Like a fairy-tale kingdom released from its spell of winter.

I look for a bench in the southeast corner of the park to sit and wait for Jack, but he's already there. Another surprise—he's usually late. He's changed out of his usual paint-splattered T-shirt into a soft blue denim shirt—faded but clean and ironed. Is it the shirt that makes me notice—for the first time in years it seems—how blue his eyes are? Or is it that I hardly ever see him in the daylight anymore? How long has it been? What time he has left over from his teaching schedule at The Art School and Cooper

Union he spends in his studio painting. His best working hours—and the best light—are in the early morning. He likes to wake up in his loft and start painting right away. So he comes over to my apartment Wednesday and Saturday nights, but never stays the night even though we see each other again on Sunday night. Sometimes he cooks me dinner in his loft (Jack's a great cook and in the summer he grows his own tomatoes and basil on his roof), but I've never spent the night there.

Aunt Sophie says I've done a Lee Krasner, subordinating my art to his. Which is pretty funny considering Sophie gave up her own studies at the Art Students League to join her brother in upstate New York when the hotel desperately needed a bookkeeper. Or maybe that's exactly why she's so anxious I not repeat her mistake.

What she doesn't understand, though, is how well our arrangement suits me. I've always felt that we were just the same and, since we met ten years ago in a "Drawing on the Right Side of the Brain" class at the Omega Institute, lucky to find each other. How many men would put up with my erratic work schedule and understand the time I need to write? How many would understand the hours I spend in the late afternoons, sitting at my desk, staring out the window and waiting for the muse to wing over from New Jersey?

But as Jack rises to greet me—shifting a green paper cone in his arms (Why, he's bought me flowers!)—I think two things at the same time. One is that there is something odd, even vampirelike, about a relationship that is always conducted outside the light of day, and two, How handsome he is! How much I love him!

"Hail the conquering hero," he says presenting the bouquet—white irises, my namesakes—with a sweeping flourish. When he leans down to kiss me I notice specks of light in his hair, which I think are paint splatters, then petals, and then, I finally realize, are just streaks of gray. Honestly, how long has it been since we did something as simple as meet in the park?

"I thought we could eat at Mezzaluna," he says. It's our favorite restaurant in Little Italy, but it's been so long since we've been there that I'm not even sure it's still in business. We head south on Thompson, though, and continue on West Broadway. Usually walking through Soho annoys Jack.

He can remember when the area was abandoned warehouses and a few health food stores. Now it's overpriced clothing stores and trendy galleries geared toward a tourist mentality. I expect him to rant about the various gallery owners and artists who have "sold out," but instead he asks me about the story that *Caffeine* is going to publish.

"It's an essay really, a memoir about my mother."

"Memoir?" he says suspiciously. "Since when do you write memoirs?"

"Well, it's not a memoir about me." I know Jack's opinion about the spate of self-absorbed memoirs to hit the bookstores in recent years. "It's really a retelling of a fairy tale that my mother—and then Aunt Sophie— used to tell me. I asked my students to write about a favorite fairy tale and so I did too. You know, as a model."

"Well, I'm glad something useful came out of those classes you teach." Another of Jack's saws: any time not spent doing your art is wasted time. Teaching is a necessary evil. I used to tell Jack that I actually liked teaching, but I gave up, not so much because he didn't believe me as that the more I tried to convince him the less I believed it myself. "I just hope you're not going the memoir route because it's commercial."

"I didn't write it because memoirs are commercial," I tell Jack. We've come to Mezzaluna, but we pause outside the restaurant while Jack waits for me to presumably tell him why I did write it. Because obviously he's not buying the idea that I wrote it for my students. That would be like him doing a painting to match a client's decor. And suddenly I'm not sure how I did come to write "The Selkie's Daughter"—did I write it to model an assignment or did the assignment come after?

"I've been thinking about my mother a lot lately," I say, "the way she told those fairy tales and then the fairy tales became part of her novels. I was wondering if I went back to her books and looked at all the fairy tales she used if I could figure out what would have come next. I mean, why she didn't finish the third book in her trilogy. Maybe there was something about that third book that made it too hard for her to write—the way John Steinbeck stopped writing the King Arthur stories when he got to the part where Lancelot and Guinevere kiss."

"So you think if you figure out her writer's block you'll break your own?"

It's the closest he's come to being mean tonight, but when I look at his face I see that he really didn't intend to hurt me. Jack can be brutally honest, but only because he thinks it'll help in the long run. Still, he must see the tears in my eyes because as he escorts me into Mezzaluna he whispers into my ear, "Maybe you're right. It's already worked hasn't it? After all, you're writing again."

I turn to him, but the maître d' is approaching us with two menus in his hand and Jack is smiling and greeting him by name. By the time we're seated and Jack has ordered a bottle of wine, I think I'll change the conversation. Ask him about how his paintings for the faculty show at The Art School are coming. But Jack still wants to talk about my work.

"I mean it. You look different. I can always tell when you're working. You get a certain glow."

I blush. The truth is that I haven't written anything since I wrote "The Selkie's Daughter"—I've had all those fairy-tale papers to grade—but I do something that I've never done with Jack before. I lie. "Yes," I tell him, "I have been writing. Something new. I think it's going well."

"That's great, Iris. To tell you the truth I was a little worried, but I didn't want to say anything."

I smile and pick up my menu. When Jack and I first met I thought it was wonderful to find someone who loved me for my writing, but then I started wondering what would happen if I stopped writing. Would he stop loving me?

"Tell me," I say, desperate now to change the subject, "what's your favorite fairy tale?"

Jack laughs, spraying a few crumbs of the bread he's been chewing. "Can't you guess?" he asks.

I shake my head and take a sip of the wine that the waiter has poured for me.

" 'Jack and the Beanstalk,' of course."

"Oh, come on. That can't be it."

"Really. 'Jack and the Beanstalk.' "

"Just because of your name?"

"Yeah, maybe at first. Why, what's wrong with 'Jack and the Beanstalk'? Is it because it's not as creepy as your tortured-maiden tales?"

"I don't know—it's kind of obvious, isn't it? And then I've got the Mickey Mouse version stuck in my head and that vine always struck me as obscene . . ."

"It's a good story—clever boy makes good—tricks the bad old giant and escapes with the magic harp—cuts down the beanstalk and lives happily ever after."

"Oh, I see, the mean old giant is the art establishment."

"Hey, I didn't psychoanalyze your fairy tale." Jack looks genuinely hurt.

"Sorry. You're right. It's your fairy tale. At least it doesn't have a mean old witch in it."

"Yeah, and it's got gardening."

Of course. Jack's an avid gardener, not an easy feat living in New York City. But Jack is one of those New Yorkers who goes about his daily life as if he's living in rural Nebraska. He has his coffee and eggs at the same local diner every day (where he gossips about art auction prices instead of feed prices), shops at the Greenmarket in Union Square twice a week, and grows tomatoes on his rooftop in old discarded tin drums. In his faded denim shirts, paint-splattered jeans, and the kind of boots you can order from JCPenney, he looks more like a farmer than an urban artist. He even has a pickup truck.

". . . I'd like to do some real gardening," Jack is saying. "You know, like in the ground, not five stories above concrete."

"Oh, come on. What are you going to do? Move to Long Island?"

It's long been a tenet of Jack's that outside the city limits lurk all the traps that can ensnare the artist. Two-car garages, mortgage payments, lawns to mow on Saturdays, nine-to-five jobs, kids to feed and send to college . . . we agreed a long time ago that such a life would be death to at least one of our artistic careers. Jack had generously pointed out that it was usually the woman's career that suffered first.

Jack shakes his head. "Not Long Island, no way. But I have been thinking it would be nice to get out of the city for a while. I don't know if I can take another summer here. It might be nice to go upstate for a while. What do you think?"

Is Jack asking me to spend the summer with him out of town?

"I think it would be nice," I say cautiously, taking a sip of my wine. I already have a vision of us in some little cabin in the woods, where Jack can paint and I can write, a creek nearby where we skinny-dip, a wide brass bed covered with a faded quilt where we make love in the middle of the afternoon.

"Well, let's think about it," Jack says. Our food comes—linguine and mussels in garlic—and we drop the subject for now, but that vision stays with me so that when we make love that night back in my apartment, the streetlight that filters through my windows and bathes my narrow bed feels warm as sunlight.

The next day I'm still basking in the glow of Jack's enthusiasm—from the subtle shift I feel in our relationship—and I decide to share my good news with my aunt Sophie. As soon as I hear her voice—Ramon, the desk clerk, has transferred my call to the laundry room where she is inventorying the linen and I can tell from the snap and rustle in the background that she is still folding sheets while taking my call—I know I've made a mistake. Good news and Aunt Sophie don't go together. If good news is a light source, Aunt Sophie's a black hole sucking all its rays into her gravitational orbit and extinguishing them. I tell her about *Caffeine* taking the story—I tell her it's for the Mother's Day issue and I'm planning to send her a copy, hoping to kindle her maternal instincts—and I hear that little pocket of silence where there should be exclamation points. I listen to the rustle of heavy linen, as of wings beating the air, and then comes the inevitable question.

"So, what are they paying you for this seal story?"

"Aunt Sophie," I say, "I've told you before. Literary journals can't afford to pay. But it's a credit . . ."

"You mean they owe you the money?"

"Not that kind of credit." She knows this. At seventy-six Aunt Sophie is as sharp as a tack. She's kept the books for the hotel for fifty years and never been off a penny. "It's like an honor. I list it on my next submission letter and editors are more likely to publish my next story."

"And then you get some money?"

"Well, maybe," I lie. "If it's a big enough magazine. *Caffeine* is a pretty good credit . . ."

"And what kind of name is that for a magazine? *Caffeine?* What are they selling? Literature or Maxwell House?"

"The idea is that it's read in cafés and it's stimulating—like coffee. It's a good journal. John Updike had a story in it last year."

"Well, Mr. Updike can no doubt afford to give away his stories for free, but you—on the money you make? How much did you gross last year?"

"Eighteen thousand," I say, my heart sinking. She knows this too. She always does my tax return.

I hear a sharp snap that sounds like bones breaking, but then I realize it's just her shaking the wrinkles out of the sheets. I can picture her, in the laundry room behind the servants' quarters in the North Wing. The folding table is beneath a row of windows facing the circular drive at the back entrance to the hotel. When I was little I used to climb up onto the folding table and wedge myself between the stacks of folded linens—still warm from the dryers—clear a circle in the steamy windows, and watch the guests arriving. It was the perfect vantage point from which to see while remaining unseen. I can hear over the phone line the hissing of the steam irons and I switch the receiver to my left ear and shake my head as if to dislodge water. I could say that it's none of her business how much money I make, but it is. She sends me a check every month to supplement my meager salary. Otherwise I wouldn't even be able to afford this little rent-controlled apartment. Even the apartment is thanks to her—handed down to me by an old friend of hers from her Art League days.

Switching the receiver again, I wait for the other shoe to drop. Usually the mention of my puny adjunct salary is followed by the salary I could make if I gave up my silly notions of being a writer and came back to the hotel to take over my father's old job as manager. Since my father died last year the Mandelbaums, the hotel's owners, have made it clear that I could have the job whenever I wanted.

"You could still write," Cora Mandelbaum has said to me, "in the evenings after your work was done. Your mother wrote here."

But my mother wasn't the manager. Although she started out at the Hotel Equinox as a maid, once she married my father the only work she did was as unofficial hostess and greeter during the season. In the off-season, between October and May, she devoted herself to her writing. My father, though, worked hard even in those off months. There were repairs to be done, supplies to be inventoried. Although it was true that I would probably be able to find some time to write during the off-season I have always been afraid that the responsibilities of the hotel would weigh too heavily. I know that my father, after fifty years of running the Hotel Equinox, had seemed bowed down by the weight of it, as if its stately six stories had pressed down upon his head. Besides, I don't want to leave the city.

I wait some more, but my aunt's usual offer of employment is not forthcoming.

"The hotel's opening next week, right?" I finally ask. "Everything ready?"

Now I'm almost begging her to regale me with the usual stories of last-minute foul-ups and colossal mismanagement that I, if I only saw fit to, could remedy by stepping into my father's managerial shoes.

"I suppose," she says. "It hardly seems to matter now. What with the hotel closing at the end of this season."

"Closing?" I say, but it comes out more as a gasp than a word, all the breath having swooshed out of me. No wonder my aunt has been so calm this morning, with this bombshell under her hat, so to speak.

"Yes, Ira and Cora have finally had enough. They've bought a little motel in Sarasota to manage. If I'm lucky, they'll take pity on an old lady and let me night clerk and make the beds for them. But it's you I'm worried for, *bubelah*, because I won't be able to send you money anymore."

Bubelah. Now she's maternal. Now that she's spilling the bad news.

"Aunt Sophie, are you sure? The Mandelbaums have talked about retiring for years, but that hotel's been their life . . ."

"Sucked the life out of them more like. Yes, I'm sure, I'm not senile yet. They've bought their motel, given notice to the staff, and put the hotel up for sale."

"So maybe someone will buy it. Maybe you could work for the new owner." Maybe I could still have my manager's job. Now that my dreaded backup job has vanished I feel suddenly unmoored.

"Who would buy this old white elephant? It would take a fortune to do the work that needs to be done and what for? We haven't had a booked season for twenty summers. Truthfully, we've been less than half full for the last ten years. We haven't shown a profit in twice that long. There are liens on the property and back taxes. I don't know why Ira and Cora held on so long."

"But then what will happen if no one buys it?"

"They'll tear it down of course. They can't just leave it here as a ruin to molder away. Kids would get in and get up to no good. They'll tear it down and make the property into a park."

"But they can't just tear it down. It's over a hundred years old. Shouldn't it be a national monument or something?"

Aunt Sophie sniffs. For a moment I think the idea of the old place being torn down has gotten to her too, but then I remember how warm and humid it is in the laundry room and realize it's probably just her sinuses acting up. As for me, I have swiveled my chair around to look north out my window at the river as if, if I stared hard enough, I could see the white columns of the Hotel Equinox rising above the western banks of the Hudson. Over a hundred miles to the north, but still, I have always felt the pull of the place, like an anchor tethering me to the surface of the water here at the mouth of the harbor.

"I can't imagine it not being there," I say.

"Nothing lasts forever, *shayna maidela*." *Shayna maidela*. It's what my father used to call me. Pretty girl. I can't remember my aunt ever using it before, but today she's suddenly a font of Yiddish endearments. "Don't spend so much time worrying over the past. And with such good news about your story in that fancy coffee magazine! Go out and get some sun, you spend too much time sitting at your desk fretting about the past. Like your mother. So morbid. Don't you worry about an old hotel and an old woman. Go out and enjoy the sunshine."

Chapter Six

As if in direct response to my aunt's advice to enjoy the sunshine it rains all the next week. The rain strips the trees of their white petals, leaving bare limbs and a litter of soiled blossoms like muddied slush on the sidewalks. It might as well be the middle of winter.

Jack cancels our Wednesday night together—so he can catch up on the work he missed going out with me on Tuesday—and I realize that instead of a sea change, our Tuesday night together was merely a misplaced entry on the ledger books to be made up somewhere else.

I collect the fairy-tale papers from all my classes. Eighty-six of them altogether, including Aidan's hand-delivered essay, which I put on the pile with the papers from Grace College when I get his transfer notice in my mailbox. By the time I wade through the misspellings and incorrect usages, the fragments and run-ons and comma splices, the stack of red-marked essays are so much bloodied paper and my red-stained fingertips the hands of a butcher.

At the end of each day—when I've taught my classes and marked the requisite number of papers I've assigned myself—I sit at my desk and try to do my own writing. I stare out the window where, some days, just before dusk, the cloud cover lifts for the moment before sunset, releasing a thin band of copper-colored light above the New Jersey skyline. I tap my pen against my desk to the tune of *follow-up piece* and *possibly publishable*. I try to think about my mother—about what I might write about her next. But instead I think about my father, about how saddened he would be if he knew the hotel was going to be torn down.

The hotel was his whole life. He'd come there straight out of the war, wearing the one suit he owned—other vets dyed and wore their uniforms but my father burned his—with nothing but his own father's warnings ringing in his ears. What kind of job is that for a Jew? A *hotelier?* my grandfather had said to him. He was supposed to go to City College and become an accountant, but on the first day of classes he caught a train north and answered the ad the Mandelbaums had placed in the *Times* for a night clerk at the Hotel Equinox—"a family hotel in the heart of the Catskills overlooking the beautiful Hudson River."

"I liked that," my father would tell guests over a cigar and a glass of seltzer in the Sunset Lounge (my father never drank hard liquor). "A family hotel. At the end of the war a French family put me up in their hotel while I recuperated from pneumonia. I got to like the hotel life. Of course, I thought the Mandelbaums were Jewish."

They weren't. They were Quakers. The hotel wasn't in that part of the Catskills—it was north and east of Grossingers and the Concord, isolated on a narrow ridge above the Hudson River. It was the kind of place where wealthy families from the city had summered for generations, hiking and swimming in the cold lake—not playing bingo and canasta by a pool. The nightly entertainment was more likely to be a lecture on birding or "folk songs around the campfire" than a Borscht Belt comedian or social dancing. But the Mandelbaums didn't care that my father was Jewish or that he'd never worked in a hotel before.

"I liked how clean he looked," Cora Mandelbaum once told me. "I knew he'd be a hard worker. He's never let us down."

And he never did. Not until last spring when he came back from the hospital in Albany with the news that the touch of indigestion he'd been getting every night after dinner wasn't Cora's stuffed cabbage, it was a tumor, high in his stomach, too close to his heart to operate. The doctors gave him eight months.

"This season you'll be our guest," Cora told him. "You'll sit in a lounge chair and take it easy. Let the college kids do the work."

But my father wasn't one to lounge. He'd seem to sometimes. To keep a guest company he'd sit with his seltzer and cigar and admire the sunset, looking like he had all the time in the world. My father never hurried. But always, he'd have one eye on the new bartender, an ear cocked for late arrivals, for the crunch of gravel on the driveway and the ping of the bell at the front desk. He worked through that last season with the same unhurried grace and when the last guest checked out he went back to the hospital in Albany—as if keeping a date—and died.

Maybe, I think now, it was better he didn't live to see the hotel sold or torn down. But the thought fails to console me. Even my lunch with Phoebe Nix—*lunch with my editor,* I hum to myself—fails to lighten the gloom I seem to be sinking toward.

We meet at Tea & Sympathy, a mousehole of a restaurant on Greenwich Avenue for expat Brits homesick for bangers and mash, bubble and squeak. When she named the place I remembered that her famous poet mother had been married to a British lord something-or-other and I thought I'd be treated to high tea and expansive anecdotes of life across the pond.

But there is nothing expansive about Phoebe Nix. I'd forgotten, from our one meeting at the reading, what a stern young woman she is. There's not an ounce of spare flesh on her T-shirted, black-jeaned figure, which makes it far easier for her than for me to fit into the narrow slot allotted us by Tea & Sympathy. Her fair, baby-fine hair is shorn so close to the skull I can see the pale blue veins throb at her temples beneath its colorless sheen, like blue-veined rocks under a mountain stream. Her only adornment is a delicately engraved wedding band that she wears on her right thumb.

"My mother's," she says when she sees me looking at it. "It's the only thing of hers I got. All her other jewelry went back to the family estate, but I didn't want any of that ancestral crap anyway."

"It's lovely," I say, leaning over our tiny table—and knocking over a tea strainer—to get a better look at Phoebe's thumb, which is splayed over the painted roses on her china teacup.

She slips the ring off her thumb and hands it to me. I hold up the thin band of silver—terrified that I'll drop it into my Earl Grey—and study the design. It takes me a minute to realize that the band is engraved with an interlocking pattern of barbed wire and thorns. And then I do drop it—into the sugar bowl.

"Wow," I say, fishing the wedding ring out of the sugar. "Your mother and father must have had some interesting wedding vows."

Phoebe shakes her head and blows on her hot tea (chamomile—the same color as her hair—unsweetened).

"I did the engraving," she says. "I took a class at Parsons just so I could do it myself. I wanted to remember every time I looked at it that marriage is a trap. It killed my mother. Kept her from writing and then she figured she might as well be dead if she couldn't write."

"Wow," I say for the second time today (I'm really impressing her with my writer's vocabulary, I think), "their marriage was that bad?" I hand Phoebe back her mother's ring.

"*All* marriage is that bad," Phoebe says examining the ring for sugar crystals. She pops the ring in her mouth, sucks, and then spits it out into her napkin. For an instant before the ring reappears on her thumb I think I see blood on the napkin—as if the barbed wire and thorns on the ring sprang to life in Phoebe's mouth—but then I see it's just a spray of embroidered roses on the cloth. "But you must know that. I mean 'The Selkie'—the story you chose as a vehicle for your mother's story—is a classic entrapment tale. The woman's true nature—her skin—is stolen by the bridegroom. He holds her captive by hiding her skin. That's what my father did. He promised my mother financial support so she could write but then when she didn't want to have children right away—she was over forty when she had me—he was furious at her for not providing an heir to carry on the Kron name. He made her life a living hell—drinking, having affairs—and when she finally gave in and had a child he was pissed off I wasn't a boy. My mother killed herself six months after I was born."

Phoebe takes a sip of tea and I study a portrait of Queen Elizabeth hanging on the wall behind her because I can't think of anything to say.

The worst part, I imagine, is knowing your own mother chose to die so soon after giving birth. At least I was ten when my mother died.

"Our mothers had a lot in common," she says after a moment's silence. "It would be interesting if they had known each other."

"Did you look in your mother's journals to see if they did?" I ask.

Phoebe studies me closely and then makes what for her constitutes an expressive gesture. She tilts her narrow hand over to show an empty palm. "She mentions a Katherine in her early New York journals, but I'm not sure if it's your mother. Her later journals are at my place in the country. I'll look through them when I go up there this summer. Even if they didn't know each other, their stories have remarkable similarities. My mother stopped writing the year before she died and your mother was unable to finish her third book. Don't you think that had something to do with her marriage?"

I shake my head. Although I'm flattered that Phoebe has included me in her sorority of writers' daughters—after all, her mother was a famous poet, while my mother was a has-been genre writer whose two fantasy novels are out of print—I can't allow her to lay the blame for that unfinished third book on my father. "Actually, my father was really supportive of my mother's writing. When they met she was a maid at the hotel—he found pieces of her novel under the stacks of linen and instead of firing her, he gave her one of the guest rooms to write in."

I watch Phoebe's eyes, over the rim of her teacup, widen, but I go on.

"When he found out she only liked to write on hotel stationery—the expensive kind with a watermark—he ordered an extra ream for her personal use. He bought her a typewriter when he proposed to her instead of a ring. An Underwood," I finish lamely. Fortunately our lunch comes—a plate of undressed baby greens for Phoebe, Welsh rarebit and scones for me—or I'd still be rambling on, singing my father's praises and the joys of matrimony.

Phoebe spears a clump of prickly escarole and waves it at me.

"Then why, if your father created such a perfect atmosphere for writing, didn't your mother write her third book?"

I look down at the pool of melted cheese on my plate and shrug. Even shrugging is too expansive a gesture for the cramped confines of Tea & Sympathy. The motion of my shoulders dislodges from the arm of my chair my umbrella, which unfurls and flaps to the floor like a large, damp bird.

"She wrote her first two books before I was born," I say, bending to retrieve my umbrella and knocking my head on the next table. "So I have to assume her inability to finish the third one had more to do with being a mother than being a wife."

By the time I leave Tea & Sympathy I'm almost surprised that Phoebe Nix still wants to publish "The Selkie's Daughter" in *Caffeine*. But she's given me a sheaf of galley proofs, which I've slipped underneath my raincoat to keep dry, so I suppose she still means to go ahead. I feel, though, that I've totally muffed my first editorial luncheon. The rain doesn't help. My umbrella— having acquired an energetic life of its own at Tea & Sympathy—promptly turns itself inside out and wings east toward St. Vincent's Hospital. There's nothing to do but bow my head to the onslaught of rain and head west on Jane, toward the river, where all this rain and wind seem to be coming from.

By the time I make it home the galley sheets are limp and waterstained. I read over my essay, which instead of gaining stature in set type seems to have shrunken and withered. The little that still sounds good to me feels appropriated. I'm telling a story told to me by my mother, who heard it from her mother. When I wrote it that seemed to be the point— the way fairy tales are handed down from mother to daughter. But instead of a sense of matriarchal bonding there is now a whiff—like the dead fish smell coming off the river tonight—of theft. Aren't I just stealing my mother's story? Even the title, "The Selkie's Daughter"—which Phoebe admired and which I thought was an original variation on "The Selkie"—rings false to me, as if I'd heard it somewhere else. I even search Amazon.com for other books with that title but the closest match I find is *The Optimist's Daughter* by Eudora Welty.

The rainy weather lifts in the next weeks, but instead of lightening my gloom it just makes me too edgy to sit at my desk. I make no further progress writing about my mother and fall shamelessly behind on my grading. I feel bad because my students were truly excited by the fairy-tale assignment and each time I come to class empty-handed they look disappointed not to get their papers back. I decide, one Monday toward the end of April, that I simply have to finish grading the papers before that night's class at Grace, but when I read Mrs. Rivera's paper, which retells a Mexican version of "Rapunzel," I suddenly have an overwhelming urge—like the pregnant mother in the story—for fresh greens. There's no witch's garden to steal from so instead I head across town to the Greenmarket in Union Square. I tell myself that I'll just pick up some salad for lunch, but I know I'm also hoping to run into Jack.

Instead I run into Gretchen Lu.

She's standing by a vegetable stall, taking two large plastic garbage bags from a young woman in overalls.

"Professor Greenfeder," she says, holding up her bags in two white-gloved hands. "Are you coming to the opening tonight?"

I rack my brain for knowledge of an opening, but give up.

"I'm sorry Gretchen, I don't remember . . ."

"The student show, Professor. My installation piece was inspired by your fairy-tale assignment."

Oh yes. Dead fish. "That's right. You did 'The Little Mermaid,' right?"

"Oh no. Too Disney. I changed my mind. Haven't you read my paper?" I picture Gretchen Lu's paper at the bottom of a stack on my desk, but she's gone on, oblivious to the slothful practices of her English Comp teacher. "I wanted something more connected to my major—you know, textiles? So I reread Hans Christian Andersen and you can guess which fairy tale I came up with."

I can? I run though my list of Hans Christian Andersen stories in my head—"The Snow Queen"? "The Little Tin Soldier"? "The Ugly Duckling"?—but can't come up with a textile motif. I'm distracted by the piles of fresh greens all around us, lying in damp bunches as if just picked in a dewy field somewhere in the country.

"The Wild Swans!" Gretchen says. "You know, this little girl Elisa? Her eleven brothers are changed into swans? And she has to knit eleven shirts to change them back? And she can't talk to anyone until she finishes knitting? And her mother-in-law makes it look like she's killing her babies by smearing her mouth with blood? And she can't defend herself because she can't talk?"

Although she ends every sentence with the upward lilt of a question, Gretchen doesn't pause for answer, so I find myself nodding, spellbound, along with a small circle of farmers and shoppers here in the Greenmarket also drawn in by her story.

"So she's going to be burned as a witch? But she keeps on knitting and finally she's finished all eleven shirts except for the sleeve on the last one and her brothers fly into the town square where she's going to be burned and she throws the shirts over them and they change into boys again except for the youngest one? The one who gets the unfinished shirt? He has a broken wing instead of an arm."

Gretchen takes a deep breath and I notice that the little circle we've drawn also seems to take a breath and turn back to their purchases of herbs and goat cheeses and fresh-picked wildflowers. Are there really wildflowers like this growing somewhere? I wonder. Is the pine forest around the lake—Tirra Glynn, my mother called those woods—full of violets? Are there lady's slippers growing by the pool below Two Moons? Is it really almost May?

"Isn't that the creepiest detail? The winged arm?" Gretchen shivers with pleasure and the garbage bags in her gloved hands shake like cheerleader's pom-poms.

"Yes," I say, wondering what she's made of this detail in her installation piece. It's got to be better than dead fish, right?

"What time is the show, Gretchen? I'd love to see your piece."

Gretchen holds up her left hand to look at her watch. I notice, for the first time, that what I had taken for gloves are in fact bandages.

"Eight," she says. "Only seven hours away and I've got three more shirts to knit. No one's going to burn me," she says, giggling, "but I know how Elisa felt."

"What are you knitting them from . . ." And then of course I remember. I don't have to look into the garbage bag that Gretchen has obligingly spread open with her scratched and bandaged hands. Nettles. That's what Elisa knitted the sweaters out of in the story. Stinging nettles.

"Jesus," I say to Gretchen, touching her right hand gingerly. I notice that above the white line of bandage the skin is dotted with red pinpoints, like tiny drops of blood. I fell into a patch of nettles once. The rash was so bad my mother had to soak me in oatmeal baths for a week.

Gretchen only shrugs at my concern and smiles. "You know what they say, Professor Greenfeder, 'You have to suffer for your art.'"

Chapter Seven

Considering that she has maimed herself in the execution of my assignment, I figure that the least I can do is go to Gretchen's show. The only problem is that my class at Grace doesn't end until eight-thirty. It occurs to me, as I hurry through the rest of the papers I have to grade, that it might be pedagogically defensible to dismiss my class early and invite them to the student show at The Art School. Gretchen has given me a handful of flyers and I see that the theme of the show is *Dreams and Nightmares: Childhood Memories*. Someone has drawn a picture of a leering wolf in granny bonnet underneath the location and time of the show. I know that at least a few of my students will have done pieces based on fairy tales, so really, it ties in beautifully with the assignment my Grace students have just completed.

By four o'clock I've finished all but one of the papers—Mr. Nagamora's, which I've saved for last because his English is so faltering that it's painful to read and agony to correct. I decide to take a break and make a light dinner before trying to untangle Mr. Nagamora's knotted syntax. I sauté the rhubarb chard and dandelion greens I bought at the Greenmarket in olive oil and garlic and toss them into a bowl of capellini. I rarely go to this much trouble to cook for myself, but the fresh greens seem to demand some extra respect. I don't actually have a kitchen table (I certainly don't have a dining room table!), just a counter and one wobbly bar stool, so tonight I eat at my desk, looking out the window. Although the stretch of Jersey shore I face is mostly warehouses and docks, I think I see a bit of green in the shoreline to the north. The last few train rides I've taken to Rip Van Winkle have been on rainy days, so I hadn't noticed the greening of the forested parts of the Palisades. Nor have I spoken to Aunt Sophie since she told me the news that the hotel was up for sale. Surely, though, it would be a little while before the hotel was sold or before anyone decided to tear it down. Time enough for me to go up there when classes are done and spend some time walking in the green woods behind the hotel. Time to swim in the lake.

I finish my pasta and greens and although full I realize I'm not sated. Like Rapunzel's mother, this longing I have for greenery transcends carnal appetite. The green I'm longing for is the translucent dappled green of a forest glen, pale fern green, shadowy pine green, sunstruck lake green. Although I've always felt I belonged here in the city, I hadn't realized until now how much I depended on that pocket of country a few hours north to retreat to—if only in my mind.

I startle out of my reverie of green, realizing I'm going to be late to class. And I still haven't graded Mr. Nagamora's paper. All the work I've done today will be worthless if I can't hand back all the papers at once. I decide to read his paper quickly without correcting anything, just to get a feel for it.

At first I'm surprised at how hard it is for me to read without the red pen in my hand. I reach for it twice, but then the sheer beauty of the story, visible like the warp thread in an elaborate brocade, wins me over and I sit reading with my hands clasped in my lap. I know when I've finished that if I were to subtract for every error Mr. Nagamora has made—every crime against English usage—he would get a failing grade. So instead—because the story is so beautiful and because I am out of time—I scrawl a large A on top of his paper and shove it into my book bag before I can change my mind.

On the way to class I justify Mr. Nagamora's A by deciding to have him read the story out loud to the class. The story about a poor Japanese weaver who marries a mysterious woman who is able to weave a magical cloth for sails will be a perfect introduction to how textiles figure in fairy tales. There's "Rumpelstiltskin," of course, in which the miller's daughter has to spin gold out of flax, and "The Three Spinners," whose heroine also finds a surrogate spinner to do her work—but instead of a dwarf she finds three deformed sisters to do the work for her and when the prince meets the hideous threesome on the wedding day and learns that their deformities are caused by years of spinning he forbids his young bride from ever spinning again. There seems to be a subversive thread running through these stories protesting the drudgery of women's work. I think of the banishment of spindles in "Sleeping Beauty." I think of the selkie in my mother's story who is unable to knit, but weaves a wreath out of salt spray in her daughter's hair as her parting gift. I think of Gretchen Lu's maimed hands. It will be perfect, I think. We'll hear Mr. Nagamora's story and then go see what Gretchen Lu has made of "The Wild Swans."

. When I tell the class we're ending early and going on a field trip there's an agreeable ripple of excitement but also a slight frisson of anxiety. I have to assure Mrs. Rivera that she'll be able to catch the nine forty-nine back to Great Neck (the family she lives with expects her back to sleep in the house even on her days off—in case one of the children wakes in the night) and give Amelie alternate subway directions so she can make it back to Queens without walking back across town. Aidan is quiet through all this, but it occurs to me that there's probably a curfew at the detention house where he stays. I tell him it's all right if he can't go to the show, but he grins and tells me he wouldn't miss it.

I hand back their papers during this flurry of negotiations—grateful really that the noise cloaks the disappointed sighs and the little gasps of pleasure with which my students react to their grades. After all these years I am still not comfortable being the giver of grades, the passer of judgment. I worry I've been too harsh with the poorly graded and too lenient to the ones getting good grades. When I hold out Mr. Nagamora's paper I almost decide to pull it back—so sure I am now of the recklessness of that A—and the pages quiver midair between us for a moment before they float down to his desk. I see the creased lines of his face tighten as he looks down at the grade on top and for a second I think he has misunderstood. Does an A mean something else—something shameful like Hawthorne's scarlet letter—in Japan? But then I realize that the tension in his face is only his attempt to stem the smile that finally floods across his face.

"So many mistakes I'm sure I make . . ." he begins, looking up at me.

"But the story is so beautiful," I say. "Would you read it to the class? I think if you read it aloud you might be able to correct the errors yourself later."

See, I say to myself, I haven't totally abandoned the cause of grammar. I'm sure I read somewhere that this reading-the-text-aloud-as-proofreading is a legitimate rhetorical procedure.

Mr. Nagamora blushes so violently that I fear he will be too shy to read his paper to the class, but he rises instantly to his feet, electing on his own to stand before the class where the only sign of his nervousness is the slight trembling of the pages in his hand as he tells us the story of "The Crane Wife."

"In Japan too we have a story of a man who marries a woman who comes to him in much mystery like your Irish farmer who marries his seal bride. Your story reminded me of a story my father told me and for many years I thought it was a true story. That is because the story is about a silk weaver and that is what my father was back in Japan."

Mr. Nagamora takes a deep breath and looks at me. I nod for him to go on. What amazes me is that the grammatical errors I know are there on the page are vanishing as he tells his story aloud.

"The silk weaver in the story, though, made sails for boats and my father wove silk for kimonos. There was one pattern that my father was most famous for—a pattern called Dancing Crane—and when he worked on this pattern he would tell this story about the sailmaker.

" 'Once there was sailmaker who lived by himself,' my father told me."

I notice that Mr. Nagamora's voice changes now that it's his father telling the story. Also his spine straightens and the pages in his hand cease to tremble.

"And he was very lonely because he had no bride. In spring he watched the cranes dancing their mating dance together and although their dance was beautiful it made him sad because he had no one to share his rice with at night, no one to help him weave his cloth or admire how light and fine the sails were when they were done. One autumn night he heard the lonely cry of the cranes flying south for winter and the sound made him so sad he stood at his door for a long time—far into the night—watching the birds fly across the moon. He raised his arms and the long sleeves of his kimono flapped in the wind. It reminded him of the way the cranes flapped their wings in their dances and before he knew what he was doing the weaver was dancing on his doorstep, turning in great circles, dipping up and down, just like he had seen the great birds do."

One of the younger women in the back giggles and Mr. Nagamora lowers the paper and looks at her. I start to shush her but Mr. Nagamora grins and says, "Yes, I thought this sounded silly when I was young too and I always laughed at just this part. 'Oh you think that's funny,' my father would say and I would be scared that my father was angry but then he would leap up from his loom and dance around the room like a crazy man." Mr. Nagamora waves the pages above his head like a tambourine and swoops down to the giggler who shrieks with surprise and delight. He takes a spin around the room, flapping his arms so that the sleeves of his baggy cardigan flutter like wings. Aidan Barry claps a rhythm and for a moment I have the unsettling feeling that my class has slipped out of my control, but then Mr. Nagamora glides back to the front of the class, clears his throat, and continues reading as if nothing has happened. The class, which was whooping and shrieking at Mr. Nagamora's dance, falls silent instantly, as if under a spell.

"The weaver danced so long into the night that he slept through half the next day and when he awoke he felt ashamed that he had wasted a day of work. He was supposed to deliver a sail the next day to a ship's captain, which he had not even begun to weave. But then he heard the sound of the shuttle knocking against the loom in the weaving room. He thought he was dreaming but when he tried the door he found it was locked. A voice from inside—a beautiful voice, a woman's voice—called from inside. 'Please wait and all will be well.' The weaver was confused, but also tired and hungry, so he boiled water for tea and waited. All through the night the door remained locked and the sound of the shuttle knocking against the loom went on without a break. 'Whoever is in there is the strongest weaver there ever was,' the weaver thought. 'Even if she is ugly, I will ask her to marry me.' But in the morning, when the weaver awoke, the woman who knelt by his side, holding the finished sail, was not ugly. She was the most beautiful woman he had ever seen, with skin as white as down, and eyes black as night. She held out to him the bundle of white silk, which when he took it in his hands was so light it was as if he held the wind.

" 'This is my dowry,' the woman said to him, 'if you'll have me as your bride.'

"Of course, the weaver was delighted to have this woman, who was not only beautiful but skilled and useful, as his bride. When he delivered the sail to the ship's captain he was paid twice what he had been paid before because the sail was so fine and light.

"The weaver and his bride lived happily all that winter on the money from that sail, but in the spring the money was gone and the weaver knew he must make another sail. A messenger from the ship's captain had come to ask for another sail like the one he had bought before. A sail that seemed to coax the wind out of the sky.

" 'Only you can make a sail like that,' the weaver told his bride. 'Will you make me another?'

"The weaver's bride was slow to answer, which surprised the weaver because she had always been happy to do all that he had asked. Finally she answered, 'I do not think you understand, my husband, what you ask of me. The work takes so much out of me. I was glad to do it as my dowry, as a gift from my heart, just as your dance was a gift from your heart. But if you want me to do this, I will do it for you this once.'

"The weaver was ashamed by her words and he didn't like to feel ashamed. 'Yes, wife,' he answered, 'I want you to do this for me.'

"So she went into the weaving room and locked the door and for two days and two nights the weaver heard the sound of the shuttle knocking against the loom without stop or rest. Finally his wife called from inside that the work was done. When the weaver came inside he found his bride leaning against the loom, her poor hands still clutched around the shuttle like birds' claws. On the floor by her side was the sail, as flawless and light as the last one.

"The weaver sold this sail for twice again what he sold the last one for and they were able to live two years from the money, but at the end of those two years the money was gone again. When he went to his bride she knew what he was going to ask, before he spoke.

" 'Do not ask this of me, husband,' she said. 'You ask me to give all of myself.' Again the weaver felt ashamed and he did not like feeling ashamed. 'As a good wife should,' he answered her and showed her to the loom. This time she worked three days and three nights without rest or stop. The weaver waited for her call to come inside but when it did not come he began to grow worried, and then afraid, and then angry. 'What is so hard about her weaving that she makes such a fuss,' he said to himself. 'I will see.'

"When he forced the door open he saw a sight that he would never forget for as long as he lived. Trapped inside the loom stood a huge crane. In its claws it held the shuttle. Its long neck bent down to pull a feather from its wing and then the bird used its beak to feed the feather to the shuttle, weaving the cloth out of the downy white feathers. The silk that fell from the loom shook with the rocking of the bird, trembling like feathers in the wind. As he stood in the doorway, his mouth wide open, the bird turned to him and he saw his wife's sad black eyes looking at him. When she saw him she dropped the shuttle and flew out the window.

"The weaver called her name and followed her but although she flew slowly and close to the ground he could not keep up with her. Even after he lost sight of her he followed the path of bloody feathers she left behind her but he never found her."

Mr. Nagamora lowers the papers. Suddenly he looks as tired and worn out as the dying crane. Gone is the youthful man who danced a moment ago; now he looks old and bewildered, looking out at this little group of strangers. I get up from my perch on the edge of one of the student's desks to relieve him of the spotlight, but he holds up his paper and waves me away.

"When I was a boy I thought this a very sad story," he says. Several of the students nod. "But now when I tell it what I remember most is my father dancing. And I'm glad I have this story to remember him by."

Mr. Nagamora gives a little bow and the class begins to applaud—I think it's Aidan who starts it—as he walks back to his desk.

I haven't a clue how to follow up his performance—no pithy, teacherly comment to bring closure to the lesson. And so I suggest we adjourn to The Art School to see what my other students have done with this assignment I've given—an assignment that seems to have taken on a queer life of its own.

We walk across town in a straggling clump. I notice that Amelie and Mrs. Rivera walk protectively on either side of Mr. Nagamora as if he were one of the young children they nanny for their livelihoods. I'm glad to see him in good hands. Aidan Barry gravitates to my side and tells me about his work-release job at the printing press. He doesn't really like it, he says, and he's afraid he's not learning the trade fast enough. If he loses the job, he tells me, it won't look good to the parole board.

"What did you do before . . ." Before I'm forced to say *before prison* he answers, "I worked at a hotel in Midtown. First as a doorman, then a desk clerk. I liked it. Hotels are classy. If my family had a hotel like yours I'd definitely work there, learn the business, maybe run it someday."

"My family doesn't own the Hotel Equinox," I remind him. "My father was the manager, but he died last year, and my aunt Sophie's just the bookkeeper—although she tends to put her hand in everywhere. Besides, it's up for sale and if no one buys it it'll probably get torn down."

"That's a shame," he says. "Maybe you could find someone to buy it."

I laugh. "I don't know anyone that rich, and even if I did, who'd want it? It would cost millions to renovate and even though the setting is really spectacular it's not exactly in a prime tourist location. No one goes to the Catskills anymore."

Aidan shakes his head. "You shouldn't give up so easily on the family business."

"It's not the family business . . ." I begin, but he doesn't hear me. We've come to The Art School's student gallery and he springs ahead of me to open the door, a gesture that amuses the crowd of slouching smokers lounging on the front steps. Unfortunately I prolong the embarrassment by freezing at the entrance.

The student gallery is a long stretch of glass-fronted, stark white space facing Fifth Avenue. It's a venue that can make even the most mild-mannered of student efforts striking. The tableau mounted at its center tonight doesn't need any help. My first reaction is that Mr. Nagamora's story has come eerily to life, at least that last part when the crane flies away leaving a trail of bloody feathers. There's a lot of feathers and a lot of blood. Well, red paint, no doubt, but still . . . it looks as if there's been a lethal pillow fight—the My Lai of pillow fights. Giant white birds are suspended from the ceiling, white feathers drifting from their ruptured bellies like candy from piñatas. The feathers drift steadily—how Gretchen has engineered this part is a mystery—onto a scene of bizarre carnage. Eleven—I know it's eleven without having to count—baby dolls sit in a circle around a pyre of wood. In the center of the pyre a mannequin in a torn Disney princess nightgown sits cross-legged, knitting. Even from out here on the sidewalk I can see the bloodied bandages on her hands. She's knitting a shirt made up of prickly green leaves—the nettles, no doubt—and, more disturbingly, barbed wire. Ten of the eleven dolls wear shirts made of this strange fiber. The eleventh doll is standing reaching its one chubby baby fist up toward the girl on the pyre. Its other arm has been ripped off. Feathers and blood pour out of the little gaping hole.

The fact that attractively dressed people—mostly in black—are standing around this scene, gesturing toward it with their plastic tumblers of wine, only makes the whole thing more unsettling.

My little crew of Grace students have come up beside me. We've lost a few in transit—but here are Mrs. Rivera and Amelie and Mr. Nagamora. What in the world will they make of this?

I would like to flee the scene, but how would I possibly explain that to my students? Besides, as I stand here, foolishly keeping Aidan holding the door, Gretchen Lu spies me from inside and comes running out to get me.

"Oh, Professor Greenfeder, thank God you're here. It's turned into a real circus. The board of trustees was invited, and there are some reporters, and everyone's asking me what my inspiration was? So now that you're here you can explain everything, right?"

Chapter Eight

Gretchen Lu takes me by the hand—even if I wanted to resist, the blunted shape of her bandaged hand, soft as a kitten's paw, totally disarms me—and leads me to a small group standing next to her project. I recognize a few of the teachers—full-timers for the most part—and the head of the English Department, Gene Delbert. Gene, in black jeans and leather jacket, is nervously swirling red wine in his tumbler while talking to a small group of older men and women whom I guess to be trustees. I notice there's a feather sticking out of Gene's hair and resist the temptation to pluck it loose. Several of the men and women standing around have feathers in their hair or clinging to their clothing. As a result their serious expressions seem feigned, like children who've been surprised in a pillow fight, pretending innocence.

"Oh good," Gene says when he sees Gretchen leading me forward. "Here's the instructor who gave the assignment. I'm sure she can make clear her intent."

Gene says *intent* the way a lawyer might use the word in phrases like *with harmful intent*. I also notice that he's called me an instructor, not professor, making clear, I'm sure, to the college trustees that I am an expendable part-timer. There'll be no sticky tenure issues to cope with when they fire me for inspiring this scene of feathery carnage.

I take a deep breath and, dropping Gretchen's hand, gesture toward Elisa on her pyre. I notice, now that I'm closer, that the mannequin's mouth is sealed with silver electrical tape. I open my mouth to speak but the voice that I hear isn't my own.

" 'The Wild Swans' is yet another allegory of the silencing of women's creativity," the voice explains much more eloquently than I could have hoped to. "While Elisa works she is sworn to silence, just as the woman artist is forced to give up her true voice in order to produce in a man's marketplace."

I turn around and find Phoebe Nix behind me, one hand on my shoulder, the other gesturing toward the tableau. I'm so relieved to have her explaining the piece that I forget for a moment to wonder what she's doing here.

"But what does the woman artist produce without artistic freedom?"

Phoebe pauses while we all consider this question and Gretchen's work. I notice that the little shirts worn by the baby dolls are not just knitted in stocking stitch, but in alternating cables of nettles and barbed wire. If I'm not mistaken, Gretchen has even managed to work in a blackberry stitch within the cables. What attention to detail! Even if she's gotten me fired, I'll have to give Gretchen an A+.

"Bad clothes?" I hear Mark Silverstein mutter his answer to Phoebe's question somewhere behind me. I try, out of the corner of my eye, to see Mark's piece on "The Emperor's New Clothes" but his unprepossessing assemblage of naked mannequins has been crowded into a corner like uninvited guests. No wonder he's pissed off at Gretchen.

Phoebe ignores Mark's comment and answers her own question. "She creates a prison for her offspring, crafting a garb of barbed wire for her daughters out of the old myths and collusion of silence."

I'm tempted to correct Phoebe's version of the fairy tale. The baby dolls in their barbed wire and nettle shirts aren't Elisa's daughters, they're her brothers. But then I notice that several of the older trustees and most of the full-time professors are nodding eagerly. Only one man—a much older man in a beautiful charcoal gray suit—is not nodding along with the others. Instead he is staring at me as if challenging me to unmask Phoebe's mistake. But there's no way I'm going to turn back the tide of acceptance and approval that sweeps over the crowd. I can feel the tension in the room dissipating. Conversation resumes, the crowd breaks into groups of twos and threes, again happily swirling the wine in their tumblers and picking feathers out of their hair like friendly chimps picking out each other's nits. I notice Aidan Barry chumming up to Natalie Baehr and smile and then think *Oh my God, should I tell Natalie he's an ex-con?* and then, once again, I catch the old man in the gray suit staring at me.

I turn away from him and find Phoebe at my elbow.

"Thanks for that speech," I tell her. "I'm lucky you turned up here."

Phoebe doesn't shrug or smile or even lift an eyebrow. She is one of the most gesture-free people I've ever met.

"I came with my uncle Harry; he's on the board. I thought it would be a good venue to give away some copies of the journal. If you had told me you were involved in the show I would've planned a tie-in with this month's issue."

"You mean it's out?"

"Yes, we got to press a little early. There's a stack by the door." I turn toward the entrance and suddenly notice that several of the people in the gallery are leafing through a pale lavender magazine. The thought that some of them might be already reading my piece makes me feel strangely queasy.

Misreading my wave of nausea as excitement—I suppose a person who doesn't use facial expressions can be excused for misreading them—Phoebe says, "I've got some copies for you in my bag, but first I want you to meet my uncle. He's an imperialistic fossil, but he's rich as Croesus and a great patron of the arts, so you might as well know him."

Phoebe takes me by the hand, her grip surprisingly firm, and pulls me over to the man in the gray suit who is facing away from us.

"Uncle Harry, I want you to meet Iris Greenfeder, one of the writers in this month's issue of *Caffeine*."

The man turns toward us, his blue eyes vague but not unkind. I can see him assembling his features into an expression of polite interest. For a moment I feel sorry for him. He's older than I thought at first, my father's age at least—or the age my father would be if he were still alive. I remember how, as my father got older, his feet would bother him if he had to stand still for any length of time and how he hated being in a crowded room with lots of people talking; he said he found it hard to hear what people were saying. I imagine the effort it takes for this man to feign interest in his niece's half-baked writers. To his credit, though, I see his vague over-the-shoulder look resolve into something unexpected—perhaps to him as much as to me: genuine interest.

"I'm afraid I didn't catch your name," he says.

I tell him—trying to pitch my voice loud enough for him to hear but not so loud as to seem to be shouting—and he repeats it, taking a sip of red wine from his tumbler and wincing. He is, no doubt, used to a better vintage.

"Iris is writing a memoir about her mother who was a fantasy writer," Phoebe says.

I am?

"Well, I've just gotten started."

"Who was your mother?" he asks me so avidly that I'm a little taken back.

"She wrote under the name K. R. LaFleur," I tell him. "You probably wouldn't have heard of her."

"LaFleur." Phoebe's uncle swishes his cheeks back and forth as if he's at a wine tasting. I half expect him to spit. "The flower. Perhaps her first name was a flower name?"

"No, her name was Katherine, but everyone called her Kay. I don't know why she chose LaFleur . . ." *One more thing I don't know about my mother,* I think. Perhaps sensing my confusion Harry Kron comes to my rescue.

"I'm sure she had her own reasons. My name for instance, *Kron,* means 'crown' in German and so that is what I named my first hotel."

He pauses—a little pause like an orator who's penciled in the spaces for applause or laughter—and I realize that I'm supposed to recognize the name. The name *Harry Kron* doesn't register at first, but then the words *crown* and *hotel* do.

"The Crown Hotel," I say, "near Grand Central? My father always said it was the best-run hotel in New York. He admired the whole chain. He modeled our hotel's management on the Crown Hotels."

I notice Harry Kron grimace at the word *chain* and realize I've blundered. Holiday Inn is a chain, Hilton even, but the Crown Hotels, a dozen gemlike establishments known for their luxury and exclusivity, are more like a line, as in a line of purebred racehorses or the descendants of royalty. "Jewels in the Crown," they're called, all listed in the blue Michelin guides my father kept on the shelf above his desk in the front office. I feel an ache in my throat. The sight of old men sometimes does this to me. This is what my father would have looked like if he were still alive. (Curiously, the sight of old women never has this effect on me; I can never picture my mother as old.) But this man has not only attained an age my father never will, he is everything my father always wanted to be—the quintessential hotelier.

"Ah, your father ran a hotel and your mother wrote . . . what an intriguing combination. Perhaps I knew your parents . . ."

"Oh no, I doubt it. It's a small hotel upstate—the Hotel Equinox. My father was the manager for almost fifty years. He died last year."

"I'm so sorry. And your mother?"

"My mother died in 1973, when I was ten."

"Ah, like my sister-in-law, perhaps, Phoebe's poor mother, too sensitive to live in this world."

"She died in a hotel fire—not ours—I mean she was staying at another hotel. The Dreamland in Coney Island." ·

Something like distaste passes over Harry Kron's face and I'm not sure if it's the mention of such a déclassé hotel or the idea of a hotel fire—every hotelier's worst nightmare.

"Yes," he says, "I remember the incident. So tragic. Fire is a hotel's greatest danger and fire regulations were once quite lax. Even now not all managers are as scrupulous as they ought to be in fire prevention. The Crown Hotels have been leaders in fire prevention in the field. We installed emergency exits and sprinkler systems long before we were required to."

"Yes, I know," I say excitedly, "my father told me that. He installed pumps to draw water from the lake and trained the waiters in fire-fighting procedures. My mother was especially terrified of the idea of a fire . . ."

I stop, interrupted by an image of my mother, a picture of her I didn't know I possessed, walking the hotel halls with her hands on the walls, like a blind person, feeling for electrical fires in the wiring.

Seeing the emotion on my face, Harry Kron gallantly rescues me. "How doubly tragic, then, for her to die in one. What was your mother's maiden name?"

"Morrissey," I say. "Katherine Morrissey."

"Ah," Harry says, "I thought I saw a touch of Irish in you. You must look like your mother."

I smile. I'd like to think I look like my mother because she was beautiful. It's true I have my mother's dark hair and pale green eyes, but I'm built more solidly than she, more like my father's sturdy eastern European stock, and I've got a touch of his sallowness in my skin.

"Morrissey," he repeats. "Interesting."

"Well, you'll have to read Iris's piece in *Caffeine*, Uncle Harry." I've almost forgotten that Phoebe is still standing there.

"Oh, I will, I will." I can tell it's more than a polite lie and I'm ridiculously flattered by the idea of this urbane man reading my piece. "A writer living in a hotel. I think that's most interesting. Where in the hotel did your mother write? Was she like Jane Austen, writing in the parlor and then hiding her work in a drawer when people came in?"

"Oh no, she wrote—" I'm interrupted by Aidan Barry who's come up with Natalie Baehr in tow.

"Professor Greenfeder, you've really got to see what Natalie's done— it's small so I'm afraid you'll miss it."

I hold up a finger to signal to Aidan I'll be right with him, but Harry Kron smiles magnanimously and stretches his arms out as if to embrace me and Aidan and Natalie. "I've monopolized you far too long, Miss Greenfeder. Please, let's see your student's work."

I'm pleased, both for me and Natalie. After all, Phoebe said her uncle was a patron of the arts. Maybe he could do something for Natalie.

We walk over to a glass case in the corner of the room. Aidan's right. Natalie's display is so small and tucked away that I would have missed it. And I wouldn't want to miss this. Suspended on wires within the case—so that it seems to float—is a circlet of crystal and pearls so fine it seems spun out of dew. The piece could be worn as a necklace or headpiece, but floating as it does it seems to be something more than just a piece of jewelry, something elemental. In fact it seems to partake of all the elements: water frozen, shaped by wind, sparkling like fire, tethered to the earth by a single green teardrop. Natalie has crafted the wreath described in my mother's version of "The Selkie."

"Natalie, you made my mother's necklace," I say, so touched I barely trust myself to speak.

Harry Kron, who has taken out a pair of reading glasses to read the index card on which Natalie has typed the part of my story that describes the Selkie's necklace, turns to stare at me, his eyes disturbingly magnified by the lenses of his glasses. "Your mother had a necklace like this?"

"Oh no," I say, laughing, "my mother hardly wore jewelry at all—just some fake pearls." Just as before I'd had an image of my mother touching the hotel walls now I almost hear the sound my mother's pearls made when she leaned over me in bed to kiss me good night. "She described it in her books—the net of tears, she called it, but I think she got the idea from the selkie legend . . ."

I falter. Did she? Actually, now that I think of it, I've never seen a version of "The Selkie" that mentions any necklace at all.

"Or she added it to the fairy tale when she was writing her books," I say. "She did that. She took fairy tales and then changed them and created a whole fantasy world based on these altered fairy tales. I've always thought that the places where she changed the fairy tales might be where she's talking about herself, about something that happened to her . . ." I trail off. This had been the thesis of my dissertation and I've never been comfortable articulating it. Which is probably why I'm ABD.

"You'll have to explore that in your memoir," Phoebe says, "the intersection of your mother's life with her art."

Harry Kron nods, looking back at Natalie's necklace. "Yes. I'd very much like to know the real-life inspiration for this."

I stay another hour and drink three (or is it four?) tumblers full of sour, greenish wine. By the time I walk home my head is spinning. I haven't even looked properly at the magazines Phoebe slipped into my book bag before I left. I stop at Abingdon Square under a street lamp and pull out a copy of *Caffeine*.

The sight of my name on the cover has the unexpected effect of making me feel lightheaded. Or maybe it's just the wine. I should be pleased. My name comes first on the list of contributors. The drawing Phoebe's chosen for the cover even refers to my piece. It's a pen-and-ink drawing of a naked woman sitting on a rock, her long hair spread out around her like a fisherman's net. Caught in her hair is a naked man. In the borders of the picture, enclosed in Celtic spirals, swim sinuous seals. It's the same illustration that's on the cover of the book Aidan gave me. What an odd choice for the Mother's Day issue, I think, but then I notice the caption at the bottom of the cover. "Rewriting Our Mother's Lives: Cutting Loose the Ties That Bind."

I can scratch the idea of sending this to my aunt Sophie for Mother's Day. I'll have to go out tomorrow and buy her a nice cardigan to go with the MOMA address book I'd already gotten her.

By the time I get home the mood of exhilaration I'd felt at the party has evaporated and turned as bitter as the smell of cooked greens that permeates my one-room apartment. I'm replaying every conversation, looking for the missteps like hunting for dropped stitches. How could I have referred to the Crown Hotels as a chain? Or gone on and on about how my father emulated Harry Kron's management techniques? Although he'd politely told me that he'd be "keeping an eye on me" it was Natalie Baehr he'd singled out and given his card to.

"I've been thinking of revamping the logo of the Crown Hotels," he told an awed and speechless Natalie. "I think I could do something with this extraordinary tiara you've created."

Well good for Natalie, I think, unfolding my futon couch so violently I catch my hand in the wooden slats. I should be glad for her. I should rejoice in my student's success.

Lying in bed, though, thinking of the odd mix of my students at the show, I kick at the sheets and thrash uneasily. What a mistake! Harry Kron wasn't the only one to give Natalie Baehr his number. I'd seen Aidan and Natalie exchanging telephone numbers. How was I going to explain to Natalie that Aidan was an ex-con!

I flip over and try to think of something positive from the evening. Some of my Grace students looked like they were having a great time. Mrs. Rivera struck up a conversation with several textile majors about Mayan embroidery. I'd rarely seen her look so carefree. But then I noticed Mr. Nagamora. Only minutes before I left did I realize he had been standing in a corner, smiling and nodding at the groups of people who were, on the whole, ignoring him. I told him again how much I'd loved his telling of "The Crane Wife" and offered to walk with him across town, but then Phoebe came up with those issues of *Caffeine* and when I turned back Mr. Nagamora was gone. I scanned the room for him, but he'd fled as abruptly as the bird in his story, leaving behind the same trail of bloodied feathers.

I close my eyes and moan aloud at the picture waiting for me there— the papier-mâché geese suspended from the gallery's ceiling, their ruptured bellies disgorging white down.

I get up, walk to my bathroom, and throw up. A sour greenish bile that looks like dirty seawater. Feeling slightly better, I remake my bed and try to sleep. Just as I'm drifting off, though, I hear the question Harry Kron asked that I never got to answer. *Where in the hotel did your mother write?*

The answer is that she wrote in every room of the hotel, between the months of October and May when the hotel was closed. She wrote everything in longhand first, usually on hotel stationery—which of course made my aunt Sophie furious because it was so expensive. It wasn't bad enough that she used the paper, Aunt Sophie used to complain, but she was always stealing it out of the drawers in the guest rooms so that my aunt had to always check and replenish the supply before the hotel reopened. Even when my father ordered her a stack of the same paper she left that stack untouched until it was time to type. She preferred to wander from room to room until she settled on one she wanted to write in. Then she would perch at the desk, slip a sheet of letter paper from the drawer and take out the fountain pen she always kept in her pocket, and she'd write until she'd exhausted that supply of paper in the drawer. Then she would move on, sometimes leaving the thin sheets of handwritten pages behind her or carrying them so carelessly to the next room that some would slip from her grasp and flutter down the long empty halls, the loose white sheets trailing behind her like the feathers of a molting bird.

My father or aunt, or later I, would gather them and return the pages to her, which she would shuffle haphazardly into a pile that slowly grew over the winter like a snowdrift, until sometime near spring she would come to roost in one of the rooms and then, after a period of silence, we'd hear the typing begin: a steady, rhythmic beat that sounded like rain falling on the roof.

It was hard to imagine a finished novel coming out of those haphazard wanderings—and yet two books had. Only after I was born had something gone wrong. The pages had accumulated, the typing had begun, but years went by and no book appeared. It was as if she were weaving on an empty loom.

Sometime in the middle of the night it begins to rain and it's that sound that finally lulls me to sleep and follows me into my dreams. In my dream I am walking through the halls of the Hotel Equinox, not fleeing the sound, but following it, trying to find its source. As I walk up the main stairs, I run my hands along the walls, feeling for the vibration. At first I feel only a faint tremor, but then the walls begin to shake with the concussive beating and I realize I'm getting closer. The chandelier on the second-floor landing is shaking so hard its crystal drops sing like window chimes. This violent clatter, which shakes the old hotel like an earthquake, is coming from the room at the top of the stairs, the door of which is vibrating on its hinges.

Only when I touch the cut-glass knob do I remember that this is a room I'm not supposed to enter—it's a suite reserved for very important guests—but it's too late, the door is swinging open, the awful sound is stilled, leaving an even more awful silence behind it. Something turns to me from the black cage at the window but then there's a great rush of wind that hits my wide-open eyes and blinds me for a moment. When I can see again the room is empty, only the stir of breeze from the open window a reminder of those wings that have grazed against my damp face.

When I open my eyes it is morning. The window above my bed has come open in the night and the rain has soaked my sheets. The phone is ringing. I answer it and hear a voice that's more like a croak and for a moment, still half asleep, I think of the giant bird suspended above the old black typewriter. In my dream the bird was pulling feathers from its breast and feeding them into the typewriter's smooth black roller. Someone on the phone coughs and I switch the receiver to my other ear.

". . . feder?" I catch only the last bit.

"Yes, this is Iris Greenfeder," I say.

"This is Hedda Wolfe. I was your mother's agent. I want to see this memoir you're writing about Kay."

Chapter Nine

"The Wolf? Hedda Wolfe, the literary agent?" Jack asks that night. When I called and told him about Hedda Wolfe's call he said he'd come right over even though it was a Tuesday.

"The same," I say. "I read an article in *Poets & Writers* that said her workshop is called 'the wolfshop.' Some say she devours writers."

"Or makes them," Jack says. "I hear she got a six-figure advance for some twenty-year-old's first story collection."

I'm surprised that Jack—usually so outwardly disdainful of commercialism in the arts—knows and cares about a six-figure advance. I dip an asparagus spear in the hollandaise sauce I decided to make when Jack showed up at my door with a bundle of pale thin asparagus spears and an armful of lilac boughs. The sauce is lumpy because he'd come up behind me while I was stirring it at the stove and leaned his cool cheek against the back of my neck and folded himself into the curve of my back. This is new, I thought, as I switched the gas off under the saucepan and turned in the circle of his arms like something tightly rolled unfurling. I kept that feeling while we made love, of something wound close uncoiling slowly, but with an urgency I had thought we'd lost a long time ago. We had it once, I remembered when Jack, too impatient to fold out the futon, lifted me onto the wide window seat.

When we'd first met we were both dating other people—he, an art student at Cooper, me, my Medieval Lit professor at City University—but his ardor had totally swept me away. I remembered the first night I brought him back here and we made love standing against this same window ledge, so recklessly that the glass shivered in the panes, and then again, in the bed. And then in the middle of the night I'd woken to find him stroking me. As soon as I opened my eyes he entered me and came, quickly, without waiting for me, without apology. I hadn't minded, but felt instead awed by his need of me. It never happened like that again. He's been a courteous, generous lover for these last ten years but I sometimes feel that that third time we made love on our first night was the last time he wanted me more than I wanted him. That some extra edge had dulled then, a slight shift of desire that left me the one always wanting more.

Lover and beloved. Didn't there always have to be one of each? I've felt like the lover for close to ten years now, but tonight I feel a slight shift, something subtle as the fine mist of rain that seeped through the screens and soaked my back at the window, a shift in how his eyes followed me when I went to the stove and finished stirring the hollandaise sauce and steaming the asparagus. A shift in how he watched me put down the plates on the bed as though I were some powerful sorceress and this lemony butter sauce steaming the air around us a spell I'd woven. Even the lilacs, which had been cool and disappointingly odorless when Jack brought them, have opened in the warmth of the apartment, opened in the heat of our love-making, and released their heady purple scent—that smell of flowers that bloom briefly and only once—into the air.

It's only when we're eating the asparagus and lumpy hollandaise sauce that I wonder how much this change is attributable to my newfound success and I feel compelled to confess my reservations about Hedda Wolfe.

"My mother had a falling-out with her," I tell him.

"Do you know what it was about?"

"I overheard my mother say to my father, 'She'd have me give up everything for writing—even my family.' "

"What do you think she meant?"

"I think she told my mother not to have me. I imagine she thought that having a child would be bad for her writing career."

"And she was right."

I laugh so Jack won't see how hurt I am by this remark. Also, it is kind of funny. Hedda Wolfe—literary arbiter, maker and breaker of authors—nearly blue-penciling me out of existence thirty-six years ago like an ill-conceived metaphor or a wordy passage.

"Thanks, Jack," I say, trying to keep my tone light. "In other words you think it would have been better if I hadn't been born . . ."

"You know I don't mean that, Iris, but I do think that your mother's story is about the consequences of giving up your art. It's a cautionary tale."

"Well, maybe a cautionary tale against staying in cheap hotels with illicit lovers . . ."

"What drove her there? Do you really think she'd have been in that hotel if she'd kept writing? Would she have had to look elsewhere for satisfaction if she had finished her third book?"

It seems an unlikely explanation, but this is the first time I've heard Jack profess a belief in monogamy and marital fidelity as the badge of the fulfilled artist. It's an appealing thought. Maybe this is what's kept him at arm's length from me all these years—a sense that I was incomplete as an artist. Maybe there will be more than a six-figure contract to come out of this book.

"I'd have to do a lot of research," I tell him. "I hardly know anything about my mother's early life. I might have to spend some time up at the hotel this summer, especially since it looks like this will be the Hotel Equinox's last season."

"It'll be good for you," he says stroking my hand and then moving closer to me and touching my face. His hands, I notice, smell like butter and lemons. "I'd like to get out of the city when classes are over."

"I think my aunt would let us have the attic rooms," I say, sliding down beside him, pressing into his hands. "The light is good, the views are amazing."

Jack doesn't bother to tell me, as he usually does when I mention the famous view from the Hotel Equinox, that he's not a landscape painter. He's too immersed in the landscape of my hip, the small of my back, the hollow behind my knee. That slow unfurling I'd felt before becomes a flutter now as if what I'd thought was something green and root-bound had been, all along, the beating of wings against the chrysalis of my flesh.

Walking to Hedda Wolfe's apartment the next morning I carry with me the memory of the night with Jack like some secret hidden power: X-ray vision or the ability to fly. I've become one of my mother's superheroes, those creatures she wrote about who hid their wings between their shoulder blades and possessed gills pleated between their breasts. I even imagine that I smell lilacs, and then realize that of course I do—the florists and Korean grocers on Washington Street are full of them. Great nodding heads—like dopey, long-eared spaniels—of the purple blooms are at every corner. Where do they come from, I wonder. They're not a flower that's grown in a hothouse or nursery. I remember the shaggy bushes that lined the hotel's drive and bloomed for only a week or two in May. Hardly worth the trouble, my aunt Sophie would say and try to convince Joseph to uproot them and plant something tidier like box hedge or yew trees. But Joseph knew that the lilacs were my mother's favorite and wrapped their roots each fall to help see them through the cold winter. What would become of them if the hotel was sold and closed? For that matter, what will become of Joseph, who must be close to eighty now.

When I turn on 14th toward the river the scent of lilacs is replaced by something metallic and acrid. I pass a large open stall where a man is hosing down the sidewalk. White shapes hang in the shadows and I quickly look away, toward the river, where the low buildings afford an unusual view of open sky and sunlight. I notice a new café on the corner—modeled after the open-air market cafés of Paris—and the sleek white facade of a new clothing store. I check the address Hedda gave me and hope I haven't copied it down wrong. Although this part of the meatpacking district has boutiques and restaurants now, I didn't think it was zoned for residences, and she made it clear on the phone that she was inviting me to her home.

"After all," she said, "I knew you when you were a baby."

When I finally locate the number it's an industrial building, an old warehouse. I ring the buzzer and struggle with the heavy, steel door. I have to ring three times before I'm able to get it open.

The bottom floor is unfinished industrial space—something you don't see too much of anymore in the city. The ground floor of Jack's loft looked like this ten years ago, but now it's a South American furniture store. I notice in the dim recesses of this cavernous space a massive floor scale with an enormous grappling hook hanging above it. An image of the white carcasses I'd seen on the street comes briefly to mind, but of course the space is empty here. Instead of the smell of blood from the street there's the faintest whiff of coffee beans. To the right a flight of stairs climbs steeply up to a steel door.

I start up the stairs, which are corrugated iron, rusted in spots so that you can see through to the floor below. So far this isn't at all what I thought the famous Hedda Wolfe's home would look like. I'd expected something tweedy and book-lined—a town house in Chelsea with flower boxes and first editions in the built-in bookcases.

I knock on the metal door and hear that instantly recognizable voice call "Come." Like the captain of a ship, I think, turning the knob.

The space I enter is somewhat shiplike. Maybe it's the enormous floor-to-ceiling half-moon windows that give the impression that you're standing on the deck of a luxury liner, or the shifting light that undulates along the pale green walls like the reflection of water in an underground cavern—only here the effect comes not from water but from branches moving outside the opaque window. A long low backless couch runs under the windows, a few feet out from the wall, like something you would perch on for a moment to admire the paintings—or in this case, the viewless windows.

On the opposite wall there's a row of straight-backed metal chairs. I imagine they're pulled into a circle when she holds her workshop.

At the far end of all this shifting light sits Hedda Wolfe behind a wide desk, an almost empty expanse of some kind of green-black stone beneath another half-moon window, this one glazed with clear glass instead of frosted. Only when I step forward does she stand and come out from behind the desk to greet me. I have a feeling she's used to guests pausing, disoriented, on her threshold.

I walk across the wide-planked floor, my hand out to shake hers, but remember, only when she lifts both her hands and lightly touches my arms just above the elbows with her fingertips, that I once heard that Hedda Wolfe has severe arthritis—so severe she can't shake hands. Deprived of the conventional greeting I stand still as she studies me with her large, slightly hooded gray eyes.

If I hadn't heard her voice, I'd doubt this was the woman I spoke to on the phone. I'm not sure what I've been expecting. Talons, perhaps? Gloria Swanson in *Sunset Boulevard*? Certainly not this slight, elegant woman with chin-length silver hair, pale violet silk dress, and ladylike pearls at her throat and earlobes.

"Yes," she says, her soft, crumpled hands fluttering down from my arms. "I can see Kay in you, and Ben too. I was sorry," she says, still holding my gaze, "to hear about your father last year. I wrote to Sophie and asked her to convey my sympathies to you. But perhaps . . . well, at any rate, I am sorry. He was a fine man, your father. A prince."

She holds my gaze another moment, long enough to see my eyes well up, and then gestures for me to be seated in one of the two armchairs in front of the desk while she takes the other one.

"So tell me about this book. What made you decide to write it? Why now?"

"I'm not sure," I tell her honestly. "I started thinking about that story my mother used to tell me—the selkie story—and I used it for an assignment with my classes. I was surprised at how powerfully my students reacted to the idea of retelling the fairy tales they'd heard as children . . ." I pause for a moment, thinking of Gretchen Lu's maimed hands, and realize I'm staring at Hedda's hands, which lie, palms up, in her lap, curled in on themselves like a piece of knitting that's been stitched too tightly. I quickly look up into Hedda's face, surprising a look of impatience in her eyes.

"So it's not that you've found any new material? Letters . . . or a manuscript?" She leans toward me, her hands stirring in her lap as if grasping at something, but I remind myself that it's only her arthritis that make them seem like a witch's claws. I can see, though, why people are afraid of her. It occurs to me that she's the last person I'd like to have read anything I'd written. That sudden conviction gives me the nerve to be honest.

"To tell you the truth, I'm not sure I even want to write about my mother. Or that I can write about her. I don't know that much about her. She never talked about her childhood, or family, or anything that happened to her before the day she showed up at the Hotel Equinox with her one suitcase . . ."

"No," Hedda says, leaning back, the expression on her face softening. "Kay would never talk about her life before she came to the hotel. Not to anyone."

I shrug. "Maybe there wasn't much to tell. Maybe she had a boring life and that's why she created a fantasy world. Tirra Glynn. A magical land populated by changelings and shape-shifters."

"Exactly." Hedda Wolfe leans forward again in her chair, her eyes gleaming with interest. It's almost thrilling to feel that intelligence trained on me and I imagine this must be the flip side to her harshness—to excite her approbation must feel like having the sun shine on you. She lifts her hands from her lap and tries to interlace her fingers, but they splay limply on the folds of her silk dress.

"Exactly what?" I whisper, more than a little horrified and ashamed. Those hands. It strikes me how awful it is that this woman who has spent her life nurturing writers probably can't even hold a pen.

"Changelings. Shape-shifters. I think Kay left behind a life when she arrived at the Hotel Equinox. It's as if she sprang into existence there: twenty-five years old on a summer day in 1949. She made herself up like one of her own characters. But whatever she was fleeing from kept coming up in her books. That's why she didn't want the second one published."

"She didn't want the second one published?" I repeat stupidly. The idea of anyone not wanting their book published is so foreign to me I know I must be gaping openmouthed.

"Truthfully, she didn't want the first one published either. Didn't your father ever tell you?"

I shake my head. After my mother left I tried not to bring her up in my father's presence; it was too painful to see the look in his eyes at the mention of her name.

"He's the one who showed me her first book. I stayed at the hotel every summer with my grandmother and then in my twenties—when I had my first job at a literary agency—I'd still come up on weekends. Your mother always fascinated me. She was . . . so beautiful, even when she was still a maid, you'd come into your room and find her making your bed and you felt like you were the intruder. And when she married your father . . . well, even the guests—the regular ones who'd been coming for years—attended the ceremony in the rose garden. It was like a fairy tale, you knew she was someone special, and when I heard she spent the winters writing I just had to see what she wrote. I asked your father and he showed me the draft of her first book."

"Without telling her?"

"Yes. I'm afraid I talked him into it. I told him she was probably just afraid it wasn't any good and that no one would want to publish it. But that wasn't it at all."

"But she had to agree to let it be published . . ."

"Of course, but by the time she knew I'd gotten ahold of it I'd secured an offer from a publisher for what seemed like a lot of money back then. How could she turn it down? They needed the money . . ."

"For me? Because she was going to have a baby?"

Hedda Wolfe lifts one of her crumpled hands to her brow to shade her eyes from the sun and stares at me. "Darling, that was years before you were born. But yes, because she thought she was having a baby. That was the first miscarriage, I believe . . ."

My mouth is suddenly dry. This is the first time I've ever heard of a miscarriage, but then, who would have told me?

"The first?" I ask.

"Didn't you know? She had two before she had you. You have no idea how thrilled she was when you were born. We were all so happy for her."

"You mean you didn't disapprove . . ."

Hedda laughs, the first time I've heard her laugh, and the sound takes me by surprise, it's so unexpectedly light. "Why in the world would I disapprove? I was thrilled for her and, frankly, from a selfish perspective, I thought it would keep her from flying off. You always had the feeling with Kay that she could be gone any second, like some shy woodland creature that was ready to bolt. I wanted her to stay put and write her books, which she did . . . at least for a while."

"But she wasn't able to finish the third book."

"No? But she was still writing, wasn't she?"

I look out the window behind her desk where sycamore branches scrape the glass. That first tender green of spring is turning darker on the branches; a sparrow forages in the leaves for seeds. I remember the dream I had of my mother as a large bird tearing her own feathers out to feed into the cagelike typewriter, the tapping sound that followed me down the halls.

"Yes, she still wrote in the guest rooms on the hotel stationery . . ." I notice that Hedda smiles at this, as if it's an endearing trait she remembered. ". . . and I remember hearing her typing . . . but years went by and no book appeared."

"That doesn't mean she didn't write it. I have reason to think that she did finish the third book."

"But how would you know? I thought you and she had argued . . ." I hadn't meant to bring up their argument, but I'm past thinking I can direct the course of this conversation. Clearly, Hedda Wolfe has held the reins all along.

"Ben told me. We still talked. He was worried about her . . . she'd disappeared several times and seemed distracted. He said that she had finished the third book, but that she didn't want to publish it. Of course she'd said that before and relented and she'd seemed more peaceful after each book came out. Ben thought that if I could convince her to publish the last book she might attain some sort of closure on whatever she was afraid of. He was able to convince Kay to speak with me on the phone. She told me I might not like the third book but she agreed that I could see it when she was done. She was going to bring it with her into the city when she went to that conference, only she never made it there."

"If she had it with her it would have burned in the fire. We'll never know . . ."

Hedda Wolfe shakes her head impatiently. "She always made a carbon copy. Ben said he couldn't find it; I think she hid it before she left for the city."

"And you think it's somewhere at the hotel." I can't hide the disappointment in my voice. This is what the great Hedda Wolfe wants with me: a finder for my mother's lost manuscript. I should be excited, I suppose, over the idea that such a manuscript exists. Haven't I spent my whole life poring over my mother's two novels, trying to decipher from her mythic fantasy tale some message for me? And always I'd felt right on the brink, as if the winged men and half-aquatic women would suddenly spring off the page and tell me why my mother left me when I was ten years old to meet a strange man in a hotel and die there. But if the first two books have failed to answer this question, why should I believe that a third would?

"I thought you might have already found it," Hedda says. "That's why the title of your essay struck me so forcibly. It's what your mother was calling the last book in her trilogy: *The Selkie's Daughter*."

Chapter Ten

I am too preoccupied thinking about all I learned in Hedda Wolfe's office to teach that night, so I tell my Grace students to write a five-paragraph essay on "What the New Millennium Means to Me." I know that later, when I have to add twenty new essays to my stack of ungraded papers, I'll regret giving the assignment, but at least it buys me time to stare out the window at the stream of traffic inching toward the Lincoln Tunnel while I try to sort out what I'm feeling.

I should be overjoyed. Not only have I signed my first contract with an agent—a renowned agent, no less—I've learned two pieces of information about my mother that should relieve at least some of the burden I've been laboring under all these years. The first bit of knowledge is that my mother was happy to have a child. I'd always imagined that she'd avoided having a child for as long as she did (how many women of her generation waited until they were thirty-eight to have their first child?) because she thought motherhood would interfere with her writing. But if what Hedda Wolfe told me is true and my mother had two miscarriages before giving birth to me, then she must have wanted a child all along.

The second piece of information seems even more important: my mother finished the third book in the Tirra Glynn trilogy. I've always believed that my mother wasn't able to finish her third book because of me. All those times I followed her down the hall, picking up the stray pages she would drop, and later, listening for the sound of typing so I could trace it to its source . . . I couldn't leave her alone. I tracked her down wherever she was—no wonder she wrote in so many different rooms!—to demand a game, a story, her time, her attention. She would look up from the page or the typewriter and for a moment—just a moment—her eyes would be blank. As if she'd forgotten who I was. The next moment she would look sorry and give in to my demands—especially the ones for a story. She must have felt guilty for that initial lack of recognition—how could a mother forget her own child!—and I learned to take advantage of that guilt even though no amount of attention—and all the stories in the world—could ever completely make up for that moment when I didn't exist in her eyes.

I shiver and Mr. Nagamora offers to close the window. I look out at my class and notice that most of them have finished. Only Mrs. Rivera is still frantically scribbling into a spiral notebook.

"You can go if you're done," I tell the class. "Don't forget to finish Rodriguez's *The Hunger of Memory* for next week."

I turn my back on the class to wrestle the window shut. I'm trying to discourage stragglers. I just don't feel up to conversation tonight, the excuses for late papers from the poor students, the small talk and questions from the good ones. When I turn around, though, Mrs. Rivera is still there and when she looks up from her notebook I can see from her swollen and red-rimmed eyes that she's been crying.

"Mrs. Rivera," I say, "what is it? What's wrong."

Mrs. Rivera takes out a flowered handkerchief and blows her nose. "I'm sorry, Professor, I don't mean to bring my troubles to you."

I come around my desk and sit in the chair next to Mrs. Rivera's. I try to sit sideways so I can face her, but the attached desktop makes that impossible. I swivel the whole desk and chair around, feeling clumsy and loud, while Mrs. Rivera takes large gulps of air, struggling to control the tears.

"It's okay." I fold her hand between mine. Although she's about the same age as I am her hands feel leathery. I can feel the calluses and the roughness—the maids who worked in the laundry always had hands like this and I remember Mrs. Rivera saying she used to work in a hotel.

"Is it the class, Mrs. Rivera? You're doing fine, you know. Your last paper—the one on 'Rapunzel'—showed a big improvement. Only two sentence fragments and one run-on. I'm sure you'll pass the final." I'm really not sure at all but I'm desperate to halt her tears before they get to me. Already I can feel a sympathetic tightening at the back of my throat.

"No, it's not the class, Professor Greenfeder"—she pronounces my name *fedder* so that it sounds like what it means in German: green feather—"your class is the only thing going right for me now. It's all my fault. I was having such a good time last week at the art show you took us all to—you know you're the only teacher here who does those kind of things for us and really cares about us . . ."

I wince, thinking of my own selfish motives for taking the class to the gallery last week.

". . . so it's not your fault at all."

"What's not my fault?"

"Getting fired from my job. The Rosenbergs have let me go."

"Just for getting back late? That's awful! Look, can I write them a note, or call them . . ."

Mrs. Rivera shakes her head. "They said they smelled liquor on my breath—I only had one glass of wine, Professor, I swear it to you, I don't even like to drink. They've already gotten a replacement and told the children. They won't change their minds after they've told the children. They never go back on their word once they've told the children."

Every time she says the word *children* Mrs. Rivera's chin wobbles and yet she seems to purposely repeat the word as if to inure herself to the memory of her former wards. She's lost not only a job but her connection to children she's taken care of for several years now. And at least partly because of me.

"Let me at least try to talk to them—I mean, just because they've told the children one thing doesn't mean they can't change their minds."

"Oh no, they say going back on a decision would destroy their . . . how do you say . . . *creer?*"

"Credibility?" I ask. She nods.

I can just imagine the Rosenbergs of Great Neck. Principled people who pay their nanny's insurance (just in case they decide to run for public office) and restrict their children's sweets and TV.

I pat Mrs. Rivera's work-roughened hand. "Maybe I can get you another job," I tell her.

I try my aunt Sophie once more before leaving for Rip Van Winkle on Thursday. I've been trying her all week. Ever since I had the idea of getting Mrs. Rivera a job at the hotel I've felt better about the whole memoir thing. Not that it makes that much sense, but the idea that my plans to spend the summer at the hotel—quizzing my aunt and older staff members and regular hotel guests who knew my mother and ransacking the premises for a lost manuscript—might also enable me to keep Mrs. Rivera from being deported back to Mexico makes the whole thing seem a little less mercenary. Still, it all depends on Aunt Sophie's go-ahead and suddenly, just when I finally want to take her up on the job she's been pushing on me for years, she's unavailable. Janine, the hotel operator, sounded embarrassed the last time I called and I'm beginning to wonder if my aunt is avoiding my call.

"She was just here a minute ago," Ramon tells me Thursday morning. "She has been like a whirling dervish all week but will not say why. We all suspect an important dignitary is due at the hotel . . . should I have her call you back?"

I tell Ramon that I'll be gone most of the day, but that she should call me tonight. All the way up to Grand Central I wonder if what Ramon said was just idle gossip. An important dignitary? At the Hotel Equinox? Maybe a hundred years ago. Presidents have stayed at the hotel, movie stars, baseball players, a Mafia don—whom my father pointed out to me strolling in the rose garden—and once, my aunt claims, a Russian princess. But those days are long gone. The hotel's dwindling clientele, these last twenty years, has been a motley assembly of émigrés, musicians, watercolorists, birdwatchers, and, mostly, the now elderly grandchildren of families who used to summer at the hotel and still retain a nostalgia for those halcyon days.

The only person my aunt could be taking so much trouble for would be a prospective buyer.

The idea makes me pause in the middle of Grand Central Station so abruptly that commuters flooding up the platform ramps and heading for the street bump into me. I move into the shelter of the information kiosk and stare up at the blue-green barrel vault far above me as if trying to read my future in the constellations painted there. My future. The hotel's future. Of course a buyer would be a good thing. But what if the buyer wants to tear the hotel down and start all over again? It could take years to rebuild—years that the hotel would be closed. No job for me or Mrs. Rivera—not to mention my aunt and Joseph or Janine, who must be well into her seventies by now.

I look at my watch and see I'm still early for my train to Rip Van Winkle. I usually take a bus to Grand Central (subways make me feel claustrophobic) but this morning I'd felt expansive—still floating on the promise of my meeting with Hedda Wolfe—and splurged on a cab.

"I think I could sell your memoir whether you find your mother's third book or not," she said, "but if we could bring out your mother's third book at the same time I think I could get you a very nice advance indeed."

A very nice advance indeed. I didn't have an exact monetary value to attach to Hedda Wolfe's idea of a nice advance but I had a feeling it was more than I had ever dared hope for. Not that the money was the most important thing. For years I've sent my stories out to little magazines, attended workshops and writing groups, gone to readings and seminars, revolving in the margins of New York's literary life like so many others. And still the idea of being a published author has remained as distant as one of the tiny glittering lightbulbs dotting the painted ceiling above me. If I can't spend the summer at the hotel, if I can't find the manuscript of my mother's third book, that's what my dreams will remain, a faint and distant dream.

I step out of the shade of the kiosk smack into a sheet of sunlight streaming through the three massive arched windows on the east wall of the terminal. It's like taking a bath in light. As I make my way through the crowds I can't make out the faces of the strangers heading toward me because their backs are to the sun. The light is so strong it acts almost like a fog, blurring the edges of the figures approaching me. I tilt my chin down, shading my eyes with my hand, and head toward my train, but I'm stopped by a dark figure blocking my way. I can't make out his face, but I can see he's a large man in a dark suit that gleams richly in the strong sunlight, like an animal's fur. Cashmere, I think, or alpaca. The fabric makes you want to stroke it. The way the man stares at me—I assume he's staring at me from the tilt of his head—is unsettling and I try to keep walking but when I try to move around him he lays two fingers on my elbow and turns to keep up with me. As soon as he's facing the light I recognize him. It's Harry Kron.

"Ah, Miss Greenfeder," he says, "I've been thinking about you." He hardly seems surprised to run into me here in the middle of Grand Central Station. "What train are you taking?"

"The eight fifty-three Metro-North," I tell him.

"Hm. Wait a moment."

We've reached the platform gate where my train is posted. He looks up at the listing of stops and nods his head.

"I was going to take an express, but this will do . . ."

"But I wouldn't want to delay you . . ." I'm amazed that Phoebe Nix's rich uncle would even take the train. Shouldn't he be in a limousine behind tinted windows?

"I love trains," he says, as if reading my mind. "And the Hudson Line is one of my favorite routes. I can't think of a better way of spending a spring morning than a train ride along the Hudson with a lovely, talented writer for company. Unless, of course, you have something else to occupy you for the trip."

I think of the ungraded essays in my book bag but it would be like telling a little boy you couldn't take him to the circus because you had work to do.

"I would love the company," I say.

"Ah, then, shall we?" Harry Kron waves a hand toward the sloping ramp as if escorting me onto a dance floor. He switches his briefcase to his right hand and tucks my hand under his left elbow and we descend into the bowels of Grand Central where the eight fifty-three is waiting for us. The train, running against the commute, is almost empty and we quickly find two seats facing each other, next to the window on the river side. He gives me the forward-facing seat and sits across from me. He's so tall our knees nearly touch.

"So," he says when the train begins to move, "where are you heading this lovely spring morning?"

I tell him about my job at the prison and he furrows his brow with concern.

"But is that safe?"

"There's a guard in the hall at all times and all my students are from the medium-security prison."

"Well, then, small-time thieves and drug dealers. I can't imagine it's a productive outlet for your talents. I very much enjoyed, by the way, your essay in my niece's magazine—which is more than I can say for most of the nonsense she publishes."

We've come out of the tunnel and emerged into sight of the river so I'm able to look modestly out toward the view while I thank him for the compliment.

"You ought to be spending your time writing instead of wasting your talent on illiterate criminals."

I'm torn between indignation on behalf of my students—I think of Aidan and his beautiful rendition of Tam Lin—and gratitude for being considered talented. I settle for honesty.

"I need the money," I tell him.

He scowls at the window and looks slightly embarrassed, as if I had just mentioned some shameful bodily function.

"You must get a contract for this memoir of yours. Do you have an agent?"

I tell him I do. "Hedda Wolfe," I say.

His eyes widen. "Really. Hedda."

"You know her?"

"Oh, yes," he answers. "We serve on many of the same boards. Surely she can secure you an advance so that you can work on your book in peace."

"Well, she says I need more than the first chapter and it would help if I could find my mother's third book."

"She wrote a third book? I thought she only wrote the two." Harry Kron snaps open his briefcase and, amazingly, extracts a paperback copy of my mother's two novels—a one-volume edition reissued in the 1970s during the Tolkien craze. I remember that the cover illustration of a sexy red-headed mermaid enraged my father. "There are no mermaids in her books," he'd ranted for days. "Did those people even bother to read her books?"

"Maybe we'll at least see some royalty checks," my aunt had replied. And, in fact, the royalties from that edition paid for my college and first year of graduate school.

"You see, your little essay inspired me to look up your mother's work. I'm afraid I'd never read them." He shakes his head and looks genuinely regretful. "I'm not usually a fan of science fiction—or do you call this fantasy?—but I found your mother's books an exception. It's quite fascinating how she's taken these Old World legends and turned them into a fantasy world. These selkie creatures, for instance, who are searching for a lost necklace—where do you think she got that from?"

"Well, the selkies are from an Irish folktale, but I've never been able to find a version of the story that involves a necklace. Of course the search for a lost piece of jewelry is a common archetypal quest motif—like the ring in Tolkien or the Grail in Arthurian legends . . ." I notice that Harry Kron's eyes are glazing over as most people's do when I start in with words like *archetypal* and *motif*. "Anyway, I've never been able to figure out the significance of the necklace—the net of tears, as it's called. It's supposed to be a gift from a mother to her daughter, but then it's stolen by the evil king Connachar, and recovered by the hero Naoise in Book Two."

"Shouldn't that be the end of the story?"

"Unfortunately for Naoise—but fortunately for readers who like a sequel—the necklace brings nothing but trouble for him. By the end of Book Two, the selkie Deirdre knows she must find the necklace and destroy it. Presumably that's what she'll do in Book Three and that's when we'd learn the significance of the necklace."

"And what makes you think there is a third book?"

I tell him what Hedda Wolfe said. He looks out the window as I talk, more engrossed, I think, by the red cliffs of the Palisades and the hard blue glitter of the Hudson than by what I'm saying.

"So my plan is to spend the summer up at the hotel looking for the book and talking to people who remember my mother."

"Are there many left?" he asks, stirring from his drowsy contemplation of the river. The rhythm of the train and the glare off the water have made me sleepy as well and I have to stifle a yawn while I answer him. "Oh, my aunt and the gardener, Joseph, and Janine, the telephone operator. Some of the regular guests maybe—but that will depend on how many come this summer." I explain, then, about the hotel's financial troubles and he perks up a bit. This is more up his alley than obscure mythological fantasy creatures. We talk about hotels for a bit and he becomes more and more animated, telling me about his favorite hotels in Europe, the Villa d'Este on Lake Como, the Hotel Hassler in Rome ("The first hotel I worked in after the war was in Rome, where I'd studied art before the war," he tells me), the Ritz in London, the Hotel Charlotte in Nice. Many of the names are familiar to me from my father's reminiscences of Europe after the war and I tell him which ones my father loved.

"I think the Hotel Charlotte is where he met Joseph, our gardener," I conclude. "He said it was how he got the idea of running a hotel, the time he spent in Europe at the end of the war."

"Ah yes," Harry Kron says, his eyes lighting up, completely awake now. "For many of us the war opened our eyes to a whole new world. That might sound like a paradox—that good could come out of so much horror and destruction—but it's true, or at least it was for me. It wasn't for my brother Peter, Phoebe's father; he spent a year in the Udine POW camp in northern Italy and then, after Mussolini died, he escaped and hid at a villa near Ferrara that belonged to an old friend of our family."

I'm remembering what Phoebe said about her father, how she painted him as the villain in her parents' marriage. "Was he very traumatized by his experience in the camp?"

"He would never say very much of it; he preferred to regale us with stories of the Countess Oriana's wine cellars in which he hid for several months and hairbreadth escapes on Alpine passes. He treated it like a romantic adventure. I suppose ordinary civilian life seemed dull to him after the war; he was never able to settle down to anything, whereas the war pointed me toward my future. I had the great opportunity to serve as a Monuments officer."

"What's that?"

"We were in charge of protecting works of art and monuments of national artistic significance. I was recruited out of Cambridge because of the time I'd spent in Italy. I was instrumental in recovering a trove of Florentine treasures that had been removed from the Uffizi by the Nazis."

"That must have been gratifying."

"Most gratifying. I became friendly with a number of Americans and I decided that after the war I'd bring European culture back to America. You Americans discovered Europe after the war. Tastes in food, wine, and art were transformed. So many new possibilities. That's what I saw when I came to New York . . . it's not just that there was money all of a sudden, but what people were willing to spend it on . . . good food, wine, elegant hotels like the great hotels in Europe."

"So you bought your first hotel—the Crown Hotel in New York?"

"Yes," he smiles at me for remembering. "And your father too went into the hotel business."

I nod. Of course my father didn't have the money to buy a hotel. Nor do I think he quite shared Harry Kron's entrepreneurial vision. He saw life in a hotel more as a refuge, I think, a corner of peace after what he had seen in the war.

"The country was reinventing itself," Harry is saying. "And I thought, what better way than with travel and hotels. There is, in a beautiful hotel, the possibility of inventing oneself anew."

"Yes, my father said that too. He said vacations gave people the opportunity to be their best selves and that's what a good hotel should bring out in people: their best selves."

Harry Kron smiles. "I would have liked to meet your father."

I nod, too close to tears suddenly to speak, and we both look out the window at the bright blue ribbon of river, our constant traveling companion. I realize from the terrain that we're nearing my stop and then the conductor calls the name of the prison, which is also the name of the town.

"Well," I say, slinging the strap of my book bag over my shoulder, "the trip has never gone so fast for me. I really enjoyed your company."

"And I yours."

"Please don't get up," I say when I see him preparing to.

He gets up anyway and opens the corridor door leading to the platform between cars and stands with me there while the train comes into the station. The outside door is open and I can see the rails flashing under us like the spokes of a wheel, blurring one into another. It makes me dizzy for a moment and Harry Kron puts his hand over mine on the handrail I'm grasping to steady me. I realize he must be a little unsteady himself because he grips my hand so hard I have to bite my lip not to call out. When the train finally stops I have to wrench my hand out from under his.

"Well good-bye," I say, walking down the iron steps. I turn when I'm on the platform. "Have a good trip . . ." I start to say, but the space between the cars is empty and I suddenly realize I never even asked where he was going.

Chapter Eleven

My class at Rip Van Winkle is three hours long. There's not much point to giving breaks because none of us can go anyplace and so the session usually seems interminable. Today, though, they're writing their final essays. I manage to finish grading all their previous assignments by the time they finish writing. I can't dismiss them early—or let them go one at a time—so we're stuck making small talk until the officer comes to escort us back across the courtyard. We talk about the movie version of *Othello* that I showed them last class—the one with Kenneth Branagh and Laurence Fishburne. It had been a challenge to get them through Shakespeare and I'd thought the movie would help. It had. They'd liked the crafty Iago, the sword fights, Laurence Fishburne's regal bearing. What had unnerved me was that when Othello killed Desdemona they had cheered.

"The bitch got what she deserved," one of my students informs me today.

"But she didn't do anything—she wasn't unfaithful," I try to explain.

My point falls on deaf ears. Desdemona's innocence seems beside the point. Maybe because they're used to such claims. *I'm innocent, I didn't do it* doesn't carry a whole lot of weight around here. Even Emilio Lara shrugs as if he agreed with Desdemona's fate but is too much of a gentleman to say so. By the time the officer comes I feel dispirited and depressed. I realize as I'm checking out at the front gate that if I could grade their final exams and average their grades right now I wouldn't have to come back here next week. Maybe it's Harry Kron's comments that have gotten to me—wasting my talent on illiterate criminals—or the discussion on Othello. Or maybe it's that Aidan's no longer in the class. I'm suddenly desperate to be through with this prison.

I go to a coffee shop on Main Street and over a Greek omelet and several cups of coffee read my students' finals, average their grades, and bubble in their grade reports. By the time I turn in the grades and walk back down to the station the sun is already beginning to approach the mountains on the other side of the river. I've spent the whole day here, but at least I feel a sense of completion—a rare thing for me.

I've got half an hour before the next southbound train so I walk to the north end of the platform and lean on the chain-link fence separating the train yard from the river. The river is wide here, a fjord really, which, when I once looked it up, I found meant that it was a river that had been drowned by the sea—just like the river in my mother's books. *In a time before the rivers were drowned by the sea . . .* she would start her story each night. Which I suppose is just another way of saying once upon a time.

As the sun sinks toward the Catskills on the west bank the river turns a cold slaty blue—tinted, I imagine, by an infusion of Atlantic water sweeping up from the sea. The low mountains on the other side fold the light into jeweled bands: emerald, sapphire, pearl, and amethyst. It's hard to tell where the mountains end and the clouds, purpling as the sun sets, begin. It's as if the mountains were pulling the water-dense swaths of pink and violet clouds to them, like a woman drawing a cloak over her shoulders. No wonder the early Dutch settlers thought the mountains were the home of storm gods and ghosts. It looks as if they are drawing a storm down right now. I close my eyes to feel the last warmth of the sun before the rain reaches down here. I've still got my eyes closed when I feel a hand touch my shoulder.

I turn around to find Aidan Barry, shading his eyes from the sun, squinting at me.

"Professor Greenfeder? I thought that was you."

"God, Aidan, don't creep up on me like that. Especially so close to the train tracks." It's an absurd comment—we're a good eight feet from the edge of the platform, but I'm trying to cover my embarrassment with teacherly admonishment. Lately I've found with Aidan that I have to keep reminding myself that I am his teacher and that I'm a good seven years older than he is.

"Och, I wouldn't let you fall on the tracks like poor Anna Karenina. At least not till I get the letter of recommendation I'm after asking you for." Aidan winks at me to accompany his suddenly exaggerated brogue—or maybe it's just the sun in his eyes. I turn to walk back down the platform so he won't have to look into the sun to talk to me (not, I tell myself, because I'm nervous being alone with him at this deserted end of the platform) and he falls into step beside me.

"What letter is that?"

"My parole officer just now—" He jerks his chin in the general direction of the prison. "—says I should get a letter from one of my teachers saying what a good citizen I've become, a reformed man, you know. I thought you could write it for me. None of my other teachers has so much as bothered to learn my name."

"Oh, I bet that isn't true." I can't imagine having Aidan in a class and not knowing exactly who he is. Sneaking a sideways look at him I notice that since he's gotten out of prison he's filled out a bit and gotten some color in that pale skin of his. He's let his hair grow and it curls just a bit over his ears and at the nape of his neck.

"I'm happy to write you a letter, Aidan; you've been a fine student. If there's anything else I can do . . ."

"Well, there is one thing . . . but let me tell you on the train." He cocks his thumb over his shoulder and I look behind him. Far down the tracks, barely visible, I make out the silver glint of the southbound train.

"How'd you know the train was here?"

Aidan grins and rocks back on his heels. "Old Indian trick. The tracks run right through Van Wink. I got used to feeling the vibrations before it came. I guess that's something you don't forget." That momentary glint of pride fades, replaced by something else, sadness or shame, or some mixture of the two. I try not to think of what else he's learned in prison and wonder if he'll always live under that shadow.

We board the train and find two seats next to each other. He takes the window seat, which means I can look at him and still see the river. I can't help but compare the southbound trip with the northbound. The sunlit trip north, the gathering clouds heading south. My two gentleman admirers! One old enough to be my father, the other young enough to be . . . what? A younger brother, I suppose . . .

I'm so caught up figuring out what our age difference adds up to that I miss something Aidan is asking me.

". . . so do you think there's any chance you could look into it for me, I mean, I know, no one wants to hire an ex-con." That look of shame passes over his clear blue-green eyes, like the rain shadow I watched pass over the mountains before, and it pains me to see it.

"I would personally vouch for you to any potential employer," I say, gratified to see that shadow lift from his eyes. We've reached the outskirts of the city, the Bronx a dark silhouette against a moist purple sky. The heavy clouds I saw massing over the Catskills have followed us south. I see the lights of the skyline over Aidan's shoulder and then a curtain of rain extinguishes them.

"Brilliant," Aidan says, flashing me a smile so expansive I feel something let go inside my chest just as the clouds have released their rain. "I know hotel work's the line for me. You won't be sorry."

I am sorry, though, for the rest of the train ride but I can't think of any way to explain to Aidan that I misheard him—that I wasn't paying attention because I'd been too busy rationalizing a relationship I don't plan to have. He, innocently unaware of my remorse, is filling me in on his varieties of hotel experiences. He comes from a long line of hotel workers, he tells me. Even back in Ireland, the men in his family would go over to London to work in the big hotels—the Connaught, the Savoy, the Ritz, the May Fair—and send money back home. "That's how my mom met my dad— she was working as a maid and he was the night clerk. They came over here because they had a cousin who'd promised them work in a New York hotel, but by the time they got over the hotel had closed down. That's when my dad started drinking—like he'd decided the world had no good in store for him anymore. Anyway, I've always felt the business was in my blood. You understand, coming from a hotel family yourself."

I could explain that I've spent most of my life trying to avoid working at the hotel. It would be a good preamble to telling him I can't really get him a job at the Hotel Equinox—but knowing, as I do, that I'm planning to ask my aunt for a job myself, I can't. As the train pulls into the station I tell myself that in a few days I'll just tell Aidan that I asked my aunt Sophie for a place for him at the hotel and that there wasn't one. I shoulder my book bag and button up my raincoat with that resolve in mind. We both walk briskly up the platform toward the main terminal, both of us resuming a city pace until we hit a wave of commuters heading down to the trains, the great tide flooding back out of the city. Aidan takes my arm and steers me though the crowd. The vaulted space above us is dark now, the lightbulbs in the constellations twinkling a little brighter in the gloom.

Would it really hurt, I wonder, just to ask? Chances are there won't be a job for me, or Mrs. Rivera, let alone Aidan. The hotel might not be open this summer. I'll ask and then I can tell Aidan the truth and it'll just be one more disappointment to him, but it won't be my fault.

I feel better, then, turning to say good-bye to him at the Vanderbilt exit. I tell him I'm going to take a bus home because of the rain. But instead of shaking the hand I hold out to him he holds both his hands up, wrists bent, palms up, so that he looks like some ancient figure representing justice or balance. It's a full thirty seconds before I get the purpose of his pantomime. It's not raining. The thundershower that rolled off the western mountains and bowled its way down the alley of the Hudson was an isolated salvo. The rain has glazed the streets, freshened the air, and moved on.

"It's a beautiful night," he says, "let me walk you home."

And since I can't dispute the truth of the first part of his statement, I see no reason not to assent to the second part.

We walk west on 42nd Street and cut across Bryant Park just because the trees are so beautiful there. The leaves are still that new spring green, not full enough yet to hide the elegant bone structure of their limbs. The street lamps make spiderwebs out of the slick wet branches. Aidan tells me more about his family, about growing up in Inwood and how even though his dad wasn't much on the scene he'd had his grandmother, aunts and uncles, and scores of cousins to take up the slack.

We weave through the streets of the garment district and end up on Ninth Avenue and 38th Street, the southern edge of Hell's Kitchen.

"Does your family still live in Inwood?" I ask Aidan as we turn south on Ninth.

"My mother's still there—my dad died a couple of years ago. Most of my cousins live in Woodlawn."

"That's nice you're so close to your family," I say.

Aidan makes a face. "Oh, it's a bit clannish for me. That's how you find work, though, by staying in touch with all the boys, only . . ."

Aidan pauses and I can tell, looking over at him as we pass under a street lamp, that he's not so much at a loss for words as trying to edit something out for my benefit. I wonder what it could be.

"Only sometimes the work's not to my liking."

Aidan looks over at me and I nod. In other words, sometimes the work's not legal. That's what he's trying to tell me. That if I don't find him work at the hotel he'll end up in the same old crowd. I remember what he said in his paper, about watching the ex-cons fall back in with their old ways because no one was willing to take a chance on them and give them a fresh start. Unless there was someone like the girl in the fairy tale who held on even when the boy she embraced turned into a snake, and then a lion, and then a pillar of flames.

Was it too much to ask to look beyond what he appeared to be now, to what he could become if only someone gave him a chance?

Although I assure Aidan that I don't need him to walk me all the way home he says he's glad to. That he's enjoying the air and the company. When we pass a bar in Chelsea, though, I see his eyes flick sideways and the young men standing around outside smoking cigarettes call his name.

"Friends of yours?" I ask as we approach the bar—which, I notice, is called the Red Branch.

"Aye, like I said, I know half the Irish population on the isle of Manhattan."

"Well, don't let me stop you if you want to go in. I'm more than halfway home."

Aidan smiles, I think because I've released him, but then he puts his arm around my shoulders and pulls me close enough so he can whisper in my ear.

"Would you mind coming in for a drink?" he asks. "It'll mean a lot to these lads that I'm seen with such a classy lady."

I can't help smiling at that any more than I can help that flutter I feel in my chest every time Aidan looks at me. It's not a night Jack comes over, so why not? Haven't I earned a little time off after all the grading I've done today? The pub looks bright and inviting, not one those derelict Irish bars near the train station. I can see through the door a mix of young and old people and I can hear live music wafting out onto Ninth Avenue. There are tables with candles flickering in stained-glass holders and a beautiful stained-glass window set into the fanlight above the door, which depicts three men struggling through a raging sea, a woman in a red cloak perched on the shoulders of one of the men.

"You see that window?" I ask Aidan, buying myself time while I decide if I should take him up on his offer or not. "It's from a story called 'The Sorrows of Deirdre.' Have you ever heard of it?"

"Wasn't it Deirdre who got her husband and his two brothers slaughtered?" Aidan asks, looking up at the window. "I always wondered why it was called 'The Sorrows of Deirdre' when it was she who caused all the sorrows."

"Just like a man," I say. "Always blaming the woman. It wasn't her fault that Naoise fell in love with her."

"Naoise?" It's one of those names that sounds—NEE-sheh—nothing like it's spelled, but Aidan pronounces the name just as my mother did.

"That's the fellow whose shoulders she's on. He falls in love with her and they run away, along with his brothers Allen and Arden, because she was supposed to marry the king, Connachar Mac Ness. They all live happily in Scotland for a while, but then they're tricked into coming back and Mac Ness tries to take Deirdre back. When they try to escape again, Connachar orders his druid to conjure up an ocean to stop them. That's them trying to get across it."

"Do they make it?"

"No. Mac Ness orders them to be beheaded. Deirdre throws herself into their burial pit and dies in Naoise's arms. That's why it's called 'The Sorrows of Deirdre.' Her sorrows are over having caused so much death. My mother named the main character in her books Deirdre and there's an evil king named Connachar and a hero called Naoise, but she doesn't really follow the story. I think, though, that she used the names to allude to the danger of love—what might happen if you followed your heart."

Aidan is still looking up at the window. The light, coming through the stained glass, casts jeweled shadows on his face—emerald, ruby, and sapphire. When he turns back to me I notice that his eyes are the same sapphire as the glass in the window.

"It seems to me there's more sorrow in not following your heart," he says. "So are you coming in?"

I shake my head.

"Then would you like me to take you home?" I notice he says *take you home* not *walk you home*, but I choose to answer as if he said the latter.

"No, Aidan I'll be fine, it's a lovely night and I'm almost home." He shrugs and turns his shoulder so I think he's heading back inside but instead he leans in and kisses me lightly on the cheek, saying something I don't quite hear. Then he's gone. I turn and walk south. I've gone two blocks before I realize what he said. "Well, maybe another time then."

Chapter Twelve

At home there's a message on my answering machine that sounds like running water. When I turn up the volume a notch it sounds like running water with a Brooklyn accent. Only when I've turned the volume as high as it goes do I make out my aunt's message.

"I'm calling from a cell-yu-lar phone," she says, drawing out each word as if to make up in slowness what she lacks in volume. "I have some news to discuss with you that I cannot relate over the switchboard. I'll be in the Hoo-Ha by Sunset Rock precisely at ten o'clock P.M. I'm assuming you'll be home by then. The number is . . ."

I have to replay the message six times to transcribe the number of my aunt's new cellular phone. By the time I've got it, it's ten minutes before ten.

The Hoo-Ha my aunt is referring to is a little wooden structure with a bench and a cedar shake roof, one of the dozen little buildings built by Joseph over the years. Our guests usually refer to them as the gazebos or summerhouses, which is what they're called by another hotel to the south of us. Joseph, though, always called them *chuppas*, like the rudimentary shelters used in Jewish wedding ceremonies. My aunt thought our gentile guests would be put off by this designation so whenever she heard Joseph use the word *chuppa* she would pretend to correct his pronunciation and say, "He means Hoo-Ha—that's what the English call them." By the time I learned that the British designation for this kind of garden folly is a "Ha-Ha" it was too late to break her of the habit.

This particular Hoo-Ha, the one by Sunset Rock, is on a trail in the woods about a quarter mile from the hotel. I can't imagine my aunt making this journey in the daytime let alone in the dark. The path she has to take goes across a bridge over a waterfall and along a ledge with a forty-foot drop on the other side. What in the world does she have to tell me that would require this level of subterfuge?

I dial the number and my aunt picks up on the eighth or ninth ring as if she were in a large mansion instead of a three-by-five-foot lean-to. "Hello, Mata Hari," I say, "this is your niece, code name Hoo-Ha."

"What? Is that you, Iris?" my aunt yells into the phone as if she's calling down a deep well. "I don't think this thing works too well."

"I can hear you fine, Aunt Sophie."

"Ah, that's better. I didn't want to hold this thing too close to my ear in case it gives you brain cancer, not that at my age a tumor would matter much—"

"Aunt Sophie," I interrupt, "why are you out in the middle of the woods? What's up?"

"I didn't want Janine to hear. You know Janine—a bigger yenta you never met."

Actually I've always thought that Janine, the hotel operator for over forty years, has the discretion of a priest in the confessional. Especially considering all she must have heard over the years. She showed me when I was only ten how to listen in on calls without "the party" catching on, but the only time she divulged the information she had overhead was when, as she put it, she was "privy to information of a dire or life-threatening *nachure*." When Mrs. Crosby in Room 206 told her estranged husband she was planning to swallow a bottle of sleeping pills, for instance, or when she overheard the "millionaire" occupying the Sunnyside Suite for the whole summer discussing his imminent bankruptcy with his lawyer, Janine alerted my father. "For the good of the hotel or the good of the guest," Janine liked to say. "Otherwise: zip," and she would draw her lacquered red fingernails across her matching shade of lipstick in a pantomime of confidentiality. But surely my aunt has not braved wildlife and brain cancer to discuss Janine's character.

"So what do you have to tell me?" I ask.

"Well!" I can tell from the explosion of breath that my aunt would like to draw out this piece of news but either her dislike of being outdoors or consciousness of how much this call must cost compels her to be brief. "The hotel has been sold. A big-shot hotel man from the city has bought the place, lock, stock, and barrel."

"A hotel man," I say. "Then it won't be torn down? The hotel will be open this summer?"

"Open and running at full capacity. Mr. Big-Shot Hotel Man says he wants extra staff put on, everything spruced up, advertisements in all the papers. He wants to see what the hotel can do and then he'll 'determine the direction of the Hotel Equinox's future' at the end of the season."

"In other words . . ."

"In other words, we have the best season we've had in twenty years or he'll tear it down and write it off as a tax loss."

"Well, that should make for a relaxing summer."

"Relaxing is for the guests," my aunt tells me, something she's said to me all my life. "Of course, it doesn't help that I'm surrounded by geriatric staff. What we could use up here is a little fresh blood . . ."

"I'll come up," I say. I could drag it out, I realize; she obviously needs my help more than ever, but I have an image of my aunt in the deep pine woods, peering anxiously into the shadows for rabid wildlife ready to spring out at her. "I want to work there this summer . . ." What I'm about to say is that I want to work on the memoir I've just contracted to write, but when she cuts me off—obviously misinterpreting what I mean—it occurs to me that maybe I shouldn't tell her about the memoir yet. Why get her hopes up? Why expose my new good luck to her withering scrutiny?

"Excuse me," she says, "I must have a bad connection. Miss I-have-to-be-in-New-York-City-to-write wants to work in the hotel this summer?"

"Very funny. I've even got a maid and a night clerk for you. Two students who need work. If you want them."

"Are they under ninety?"

"Yes, only I should tell you that the man . . ."

"Any experience in the hotel business?"

"Yes, Mrs. Rivera worked at a resort in Cancún; Aidan was a bellhop at a hotel in the city, but you should also know . . ."

"I'll hire them. No. You'll hire them. That's part of your new job as manager. See if you can find a good carpenter while you're at it. All these Hoo-Has need to be resanded; I've gotten half a dozen splinters in my *tuckis* while we've been talking."

"Don't you have to okay hiring me with the new owner?"

"Nah. He already asked for you. I told him you'd always refused to work at the hotel but he said he thought you'd feel differently this summer."

"It's Harry Kron, isn't it?" I feel so stupid I could smack myself. Not only for not guessing the identity of the new owner—of course that's where he was heading on the train today—but for buying into my aunt's whole "poor me, you probably won't take the job" shtick. She'd known all along I'd say yes.

"That's right. We're the newest jewel in the crown. So when can you get up here?"

I manage to give my aunt a rough picture of my finals and paper-grading schedule and by the time we've settled on an end-of-May arrival date the connection really is breaking up.

"Be careful walking back," I shout into a rush of white noise that might be cellular static or my aunt tumbling into the falls. It's only when I hang up that I realize I never got around to telling her about Aidan's questionable credentials.

Mrs. Rivera bursts into tears when I tell her she has a job. Aidan is less demonstrative, but on the back of his final paper he scrawls the message, "You've saved my life. I promise, you won't be sorry." In the face of their gratitude I feel expansive and generous. I feel, I suppose, like a hotelier.

Jack is delighted that the plans for the book are running so smoothly. We spend a happy afternoon at the Met looking at his favorite paintings.

He talks of wanting to paint in the open air, of larger canvases, of limitless skies. He tells me he's "almost a hundred percent sure" he'll be able to spend the summer with me at the hotel.

I finish grading my papers in record time and a record percentage of my Grace students—including Aidan, Amelie, and Mrs. Rivera—are passed by the grading committee. I make an appointment with my thesis adviser (who is, understandably, surprised to hear from me after a silence of two years) and launch a proposal to substitute my forthcoming memoir about my mother for my dissertation. She's skeptical at first, but when I tell her I've signed a contract with the agent Hedda Wolfe I see a little light go on in her eyes.

"Have you thought of someone to do an introduction? An impartial scholar in the field of women's studies to assess K. R. LaFleur's place in twentieth-century feminist dialectics?"

"I was hoping you would do it," I say.

Within minutes we've settled on a schedule of deadlines and submissions.

Phoebe Nix calls and congratulates me on signing with Hedda Wolfe and asks if I would consider publishing a series of excerpts from the memoir in *Caffeine*. I tell her I'll have to talk it over with Hedda, but that I like the idea.

"Don't let Hedda boss you around," she says. "She's been know to bully her writers."

"Don't worry about me, " I say, and then, to change the subject, I tell her how grateful I am that her uncle Harry decided to buy the Hotel Equinox.

"Yes, Harry's quite the knight in shining armor. You won't recognize your little hotel when he gets done with it. He's got the Midas touch, Harry does."

I get off the phone unsettled by that last image. I've always hated that story—the little girl running into her father's arms and turning into hard and lifeless gold. Alchemy gone wrong. I decide that Phoebe Nix can be a bit spiteful—think of that wedding ring engraved with barbed wire! Harry Kron is a godsend. Not only has he rescued the Hotel Equinox but, I learn at my last class at The Art School, he's also hiring art students to restore the summerhouses at the hotel and sponsoring a competition to design a series of new summerhouses. The contest is called "Follies in the Garden, Whimsies in the Woods." I spend the last class describing some of my favorite Hoo-Has—Half Moon, Evening Star, Sunset, Two Moons, Brier Rose—and telling the Hoo-Ha/*chuppa* story. I notice that both Gretchen Lu and Natalie Baehr take copious notes and are already sketching ideas as I talk.

I'm inspired after the class to write a note to Harry Kron, telling him about my students' enthusiasm for his contest and, of course, how glad I am that the Hotel Equinox will be in such good hands. It gives me a chance, as well, to take care of another loose end. I mention in the note that I haven't told my aunt about my memoir project or the contract I've signed with Hedda Wolfe. "I don't want to get her hopes up prematurely," I write. Would he mind not mentioning the matter to her?

Sending the note eases my mind for a day but then, like the uninvited fairy at Sleeping Beauty's christening, Phoebe Nix's warnings about Hedda Wolfe and her prediction of the hotel's imminent transformation under her uncle's aegis begin to cast a pall on my leave-taking. As I tick off each chore that lies between me and my departure date—books crated and UPSed upstate, *Times* delivery canceled, mail forwarded—a feeling of unease settles over me, a malaise that not even the end of the rainy season and a run of flawless spring days can dispel. The cool efficiency with which I dispatch all these errands begins to feel like the settling of affairs of a condemned man. It's like I'm preparing for death instead of a summer in the country.

"Maybe you're just not cut out for happiness," Jack says to me one heartbreakingly beautiful May morning when I call him up to confess my second thoughts about the summer. Although I know he doesn't mean to be unkind, the remark hurts me. It's what I've always suspected my mother suffered from—an inability to be happy. Even when she was laughing with guests or flirting with my father there was always a shadow of unhappiness I'd see whenever she thought no one was looking. Some lingering sorrow that drove her each winter to that feverish typing that sounded to me as a child like an animal trying to tap its way out of a shell.

"You're right," I say. "It's going to be a great summer. After all, you're going to be there."

In the pause that follows I guess everything Jack is about to say. I don't really need to hear the details about the residency he's just been awarded at an artists' colony in New Hampshire. An eight-week residency.

"But of course, I can come over to the hotel for a few weekends. It's not far. But you know how much this means to me . . ."

"Of course I do," I tell him. "I'm really happy for you, things are working out for both of us. But you know, I'd better go, there's some research I wanted to get done at the library before I go upstate."

"I didn't mean to tell you over the phone," Jack says, "I was going to tell you tonight. I just found out about it yesterday."

"It's okay," I tell him. "Really. I'll see you tonight."

I get off the phone and stare at the flawless blue sky over New Jersey, the little whitecaps on the Hudson. I'd made up that part about needing to go to the library, but suddenly it seems like a good idea. Anything to get out of the apartment right now.

I grab a notebook and pen and walk uptown fast, giving myself ten blocks to cry and ten blocks to be angry. By the time I'm in the twenties, though, I can see Jack's side of it. After all, if I had been awarded a residency at Yaddo or MacDowell I'd certainly want to go. I know that if the situation were reversed Jack would be nothing but supportive. It's why, after all, we've stayed unmarried and childless all these years—so we can take advantage of opportunities like this.

By the time I'm crossing through Bryant Park I feel almost happy. The white-limbed London plane trees, which were just beginning to bud that night I walked here with Aidan, are leafed out now, their greenery filling in the tangle of branches. The back of the library is gleaming in the sun. I'm not like my mother, I think, walking around to the front and mounting the steps past the two marble lions, I am capable of happiness. Why wasn't she? Standing in the marble foyer of the library I try to think of something I could find out about my mother here. Some piece I can take up to the hotel with me. After all, this is where she started out from. Somewhere in the city. Did she feel the same mixture of hope and apprehension about leaving that I do?

Her first book begins with a mysterious creature—half woman, half seal—journeying up a river—the drowned river, it's called—fleeing an un-named pursuer. The journey literally transforms the creature. "Where the river turns to salt the selkie sheds her skin and becomes a woman." Was she talking about her own journey up the Hudson and how it transformed her?

I'll write about the day she arrived at the hotel, I decide. I'll compare her train trip up the river to the journey she describes in her first book. Just as the selkie of her story sheds its skin halfway up the river, my mother shed her past and was reborn on the day she arrived at the Hotel Equinox. June 21, 1949.

I know the date because it's also my parents' wedding anniversary. They were married on the one-year anniversary of her arrival. "She came on the first day of summer," my father always said. "Trailing clouds of glory . . ." The old lady guests loved that part and as corny as it was you could tell my father really meant it. Her arrival at the hotel had been the beginning of his life—but what had it been to my mother—a beginning or an end?

I turn left and go down the wide hall to Room 100, the microfilm divi-sion of the Periodicals Department. Of all the rooms to work in at the li-brary it's my least favorite. It doesn't have the beautiful publishing-row murals of the Periodicals Reading Room across the hall or the blue-sky ceil-ings of the Rose Reading Room on the third floor, but it does have the roll of microfilm containing the *New York Times* for 1949, June through Decem-ber. I find a free microfilm viewer, buy a copying card, and, after a few mis-feeds, scroll the film to the front page of Tuesday, June 21, 1949. There's a picture of four men shaking hands, with the caption "As the Big Four Conference Ended in Paris," a story about Pope Pius's excommunication of Czechoslovakian leaders, and a small article about a peace treaty in Aus-tria. Postwar stuff, nothing all that exciting, but I make a copy of the first two pages to read later because I find it hard to read directly from the screen. I scroll through the rest of the paper, stopping to notice—and copy— a story about the weather: "Summer arrives with no relief from worst drought in 41 years." Dry summers were always big news up at the hotel because of the acres of pine forest surrounding it and the ever-present threat of forest fires. I'll have to ask my aunt whether there were any fires that summer.

I make copies of the entertainment pages for the movie listings. This is what my mother could have gone to see in the weeks before she left the city: Joan Crawford in *Flamingo Road*, Vivien Leigh in *Anna Karenina*, Anna Magnani in *The Bandit*. Also, at the 50th St. Beverly Theater, "your last chance to see," *Gone With the Wind*. I've used up most of the credit on my copying card when I decide I ought to look at June 22 as well. After all, anything that actually happened on the day my mother arrived at the hotel wouldn't show up in the paper until the next day. Again, there's nothing too exciting in the first pages so I scroll through quickly, the whir of the film making me sleepy in the stuffy room. My eyes are half closed when a familiar name flashes by.

I stop the film and scroll backward. It's a small story, and the name doesn't appear in the headline—"Brooklyn Woman Killed in Train Accident"—but in the next line, "Death of Rose McGlynn Called Possible Suicide." When I notice that the dateline is Rip Van Winkle, New York, my hand slips on the knob and the film jumps forward several frames. By the time I manage to scroll back and find the story I'm nearly hyperventilating in the stifling low-ceilinged room. I decide to copy the article and take it upstairs to read.

I walk up the three flights of stairs to the Rose Reading Room, clutching the Xeroxed newsprint in my now sweaty hands. It's not just that I need more air, but that I have this inkling that what I'm about to read is going to be important. I don't want to have that kind of revelation in Room 100. The Rose Reading Room, with its gilt-coffered ceilings and gleaming wood tables, is where the real writers work. This is where famous biographers toil away on decades-long projects. When I look back on this day, I want to remember that this is where I started to tell my mother's story. I find a seat at the south end of the north gallery and read my article.

Tragedy struck at the Rip Van Winkle train station yesterday when Rose McGlynn, of Mermaid Avenue, Coney Island, fell beneath the northbound train. She was killed instantly.

Onlookers disagreed as to why the young woman fell, but at least one witness reported that Miss McGlynn appeared to wait for the approach of the train and then "she kind of leaned forward and fell onto the tracks."

No family members could be found to comment on this possibility. Miss McGlynn's mother died in 1941, when Rose was seventeen, at which time her three younger brothers were remanded into the care of the state. Her father, John McGlynn, died four years later. Neighbors said that she had recently lost her job. A young woman traveling with Miss McGlynn, who asked that her name be withheld, said that they were both traveling north to the Catskills to look for work in the hotels. "She wanted to start a new life, but now she'll never get the chance."

I sit back and stare up at the clouds and blue sky in the painted ceiling above me. Tirra Glynn is what my mother called her imaginary world in her fantasy books. She and her unknown companion were registered under the names Mr. and Mrs. McGlynn the night she died in the fire at the Dreamland Hotel. On the day my mother arrived at the Hotel Equinox, Rose McGlynn—an Irish girl who came from Brooklyn, just like my mother— killed herself. I'm instantly sure that the unnamed traveling companion must have been my mother, which means she saw her friend throw herself under the train. Two girls, very much alike, trying to change their lives, only one is killed in the process: the events mirror the story line of her fantasy world in which the selkies shed their skins to live new lives—only some of them die in the attempt.

I gather up the copies I've made and leave. I've been sitting under clear blue skies inside so it's a surprise when I get outside to see that the sky has turned to violet and the street lamps are on in Bryant Park. This story of tragic death should, I suppose, have deepened my unease about my summer plans, but instead my fingertips are nearly tingling with excitement, with the urge to get home and start writing. It's a feeling I've been waiting for all my life: I have a story to tell.

PART II

The Net of Tears

Chapter Thirteen

THE BROKEN PEARL

Once there was a great serpent who lay at the bottom of the ocean in the land of Tirra Glynn and in his mouth he held a pearl that was the soul of the world. But the king Connachar desired the pearl for himself and he dived under the sea and stole it from the serpent. Before he could swim to the shore, though, the pearl shattered into a million pieces. All around him the water glowed white with the shards of the pearl and when he dragged himself onto the sand and looked back at the ocean he saw the glowing slivers in a path that led to the moon. He dipped his hands in the surf's foam and tried to scoop up the glittering sand but the pieces of the pearl slid through his fingers.

From that time on the selkies were banished from Tirra Glynn and cursed. We can never return to the sea. Our only means of escape is the drowned river that twice a year flows backward from the sea. But even if we can catch the current and shed our skins where the salt water becomes fresh, we're still trapped in a skin not our own. We can shed a million skins and still not be ourselves.

As for Connachar the shattered pearl had soaked into his skin and formed a carapace around his heart, because that's what happens when you long for one thing, and one thing only, and then you lose it.

To go to the Hotel Equinox I take the same train I take every Thursday to teach at Rip Van Winkle. It's the same train my mother would have taken in 1949. This is how my mother described her first trip to the Hotel Equinox: "It was the farthest I'd ever gone from home," she would say. "I'd only ever taken the train into Manhattan for work. Even the Bronx seemed far. Another world. If you went to a dance and met a boy from the Bronx you'd say—even if you liked each other—too bad. But I'd heard about the job from a friend and that summer . . . 1949 . . . it was so hot working in the city. I had to get out. So a friend told me they were still hiring at one of the hotels in the Catskills and I wrote and someone—well, of course, it turned out to be your aunt Sophie—wrote back and said my references sounded fine and even though they'd already hired for the season they could use another girl. The hotel was having a good year. You see, all the men were home from the war now and people had, well, a little more money, at least more than anybody'd had for a while.

"So I took the subway into Grand Central and I missed the train I'd meant to take. I had to wait another hour. I was too nervous to sit. I walked back and forth looking up at the ceiling, at those drawings of the constellations. You know what I thought? I thought I might as well be going there, to the Milky Way, to where all those stars were, to another planet as to someplace in upstate New York. I almost took the subway back to Coney Island."

My mother must not have known how unbearable this part of her story was to me. She was trying to show, I suppose, all the obstacles fate threw up between her and her eventual destination, but for me it was unimaginable. How could she not get on the train that took her to the Hotel Equinox? To my father. To me.

"But I didn't, of course; I took the train upstate. Oh, I almost changed my mind again when we had to change trains at Rip Van Winkle. Such a funny name, like a fairy tale, I thought, but not funny because it was also the name of a prison. The northbound train was delayed and when I saw the southbound train pulling in I almost crossed the tracks and took it back to the city." Again she would pause. Tauntingly, I thought as a child, drawing out my panic. Later I would think it was funny that this stop was the one I got out at every week to teach at the prison. There were days when, after I'd taught my class, I'd come back to the station and feel an overwhelming urge to cross the narrow bridge spanning the tracks and wait on the other side for the northbound train. It seemed such heresy to leave this station southbound; as if by doing so I was rewriting my mother's decision and so writing myself out of existence.

Today, when we stop in Rip Van Winkle, I think of the woman who died on these tracks on June 21, 1949, and wonder if that's why my mother always paused when she told me this story. Was she editing out the memory of that horrible death? Had she seen it? Did she know Rose McGlynn? As the train starts again, the thing that strikes me the most is that my mother might have witnessed that death and she still got on the northbound train—when the tracks had been cleared of Rose McGlynn's body—and continued on her journey. I stare out the window at the river and the low blue mountains on the other side, straining for a glimpse of the hotel, but there's a light haze today rising from the mountains and I miss it and before I'm quite expecting it the conductor calls my stop.

When I get off the train I recognize the old caramel-colored Volvo station wagon that Joseph has driven and nursed along for so many years. I almost expect Joseph to get out of it and come limping across the parking lot (one of his legs was broken in the concentration camp and it didn't set right) to wrest my luggage away from me, but I'm sure my aunt said that Joseph had gotten too old to drive. Still, I would be less surprised by the sight of ancient Joseph hopping spryly from the car than by the figure I do see walking around the car, heading toward me with a wide, mischievous grin.

"What's the matter, Prof, did you think the management would leave you stranded?" Aidan says, releasing my suitcases from my grip. He swings the smaller bag under one arm and carries the large bag in the same hand, leaving his right hand free to tip an imaginary cap at me.

"I'm just surprised to see you doing car service—I thought you were bellhopping." What I'm really surprised at is Joseph letting him drive the beloved and ancient Volvo.

"That's what I thought, but your aunt took one look at me and said I'd better help Joseph. Seems most of your bellboys are over sixty and arthritic or skinny college kids who've never worked with their hands a day in their lives. So I've been given the heavy lifting jobs, carting shrubbery back and forth until Joseph decides where he wants them, hauling wood for the new summerhouses, shoveling gravel for the garden paths . . . not that I'm complaining . . . Want the full chauffeured experience, mum?" he says opening the back door for me and presenting the Volvo's cracked leather rear seat with a flourish of his gloved hands. "I've got a nice champagne chilling in the mini fridge and CNN on the porto-telly."

"No, thanks," I say, opening the front passenger's door for myself. "Champagne and TV make me carsick. I'll ride in front. I am staff, you know."

"Management, Professor," he says, getting into the driver's seat. "And don't you forget it."

"Barely. I'll be lucky if my aunt doesn't have me hauling gravel. Look, you might as well drop the *Professor Greenfeder* bit too. No one at the hotel has called me anything but Iris since I was two."

"Not Miss Iris?"

I shake my head. "My father didn't want me turning into a hotel brat like Eloise at the Plaza." Aidan cocks his head at me before starting the car. "Okay," I admit, "it didn't work. I still ended up a bit of a hotel brat."

Aidan grins. "Joseph calls you Miss Iris. To me at least. I think he's making it clear you're above my station."

"Oh please. Joseph's just old-fashioned and . . . well, he sort of looked out for me after my mother died. He must think well of you to let you drive his Volvo."

"No choice. I'm the only one about who knows his way around a stick shift. No, I'm afraid your Joseph isn't crazy about me. I think he's trying to load me down with enough heavy work so I'll quit or have a heart attack."

"I'm sorry, Aidan, I didn't mean to get you such a miserable job." What really bothers me is the idea that Joseph and Aidan don't get along. Although he never spoke much, I'd always found it soothing just to be around Joseph, and after my mother was gone he'd let me help in the garden. We'd work the flower beds together in companionable silence and overhear all sorts of things the guests said among themselves without noticing us. Joseph never commented on these overheard conversations, but I'd know by a wink or a nod or a grimace what he thought of the guest and I came to trust his judgment about people. "Do you want me to speak to him?"

"Nah, don't bother, I think that would make it worse. I'm used to this kind of thing—I've had guards who had it out for me who could do me a lot more harm than an old, lame gardener can dish out."

I look over at Aidan—we're crossing the Kaatskill Bridge and he's looking straight ahead, concentrating on the narrow causeway—and see that flicker of shame that crosses his eyes whenever he talks about prison. Is this maybe what Joseph has picked up? It's something I imagine that Joseph—after his experience in the concentration camps—might sense.

"So is the place all aflutter at the new owner's imminent arrival," I say, trying to change the subject. "When's he supposed to get here?"

"Oh, you mean Sir Harry?"

"Sir Harry?"

"Didn't you know? He was knighted by the queen for his war efforts. He saved some famous paintings from the Nazis and restored them to their rightful owners after the war."

"Really? I knew he was a Monuments officer in the war, but I didn't know he'd been knighted." What had Phoebe called him? A knight in shining armor? "He doesn't really expect us to call him Sir Harry?" We've come to the crest of the bridge and I can see the blue hills of the Catskills receding before us like ripples in water, a narrow band of cloud separating the mountains from the river so they appear to be floating. Whenever I see them like this I remember that Washington Irving called them a "dismembered branch of the great Appalachian mountains." They seem somehow transplanted from someplace else, exiled mountains floating in a foreign land. It's what my mother called the mountains in her fantasy world: the Floating Mountains. And there, rising from a blue fold, are the white columns of the Hotel Equinox, like a Greek temple in Arcadia.

"Nah, Mr. Kron. But down in the under cellars we serfs refer to him as Sir Harry. Gives the enterprise a touch of class, don't you think?"

We're past the glimpse of Arcadia from the bridge and driving through the town of Kaatskill. I'd heard that some restaurants and antiques dealers had moved to downtown, but there are still more abandoned storefronts than occupied ones and most of the stores are the same sad and dusty gun shops and taxidermists that I remember from my childhood. Hunting and fishing are still the region's most profitable tourist draws. On the outskirts of town faded and peeling signs advertise hotels and resorts long out of business. We pass the Agway advertising deer feed and kerosene for home stoves. I'm looking for the little green-and-white sign, with its fringe of pine trees carved years ago by Joseph and painted by my mother, that is the Hotel Equinox's only advertisement. But instead, as we turn off the county route onto the long private drive that climbs the mountain to the hotel, I see a new sign, cream with glossy purple lettering. THE NEWEST JEWEL IN THE CROWN . . . the sign reads, THE CROWN EQUINOX.

"The Crown Equinox? He renamed it? My aunt didn't tell me."

"He renames everything that's his," Aidan says taking a curve a bit too fast, "like God."

I take a deep breath and the smell of pine instantly calms me down. Of course the hotel would be renamed. What does it matter? What matters is that the hotel is still here. I roll down the window all the way to inhale more of the warm resiny smell. Through the dense stands of trees I catch the flash of water, the stream coming down from the falls. We're the only car on the road and except for the sound of the Volvo's engine and the flowing water there's silence—a quiet I remember as peculiar to these woods as if the dark dense stand of pines absorbed all sounds.

"The pines look dry," I say, anxious to divert the conversation from Harry Kron's alterations—after all, he can't change the woods, or the mountain, or the falls. "We had such a rainy spring."

"That's what I thought when I got up here, but apparently we got all the rain in the city and they didn't. Joseph says it's to do with the rain shadow . . ."

"The mountain draws down the clouds but it rains on the other side of the mountain. The east side. I never quite got that."

Aidan shakes his head and grins. "Me neither, but I learned pretty quick you might as well question a statue as ask Joseph what he means by something."

"And Joseph thinks it's going to be a dry summer?"

"Worst drought in fifty-one years, he predicts. But at least the lack of rain should be good for business. No one wants to spend money for a hotel room way up in the country and then sit inside and watch it rain."

I nod, even though Aidan is concentrating too hard on the twisting, steep road to see me. It's true, I think, guests hate the rain. It's not their problem if the water level in the cisterns is low or the pine needles in the forest are dry as tinder. All they care about is good hiking weather and dry tennis courts, clear sunrises to paint and sunsets to decorate the windows of the lounge while they sip their aperitifs. It's only when we're on the final approach to the hotel that I take in fully what Aidan said. The worst drought in fifty-one years. It's exactly what I read in the paper at the library, about the summer my mother arrived here, only then it had been forty-one years since the last drought. It makes me anxious to arrive at the hotel, to make sure it really is still standing, and that it hasn't been destroyed by a fire while Aidan and I have made our way up the mountain.

Of course it hasn't. As we round the last curve in the road the hotel appears, cool and white on its ridge above the Hudson Valley, its slender Corinthian columns echoing the encircling white pines. No wonder. The wood for the hotel was hewn right on this spot and carved into these columns by local craftsmen. It's almost as if the northern white pines had sprouted a crown of tropical foliage. "If you look closely," Joseph once told me, hoisting me up on his shoulders and pointing to the carved capitals, "you can see they mixed acorns and pines boughs in among the Greek frippery. And here, at the base"—he swung me down to the ground and lowered himself slowly to his knees—"if you feel under the paint . . ." He held his large, rough hand over my small one until I could feel the pattern carved in the wood.

"An arrow!" I said, proud to find this secret mark. "But what's it for?"

"Mark of the British Crown," he said, pointing toward the woods surrounding the hotel. "You'll find it on some of the oldest trees in the forest. They were meant for the ship masts for the British navy."

It's what the hotel looks like to me now. A white ship floating on a sea of blue sky—the ghost of Henry Hudson's *Half Moon* perhaps—hovering above the Hudson, waiting for the right tide to take it home.

"Look who's waiting for you," Aidan says as we enter the circular drive. "He couldn't stand not coming for you himself."

"I think it's the Volvo he hates to let out of his sight," I say, but truly I am touched to see Joseph standing in the flower bed framed in the arch of one of his summerhouses, watching our progress along the circular drive. He stands so still, in fact, that for a moment I have the unnerving sensation that he's a statue, that he's become an ornament in his own garden, but then he lifts one hand, retrieves a folded red bandanna from his shirt pocket, and passes it over his face. It's as if the cloth releases the deep creases around his eyes and mouth. He doesn't so much as smile—I'm not sure I've ever seen Joseph smile—as he relaxes his face, looking toward me with the softness he usually reserves for tree roots and tulip bulbs.

We pull up under the porte cochere and a uniformed bellhop—a skinny, pimply kid who looks about sixteen—reaches to open my door, but I've already slid out the driver's side behind Aidan so I can greet Joseph first. There's a little cluster around the entrance and I have the feeling that once I go in that way my job as manager will have really started. For just a moment I want to be the hotel brat again.

"*Shayna maidela,*" Joseph says hoarsely as I reach up to kiss his lined cheek. Pretty girl. It's what he always called my mother. "You look more like your mother every day."

I shake my head. I know I'll never be as beautiful as my mother, but I'm always grateful for Joseph's lie. It's a lie he tells for himself, I think, as he pulls out the square of red cloth and passes it over his face again, as much as for me. So he can see my mother back here again.

"You, though, really do look just exactly the same." This is actually true. Joseph looked ancient, I imagine, from the day he set foot in this hotel. "And look at your roses," I say waving my arms at the spray of deep red climbers trained over the arch of the summerhouse, knowing that Joseph will be more comfortable with praise for his flowers than for his own person.

"It's a wonder they're doing this well without rain. I've been hand-watering them from the lake every day."

"You're hauling water up from the lake?"

"Oh, I've had a hand." Joseph cocks his thumb over his shoulder at Aidan who has come up behind him carrying my suitcases. Behind Joseph's back Aidan rolls his eyes and mouths, "Thirty buckets a day he has me bring up."

"What about the pump from the lake, doesn't that still work?" This had been one of my father's inventions, a hydraulic pump that drew water from the lake to supply the hotel with water for the gardens and, most important, in case of fire. Drinking water had always been supplied by a spring near the hotel, but even in wet summers it didn't give enough water for the gardens and it would never have been enough to douse a fire.

"Your Mr. Kron has shut it down for repairs."

"He's not my Mr. Kron," I say defensively, although in truth I had been proud of delivering the hotel's savior.

Aidan has come around by my side and is inspecting the roses climbing over the arch. Joseph cranes around and looks at the Volvo standing with the driver's-side door still open. I think he's looking for signs of wear in his precious car, but then he looks back at Aidan and me, scowling. "Where's your man, then? Wasn't he coming up with you?"

"Oh, Jack?" I remember now that when we'd come up last summer Jack had followed Joseph around the whole time asking him gardening questions. "He couldn't come. He was awarded a residency at an artists' colony. A prestigious one . . ." I falter under Joseph's stare and, I notice, Aidan's raised eyebrows.

"Yaddo?" Joseph asks. "MacDowell?" I shake my head, amused that Joseph has picked up the names of these institutions from listening in on painters' conversations, and name the somewhat less renowned colony that Jack has gone to.

Joseph flaps a large, callused hand in the air. "He would have done as well to come here and paint. Keep you company." Joseph glares at Aidan and suddenly I realize what he's worried about. He thinks there's something going on between me and Aidan. And here we are, standing together under the arch of one of his *chuppas*—Brier Rose, this one's called—on the exact same spot where my mother and father were married. I take a step out of the shelter of the arch, but Aidan happens to step with me and our shoulders bump together.

"Well," Aidan says, "I'll be getting Iris's bags upstairs."

Even though I've told him to use my first name it takes me by surprise to hear him say it.

"There's bellhops for that," Joseph says turning toward the front door. "I've got some work for you."

While Joseph's back is turned Aidan nimbly plucks a rose from the bower and palms it behind his back so Joseph won't see. Then he winks at me. I'm trying to keep a straight face as we walk past Joseph.

"I'll come down later to see the rest of the gardens," I tell Joseph.

"And I'll just get these into the lobby," Aidan says, hoisting up my bags.

I can't help but laugh when we've gotten around the car and Aidan presents me with the rose. "Joseph will have your head for that. He's the only one supposed to cut the flowers."

But Aidan pulls the rose away from me teasingly. "Aye, he's already had his revenge. Look." Aidan holds up his hand and I see a long bloody scratch on his palm. "I'd better hold this for you until you have something to put it in. Do you think he breeds them extra thorny?"

I reach into my pocket and find a tissue, which I press into Aidan's hand. And that's how my aunt finds us, holding hands on the threshold of the hotel.

Chapter Fourteen

THE BROKEN PEARL

When my mother told me the story about the selkie who leaves her children to go back to the sea I asked her if she ever came back.

"No, but someday the daughter will join her mother under the sea. That's why she wove for her the wreath out of sea foam and dew and her own tears. If the daughter throws the net of tears into the sea it will turn into a path of moonlight that leads back to the land under the sea—to Tirra Glynn."

It wasn't until I was older that my mother told me that the net of tears had been stolen from us. Connachar had taken it to the Palace of the Stars and as long as he kept it there was no returning to the sea. "You are old enough now to know," she told me, "and old enough to take care of your brothers when I go. Promise me you'll take care of your brothers." I promised her.

The next day my mother was gone. She slipped away like a breeze moves through a room, leaving emptiness and silence. I knew that my job now, like the selkie's daughter in the story, was to take care of my brothers, but instead I thought of the net of tears that had been stolen from us and lay somewhere in the Palace of the Stars. So I disobeyed my mother's last wish. I left my brothers to fend for themselves and I went as bondswoman to the Palace of the Stars.

"There you are. I thought you missed your train." My aunt Sophie pulls me toward her for a quick kiss, her eyeglasses clinking against my sunglasses. She turns away, pulling me into the hotel before I have a chance to really look at her, but the first impression I have is that she's shrunk in the six months since I've seen her.

"You, Barry, are you going to take Miss Greenfeder's bags to her room or have you decided they make a nice set of planters for the lobby?"

"Joseph said . . ."

"Never mind what Joseph said. There's a large party coming in by limo from the city and we'll need all the bellhops for that."

Aidan shrugs and tucks my bags under his left arm. With his right hand he tugs a piece of his hair and then swings around and heads for the elevators. It takes me an instant to realize what he was doing. Tugging his forelock. The countryman's sign of respect to his landowner, here rendered mockingly. Even sillier, he's got the rose he picked for me sticking out of his back pocket. I struggle to keep the smile off my own face and start to follow Aidan to the elevators, but my aunt grabs me firmly by the elbows and turns me around to give me the once-over. I feel like I did when I was little and she inspected my outfit before letting me into the dining room. It gives me a chance to look at her. My aunt, like Joseph, has always seemed old to me and so I tend not to notice the signs of aging in her. Her hair has been gray since before I was born and her slightly plump face has held up remarkably well to wrinkles. In fact, she's one of those women who has only looked better as she ages. If she hadn't so convinced herself she was unlovely in her youth—she always felt self-conscious about her weight, my father told me—she might have enjoyed her good looks. I've noticed more than a few bachelors paying her attention over the years, but she's someone who still carries herself with the defensive posture of the unbeautiful.

"You'll have to change of course," she says to me now. "I hope you brought the right clothes."

Actually I thought I was wearing the right clothes. I went out of my way to wear a tailored khaki skirt and a pressed oxford cloth blouse in what I thought was a becoming shade of pink. A little preppy outfit that to me had *hotel manager* written all over it, but looking down at myself, I notice that my skirt is rumpled, my shirt is coming untucked, and my loafers are covered with grass clippings.

"I'll go right up and change," I say. "I just want to get a look at the place."

We're standing between the Sunset Lounge and the concierge's desk. When my mother first came here, my father told me, she hated the entrance to the hotel.

"It's like you're coming in the service entrance," she complained. "There's no sense of the place—no feeling you've arrived."

The problem is that the hotel faces east, perched on a narrow ridge above the Hudson. What makes it so spectacular is that view, the expanse of sky, so it only made sense to the hotel's original builder to orient the hotel toward the east. But you can't approach the hotel from the east side. The ridge is too narrow. Before my mother redecorated, guests came in the back door and worked their way through a warren of fusty, Victorian lounges before ever coming upon that spectacular view of sky and river.

My mother had the walls knocked down to create one expansive lobby and sunk its marble floor so that standing on the threshold you look over the pale green velvet sofas and rustic tables, your eye drawn to the floor-to-ceiling glass doors along the east wall, and out to a view of pure sky. The promise of the outer appearance is now fulfilled by the interior: you feel as if you're on a ship floating above the clouds.

As a child, hidden in one of the deep sofas, I'd watched guest after guest come in the entrance, nervously looking after their luggage and tugging their clothes straight after long car trips, look up and go still at the sight of all that sky. I could almost count the time it took after that pause for them to float across the lobby and out the French doors, onto the colonnaded terrace overlooking the valley. That's where I want to go now, only Aunt Sophie is pulling me toward the front desk, which runs along the south wall of the lobby.

Ramon, the head day clerk, smiles at me as we approach the desk. "Welcome back, Iris."

"That will be *Miss Greenfeder* from now on," my aunt snaps. "As befitting the new manager."

I roll my eyes behind Sophie's back and mouth "Iris" to Ramon who makes a great show of bowing his head toward me. "*Miss Greenfeder* it is then—good to have another Greenfeder in the managerial position . . ." I can tell Ramon is gearing up for a speech. Thirty years ago, fresh out of drama school, he'd come up to the Catskills to do summer stock and dinner theater and then, when the big hotels to the south and west closed, just dinner—waiting and busing tables, washing dishes. My mother found him working as a fry cook at a diner in Peekskill. She said he made the worst omelet you ever ate while reciting Shakespeare. She knew he'd never last at the diner so she offered him a job as front desk clerk—"he has just the right voice for greeting guests"—the summer before she died.

"Yes, yes," Sophie interrupts, "we're all glad she's back, now let's let her get to work. Where's the registration book?"

The heavy leather-bound ledger is lying open beneath Ramon's long, elegant fingers, but still he takes a moment to look puzzled—as if he's misplaced the twelve-pound tome—before swiveling the book around and pushing it across the marble countertop toward me. It's open to today's arriving guests and the page is full.

"Wow, I don't think I've ever seen so many guests arriving in one day."

"It's a corporate retreat for Crown Hotels International," Sophie explains. "We've got another one next week for museum curators and two in June . . ." I flip through the pages for the next several weeks and see they're almost all full. In among the blocks of rooms reserved for corporations and various fund-raising groups (I remember what Phoebe told me about Harry Kron being a great patron of the arts) I notice quite a few familiar family names.

"The Van Zandts . . . is that Bill and Eugenie who used to come every August?"

"Their son and his family."

"And Karl Orbach, wasn't he in that painting group that came for a while in the early seventies . . ."

"And did that awful mural of naked women in the Sunset Lounge . . ."

"And Claire Mineau and her daughter, Sissy, and the Eden sisters . . . It's like old home week all summer. Why are they coming now?"

"Mr. Kron went through our old registration books and sent this to any-one who was ever a repeat visitor at the hotel." My aunt unfolds a cream-colored card from her cardigan pocket and hands it to me. Encircled by a rustic border of pinecones and acorns is a lavish invitation inviting the "friends of Hotel Equinox to return to the summers of their childhoods, when time stood still and your only appointments were with the world-famous sunrise and sunset."

"Who wrote this drivel?" I ask.

Ramon coughs theatrically into his fist.

"Not you, Aunt Sophie! I thought you hated this kind of sentimental come-on."

"I am trying to save the hotel," she says, squaring her shoulders. I no-tice that even when she draws herself up she barely comes up to my collar-bone. "Mr. Kron said he especially wanted to bring back the families who used to spend their whole summers here."

"I wonder why he needs to bother when he's got all these corporate events. Still, I suppose it's nice that he wants to incorporate the old tradi-tions of the hotel into its new profile." I am thinking, really, that it will help in my research that so many of the old guests are coming back. It's the kind of altruistic motive, though, that I'd expect my aunt to sneer at but in-stead she smiles for the first time since I've arrived.

"It is nice," she says. "Mr. Kron has authorized a forty percent discount to anyone whose family used to stay here . . . so many old familiar faces . . . I only wish your father could have lived to see it." Sophie's gaze drifts away from the registration book and out the glass doors to the terrace. Abruptly her smile vanishes. "Or maybe he's better off not seeing certain people back here."

I follow her gaze to the figure of a slim woman framed between two columns, silhouetted against the blue sky. I wonder who she could be, but then she lifts a gnarled hand to adjust the scarf tied around her hair and I recognize her.

"Hedda Wolfe," I say before I can help myself.

Sophie pushes her glasses up the bridge of her nose and stares at me. "You know her?"

This would be the time, obviously, to tell my aunt about my contract, but even if I wanted to my aunt has launched into such a tirade against my new agent I wouldn't have the nerve.

"She made your mother's life a living hell those last years . . . calling constantly to ask about the next book . . . sending her assistants up here to badger Kay after your father refused to let her stay anymore. Your parents would be turning in their graves if they knew . . ." Sophie stops abruptly. My mother, of course, has no grave. Only ashes.

"I had no idea," I stammer. "I've met her a few times in the city, at readings and seminars. She speaks quite well of Mother . . ."

"Well, she should! Made her a lot of money, Kay did, and her reputation. I suppose if you already know her you should say hello to her. It's your professional duty as manager. Don't expect me to cuddle up to her though."

I can't imagine Sophie cuddling up to anyone. I nod, though, as if carefully weighing her advice. "Yes, I think I'll go say hello and welcome her to the hotel. Might as well get it out of the way." I'm afraid that Sophie will offer to come with me, but fortunately the head housekeeper—a new woman I've never met before—arrives with news of some laundry emergency and Sophie is called away. Leaving me to go out onto the terrace—as I've wanted to since I came in—and try to explain to my new agent why my aunt doesn't know I'm writing a book.

I go out the glass doors and find Hedda Wolfe sitting on the balustrade leaning against a column. With her thick silk scarf hiding her light hair and large dark glasses she looks a little like a young Jackie Kennedy—or a little like my mother. She's wearing well-pressed chinos and a pale blue oxford cloth blouse—an outfit much like the one I'm wearing, only on her it looks somehow rich. No one would send her upstairs to change. Her gaze remains on the view until I'm by her side.

"Iris," she says, making a limp gesture with her hands that manages to indicate a greeting while precluding a handshake. "I wondered when you'd arrive. Of course, I didn't want to ask your aunt."

"I'm sorry about Aunt Sophie. She can be . . . a bit judgmental."

Hedda laughs. "She would have made a great editor, more sense than half the people in the business. No, don't apologize for your aunt. I'm only sorry if I've made things difficult for you with her. I wondered if I should come when I received Harry's invitation."

"Mr. Kron invited you?" I suppose I shouldn't sound so surprised—after all, he mentioned he knew her.

"I believe he's inviting all the 'old-timers' and my grandmother came here for over twenty summers. He was kind enough, though, to include a personal note with my invitation mentioning that he had met you and commending me for my 'good sense' in fostering your writing career. So I gather he knows about the memoir?"

"Yes, I told him about it."

"And your aunt? Have you told her about the project?"

I stare off at the view to avoid meeting Hedda's gaze. It's one of the oddities of conversations held on the terrace: people hardly look at each other out here—the view is so commanding. Today the sun has bleached the color out of the valley and the river looks flat and far away. "No," I say, "I haven't told her. I'm afraid she wouldn't like the idea at all. She'd call it airing our dirty laundry in front of the world. I know it probably sounds cowardly . . ."

"Not at all, I think it's wise. Sophie never really approved of Kay's writing—if it had been up to her your mother would never have had any creative outlet other than rearranging the pillows in the lobby. I always thought it was because Sophie herself had given up her painting. There's no one more intolerant of an artist than a failed one." I'm a bit taken aback by the harshness of her tone, but then it strikes me that she may be right. Sophie had been a student at the Art League before coming up here to help her brother at the hotel. I always wondered why she didn't at least paint in her spare time, but she told me once that if she couldn't pursue her art seriously, she'd rather not pursue it at all. Still, I feel I should defend my aunt, but then Hedda lays one of her soft crumpled hands on my arm and it totally disarms me.

"Don't let her do to you what she did to Kay. You'll be far better able to ask questions about your mother and look for the manuscript if she doesn't know what you're doing. And I'll be right here if you need any advice about what you find. I plan to stay all summer."

"The whole summer!" I realize my surprise might sound ungracious. "I mean, how will you conduct your business while you're up here?"

"Oh, the wonders of the Internet," she says gesturing toward a thin silver laptop lying on one of the rocking chairs, "and FedEx. I'll probably go down to the city for a few days every other week or so, but for the most part, you won't be able to get rid of me."

After my talk with Hedda, I walk up the main central stairs, even though it's six flights up to my attic room. I am eager, I suppose, to put space between Hedda Wolfe and myself. I've never deliberately concealed anything from my aunt before and the fact that I am collaborating with a woman she hates makes it worse. As I climb the stairs, though, I feel better and not, I realize, because I am leaving Hedda Wolfe behind but because I feel as if I'm leaving myself behind—or at least that part of myself that would deceive my aunt for material gain. It's what I have to do, I tell myself, feeling lighter with every flight as the view through the arched windows on each landing grows wider and higher. It's like climbing into the clouds. The valley below recedes; the curving band of blue river unfurls into the distance. The thick carpets absorb the sound of my steps, and the stealthy glints of the chandeliers wink in the watery afternoon sunlight. Instead of feeling winded by the climb I feel as though I can really breathe for the first time in months. It's just as my father always said: a good hotel allows its guests to become their best selves.

On the fifth floor the main staircase ends and I have to walk to the south end of the hall to a door leading to the narrow attic steps. I notice along the way that the hall carpets have been replaced—instead of the old threadbare flowered ones there are cream and purple runners bearing the Crown logo. The walls have been repainted a glossy cream with lavender trim. It's a bit like being inside a candy box.

I peer into an open room that's being cleaned by a maid and notice with relief that the renovations haven't extended that far yet. My mother's choice of color scheme—forest green and white—has faded but still looks good in the muted carpets and faded silk curtains. And when I head up the attic stairs I see that nothing has been changed up here at all.

Most of the rooms I pass haven't been occupied since the new servants' quarters were built in the early 1950s. Over the years the rooms have become a repository of broken furniture—too good to throw out, though, my aunt would insist—holiday decorations, and the things that guests have left behind. "You never know when they'll realize they're missing something and expect you to have it. And send it free of shipping charge, no doubt!"

When I was little I loved to go through the boxes of things—amazed that people could be so careless as to leave such treasure. Silk nightgowns and robes were the most commonly forgotten items because, my mother once explained, guests hung them on the bathroom hooks and forgot to check the back of the door when they were packing. But there were also shoes and books and tennis racquets and paint boxes and diaries and shawls and ropes and ropes of cheap paste pearls in every color imaginable, which sometimes my mother would wear. On her they always looked real.

It's obvious that no one has bothered to go through the hoard in years. Boxes of long-discarded loot—the detritus of half a century of summer holidays—line the floors of each room. Until I get to the last room on the west side of the corridor, my old room.

Someone has gone to the trouble to clean and neaten my old room. The scarred and ringed surfaces of the night table and bureaus have been rubbed free of dust, and there's fresh linen on the four-poster bed. I touch the carved sun and moon on the headboard and I can almost hear my mother's voice beginning her story: . . . *In a land between the sun and the moon* . . . My luggage is neatly stacked on the trunk at the foot of my bed and a single red rose rests in a water glass on my night table. Aidan. I feel a rush of embarrassment to think of him entering this little room, its starkness saying more about me than I would like.

I go to the window and move the lace curtains aside to look out at the gardens. I can spot new arrivals from here—and possibly Aidan if he's still working in the garden. The driveway is empty, but I do see Joseph sitting inside the archway of the summerhouse—Brier Rose—where Aidan and I stood a little earlier. It's a sign of age, I think, to see Joseph sitting anywhere instead of trimming, or mulching, or digging—fussing over his garden in some way. Then I notice that he's not alone. The person sitting on the opposite ledge is obscured by a spray of roses. I try for another angle, so curious am I to identify Joseph's companion. It's something about being under that *chuppa* together, I think, that suggests intimacy, which is no doubt why it annoyed Joseph to see me and Aidan standing under its arch. But maybe that's who it is—Aidan, sitting while Joseph gives him his next instructions.

When I finally find the right angle, though, I see it's not Aidan. I recognize her by her blue silk scarf. It's Hedda Wolfe. While I watch she gets up to leave and Joseph stands, framed in the arch, to watch her go. I'm too far away to really tell, but when I watch Joseph pass his red bandanna across his eyes I have the distinct impression he's brushing away tears.

Chapter Fifteen

THE BROKEN PEARL

It wasn't long after I went to the Palace of the Stars that I saw the net of tears on that woman's throat, the emerald tear hanging between her breasts.

It should not have made me angry. I was used to the carelessness of these women—the way they dropped their clothes where they stood, like a skin they had shed and had no more use for. Their jewels they left in heaps too, earrings placed on bedside tables where a careless hand in the night brushed them to the floor, diamond rings resting in soap dishes and pearls draping the mirror frames. Let them lose any one of these precious baubles, though, and they knew who to blame: the selkie women who cleaned their rooms.

The net of tears was just another glittering bauble to her— something to match a new green gown, to draw the men's eyes to her breasts, and, at the end of the night, a handful of stones strewn across her dressing table among coins and soiled handkerchiefs. I could have gathered it up in my dustcloth and stuck it in my pocket—the diamonds and pearls so lightly woven they weighed hardly more than a handful of sand. I should have taken it then and run—gone to the river and thrown the stones in the deepest water—but instead I told Naoise what I had seen. And Naoise began to plan.

I checked the boxes in the attic, but I didn't have much time in the next few weeks to look further for my mother's manuscript. I had forgotten what it was like, running the hotel at the height of the summer season—or maybe it was just that we'd never had a season like this before. Harry Kron had outdone himself. In addition to the former guests whom he invited back, his name and reputation drew a wealthy and artistic clientele unlike anything the Hotel Equinox had ever seen. Oh, we'd always had artists, but in the recent past we had drawn the marginal, the struggling, the has-been. Now the registration book was full of names I recognized from the *Times* arts pages—musicians and theater people, architects and painters, writers whose work I admired and their editors and agents. It would have been a great way of making connections if I could ever have a conversation with one of them about something other than their hot-water pressure or the lack of TVs and mini bars in their rooms.

"The next one who asks me how to get to the indoor pool I'm going to send to the Holiday Inn in Kingston," I tell Aidan on a hot, flawless day in June. I'm standing behind the registration desk checking the book for to-day's arrivals. Aidan is sitting on a swivel chair midway between me and the back office where Janine is answering the phones. I notice that when-ever the phones quiet for a moment Janine steals a look at Aidan and then turns nervously back to her phones to stab at the glowing buttons. I can only hope she doesn't cut off anyone too important. The new phone system has been a challenge to her and I've had to plead her case to Harry Kron several times. "Look at this weather!" I say to Aidan, trying to draw him away from distracting Janine. "Why would anyone want an indoor pool on a day like this? What's wrong with the lake?"

"Snakes," Aidan says, "and mud. Not a very appealing combination. Have you not been down to the lake recently?"

"I've hardly made it out to the terrace," I tell him. Between attending to guests' needs and settling staff disputes I've hardly had a minute to myself since I arrived. I remember how effortless my father made the job look—he never seemed to be in a hurry. And my mother could soothe the most demanding guests. But then there were two of them and only one of me.

"We've never had a problem with snakes before and mud . . . well, what do they expect to be at the bottom of a lake—shag carpeting?"

"It's the drought," Aidan tells me. "The water level's down so the shore's muddy and the water is warmer and shallower—just the thing for snakes."

"I'll talk to Mr. Kron about bringing in sand to make a bathing beach— my mother always wanted to do that but we never had the money—but I don't think there's anything he can do about the lack of rain."

"No? Are you sure?"

I make a face at Aidan. His attitude toward Harry Kron often borders on the insolent. I've seen him standing behind the new owner mimicking his instructions to the staff. He's gotten two maids in trouble for giggling during staff meetings, including Mrs. Rivera who can ill afford to lose another job. I've seen Harry studying Aidan and I know that all he has to do is check his application file to see he's on parole. I expect, daily, for Harry to call me in to ask why I've hired an ex-con, and each day Aidan's demeanor makes it harder for me to think of an answer.

"Aidan, please," I whisper, bending down toward him, "he's the owner. Everything depends on his being happy with the way the hotel is run this summer. And think of your own position here."

I look behind me to see if Janine is listening, but all the buttons on her console have lit up at once and she's busy navigating the maze of flashing lights.

"You don't want to do anything to risk your parole."

Aidan tilts his head back and smiles up at me. I notice that a curl of dark hair clings damply to his collar, and it makes me aware of how hot and sticky I am in my panty hose (Sophie insists bare legs are unprofessional). Usually our altitude makes air-conditioning unnecessary but this summer is freakishly hot.

"Hey," he says, as if reading my thoughts, "I'm on break in an hour. What about a swim?"

"I have way too much work to do . . ."

"I think it's your managerial duty to personally check out the lake situation and set an example by swimming in it."

"I don't know—if there are really snakes . . ."

Aidan holds up his thumb and forefinger and pinches them together. "Ah, they're wee snakes and they don't like people. I will personally serve as your bodyguard and, St. Patrick–like, banish the snakes from Tirra Glynn."

I smile. It's my mother's name for the grove of pine trees surrounding the lake that does it. That and the thought of cool water . . . but still, snakes . . .

"Or we could go to the swimming hole," Aidan says. "That's where the lowly staff members slink off to."

"The pool at the base of the falls?"

"That's the one. After dark it's bathing suits optional, but my favorite time is just at dusk."

I wonder whom Aidan has been going to the pool with.

"All right," I say, looking at my watch and rechecking the registration book. "I'll meet you on the path at five—by the first summerhouse."

"The one called Evening Star?"

"Yes, that one."

I'm late meeting Aidan because there's a flurry of late-afternoon arrivals and a crisis in the kitchen involving a shipment of leeks spoiled by the heat and the new chef who refuses to substitute onion in the vichyssoise, which means all the menus for tonight's dinner have to be reprinted. I'm afraid he's gone on without me when I come around a curve and see the path in front of Evening Star deserted, but then I notice the tips of someone's black Converse high-tops sticking up above the bench inside the summerhouse. Aidan is slouched down inside, smoking a cigarette, studying the view of the valley.

"Why do they call this one Evening Star?" he asks before I think he's even heard me come up behind. I remember that day at the train station when he heard the train coming before me.

I sit on the bench opposite him and look up at the ceiling and Aidan looks up too. Most of the summerhouses have ceilings made of rough cedar shakes, but this one has a dome of smooth curved planks that Joseph has fitted together so skillfully you can't make out the seams. The carvings have faded over time but I can just make out a man with a club, cloaked in some sort of skin, reaching into the mouth of a large serpent and pulling out a round orb that is already breaking up into a stream of stars, which spills past various sea creatures until it reaches a slender woman, kneeling by the shore, who scoops up the stars into a slender amphora.

"Joseph dreamed all this up?"

I shake my head. "My mother drew the pictures, Joseph carved them."

"I didn't know your mother was an artist as well as a writer."

"She didn't think much of her drawing. She just did it, she said, to help picture things in her book. This," I say pointing to the roof of the summerhouse, "is what the ceiling looks like in the Palace of the Stars. That's where Deirdre, her heroine, starts out in the first book. The painting on the ceiling is supposed to tell the story of how Connachar stole the pearl from the serpent, how it shattered and then a selkie gathered the pieces together to make the net of tears for her daughter."

"And she got Joseph to make all these little houses to go along with places in her book."

"It sounds silly, I know."

"No, it's better than Disneyland. C'mon." Aidan springs to his feet and takes my hand. "I want the grand tour of the magic kingdom."

I laugh; but really, he's right. This was my mother's magic kingdom—a world she invented out of her dreams—a feat of pure imagination that I've always envied and felt that my own earthbound prose could never approach. I would often come upon her in one of the gazebos, jotting notes on a piece of paper or just staring into space. Sometimes if I asked her what she was doing she would tell me a piece of the story she was trying to write, but as I grew older and the third book in her trilogy failed to appear, she would wave me away when I came upon her, telling me I should go back to the hotel and offer to help in the kitchen or the laundry room. That last summer I often came upon her like that, distracted and wanting to be alone.

I notice that Aidan is staring at me—and that he still has a hold of my hand.

"You're thinking about your mother, aren't you?"

"I was thinking how much I wanted to do what she did—to create my own world. It was like nothing could really touch her because she could always slip away into a world where she made all the rules and everything had to turn out the way she said. And then when she went away I thought for a long time that that's where she'd gone. Like she never really belonged with us in this world and she'd gone back to where she really belonged. I started making up my own stories then."

"Ah, so that's how you became a writer. You made up stories about your mother coming back?"

"No," I say, looking out over the valley. The sky above the eastern ridge has turned a deeper blue and one star has risen above the horizon—another reason for this summerhouse's name. "I made up stories about a girl who lived in the woods with wild animals. As far as I remember there's never any mention of a mother in them."

I show Aidan Half Moon and Castle. Then the trail turns west, away from the ridge, and plunges downhill into a forest of white pine and mountain laurel that is just beginning to bloom. Their scent reminds me of the lilacs Jack brought me more than a month ago and I wonder if there's mountain laurel where he is and whether it reminds him of that night. Jack calls every weekend, but there's no phone in his cabin at the artists' retreat so I can't call him and I've begun to think of him as beyond my reach. The rules of the artists' colony (no talking between the hours of nine and four, no phone calls, no Internet hookup) are like some harsh and arbitrary spell he's been placed under. He might as well be on the moon.

The stream follows the path here, past the summerhouses called Floating Mountain and Sunset, down into the Clove, where it turns into the falls. One path breaks off and goes to the lake; the other, narrower, more overgrown, circles down to the pool at the foot of the falls. We stop here and look toward the lake, which I can just make out as a slightly more yellowish smudge of green beyond the darker pines. I hear voices, some children splashing in the shallows, and spy a couple stretched out on the rocks by the shore—a newspaper reporter and his wife, whom I suspect are writing a feature for the travel section. Guests. Although the staff is allowed to swim in the lake, Aidan and I both hesitate with that instinctive avoidance of encountering paying guests in our time off. Who knows what complaint or request for service they might make? To our right I can hear the steady murmur of falling water and turn toward that.

The woods are so thick here that you can't see the pool until you're almost upon it. The color of the water too, is the same black-green as the moss-covered rocks, so dark the pool has always seemed to me to be underground, like the underground lake in the story of the twelve dancing princesses. When I was little I always imagined that if you dived down deep enough you might find an underground cavern as sparkling and magical as the island pavilion where the princesses danced their shoes to shreds every night, but whenever I dived into the pool I would be too frightened to open my eyes under the water.

Aidan's already stripped down to his swimming trunks. He's so slim and white he might be a birch sapling in these dark woods. I kick my sneakers off and pull my T-shirt dress over my head. The shade here is so deep that even today's heat (a record, Joseph told me earlier) hasn't penetrated and I shiver when the air hits my sweat-damp skin. Aidan is gingerly toeing the water at the edge of the pool, but I know better than that. I scramble up the highest rock and stand at the farthest edge, pausing only a moment to stare into that bottomless green before diving straight down into the pool.

The cold water is like a blade neatly paring off my hot, tired flesh like an apple peel. This is how my mother taught me to enter the pool. Any other way, she said, was just slow torture. I often used to wonder, though, if slow torture was really any worse than quick torture. Today, when I break the surface of the water, gasping for air, and meet Aidan's admiring gaze—he's still on the edge of the pool—I'm glad my mother taught me to be brave.

"Well, what are you waiting for?" I ask, trying to keep my chattering teeth from giving me away. "The water's fine."

After our swim I show Aidan the last of the summerhouses, the double-decker gazebo called Two Moons. It's right below the falls, on the edge of the forest, but because it's completely covered by a rapacious wisteria vine very few people know it's there. It looks like an overgrown bush or a shaggy mammoth downed in the last ice age. The rock it stands on—all of the summerhouses are staked into rock with iron rods—is smooth and highly polished, engraved with small crescent moons—chatter marks left by a glacier some fourteen thousand years ago. I find the steps and hold back a curtain of vines, gesturing with my hand for Aidan to go ahead.

"It's like going inside a cave," he says, ducking his head. "A cave under water."

I nod, but it's so dark when I've dropped the vines back that I doubt he notices.

"In my mother's second book the hero Naoise comes back to find Deirdre and they meet in an underwater cave when both moons are half full . . ."

"Both moons?"

"There are two moons in Tirra Glynn—which makes for very high tides—and one waxes while the other wanes. Look." I point to a curving line that bisects the circular floor. "That's one half moon. The other's on the floor above us."

I start climbing the steep curving stairs that go up to the second level, but I've forgotten how narrow the steps are and slip on the third one. Aidan, who's right behind me, catches me before I can fall down.

"It's a good thing this place is so hard to find or you'd have guests breaking their necks in it. I'm surprised Sir Harry hasn't ordered it torn down yet."

"Oh, he wouldn't. He couldn't." I continue up the stairs, turning my feet sideways to fit onto the narrow steps and holding on to the smooth wooden railing.

"Well, it might not be a bad idea to redo the stairs at least."

"Look at this railing," I say. "Who are you going to get to carve something like this? I don't think even Joseph would be able to do it now."

Aidan looks down at the grooved wood of the railing under his hand and sees what most people miss at first. It's carved to look like a serpent. When we get to the second level the serpent wraps around the center post and then, just below the peak of the roof, its jaws gape open around a large, smooth orb.

We sit on the narrow bench that follows the curve of the circle and look up. Sunlight, tinted green by the entangling vine, slips through the cracks of the roof. We're so close to the falls that drops of water cling to the leaves, sparkling in the sun like a web of diamonds. Even with the drought, the falls fill the green space with the sound of water. Aidan—he's put on his jeans and an unbuttoned white shirt over his bathing suit—wraps his arms around himself as if he's cold even though it's warm in here under all the foliage. "I feel like that snake's looking at me," he says. "I swear it's got Joseph's eyes."

I laugh and shake out my damp hair. "Maybe. The serpent's a kind of guardian—the pearl in its mouth is supposed to be the soul of the world. When it's stolen it breaks apart into a web of pearls and diamonds—the net of tears, my mother called it—and the world falls out of alignment. When it's returned the world will right itself and everything will be in balance— good and evil, day and night, perpetual equinox."

"Now that's a fantasy."

"*Tikkun olam*, is what Joseph calls it. Hebrew for 'healing the world.' He said that's what my mother's books were about, but I always thought that's what Joseph was doing, building these little houses after all the destruction he must have seen in the war . . ." I notice Aidan is looking away and think I must be boring him, but then he puts his hands to my lips and makes a shushing sound.

"Do you hear that?"

I listen, but hear nothing above the whisper of the falls and the sound of my own heart, which Aidan's touch has set racing. His hand has drifted down from my lips and come to rest on my hand. He's looking away from me, concentrating on those sounds only he seems able to hear, so I can concentrate on him, his pale skin, cool as marble, the fine black hairs that curl at the nape of his neck. I remind myself—as I've done many times these last few weeks—of our age difference, but in this place it no longer seems to matter. A drop of water falls from the leaves above us and lands on his cheekbone. Without thinking I raise my hand to brush it away but then I hear the voices and stop, my hand in midair.

". . . she came here then to meet the man?" The voice, slightly hoarse, belongs to a woman. I lean forward to make out her companion's answer but only catch a low-pitched rumble, a few short words given grudgingly that fall into the rush of the falls like pebbles into a lake.

"I know there was someone," the woman continues, "everyone knew, except Ben of course."

The low rumble sounds angrier, like thunder on a summer day, but no more decipherable.

"Yes, I know she loved Ben. Who wouldn't? He worshiped the ground she walked on and took care of her like she was a princess. But I know there was someone before him—someone she wouldn't talk about—what if he came back? Her first love returned to her? How could she resist?"

There's no answering rumble and I'm so disappointed I almost call out myself. *She would never have done that to my father,* I want to cry, but Aidan, still turned from me, squeezes my hand. I hear Joseph and Hedda Wolfe's retreating footsteps but I let them go. I search my own memory for some evidence that Hedda is wrong—surely if my mother was meeting someone down here I would have seen them together—but then I remember that I wasn't allowed to come down to the pool by myself. My mother said she was afraid I might slip into the pool and drown. What I do remember is my mother returning to the hotel in the late afternoons, her hair damp, her pale skin cool to the touch on the hottest days. I can't swear that she wasn't meeting someone down here. Besides, who am I to defend my mother while I myself cower hidden in the shadows with a young man—who's also an ex-convict, I remind myself, as I watch a drop of water splash on his white shirt, which is already soaked through in two long stripes where the wet skin on his shoulder blades touch the cloth—two long stripes that are as waxy and opaque as new skin. I lift my hand to brush away a drop of water from his neck but he turns toward me and my hand falls on his damp chest instead. A water droplet from the leaves above us lands on my cheekbone and he leans forward and presses his mouth against the spot where it fell, while I trace with my fingers the slide of water over his throat. It starts like that; the drips of water guiding our hands and mouths to the rivulets they make on our skin. We move slowly, at first, keeping pace with the soft and steady downpour, but when he lays me down on the bench and I reach up to taste the water falling over his ribs our motion lets loose a cascade that we can't possibly keep up with, that we can only give in to.

Chapter Sixteen

THE NET OF TEARS

I owed it to Naoise to help him steal the net of tears. It was my fault he'd been changed into what he was. I could have stopped it. When a man is cast under the enchantment a selkie can save him. All she has to do is shed her skin and throw it over him. But once she's done this she can never make the trip up the drowned river, never escape her own imprisonment. These are the rules the enchantment holds us to. These are our choices: to be one thing or another. When Naoise and his brothers started to change I could have helped them. One by one I watched as they were transformed into speechless beasts—lost to me forever—and did nothing. I chose my freedom over theirs. Now Naoise was the last. I saw the signs, the stoop in his back where the wings had begun to grow, the hard black glitter in his eyes replacing what was once human. He believed the net of tears would save us all. How could I say no?

Before I began my affair with Aidan I never realized how many secret places there were in and around the Hotel Equinox—especially during a dry, hot summer like this one. There are the summerhouses, of course, Two Moons offering the most seclusion, but many of the others affording a brief screen from prying eyes, room enough for a furtive touch, a desirous gaze, a chance to let drop the mask of indifference. Then there are the woods—acres of pine forest floor covered in soft, dry pine needles. I find, later, embedded in the creases of my skin, the pale reddish gold dust the needles make when they've been crushed. I see Aidan brushing the gold dust off the back of his neck and imagine the hot prickly ground scouring my back, the cool smoothness of his chest moving over me like water. I have to stop whatever I am doing while an ache passes through my body.

My aunt thinks I've developed stomach trouble.

I wonder if this is how my mother felt that last summer—as if she were spending her days in someone else's skin—living for the brief moments when a touch would release her? No wonder she wrote about selkies, I think, who shed their true skins and are forced to live in a false shape. But then I remember that she had written about the selkies years before that summer. Had she always felt like an impostor? Had her entire life with my father and me been a false one—a hundred-years spell she had endured only until her true prince could return and cast off her enchantment?

I wish now that I had never thought of writing a book about my mother. I'm not sure I want the answers to these questions. For the first time in my life I wonder if it's all that important for me to be a writer— something I've been struggling for all my life. Why not stay here and run the hotel—with Aidan. Why shouldn't that be enough?

But I know that even if I don't ask the questions, others will. I see Hedda Wolfe every day walking through the gardens with Joseph and know she's not just quizzing him on rose fertilizers. When I talk to Joseph, though, I'm pretty sure she's not learning much from him.

"I couldn't say," he tells me when I ask him, point-blank, if he thought my mother was having an affair the summer before she left. "Your mother was always going off by herself—I understood that to be part of being a writer." There's a touch of reproach in his voice, but whether because I suspect my mother of infidelity or because I, a writer myself, should understand her need for solitude, I'm not sure.

"But did she ever talk about someone from before she came here—an old sweetheart?"

Joseph looks up from the hosta bed he's weeding and gives me that sad, disappointed look that would hurt me more if it weren't his habitual expression. "We both took it for granted we'd lost people," he tells me. "We didn't have to talk about it."

I confront Hedda one afternoon when I find her sitting alone in Brier Rose. She has a thick manuscript in her lap, but she's not reading it. I suspect that she's waiting for a chance to ambush Joseph.

"I think my mother may have been having an affair her last summer here. Do you know anything about that?"

Hedda removes the wide-brimmed straw hat that she always wears when she's in the garden and waves it in front of her face. I notice that her grip on the brim of the hat looks steadier and guess that the heat and dryness have helped her arthritis. "Why? Do you remember seeing her with anyone that summer?" she asks so avidly I'm startled.

"No," I tell her. "I mean she was always talking to some guest, but no one stands out in my mind. She did seem abstracted—even more than usual, I mean—and I remember her coming back to the hotel in the afternoons with her hair wet, as if she'd been swimming . . ."

"At the pool below the falls?" Hedda asks. "Where there's that hidden gazebo?"

I nod.

Hedda lays the hat in her lap and weaves a loose straw back into the brim. Her fingers seem almost nimble. "Your mother would never have left your father for someone new—but she had great loyalty, Kay did, and if there'd been someone she loved before she met your father, a childhood sweetheart perhaps . . ."

"But then why did she leave this other man in the first place?"

Hedda shrugs and settles the hat back on her head. "Remember, Kay grew up in the Depression and then there was the war. Maybe he was poor and went off somewhere to seek his fortune . . . maybe they lost track of each other in the war. I don't know, Iris, that's your job to find out. I think that might be the crux of Kay's story—a long-lost lover who returned to her. Have you asked Joseph?"

"He won't tell me anything."

Hedda smiles and I can tell she's glad that I haven't gotten anything more out of Joseph than she has. It strikes me as odd suddenly because wouldn't she want me to learn as much as possible to write the book? Maybe it's just her way of spurring me on—the kind of tough-love editorial style she's famous for.

"Have you tried the other employees who were here that summer?"

"Um . . . yes, I'm planning to . . . it's been a bit busy." I blush, thinking of the hours I've spent with Aidan when I might have been working on my book.

Hedda tilts her chin toward the path where two elderly women have stopped to admire a border of hollyhocks and dahlias. "They were here that summer. Maybe they saw something."

"The Eden sisters? I don't think they'd notice someone having an affair if they tripped over the naked bodies."

Hedda leans toward me as if to whisper something in my ear, but it's only to brush something off my shirt collar. Her soft fingers bat against my neck like a moth. Then she brushes the red-gold powder off her fingertips and smiles. "Don't assume everyone is as blind as they seem. You'd be surprised what people notice."

After I leave Hedda in the gazebo I catch up to the Eden sisters and walk with them around to the front terrace. I can't imagine that they really know anything, but at least it will look to Hedda like I'm trying. I offer to walk them to Sunset Rock when they tell me they've been afraid to venture there on their own.

"We don't remember things as well as we used to," the younger sister, Minerva, confides in a stage whisper. By "we" I take it she means her older sister, Alice. Alice glares at her sister and waves her cane at a daylily. "Speak for yourself, Minnie, I remember these paths like the back of my hand. There was a boy I used to meet at Sunset Rock each evening—it was a standing date."

"I bet there were a lot of secret assignations going on around here," I say, steering the sisters down the path, past Evening Star. I notice the tips of Aidan's high-tops sticking out over the wall of the summerhouse and feel a palpable ache in my stomach, but I can hardly abandon the sisters now.

"Oh, my dear," Minerva says, "I can assure you Alice's assignations were entirely innocent—if not entirely imaginary."

"Oh, I don't know," I say quickly to forestall Alice's response. "My mother always said it was a wonder you two never married what with all the admirers you both had. She said it must have been for love of your music that you stayed single."

It is true, actually, that my mother once said that Alice had real talent as a pianist, but that she'd refused to leave her younger sister when she was given an opportunity to tour. The two sisters performed "dinner music" in the big hotels for many years and when those hotels closed they'd lived for several years at our hotel—at a reduced rate in the attic rooms—until they'd gotten jobs teaching music at a girls' boarding school somewhere north of Saratoga.

"Your mother was a saint," Alice and Minerva both say in unison, like a song they've sung many times together.

It's not the best opening—and I feel a pang of guilt at undermining the sisters' loyalty to my mother—but I force myself. "No," I say, "hardly a saint, I'm afraid. After all, she died at a hotel registered as someone else's wife."

"We would never believe that," Alice says. "Kay would never have done that to Ben. She adored that man."

"But then why would she be registered . . ."

"Your father told us that the police didn't find any other remains in the room where . . . where she died. So maybe she just registered as a married woman as a safety precaution, you know, so no one would bother her. By 1973, Coney Island wasn't exactly a good neighborhood. I have always thought she went back to her old neighborhood to help someone—an old friend perhaps."

"But whom would she have been helping?" We've come to the bend where the path starts going downhill. Sunset, a tall narrow gazebo built on a large boulder, rises above us. If you climb to the top of it you can look west and see the sun set over the Catskill Mountains. I'm afraid, though, that now that we've gotten here the two sisters won't be able to make the climb up. Alice's breathing is labored and ragged.

"Minnie, go on up there and tell me if it's worth making the climb," Alice says. "I'm going to sit here on this bench with Miss Greenfeder until I catch my breath."

Minnie looks doubtful and I wonder if it's wise to let her climb the steep and narrow steps herself—but then she nimbly ascends into the summerhouse, disappearing from our view.

Alice's fingers dig into the palm of my hand so hard I'm afraid the old woman must be having a heart attack, but when I look at her I see she's positively beaming. "I didn't want to say anything in front of Minnie—she's still a child in many ways." I almost laugh to think of anyone calling Minerva—who must be in her midseventies—a child, but then I see, beneath her excitement, how serious Alice is.

"Of course she worshiped your mother. You know it was your mother who found us our teaching jobs. The headmistress used to vacation here and that summer your mother wouldn't leave the poor woman alone until she agreed to hire Minnie and me." Alice leans in closer and lowers her voice. "It was almost like she knew she was going away and wanted to see us settled."

"So you think she was planning to go away? Then she must have been having an affair."

Alice leans back away from me. She looks at me for a moment and then she looks up toward the top of the summerhouse where Minerva appears, waving a scarf at us like a departing passenger on a cruise ship. "Oh, Alice," Minerva calls, "it's just as I remember it. You can see for miles."

Alice looks back at me, her face momentarily softened by her sister's excitement, and then a tremor passes over her face and her eyes fill with tears. "She didn't act like a woman getting ready to go away with a sweetheart," Alice says to me. "She acted like a woman getting ready to die."

By the time I get the two sisters safely back to the hotel the sun is low in the sky and Evening Star is empty. I suspect Aidan has gone down to the pool and is waiting for me in Two Moons, but I remember that I'm supposed to put in an appearance at a cocktail party Harry Kron is giving in the Sunset Lounge for an arts organization whose name, at the moment, I can't remember. The group has reserved the hotel for the weekend but, Harry has told me, if they like how they're treated they might come back in August for a weeklong seminar. It amazes me how Harry, who must be rich as Croesus, worries over each and every booking like this, but maybe that's how he got to be so rich. What's clear is that he expects me to pay special attention to this group and I've got less than twenty minutes to change.

Unfortunately, both elevators are busy taking guests up to their rooms to change for dinner. I take the stairs, running up the first three flights, then slowing, out of breath, for the last two. By the time I've made it to the attic I'm drenched. There's no shower up here and I don't have time to draw a bath, so I make do with washing my face and splashing myself with cold water. I fill an old ceramic pitcher with cold water and, standing naked in the old claw-footed bathtub, pour it over my neck and shoulders. Then I comb my damp hair up into a haphazard French twist and go stand in front of my closet. None of the cotton sundresses or preppy shirtdresses look right for a cocktail party. I flip through the dresses impatiently and come, at the back of the closet, to a row of linen dress bags. I unzipper one and take out a black sleeveless cocktail dress from the 1950s. I hold it to my face and inhale, trying to catch the faded scent of White Shoulders, but all I smell is cedar from the little sachet of wood chips Sophie puts in the closets to discourage moths. I slip the dress over my head and, after only a minor wrestle with the zipper, discover it fits. I'm surprised. Although I've never been heavy I've always thought of myself as more substantial than my mother. "You've got the Greenfeder build," Aunt Sophie always tells me, "eastern European peasants—sturdy stock."

When I look in the mirror I see that the dress is shorter on me than it would have been on my mother, and it clings a little closer, but still it looks good. Except for a wisp of sheer chiffon at the shoulders and neckline the dress is plain—simple but well cut. I turn and crane my head over my shoulder for a view of my rear and see that the only thing that looks bad are the lines from my panties so I slip those off. Panty hose would probably make my stomach look flatter, but I'm damned if I'm going to wrestle myself back into those hot, sweaty things. I slip on a pair of black sandals, spritz my wrists and neck with perfume to disguise the smell of cedar, and head downstairs.

On the third floor the door to the linen closet swings open and a hand reaches out and pulls me inside.

"Aidan," I say when he moves his mouth away from my lips to my neck, "I don't think this is a good place. What if one of the maids comes in?"

"Not to worry," he says, "they've just stocked this closet with new linen and all the rooms are already made up."

It's true that the stack of folded sheets he's backed me up against are warm and smell of starch, fresh from the laundry. Aidan's skin, on the other hand, is cool and tastes of moss and mineral water.

"You went swimming in the pool," I say as Aidan lifts me onto the wide-planked shelf. I hear the wood creak but I used to climb on these shelves when I was little so I know they're sturdy.

"I was fair heartbroken to go alone. What were you doing with those two old birds anyway?"

"Fulfilling my role of gracious hotelier," I say, stroking his face, trying to guess in the closet's darkness what his expression is. There's an edge to his voice, as if he was really hurt I missed our swim. "Which is what I'm supposed to be doing now downstairs in the Sunset Lounge." The conviction in my voice fades as Aidan's hands travel up my leg, pushing the tight skirt of my mother's cocktail dress up higher.

"Ah, Sir Harry's Art Recovery party? They were still setting up when I passed by. You have time. Besides, are you really in such a hurry to join a bunch of lawyers and curators arguing about some paintings stolen in World War Two?"

I'm impressed, fleetingly, with Aidan's knowledge of the event—more than I've remembered certainly, but then Aidan presses himself between my legs. It's delicious, the sensation of being wedged between the hot soft linens and his cool, hard chest, like being suspended between land and water.

"Aidan," I say, trying one last time to sound responsible, even as he slides my leg up the length of his chest and bends to kiss the hollow behind my knee. "Mr. Kron is expecting me to be there . . ." but Aidan's discovered that I'm not wearing panties and suddenly my whole professional facade doesn't seem all that credible.

The party is just getting under way when I get downstairs. The guests have spilled out from the Sunset Lounge onto the flagged walkway and into the rose garden where little cast-iron tables and chairs have been set up and Japanese lanterns have been strung in the trellises. Harry is standing in front of Brier Rose talking to some people seated inside the gazebo so I work my way through the guests in the lounge first, hoping he'll assume, by the time he sees me, that I've been here longer. I stop and introduce myself to the conference attendees—scanning their name tags for the people Harry told me I should pay special attention to. There's the curator of a small museum in Pittsburgh who's made provenance issues his specialty, an associate curator from the Met in charge of a new provenance research project, and several lawyers who have made their reputations representing clients in restitution claims. I notice as I make my way from group to group that there's a similar thread to the conversations. The lawyers and art dealers affiliated with Art Recovery aggressively assert the culpability of museums and their negligence in establishing the provenance of their holdings, while the museum curators apologetically defend their museums' good-faith attempts to track the previous owners of all their works as best they can.

"There are always going to be gaps in the provenance of some works of art, but a gap isn't necessarily a piece of incriminating evidence," the associate curator from the Met explains to an appraiser of Judaica who works with Jewish clients to recover lost family artifacts. "If due diligence is done and the purchase is made in good faith . . ."

"Good faith?" The appraiser, a petite redhead in a St. John knit suit and Prada pumps that are sinking into the soft loam of a dahlia bed, cries, "Is that any reason not to return what's been stolen?"

I notice that Joseph, who is wandering on the outskirts of the party relighting the citronella torches, looks over at the redheaded appraiser. He's probably worried that she's impaling his dahlia bulbs with those heels. I think I'll take a moment off from mingling to tell him I'll keep an eye on the flower beds, but Harry spots me and calls me over.

"Ah, Iris," he says. "How lovely you look tonight. That dress reminds me of something my sister-in-law wore to the opening of the Cavalieri Hilton in Rome. Conrad Hilton couldn't take his eyes off her all night."

I smile at Harry. I imagine my mother—instead of his sister-in-law—dancing at the Cavalieri Hilton. In another world, it's the life she could have had, maybe if she'd had the success with her writing before she married my father and had me. She would have been free to travel.

"My mother wrote in one of her journals that she thought the Cavalieri Hilton was the ugliest hotel she'd ever seen in her life. *A mastectomy of the many-breasted city*, she wrote in one of her unpublished poems."

The voice, coming from inside the gazebo, startles me out of my reverie of my mother in Rome. I look inside and see Phoebe Nix, looking cool and tranquil in a shapeless, colorless linen shift, sitting with a slim man in a pin-striped suit and a yellow bow tie who is softly concurring with Phoebe's mother's assessment of the Cavalieri. "A travesty of Cold War architecture," he murmurs, "with its ugly American's insistence on air-conditioning and ice water piped into every room."

"Ah, but what a lovely view from the rooftop restaurant," Harry says to no one in particular, taking a sip of his martini and looking wistful.

"Phoebe," I say, "I didn't know you were here. I would have arranged for a special room for you . . ." I falter, remembering that she is, after all, the owner's niece. Surely Harry has made arrangements for her.

"Alas, my darling niece refuses our hospitality. Quite insulting, don't you think, Miss Greenfeder?"

"Gordon and I have been staying at my place in Chatham," Phoebe says, stretching her bare legs out along the gazebo's bench. "We were on our way back to the city."

Gordon blushes to the roots of his close-cropped curly brown hair. His ears, which look far too big for his small head, also turn a bright shade of pink. Men with large ears, I think to myself, should never wear bow ties.

"But your hotel is lovely, Miss Greenfeder," he says rising to his feet and putting down his drink to shake my hand. "Gordon del Sarto." I shake his hand, surprised by his courtesy and his Italian surname. "We'll certainly stay another time." He smiles so graciously I'm immediately sorry for my uncharitable thoughts about his ears.

"Oh, enough already," Phoebe says as if we'd all been haranguing her to stay. "We don't have to be back until Monday, do we, Gordon? I know you're just dying to listen to all this Nazi art stuff."

"Are you interested in World War Two art recovery?" I ask Gordon. I'm intrigued now not just by his politeness and Italian surname but by how this odd, diminutive man seems to get a rise out of the cool magazine editor.

"Well, it's a bit outside my field—I just finished doing my thesis on Renaissance goldwork—but I'm doing an internship this summer at Sotheby's in the Jewelry Department and we've had some difficulty establishing the pedigree of several recent acquisitions."

"Pedigree?"

"Old Money talk for provenance," Phoebe says, rising to her feet and beating the wrinkles out of her shift as if a swarm of bees had invaded the fabric. "Which is art world talk for previous ownership. If we're going to stay I'd better make sure of what sort of room you put us in. It has to be near a fire exit, but not too close to the elevators because they'll keep me awake. Can you show me what you've got?"

I look to Harry to see if it's all right to abandon the cocktail party. He pats my arm, as if sorry to leave me prey to his niece's demands. "Yes, I suppose you'd better get Phoebe settled. Gordon and I can discuss those recent acquisitions of his," he says and then, when Phoebe turns away to pick up her purse—a canvas book bag really—Harry leans closer and whispers in my ear, "High maintenance—just like her mother." I try to repress the smile that comes to my lips, but when Phoebe straightens up she glares at me suspiciously and I have a feeling she's overheard what her uncle said and knows what I'm smiling at.

"Come on," I say, trying to adopt a cheery managerial tone to cover my embarrassment. "I think I know just the room for you two."

"Rooms," Phoebe says when we're just out of earshot. "Gordon's not my lover. He just goes with me to these art things so Uncle Harry will get off my back about getting married. I've known him since Bennington and he's the only one of my male friends Harry can stand. Harry loves quizzing him on Italian art because it gives him a chance to relive his bohemian days as an art student in Rome before the war and the glory days of rescuing Italian paintings from the Nazis."

"Well, Gordon seems very nice," I say. We've crossed the lawn and come to the flagstone walk, but Phoebe abruptly veers off course toward the long arbor where a night-blooming moonflower vine is just opening up its pale trumpet blooms. They seem to glow under the Japanese lanterns. Phoebe dips her slender neck to one of the blossoms and inhales.

"You're not his type," she says, "so don't bother."

It's such a rude remark I have no idea what to say, so I say nothing. Although I found her a bit abrupt on our few previous meetings, she's never actually been rude to me before. Maybe she's just angry with her uncle . . . or maybe she's found out something that has changed her mind about me.

Phoebe looks up from the white flower. "Not that you look like you're hard up. You have that satisfied glow. I thought that painter boyfriend of yours was in Vermont."

"New Hampshire," I correct her and look away. I notice Joseph a little way down under the arbor, staking a droopy-headed peony.

"Then it's someone new. I hope he's not distracting you from your research. Aren't you supposed to be up here researching the book about your mother?"

She makes the remark casually while pulling one of the moonflowers down by its thick vine toward her face, but, glancing at her mother's wedding ring on her thumb, I suddenly have an idea of why she's changed her attitude toward me.

"How about your research?" I ask. "Weren't you going to look at your mother's journals while you were at your house in Chatham? Did you find out if our mothers knew each other?"

Phoebe lets loose the vine and a little puff of yellow pollen spills from the flower's quivering throat.

"Yes, they did know each other . . . but only slightly. My mother and father stayed here in the summer of 1973—just before I was born. I'm afraid my mother didn't think much of your mother's writing, but she thought it was a shame she had stopped . . ." Phoebe's voice drifts off and she turns to go into the hotel. I follow quickly at her heels, cravenly anxious to hear whatever little tidbit Phoebe has discovered about my mother.

I catch up to her on the flagstone walk, a few yards from the hotel, where she has stopped to look up at the building.

"I'd like to stay in the suite my parents had," she says. "I think it was named after some Washington Irving story."

"All the center suites, which are the nicest ones, are named after something from Washington Irving . . . a bit hokey, I know, but people still associate this area with him." I point to the central spine of the hotel where each floor has a three-sided bay window and starting with the fifth floor count down the names of the center suites. "There's Knickerbocker, Rip Van Winkle, Half Moon, Sleepy Hollow, and Sunnyside."

"How quaint," Phoebe says dryly. "I think they stayed in Sleepy Hollow."

"You're in luck, it's vacant. I'll have it made up for you right away . . . but look," I add as she starts to move away from me, "did your mother write why she thought my mother had stopped writing?"

"She wrote, *Kay spends altogether too much time with the guests.*"

"That's it? She thought my mother stopped writing because the guests kept her too busy?"

"Oh, I left out a word. What she actually wrote was: *Kay spends altogether too much time with the married guests.*"

Chapter Seventeen

THE NET OF TEARS

By the time I decided to help Naoise steal the net of tears it was back in the hands of Connachar.

"But how can we get it from Connachar?" I asked Naoise. "He's not as careless as the woman."

"He's careless in different ways," Naoise told me. "He's careless in how he looks at you."

Naoise turned away from me as he said this, pretending to check the corridor for listeners, but I knew it was because he was ashamed to look at me. I tried to harden my heart against him, but with his back to me I could see the wings forming under his shoulder blades, the skin straining over the new bone, the bone pushing to break free. Naoise would turn into one of the winged creatures soon and then there'd be no saving him.

"And that's how you want me to get the net of tears from him?" I asked him, giving him one more chance to take it back. But when Naoise turned to me I saw in his eyes that the animal growing inside him had already taken over. He touched his finger to my breastbone, his nail digging like a talon at my skin. Beneath the bone I felt the flutter of gills, the animal I had been calling to, the animal he would become.

"He won't be able to resist seeing you wear it," he said. "It's you it's made for."

The morning after the cocktail party I ask Ramon where the old registration books are kept.

"We used to store them in the attic," he tells me, "but Mr. Kron asked for all of them at the beginning of the summer so he could compile a list of old regulars to invite back. He probably still has them. Why?"

Stupidly I haven't come up with a lie. The truth is I want to look at the book for the summer of 1973 to see if somewhere among the registered guests would be a married man who might have been my mother's lover. How I'm going to recognize his name, I have no idea, but I'm hoping that something will jar my memory. My mother used versions of real people's names in her books—Glynn, for instance, which I know now comes from the girl who died at the train station the day my mother traveled here to the hotel. Maybe one of the names in the registration book will remind me of something from her books.

I decide to be truthful with Ramon—or at least halfway truthful. "I'm writing something about my mother," I whisper. Fortunately, it's still early enough in the morning that the lobby is deserted. "And I think there might have been a man staying here that summer who . . . well, who might have been her lover."

Ramon makes a soft clucking sound and shakes his head. "Not your mother. Your mother—"

"—was a saint. Yes, so everyone tells me. Ramon, you only started here midway through the summer of 1973. You hardly knew my mother."

"I know I'd still be up to my elbows in grease if not for her."

"Okay, look, maybe she wasn't having an affair. Maybe someone she used to know came up here and threatened her or asked for help." I remember Alice's theory. I don't quite buy it, but maybe Ramon will. "Maybe that's how she ended up in that hotel room in Coney Island."

"And what good would it do you to know that?"

"Well . . ." I look around the lobby as if searching for an answer. I notice we're not completely alone. A man is kneeling behind one of the couches, tape measure in hand. He's the upholsterer Harry has hired to redo the lobby furniture. The color scheme my mother chose will vanish, replaced by the Crown Hotel's signature violet and cream. "Then I'll know she wasn't planning to leave us," I say.

Ramon looks theatrically left and right—what an awful actor he must have been, I think, how fortunate my mother saved him—and then leans over the desk. "Mr. Kron has them in his suite, in the armoire, the key to which is in his night table."

I gape at him, amazed at this detailed knowledge of the owner's suite. He smiles. "Paloma—the new maid—she mentioned as much to me. She thought it was funny he went to so much trouble locking away a bunch of dusty old books."

"Paloma?" I say. It takes me a second to realize he's talking about Mrs. Rivera.

Ramon grins. "Don't tell your aunt," he says. "You know how she feels about staff romances."

Although I have a master key to all the rooms I'm not about to let myself into Harry Kron's suite and lift the registration book from a locked armoire. I'm sure the idea would never have even entered my mind if not for Ramon's detailed blueprint of the book's location. There's no reason not to simply ask Harry if I can see the registration book for 1973. After all, he is one of the few people who knows I'm working on a book about my mother.

The only problem is getting him alone for a few minutes. I can hardly ask him during the daily staff meeting with my aunt Sophie sitting across from me on his left-hand side taking minutes. I try him in the dining room at brunch, but although he usually dines alone, this Saturday he's got Phoebe Nix and Gordon del Sarto at his table. When he sees me hovering by the omelet chef he waves me over and insists I join them.

Phoebe is in the middle of giving the waiter precise instructions on how to boil her egg. I turn to Gordon and ask him if he found his room comfortable, but Phoebe, done with her injunctions to her waiter that her toast be very, very dry, answers instead. "Two of the drawers in my bureau are broken, and I tore my foot on a loose nail in the closet."

I assure Phoebe that I'll send Joseph—our unofficial carpenter—to have a look at the defective items even as I'm wondering why, since her luggage had consisted of a canvas book bag, she had needed two drawers and the closet.

"Well, my room was heavenly," Gordon interjects. "Literally. I awoke this morning to the sun rising outside my window. It was like floating in the middle of a Tiepolo ceiling."

"I thought your period was Renaissance, not High Baroque," Phoebe says to Gordon.

Gordon blushes to the tips of his large ears as if Phoebe has made an indelicate sexual reference instead of an artistic one.

"I gave you the room most popular with the sunrise school of painters who used to stay here," I tell Gordon. "If you look under the rug by the window you'll find paint splatters."

We discuss, then, the Hudson River School painters who stayed at the hotel and some more recent regional painters. I'm impressed that Gordon not only knows of these minor artists but doesn't seem to consider them beneath his notice. Harry too has an encyclopedic knowledge of local folk artists.

"I have an idea," Harry says. "Come stay—as our guest of course—the last week of August for our Arts Festival. Art Recovery has agreed to come back—" Here Harry winks at me, letting me know that the group has been well enough satisfied with their accommodations to rebook. "—and we're going to judge the 'Follies in the Garden, Whimsies in the Woods' contest. Perhaps you could put together a little program on 'The Arts at Hotel Equinox.' "

Gordon sets down his coffee cup and smiles at Harry. "It would be an honor, Mr. Kron—"

"Oh, Gordon," Phoebe interrupts, "say what you mean. You'd much rather give a talk on fifteenth-century Florentine jewelry and not some local Grandma Moses. Uncle Harry, he's got the slides in the car. Couldn't Art Recovery fit him in this weekend?"

Harry puts his toast down and gives his niece his full attention. I remember what he said last night. High maintenance, just like her mother. And then I remember what became of Phoebe's mother, Vera Nix, award-winning poet, dead at forty-four when she drove her car off a bridge. Harry must remember too because he speaks softly and gently, as if coaxing an excitable racehorse.

"Of course I would be delighted to hear Gordon speak on the subject of his expertise, and I would have asked already, only the emphasis this weekend is on works of art lost during the war . . ."

Gordon clears his throat as if to interrupt, then lapses into a coughing fit. While I signal the waiter to refill his water glass, Phoebe places a hand on Gordon's bony shoulder and takes up the gauntlet for him. I have to admit I'm touched. For all her sharp edges, it's obvious that Phoebe has a strong sense of loyalty to those she cares about. It also occurs to me their arrival here last night was not by chance—perhaps Phoebe had planned all along to get Gordon included in the weekend's program.

"He's got a painting of a lost necklace," Phoebe says. "A fifteenth-century pearl necklace that belonged to some Venetian saint and disappeared during the war."

"*Ferronière*," Gordon rasps out between sips of water. "It's a *ferronière*."

"What's that?" I ask.

"A sort of fifteenth-century headband," Phoebe answers impatiently.

"Well, that's fascinating," Harry says, "but one slide of a missing headband does not a lecture make."

Gordon holds up a finger, takes another sip of water, and clears his throat. "Actually, sir, I have assembled a rather interesting slide presentation surrounding the lost della Rosa *ferronière*. I've got portraits of the della Rosa family and several other examples of *ferronières* in Lippi and Botticelli . . ."

"Well, it sounds like quite a thorough program. I'd love to see it. Why don't we schedule your talk for tonight before cocktails? Have you got enough to fill forty-five minutes?"

"Oh, yes, Mr. Kron, I could do a good solid hour," Gordon says, beaming. I'm so pleased for Gordon's success that it takes me a moment to realize that I've missed my opportunity to ask Harry for the registration books. It's too late now. Harry is touching a napkin to his lips and sliding his chair back and Gordon is already on his feet to shake his hand.

"Thank you, sir, I'm sure you won't be sorry. And of course I'd love to do the program on local artists as well."

"Excellent. Come to my room after dinner tonight and I'll give you all the old registration books. You can comb through them for the names of artists who stayed here."

For the rest of the afternoon I kick myself for not asking for the books. I could have done it in front of Phoebe. After all, she knows about the memoir and it was she who gave me the idea that my mother might have been having an affair with a guest. In the end, though, I realize that's exactly why I didn't ask for the books in front of Phoebe. I didn't want her to know I took her suggestion seriously—or how much the idea bothers me.

I don't know why it should make such a difference if the man my mother left my father for was married and a guest at the hotel. I have, after all, come to admit that she probably was having an affair—despite all the protestations of my mother's sainthood. Maybe it's because since hearing Hedda's suggestion that it was someone she knew before coming here I've gotten a certain picture in my head. All I know about my mother's life before she showed up here is that she grew up in an Irish neighborhood in Brooklyn, attended an all-girl Catholic school, and was christened at St. Mary Star of the Sea in Brooklyn, the same church where she took me— belatedly, at my soul's great risk—when I was three to be christened. And so what I pictured when Hedda spoke of a childhood sweetheart was a young Irish boy, poor like herself, a boy who looks, in my imagination, a lot like Aidan Barry.

Only he wouldn't have been a boy in 1973. No matter how I might like to fool myself I can't tell the story that way. There's no reason to think that my mother, in her early forties in 1973, was having an affair with a man in his twenties. There's no precedent for my affair with Aidan. No excuse.

And so, after chastising one of the maids for understocking the third-floor linen closet (and remembering halfway through my lecture that Aidan and I had stuffed the soiled sheets in an unused dumbwaiter), I decide to take the matter into my own hands and retrieve the 1973 registration book from Harry's suite. Just to set the record straight. I'll wait for Gordon's lecture on fifteenth-century jewelry—a good solid hour, he said, and which Harry will of course attend—and let myself in with the master key.

I'm busy most of the afternoon setting up slide projectors and checking microphones for the evening's lectures. It's not an easy job. We're using the library and two parlors on the north side of the courtyard, across from the bar, and the rooms were meant for reading the newspaper and tête-à-têtes on a rainy day, not multimedia conferences. If Harry's vision of the hotel as an international conference site comes true the rooms will have to be completely remodeled and rewired. In the meantime, Aidan comes to my rescue with an armful of extension cords, claiming a high school AV club in his past. I don't see him as AV club material, though, and suspect it's yet another skill he's acquired in prison. Where he acquired the skill to charm the lawyers and museum curators is another question. By the end of the day the redheaded Judaica appraiser has him toting her slide carousels and setting up a display of nineteenth-century Kiddush cups along a sideboard in the Gold Parlor. I am in the library, just outside the French doors leading into the parlor, rearranging chairs, when Harry Kron comes to stand beside me. I notice that he too is paying close attention to Aidan. This would be the time—while Aidan handles the jeweled, engraved goblets—for Harry to mention any concern about Aidan's background.

"Mr. Barry seems quite an asset with the corporate clients," he says. "You did well to hire him. Perhaps we should release him from his thralldom to Joseph and give him a position of more responsibility. Say, special-events coordinator? What do you think?"

"I think he'd be very good at it," I say, relieved that the only attention Aidan has drawn from Harry Kron is positive. "And I think it would be a wonderful opportunity for him." I lay stress on the last part and hold Harry's gaze for a moment longer than necessary. If he knows about Aidan's prison record this would be the moment to bring it up.

Harry looks away from me to Aidan and then back to me. "Part of being a good manager is knowing when to take risks, how to recognize promise in unlikely places—a diamond in the rough, so to speak." I smile, relieved. He must know about Aidan. "Have I told you lately what a good job you're doing?" he goes on. "You have that rare talent, invaluable in a true hotelier, of bringing out the best in people."

I blush with pleasure—but also with the consciousness of what I'm planning to do later. It's not too late though—I can ask him right now to see the registration books before he gives them to Gordon. But before I can say anything, he leans closer to me and whispers in my ear, "I have to confess something to you, Iris."

I'm so stunned by the sudden intimacy of his voice that I laugh nervously, which draws Aidan's attention away from the redhead for a moment.

"Mr. Kron, I can't imagine you having anything to confess."

He smiles at me and touches my elbow lightly with his fingertips. "But I do, my dear. You see, I'm not always as good a judge of character as I'd like to be. I've misjudged people . . . with the direst of consequences at times . . . but never mind, this time the consequences are a pleasant surprise. You see, I didn't think you'd be much good at this."

"At this? At running the hotel?"

He nods. "Oh, I mean I knew you'd be competent, don't get me wrong, and I knew you had the right background. It's just that I feared you didn't have your heart in it. That your first love would always be writing. And this book about your mother would take too much of your time and attention. But I see now that I shouldn't have worried."

I square my shoulders and try to return his look steadily. "I wouldn't neglect the hotel." I can't possibly ask him about the registration book now, I think.

"Of course you wouldn't—and I understand that now because of your mother."

"My mother? But you didn't know my mother."

Harry smiles. For a moment I think he's going to tell me that he did know her. I think of that fantasy I had of my mother dancing at the Cavalieri Hilton in her black chiffon dress—only now, in my vision, she's dancing with Harry Kron. He must have been very handsome when young. He's still very handsome—I can tell that from the way Aidan is eyeing us from the Gold Parlor. He would have given her the kind of life she was suited for.

But instead of confessing to an acquaintance with my mother, Harry waves his hand at the black-and-white photographs lining the wall of the library. They're pictures of events at the hotel: picnics and barbecues, dinner parties and summer dances. In many of them my mother appears. A halo of black hair around her pale, delicate face, her light green eyes—startling even in these black-and-white pictures—fringed with dark lashes. She stands out in every picture.

"I feel I've gotten to know her through these," Harry says. "And from what people have told me about her. But most of all, through you. You have your mother's grace, Iris. I think you'll have a wonderful future with the Crown Hotels."

A *few months ago* I would not have thought the promise of a career in hotels would make me so happy, but I am truly touched and flattered by Harry's words. I almost decide to give up on the registration book, but then, in addition to being impressed by Harry's sense of knowing my mother through her photographs I am also a bit jealous. While he's been getting to know Kay Greenfeder, I've learned almost nothing. I have to know who she was having the affair with.

The library's ready for Gordon's lecture, the courtyard is all set up for cocktails afterward. I decide to stay for the first part of his talk and then—when he turns the lights off for the slide presentation—slip into the kitchen and up the servants' stairway. I should be able to get back before the lecture's over. I've asked Aidan to run the slide projector, so no one should miss me.

The guests take their time filtering into the library and taking their seats. They're noticeably more relaxed than last night. I notice sunburned shoulders and hair damp from lake swims or late showers. Instead of the contentious little spats I eavesdropped on last night, tonight I hear more shop talk: job openings at museums and galleries, grant opportunities, summer seminars in Prague and Florence. The burning issues of provenance and rightful ownership have ceded to professional advancement and industry gossip.

Only Gordon, hovering at the dais, flipping through a stack of three-by-five cards, seems nervous. I look around for Phoebe—surely she should be here to lend moral support—and spot her standing by the doors leading out to the courtyard. It seems to me that the least she could do for her friend would be to sit up front.

Gordon has to clear his throat several times before the crowd settles down. I find myself unbearably nervous for him and, stealing a glance at Phoebe, wonder if she feels that too and that's why she's chosen to stand at a distance.

"Our story begins not in the war-torn Europe of six decades ago, but nearly six centuries in the past in quattrocento Italy . . ."

Good, I think, six centuries in which to get up to Harry Kron's suite and back.

"It begins with a present made to a young girl on her wedding day from her mother. But before I tell you about this girl, let's imagine ourselves in fifteenth-century Italy. It's a time of great prosperity. The rich merchant guilds support not only painting, but jewelry and fashion . . ."

I look around me at this fashionable crowd from Manhattan. The women's clothes, I notice, are understated, but the shoes expensive; the glimpses of gold, pearls, or diamonds on wrists, necks, and earlobes discreet but rich. In addition to the Art Recovery participants I notice Hedda Wolfe in a middle row in a dupioni silk shift the color of eggshells, a pearl brooch like a spray of flowers on her shoulder.

". . . many painters—Ghiberti, Verrocchio, and Botticelli, to name just a few—apprenticed in jewelry workshops, leading to an increased depiction of jewelry in contemporary painting . . ."

I find myself imagining the crowd here tonight as they might look depicted by the Renaissance masters. Phoebe, with her pale skin and serious eyes, looks like one of those thin, ascetic angels of the Annunciation. Hedda would have to be something pagan instead of Christian, I think, a sibyl or a personification of something. The redheaded appraiser would be painted by Titian. Harry Kron, some rich Florentine nobleman, of course. I'm happily playing this game when I come to a figure I can't fit in because he doesn't fit here or in the Renaissance. It's Joseph, who's standing next to Phoebe in the door to the courtyard, his eyes fixed on the blank slide screen. ". . . the rediscovery of classical statuary loosened the rigid, vertical lines of fourteenth-century clothing and issued in a celebration of form over line."

The room darkens and a shadowy green wood peopled by pale gold figures in flowing drapery fills the space behind Gordon. Botticelli's *Allegory of Spring*. I look toward Joseph, wondering if this is what he was waiting for— this beautiful garden. But how would he know the program of Gordon's slide show?

Without commenting on this slide, Gordon presses the remote and the screen fills with a detail from Botticelli's painting: one of the three graces, her sinuous blond curls held up by a single strand of pearls.

"Stiff crowns gave way to loops of pearls to hold loose or plaited hair away from the face . . . this hair ornament was called a *ferronière*."

The slide changes to show a pensive Madonna, which Gordon tells us was painted by Filippo Lippi. She wears a sheer headdress, and a thin strand of pearls forms a V on her forehead. "As you can see," Gordon is saying, "the style was used for religious as well as secular subjects. Which brings us to the particular *ferronière* we will discuss tonight, the della Rosa *ferronière* . . ."

As much as I'm enjoying Gordon's lecture, I realize it's time for me to go. Fortunately, Joseph's given me the perfect graceful exit. Pretending to notice him for the first time, and pretending—to anyone who's paying attention—that the gardener must need me, I get up and slip out the door where he's standing.

"Did you need to speak to me, Joseph?" I say.

Barely taking his eyes off the slide screen, Joseph shakes his head. "I was talking to this boy today about one of the paintings he's going to show. I wanted to see it."

"Well, I'm going to just slip into the kitchen and make sure everything's going smoothly . . ." If Joseph thinks this behavior is suspicious, he certainly doesn't show it. I leave him to his painting and go out the courtyard, cut through the dining room into the kitchen, and from there to the back stairs. The servants' stairs are used by the maids in the mornings when they're making up the rooms, and later during the dinner hour when they slip upstairs to turn down beds and leave mints on the pillowcases. At this hour the maids are eating their dinner or out behind the laundry room having cigarettes, enjoying a few minutes out of sight of guests or management. I make it to the third floor without meeting anyone.

Harry's suite is called the Half Moon Suite after Henry Hudson's ship, which Washington Irving mentions in "Rip Van Winkle." In the late 1950s my mother hired an out-of-work painter who'd done work for the WPA to do a series of murals based on Irving's stories. As I let myself into Harry's room and turn on the ceiling light, I come face-to-face with a portrait of Henry Hudson at the prow of his ship, the *Half Moon*, which is floating over the Catskill Mountains. The mural is painted on either side of a large window that faces west, and the artist has managed to incorporate the view of the mountains into the painting. I'd always thought these paintings were kind of hokey, but now the cleverness of the composition takes me by surprise. I have no time, though, to admire it. I go into the next room, the bedroom, and over to the night table.

It's only when I'm sliding open the drawer that I think to worry about what else I might find there. Harry has come to seem almost like a father to me; I don't want to discover any embarrassing secrets about him. The drawer contains, though, no compromising materials. Aside from the standard hotel-issue Gideon's Bible there is only a small leather box and a tin of cough drops. I open the box and there, next to a Rolex watch, is a small key that I think might open the armoire.

I take the key out, cross to the armoire, and open it quickly. Again, I'm relieved by the neatness and ordinariness of Harry's personal arrangements. Crisp white shirts are stacked like sheafs of paper on one side, summer-weight suit jackets hang on the other. A faint scent of citrus and cigar tobacco wafts off the jackets when I push them aside to reach the stack of leather-bound books at the back of the armoire. Holding the jackets back I run my finger down the books' spines until I find the date I'm looking for: 1973. I have to use both hands to wrest it out from under the heavy books on top of it, and as I pull it out a link on my charm bracelet catches in the fabric of one of Harry's jackets. I slide the book onto one hip and try to disentangle myself, but I end up tearing the coarse nubby weave of the jacket and the registration book slips off my hip and thuds loudly to the floor.

I stand still for a moment, listening, but I know it's silly to worry. One thud in this huge ship of a hotel would hardly cause any notice. I'm less happy about the tear in Harry's jacket. He's precise enough to notice something like that. I hold the fabric up and work my hand under the lining to see if I can pull the loose threads through the back. I've almost fixed it when I notice that the piece of material I'm holding seems unusually heavy. I've got my hand in his pocket before I can think what a bad idea that is: but by then I've already closed my fingers around the hard cold metal revolver handle.

Chapter Eighteen

THE NET OF TEARS

I could say that what I did was for Naoise or that I did it for my people but that would be a lie. That watery stirring beneath my skin awakened something in me. At first I thought it was the net of tears I longed for. I knew it would look better on me than on the Connachar woman—that it was made for me. In my dreams I felt the pearls and diamonds against my skin like the coolness of dew, the spray of the ocean. I imagined the weight of the emerald against my breastbone and the absence of it began to feel like an ache—like all the things I had already lost. I burned at night and awoke from these dreams, parched and gasping for air. Only the coolness of those stones could douse this fire. And then I began to dream of his hands laying the stones upon me and I knew it was the hands I longed for as much as the stones.

I leave quickly after discovering the gun. It is, I tell myself, no reason to be alarmed. Lots of people who live in the city carry guns. Especially wealthy, Rolex-wearing executives like Harry Kron. In fact, my father used to keep a gun—we were, after all, rather isolated up here during the winter— but my father kept his in the locked safe behind the front desk. It's the casualness of coming across it in a suit jacket pocket that has so unnerved me, which I suppose is why I leave so carelessly.

I pull the door closed, but halfway down the hall I realize I didn't lock it. I go back, cursing the old-fashioned security locks that have to be locked with a key from the outside. It's one of the things we'll have to change if the hotel's to be modernized. Guests are always complaining that they forget that the doors don't lock by themselves. Worse, they lock the doors when they're inside and then misplace their keys and can't get out. My mother always said it was a horrible fire hazard and made me keep an extra room key on a ribbon hanging from my bedpost.

I'm within a few steps of Harry's door when I hear the elevator door open halfway down the hall. I stop, pretending to be looking for something in my pocket, and hope it will be a guest heading in the opposite direction. But it's Phoebe and she's heading for her uncle's suite, key in hand.

"I think you've got the wrong floor," I say to Phoebe, "the Sleepy Hollow Suite is directly below this one."

Phoebe pauses at her uncle's door and stares at me. Then she looks down at the registration book that I've got balanced awkwardly on my hip. "I know perfectly well what floor I'm on. Harry asked me to come up because he forgot his cigar."

Phoebe has slid the key into the lock.

"I'm surprised you don't mind fetching things for him. He could have sent one of the maids." It's a truly tactless thing to say, but my hope is that it distracts Phoebe enough so that in turning the key she doesn't notice the door is already unlocked. Instead it just draws attention to what she's already guessed.

"Or apparently we could have just asked you to bring some down," she says, opening the door. "Why don't you show me where my uncle keeps his cigars?"

I blush, caught in the act of petty thievery, but as I watch Phoebe smile I realize it's worse than that. She obviously thinks I'm having an affair with her uncle.

Following her into Harry's suite, I try to think of ways to disabuse

Phoebe of her mistaken notion. I'd rather have her think I'm a thief than having an affair with her seventy-year-old uncle. "Phoebe, I think I should explain what I was doing in your uncle's room."

"You don't owe me an explanation. You're both unmarried adults." Phoebe walks over to the coffee table and opens a large wooden humidor shaped like a casket. The smell of good Cuban tobacco wafts up toward us.

"But you've got it wrong. I came in here to get the 1973 registration book." I hold the book up as evidence. "Because of what you said about my mother having an affair with a married guest that summer. I thought I might be able to figure out who it was."

Phoebe eyes the book curiously. "Why didn't you just ask Harry for the book?"

I explain about our conversation earlier, about his concern that I might neglect the hotel for the sake of researching my book. Phoebe gathers up four of the fat cigars. Her slim hand can hardly contain them.

"So, you were so afraid of disappointing Uncle Harry that you decided to steal from him instead?"

I can't think of anything to say to that. I realize I'm hugging the registration book to my chest as if afraid she's going to wrest it from me, but then I see a look pass over her face I haven't seen before—a softness, something close to pity. "He has that effect on people," Phoebe says to me. "He's not a man you want to let down. Speaking of which—" Phoebe holds up the cigars. "—he'll be wanting these—and you—he told me to find you as well as his Montecristos. Hadn't you better stow that book and get on downstairs?"

"So you won't mention anything to him about the book?"

"On one condition. You tell me what you find out and let me have a first look at your memoir." Phoebe shifts her weight from one foot to the other and rolls the cigars around in her hand. It's the closest I've seen her get to fidgeting. Once again I wonder what she's read in her mother's journals that suddenly makes her so anxious to know what I might find out about my mother.

"Of course I'd be happy to get your feedback," I say. It's what you say at a writers' workshop when someone's about to tear your work to shreds and it's about as truthful a statement here as in that circumstance. Phoebe, however, seems to accept my assurance. She takes one last look around the room as if checking to make sure she hasn't left anything—or maybe that I haven't stolen anything—and her eyes light on the mural.

"My God," she says, "it's almost as bad as the one in my room, but at least there's no Headless Horseman. I've got to tell Harry to paint over these."

Up in my room I drop the book on my bed and sink down beside it. My face, when I touch my fingers to it, feels hot and there's a thudding in my chest that feels like something trying to get out. I'm not sure if it's a reaction to stealing the book and getting caught or Phoebe's humiliating suggestion that I have designs on her uncle. At the same time, a small voice is whispering in my ear: *You wouldn't have to work anymore—you could concentrate on writing.* I get up, go into the bathroom, and splash cold water on my face. I look at myself in the mirror. I'm wearing another one of my mother's old dresses, an Empire-style white linen trimmed in black velvet ribbon and a row of jet beads just below the bust. I think of how Harry looked at my mother's pictures and for a moment the image I had of my mother dancing at the Cavalieri with Harry shifts again and it's me he's dancing with.

When I come into the courtyard the cocktail hour is nearly over. Most of the Art Recovery guests have gone into the dining room. There are only a few stragglers around the fountain, too engaged in heated conversation to tear themselves away for dinner. I notice Gordon, flanked by two men—one I recognize as a curator from the Met, the other is one of the lawyers from Art Recovery.

"If the piece was recovered who would it belong to—the della Rosa family or the church? Because if it's the church—the same church that did nothing to stop the Holocaust—I can't see restituting it," the Met curator is saying as I pass through the courtyard. I catch Gordon's eye and he winks at me, obviously enjoying the debate his lecture has created.

"So what are you saying? Finders keepers?" the lawyer practically shouts. I slip into the darkened library before they can hear me giggle. Finders keepers? It's like a third-grade spat on the playground.

"What's so funny?" I'd thought the library was empty, but a flicker of light draws my attention to the back of the room where Aidan is sitting on a couch behind the slide projector.

"These art people," I say, threading my way through the tightly spaced folding chairs and perching on the arm of the couch. "I know what they're arguing about is important, but I can't help but think they're more worried about their reputations than returning a few Kiddush cups to their rightful owners." I look over toward the courtyard windows, but with the lights off in here and the Japanese lanterns illuminating the courtyard, no one can see us. I slip down from the arm of the couch and slide closer to Aidan and lean into him. He puts his arm around my shoulder and runs his fingers along the back of my neck where my hair is still damp from the water I splashed on my face upstairs.

"Where'd you go?" he asks, kissing the back of my neck. "You missed the lecture."

"Shouldn't that be my line?"

"You're not my teacher anymore," he says, "just my boss."

I pull away from him and try to look at his face but it's too dark to make out his expression.

"Does that bother you?"

He shrugs. "I don't much like all this secrecy. Would it be so awful if people knew about us?"

"Oh come on, Aidan, why would you want to be seen with an old lady like me?" Of course what I want is an assurance from Aidan that I'm far from an old lady, but he refuses to rise to the bait.

"It's not me who wants this kept a secret, Iris, and you know it. Have you told your man in New Hampshire about us yet?"

"It's not like Jack and I have a conventional relationship," I say, regretting as I do the primness of my own voice. *You're not my teacher anymore*, he said, and yet that's what I feel like. The prim schoolmarm laying down the rules.

"Look," I say, "Harry told me tonight he could see you in a management position—coordinating the corporate retreats. It would be a great thing for you and once you were settled in it . . . well, we'd both be management. There'd be no reason people couldn't know about us . . . if that's what you still wanted."

In the dim light of the library I think I see Aidan smile. He runs the back of his fingers down the side of my face and the coolness of him makes me shiver. "If that's what you want, Iris," he says, "we'll wait until I'm in Sir Harry's good graces."

When I leave the library half an hour later the curator and the lawyer are gone but Gordon is still in the courtyard and he's helping Joseph pluck cigarette butts out of the planters.

"Gordon, you'll miss dinner entirely—Joseph and I can take care of this."

"I couldn't eat a bite," Gordon says, dumping a handful of cigarettes into the bag Joseph is holding open for him. "I think the Met may offer me a permanent job."

"Miss Greenfeder is right," Joseph says, "you go on into dinner. And wash your hands first."

Instead Gordon wipes his grubby hands on his seersucker slacks and holds his hand out to Joseph. "Thank you," he says, "for the tip." He clasps Joseph's hand in both of his and then, as if embarrassed at this display of emotion, abruptly leaves.

"What was that about?" I ask Joseph, who's rooting now in a potted hibiscus.

"Nothing much. I just told him about a guest who stayed at the hotel I worked in at the end of the war—an Italian countess who might have been related to the della Rosa family. I thought if she was still alive she'd know something about that missing necklace he's so interested in. Can you do nothing about where these people throw their trash?" he says, plucking a wadded-up cocktail napkin from the hibiscus roots. "What kind of animals are they?"

By the time I make it into dinner the guests have already finished their entrées and are listening to speeches over coffee and dessert. The director of one of the Holocaust restitution commissions is just winding down a tribute to someone, so I stand by the dessert tray and wait for the speech to be over before joining Mr. Kron's party.

"... who fearlessly risked his own safety to rescue over two hundred works of art from the fascists," he says, holding a wineglass up in preparation for a toast. "Without his efforts our world would be a much bleaker place. Please join me in raising your glasses to salute our host, Sir Harold Kron."

There's a swell of murmured congratulations above which one deep, raspy voice calls out "To Harry" and the crowd follows suit, chiming in "To Harry." I look to where the voice came from and see it's Hedda Wolfe, sitting across from Harry at the banquet table, radiant in her eggshell silk and pearls. Harry rises from his seat and inclines his head to Hedda, then lifts his glass to the speaker, thanking him for what he calls his "small part in a large collaborative effort to do what little could be done in the face of monstrous evil."

"It makes you wonder," a voice at my side whispers, "if they could have hidden a few Jews for the trouble they took over their precious paintings."

I turn and find my aunt Sophie straightening a doily under the Viennese sacher torte.

"Surely it wasn't a question of one or the other," I say in a low voice, looking around to make sure we're not overheard. Of course, Sophie's always had a critical nature, but I'm afraid that if her acerbic comments get back to Harry she'll be out of a job. "I heard Harry was knighted for his work as a Monuments officer during the war, but I didn't realize he saved so many paintings."

"Not just paintings. I gather he found a trove of statues—Michelangelos and Donatellos—in a storeroom the Germans were using as a garage."

"I would think as an artist yourself you'd be impressed by that."

Sophie sniffs. "I'd trade a Michelangelo for your great-aunt Hester who perished in Theresienstadt any day." Our great-aunt Hester—a younger sister left behind in Poland when my father's family emigrated—is the one relative we know of who died in the Holocaust, and throughout my childhood Sophie would bring her up whenever I complained of some hardship—as in, "Your great-aunt Hester would have been happy with last year's coat instead of freezing to death at Theresienstadt." I had grown to dread the invocation of her name.

"Well, I'm sure Mr. Kron would have saved Great-Aunt Hester if he could have, but in the meantime I guess those Michelangelos are a good thing. I think we should be proud that our hotel's owner is a hero."

Sophie gives me a long assessing look and I find myself blushing. "I thought it would be harder for you seeing someone in your father's place," she says.

"I'm in my father's place—not Harry Kron. Dad was never the owner here, just the manager, like me—which is what you wanted in the first place, right?"

Instead of looking at me, Sophie looks around the dining room. The lighting is dimmed so that the diners can enjoy the view of the Hudson Valley and the river. The lights of the towns on the east side of the river are like scattered diamonds on the windowpanes. The white tablecloths—painstakingly bleached and starched each day—gleam like pools of ice under the candlelight. Everything gleams, the tan, well-toned bare arms of the women and their expensive silk dresses and good jewelry, the crystal wineglasses, the well-polished silverware . . . The hotel hasn't looked this good in years. "Isn't this what you wanted?" I ask.

She looks back at me and I see a look I haven't seen on her face in years: uncertainty.

"Yes," she says, "this is what I *thought* I wanted."

After dinner there's music and dancing on the terrace. I'm always nervous having events on the terrace after dark because even though the steepest drops are fenced off and posted with cautionary signs there's always the chance someone who's had too much to drink will ignore the signs and wander out onto the edge of the ridge and fall. We've had a number of sprained ankles and broken wrists and I think we've gotten off lucky—there are places where a person could fall and break worse. I would be happier prowling the perimeter myself but I've got to get upstairs and go through the registration book and get it back to Harry's room before he's ready to give it to Gordon del Sarto. Fortunately Harry is surrounded by an admiring throng clamoring to hear more about his wartime exploits. He won't be going up anytime soon. I notice Joseph hovering around the edges of the crowd and deputize him to keep any stragglers off the precipices, suggesting he start with Phoebe Nix who's wandering around the edge of Evening Star, out onto the rock ledge beyond it.

Up in my room I take out the registration book from under my mattress. I start at the beginning and read each name twice, hoping one will strike a chord. I recognize some of the names as those of families who came regularly to the hotel each summer, but I notice that many are women—widowed or never married—who came with friends or sisters or a niece, perhaps. There are, of course, men, but they're often registered for shorter times—a weekend here or there wrested from a busy work schedule. I suppose by 1973 there were fewer families who had the leisure to spend whole summers in the country, and those who did were probably buying houses in the Hamptons or the Berkshires.

The book is organized to hold a day's arrivals on one page and as I go on there are many pages with only one or two entries—or left entirely blank. It's depressing, after a while, like reliving the hotel's decline. As a child I was only half aware of the slow diminishing of the guests—it meant less work for me, more time to run free in the woods and, later, after my mother was gone and no one had time to keep tabs on me, hitch rides across the river and take the train down to the city. By the time I was a teenager I couldn't imagine anyone choosing to leave the city to come stay up here.

I am midway through July when I come across Mr. and Mrs. Peter Kron, Phoebe's parents. I notice that she was wrong about the suite they stayed in—it was Sunnyside, on the first floor, not Sleepy Hollow on the second.

I turn to the next page and a picture slips out of the book and slides onto the floor facedown. Bending down to retrieve it I see there's a stamp on the back—a circle of pine boughs with the inscription: SUMMER MEMORIES AT HOTEL EQUINOX, 1973. Another of my mother's ideas. She had a stamp made up each summer and put it on the back of the pictures the hotel photographer took. Maybe I should start doing that.

I turn the picture over wondering what it's doing in the registration books. It's a dinner-party portrait of three couples—like dozens I've seen before from this period—the women's teased hair and the men's wide ties and sideburns placing it as early 1970s. Only my mother—who, along with my father, is the only figure I recognize at first—looks timeless. Her black hair is looser and more natural than the other women's tortured hairdos. Even the one woman in the group who's adopted a more modern look—bangs and long straight blond hair, a Marimekko mini dress—looks dated. Her eyes are too heavily made up and her bangs are cut so low on her forehead, the edges tapering down over her temples, that she looks like she's wearing blinders. It gives me a little thrill to notice that not only my father, but the two other men as well, all have their eyes on my mother. I turn over the picture and read beneath the green stamp the names of the people in the picture. Dr. and Mrs. Lionel Harper, Mr. and Mrs. Ben Greenfeder, Mr. and Mrs. Peter Kron. Turning the picture over again, I look with interest at Phoebe's mother, the famous poet—who'd have thought she'd wear so much eye makeup!—and then at Phoebe's father. He's handsome in a slightly dissolute manner, his face a little too thin, his lips curved in a sensuous smile. I remember Harry said that his experiences during the war—in an Italian POW camp and then hiding out in the Italian countryside—had left him restless. I study his eyes, which are dark and ringed with shadows. They look more haunted than restless—and they're also fastened on my mother. He's obviously smitten with her. Suddenly I have an inclination that this must be what Phoebe has been hinting at—that her father had an affair with my mother. There must be some reference in her mother's journals that's led her to that assumption, and seeing the expression in Peter Kron's eyes I can believe that it might have been true. What I can't figure out is why she would want me to know.

Chapter Nineteen

THE NET OF TEARS

The first time he put the jewels on me he placed them around my neck. I knew that wasn't how they were meant to be worn, but I saw the way his eyes glowed at the sight of me and when I looked at myself in the mirror I liked how the pearls encircled my throat and the green teardrop trembled with my breath.

"Look how it matches your eyes," he said, standing behind me as I sat before the mirror, "as though it were made for you." And his hands circled my throat, pressing lightly, but I could feel the strength in them. The pearls and diamonds shook as if afraid for me. I closed my eyes and heard the roar of the ocean. I thought of the mother who wove this as her parting gift to her daughter. I thought of my mother who went too quickly to think of leave-taking presents, leaving only burdens.

I forced my eyes open. My throat was bare but I could see a ring of glistening moisture where the stones had lain—a remnant of the dew and ocean from whence they came—and I could see, in the mirror's reflection, Connachar returning the crown to its hiding place.

I flip through the rest of the book but there are no more surprises after the picture, which I decide to keep. There's no reason to think Harry would miss it. I slide it into my night table drawer, facedown, and pick up the registration book. Checking my watch I see it's only nine-thirty—early for Harry to retire. I still have time to replace the book. But when I look in my evening bag for the master key I see it's missing. I look around my room, but it's nowhere to be found. I'd been in such a hurry to get downstairs before that I'd left my room door unlocked; the last time I used the key was to let myself in Harry's room, so there's no reason to think it's in this room. Still, I get down on my hands and knees and crawl under the bed to look for it but end up with nothing but dust on the hem of my dress and a splinter under my thumbnail. I even run my hand in between the mattress and bed frame, but find nothing. Sitting back on the edge of my bed, I take the spare room key from the bedpost and press it into the palm of my hand, reassuring myself that I am not locked in, but still I feel trapped. How am I going to get the registration book back into Harry's suite? How am I going to explain to Aunt Sophie that I've lost the master key to all the rooms in the hotel?

I'll just have to retrace my steps and find it. I slip the spare room key into my purse—even though I still leave my door unlocked—and, taking the registration book, go down to the third floor. When I'm sure the hall is empty I open the abandoned dumbwaiter where Aidan and I stashed the sheets last night and slip the book in under them. At least now I won't have to go all the way back to my room if I find the key. When I find the key, I correct myself. I have a pretty good idea now of where it is—in the library where I spent half an hour with Aidan before dinner.

When I go into the library, though, I'm dismayed to discover that the folding chairs and slide projector have been removed, the rug freshly vacuumed, and the divans and easy chairs put back. The key could have been found, sucked into a vacuum cleaner, or swept under one of the big overstuffed chairs, or stuck behind the cushions where Aidan and I were. I'm ready to explore the last possibility when I realize I'm not alone.

"Are you looking for something, Iris?"

Hedda is in a high-backed wing chair facing the fireplace, which is why I didn't notice her at first. That and the fact that the reading light above the chair is unlit, leaving her in a pool of shadow. I sit down on an ottoman in front of the cold grate and see that her arthritic hands are twined around the stem of an empty brandy snifter.

"I was just checking to see if the cleaning staff put the room back all right after Gordon's lecture."

"I see you're taking your managerial role quite seriously. Harry was singing your praises this evening."

"He's brought the hotel back to life. I'm grateful—my father would have been so pleased to see it returning to its former splendor."

"Would he have? True, Ben loved the hotel but he also saw how it devoured Kay." Hedda lifts the glass up, her two hands encircling its crystal globe, and looks around the room, taking in not just the library, but the darkened courtyard beyond the French doors, the distant sounds of a band playing on the terrace, and the whole bulking weight and life of the hotel surrounding us. "Do you really think he'd want to see you giving yourself up to it?"

"I'm hardly giving myself up . . ."

"How far have you gotten on the book, then? Do you have any more for me to read?"

I look into the empty hearth and suddenly feel cold—cold enough to wish for a fire there. At least a fire would give me something to busy my hands with. Instead I notice that I'm plucking at the loose threads in the ottoman—a nervous habit my aunt had reproached me with throughout my childhood.

"I think I've found something out," I say, hoping to deflect her request for written material. At least I can show her I've been busy with something other than hotel management. "I think you were right that my mother was having an affair that summer and that it was someone she knew from before. I think it was a married man that she gave up and then he came to the hotel with his wife that summer. The affair resumed . . . and when the man went back to the city he convinced her to come meet him . . ."

"Hm. And do you have a name for this mysterious married man?"

I can hear the skepticism in her voice and indeed the story as I've reconstructed it does sound fanciful. Why would Kay and Peter Kron meet at the Dreamland Hotel in Coney Island—surely he could afford something more glamorous? And why register under the name *McGlynn*? I'm ready to abandon the whole theory, but seeing the look in Hedda's wide-spaced gray eyes—that look of cool assessment as if I were an awkward line of prose to be excised—spurs me on.

"I think it was Peter Kron," I say. "Vera Nix's husband. Phoebe's mother. Harry's—"

"Yes, I know who Peter Kron was," Hedda snaps. She shifts in her chair and the brandy snifter tilts in her hands.

"Let me take that," I offer, leaning toward her, but then I see that her fingers are frozen around the crystal stem. I can see little half moons of moisture where her fingertips press on the glass and I'm afraid the delicate crystal will break under the pressure. She manages to uncoil her right hand and then use it to loosen the fingers of her left hand. I look away, embarrassed for her. When I look back the glass rests on the table beside her chair and she is recomposed, as if the struggle with her hands was something she had observed that had nothing to do with her.

"Peter Kron," she says. "That's an interesting possibility. I knew him a little because the first agency I worked for represented his wife. The way she treated him, you wouldn't blame him for having an affair, but I don't think Kay would have been his type . . ."

"You wouldn't say that if you saw the way he looked at her in this picture I found . . ."

"Really? I'd like to see that. I suppose it is possible." Hedda's fingers have curled in on themselves, like a sweater that's been too tightly knit. "They did know each other before Kay came here."

Now it's my turn to be surprised. "How?"

"Kay worked at the Crown Hotel before she came here, and that's where Peter and Vera lived. In the penthouse suite."

"Harry's first hotel? I didn't know that's where my mother worked. Wouldn't Harry have known her then?"

Hedda smiles, as if my immediate interest in Harry confirmed something she suspected. "Well, Kay worked there as a maid. I can't imagine Harry taking much notice of a maid, can you?"

I shake my head. It's something I've noticed about Harry. Although courteous with all the staff, if he has to address one of the maids he focuses on a point a couple of inches above her head. It must be a British aristocracy thing stemming from years of ignoring the downstairs help. "But then why would Peter Kron have been any more likely to notice her?" I ask.

"Oh well, Peter . . . he was another story. He took altogether too much interest in the maids, if you know what I mean. There was always one or another he was supposed to be having an affair with . . . several girls had to be let go . . . I'm sure it was the bane of Harry's existence. And Vera! Well, you'd feel sorry for her if she wasn't such a handful herself. Imagine living in a hotel suite with all those young girls in their fetching uniforms traipsing in and out all day. There are references to it in her poems . . . 'Black and White Ladies,' 'The Dominoes' . . . she must have gotten used to it, but then if she thought one had become important to him . . ."

"Like my mother?"

Hedda nods. "And if that one turned out to be a writer . . . I think that would have killed Vera."

"When did she die?"

For a moment I think Hedda hasn't heard my question, but then she answers, reeling off the facts with a coldness that surprises me even coming from her.

"Vera and Peter died in the spring of 1974. Their car went off a cliff in the south of France. Vera was driving. The family found a note back at their villa saying she'd wanted to kill herself since the baby was born. The current theory is that she was suffering from postpartum depression."

"Damn. So she took her husband with her even though it meant leaving her baby without parents. How amazingly selfish—what could drive a woman to that?"

Hedda lifts an eyebrow but remains silent.

"Do you think it was because she knew Peter Kron loved my mother? But my mother wasn't even alive by then!"

"It would have killed her if she thought Peter still loved your mother.

She was incredibly jealous of other writers. If you can prove that Kay was having an affair with Vera Nix's husband I can tell you it would greatly increase public interest in your book. Think of it, a love triangle involving a wealthy British peer and two American writers—all of them dying tragically within one year. I'd say that story was worth more than running this damned hotel, wouldn't you?"

I leave the library so charged with what Hedda has told me I almost forget about the lost key and the registration book I still have to return to Harry's suite. I can't afford to lose Harry's good faith just yet. Not until I've learned what I can here. I stop by the front desk and check the office for a spare master key but remember that Harry'd had us remove it—"too risky, anyone could get a hold of it," he'd said. Remembering his caution I'm half sick thinking I'll have to admit I've lost mine.

I'm just leaving when I hear voices coming from the east porch, a small porch off the lobby where guests often have coffee and read the morning papers that's usually empty at this hour. I listen to the voices and recognize Ramon's. He's reciting a romantic speech from A Midsummer Night's Dream, something about the moon, ". . . the moon (governess of floods), pale in her anger, washes all the air . . ." I smile, remembering his flirtation with Mrs. Rivera—Paloma, I remind myself . . . and then realize that of course all the maids have master keys so they can clean the rooms. I peer through the half-opened door, but it's too dark to see anything. I can see why they've chosen this spot, though. With the inside light off, the terrace looks like a fairyland with its view of Japanese lanterns strung along the path glowing like fireflies and the guests, in their pale linen suits and shimmering silk dresses, aglow in the moonlight like creatures from another world.

"Ramon," I whisper into the darkness, sorry to break the spell, "are you there?"

I hear a shuffle and a little gasp and Ramon comes to the door rumpled and embarrassed.

"We didn't think anyone would notice us in here . . ."

"That's okay, Ramon. Listen, I need a favor."

When I ask him for Paloma's key Ramon nods curtly and goes back into the darkened porch without asking why I need it or what has become of my key. I am grateful, but reminded, also, of where such blind devotion springs from—my mother again. I think of the fact that Ramon knew my mother for only a couple of months and yet he has retained for almost thirty years an image of her as his savior. I can't imagine having that kind of influence over anyone.

"Paloma is a little worried about having her key back for the morning shift," Ramon says, pressing the key into the palm of my hand.

"Shh, Ramon, I told you not to bother her with that." Mrs. Rivera appears behind Ramon. Her hair, usually pulled back in a tight bun, is loose and comes nearly to her waist. She smiles at me and reaches forward to close my hand around the key. "Don't you worry, Miss Greenfeder, I can always borrow a key from one of the other girls."

"I'll get it back to you tonight," I tell her firmly, remembering that it was my fault she lost her last job. "Where will you be?"

I arrange to meet Paloma at the bottom of the back staircase at midnight. Feeling a bit like Cinderella, I slip through the porch onto the terrace. I just want to make sure Harry's still down here before heading up to his suite.

He's not among the partyers on the south end of the terrace. Tables have been set up here and most of the guests have formed little groups around them, talking over cigarettes and glasses of champagne or brandy. As I walk north along the ridge, though, I see pairs and stragglers who have slipped beyond the trail fence to sit on the flat rocks at the edge of the ridge. It's tempting, of course—I've spent many a summer night sitting out on those rocks myself, staring out into the darkness, dangling my legs over the lights of the valley far below. I know the topography of the rocks much better than these guests, though, and I worry that someone will slip. I should be herding them all back to the safety of the terrace, but if I stop to do that I'll never find Harry, never get the registration book back to the room on time. I'll just remind Joseph to do it; I'm surprised he hasn't chased them off the rocks already.

When I get to the north end of the terrace I see why. The drop below the ridge is much steeper here and most of the guests seem to realize that and have stayed on the apron of flagstone outside the dining room where the band is set up, or are sitting in the gazebos along the ridge trail. The largest group is inside Half Moon—no doubt because the two shallow crescent-shaped benches are conducive to conversation. The people inside, however, are not seated and not engaged in conversation. They're all standing on the far side of the gazebo focused on the rocks beyond.

There's a large, flat boulder here that extends out from the cliff edge and if you go to the very end it's as if you are hanging over the valley. There are, of course, signs strictly forbidding anyone from doing that but someone—a woman—has ignored them and is standing on the farthest rock, her back to her friends who are imploring her to return. One man is making his way gingerly over the rock face toward her. I notice among the onlookers in the gazebo Gordon and Harry. The woman on the rock—her thin shoulder blades standing out sharply in the moonlight—is Phoebe. The man heading toward her is Joseph.

Later I'll be ashamed to remember that my first thought was to take advantage of this distraction and run up to Harry's suite to replace the registration book, but that unworthy thought is brief, replaced quickly by one that's perhaps not all that much worthier: that Phoebe's life isn't worth the risk of Joseph's.

"What's Joseph doing out there?" I demand, coming into the gazebo. "He's too old to go out to the edge."

Gordon turns to me and quickly turns back—afraid, I think, to take his eyes off Phoebe. "I wanted to go out myself, but he said he knew the lay of the land better." Gordon's voice cracks on *better* and I feel instantly mean-spirited for thinking so little of Phoebe's life. "But how did Phoebe get out there?" I ask.

"Um . . . I think she had too much to drink . . . she's not used to it. That gardener was trying to get her to come away from the edge and she suddenly started yelling at him—" Gordon looks more nervous now than he did before his lecture.

"And then I let her know what I thought of her behavior," Harry interrupts, "and now she's making me pay for interfering. Phoebe, dear," Harry raises his voice, "I've said I'm sorry. Could we please talk about this privately? Somewhere less precipitous, perhaps?"

Phoebe doesn't respond but the sharp bones of her shoulder blades quiver like a bird's wings before flight. The image frightens me and reminds me that Phoebe's mother was a suicide. Joseph too must sense that tension because he raises his hand to silence Harry and takes another step toward Phoebe. He's only a few feet behind her. In a moment he'll be close enough to make a grab for her should she decide to jump, but will he be able to restrain her? I can't help but notice the shakiness in Joseph's step and I'm not the only one who does.

"Such a prima donna, she'll take that man down with her, just as Vera did to Peter . . ." Harry says.

I'm so surprised by the reference—coming on the heels of my own discoveries about Vera Nix and Peter Kron—that I don't react right away to what Harry's doing. It's so quick—amazing that a man his age is able to swing his legs over the edge of the gazebo and onto the rock and get to where Joseph is before any of us in the gazebo is able to stop him. No one even shouts at him to come back—there's just a collective intake of air as Harry Kron strides over the rock, throws an arm over his niece, and drags her back. Phoebe too must be too surprised to struggle. Instead she goes limp, which is almost as bad because it makes Harry lose his balance. I see Joseph step forward to keep Harry from losing his footing and for a moment the three of them sway—like a tripod with one short leg—and then steady. I can hear the release of breath around me but then something else must tip the balance out on the rock because Joseph suddenly falls.

One of the women in the gazebo screams. I'm probably the only one here who knows there's a ledge right below where he was standing and so I'm the one who rushes around the gazebo onto the rock to see if Joseph is all right—the rest of them have probably given him up for dead—and thank God I do, because Joseph has landed on the ledge but he's only just hanging on to a gnarled root poking out of the dirt. I grab his arm, yelling for help, and then Gordon is next to me helping pull Joseph onto the terrace. As soon as we've pulled him up he crumples onto the ground and I think that he must be having a heart attack.

"Joseph," I say, looking in his face, trying to assess coloring and pain through the deep lines that always seem to convey pain, "tell me what hurts."

He sees how frightened I am and pats my hand. "It's just my ankle, girl, don't fret. I caught it in a crack between the rocks. Probably saved me from going over the ledge." For a man who's just narrowly escaped death his voice is remarkably calm. "An Ace bandage and a couple of aspirins will fix me up just fine."

"I'll go get the first-aid kit and ring the doctor," I say. "Make him comfortable," I order the little crowd, "and put something over him to keep him warm." I glare at a guest who's got a pashmina shawl draped around her shoulders and only leave when I see her laying it over Joseph's frayed denim shirt.

In the lobby I run into Aidan and Ramon, who have already heard about the accident and are headed to the terrace with the first-aid kit and a guest who says she's a doctor. I start to follow them back to the terrace but then remember what else I have to do. Joseph's all right, I assure myself turning back to the elevator, and no one will miss me now.

When I get off the elevator on the third floor I see a woman at the end of the hall, but her back is to me and she's heading for the staircase. I wait until she heads down the stairs, realizing as she turns to go down that it's Hedda. Fortunately, she doesn't see me.

I get the book out of the dumbwaiter and head to Harry's suite, letting myself in with Mrs. Rivera's key. It's not until I slide the book in with the others—checking to make sure it's in chronological order like I found it—that I notice how badly I'm shaking. I lean against the armoire, breathing in the scent of citrus cologne and Havana cigars, and close my eyes. Instantly, I relive the moment Joseph fell and I snap my eyes open, shaking now not with fear, but with anger.

Damn her, I think, remembering Phoebe's rigid back, her thin arms wrapped around herself like a stubborn child, and how she went limp in

Harry's arms—like a two-year-old having a tantrum. *How dare she endanger Joseph's life with her theatrics!*

Just like her mother, Harry had said. Then I remember what Hedda had told me in the library—how Vera Nix had driven their car off the road, killing herself and her husband, leaving a six-month-old baby to grow up without either parent. Who could blame Phoebe for turning out as she had? How many times have I blamed my own failures in life on my mother's death? But at least I had her for ten years and at least I had my father after she was gone. And even though I've often blamed my mother for the circumstances surrounding her death, I still don't believe she deliberately chose to leave me—at least not forever.

But Phoebe, I recall now, has never said a bitter word against her mother—only against her father and the trappings of marriage. *I wanted to remember,* she told me at Tea & Sympathy, explaining why she had engraved a pattern of barbed wire and thorns on her mother's wedding ring, *every time I looked at it that marriage is a trap. It killed my mother.*

What if it turned out her mother had killed herself because she knew her husband had been in love with my mother? What if Phoebe already guessed—after all she has her mother's journals—but she wants me to find out so I'm forced to expose the affair in my book? Is that why Phoebe is spurring me on to write this book—to reveal my mother as the other woman, the culprit in *her* mother's death? After all, I suppose it would be better to think your mother killed herself because of an infidelity than to think it was because she was so depressed over your own birth.

I feel suddenly weak and dizzy at the thought of such an animus directed against my mother—against me. I close my eyes and remember what Gordon said. Joseph had been trying to get Phoebe to come back when she'd suddenly started yelling at him. Maybe they had been talking about something else. Had Phoebe tried to find out from Joseph if her father had been seeing my mother that summer? I can imagine what Joseph's response would be and that it wouldn't make Phoebe happy. I think of how Phoebe had collapsed and then Joseph fell. Could Phoebe have deliberately tried to hurt him, knowing how much he meant to my mother and to me?

I shake myself free from the questions, remembering where I am and that any minute Harry and Gordon—Phoebe too no doubt—could find me here. I'll have plenty of time to sort out Phoebe's motives later. For now I'll have to be wary of her. I start to close the armoire door, but I decide to do one more thing. I check Harry's pocket for the gun and am less surprised than you would think to find it missing.

Chapter Twenty

THE NET OF TEARS

When I told Naoise where the net of tears was kept he promised that he would take them to the place where the salt water turns to fresh and drop them into the river so that the net would spread a path of pearls that will lead us back to the sea. The spell would be broken and the net of Connachar's power would dissolve.

I first realized that something had gone wrong when I heard that not just the net of tears but all the jewels that the woman in the green dress had worn were gone. Naoise had said nothing about taking those. I waited and waited but nothing changed. The selkies were still enslaved within their skins, our men still bowed under the weight of their wings. Connachar still called me to his rooms each night only now instead of laying the jewels around my neck he laid his bare hands on my skin and looked into my eyes as if he would scour the truth out of me. One night he told me that Naoise had been caught and sent to the prison at the bend in the river. He watched my eyes, while he told me what had been done to him, how his wings had been severed from his body.

"And the jewels," I asked, forcing my voice to be cold, "were they recovered?"

"All but the necklace with the green stone. The one you used *to wear. But don't worry, my men will find it and when they do you'll wear it again."*

The orthopedist I take Joseph to tells me he'll be on crutches for at least four weeks. When I report the news to Harry he tells me to make Joseph as comfortable as possible and then hire a replacement.

"Hire two replacements," he says, "and have that young Irish fellow sit in on the interviews and do the training—he'll know the scope of Joseph's duties by now. When he's got them trained you can start him on planning the Arts Festival."

"Really, so soon . . . Aidan will be pleased."

Harry looks up from the accounts book and studies me. "I hoped it would please you too. What's wrong? Do you have any reservations about giving Mr. Barry more responsibility?" I notice that the vague *that young Irish fellow* is quickly replaced by a name and realize that some of Harry Kron's apparent disregard for the minor details—and minor characters—of the hotel is an affectation.

"No," I say, "not at all. It's Joseph I'm thinking of. It'll kill him to think he's being replaced."

"Well, we can't have that. I have an idea that will distract your Joseph, but I'll need him to be accessible." While Harry pauses to think I wonder what miracle could make taciturn, recalcitrant Joseph accessible. "I know," Harry says, "that run-down cottage he lives in will never do while he's on crutches. I think we should install him in one of the suites . . . let's see," he says, turning to the computer screen on his desk, "let's see, which one can we spare . . ."

"I'm not sure being in the hotel will suit Joseph . . ."

"Nonsense. How about the Sleepy Hollow Suite? My niece said there were a few broken drawers and loose floorboards . . ."

"You know, I spoke with one of the maids—Mrs. Rivera—about that and she said those drawers were fine before . . ."

Harry waves a hand, dismissing these mundane details. "However they got broken, the fact is they're broken and Joseph can putter away on them while he's recuperating. It will make him feel useful."

I'm still unsure of Harry's plan—and I can't imagine what could possibly distract Joseph from having his gardens usurped—but it's clear that as far as Harry's concerned the subject is closed. I'm turning to leave when he calls me back.

"One more thing. I think we'll have to start replacing the locks with an automated card system sooner rather than later. Something was taken from my suite last night."

"That's terrible," I say, "was it something valuable?"

"More dangerous than valuable, I'm afraid. It was my gun."

On the last word Harry looks up and catches my eye. I say in as calm a voice as I can muster, "Well, then you'll have to notify the police."

"I already have. I certainly can't have a gun registered in my name floating about, but if it had been anything else I would have handled it myself. You see, I have a strong suspicion I know who took it."

I count to ten and wait. There's a look of regret and disappointment on Harry's face that I've never seen before. It shows his age and makes me realize how fond I've grown of him. Fond, the way a daughter feels toward her father, I say to myself. It makes me see too how little I would like to be the cause of his disappointment.

"Well, it would have to be Phoebe, wouldn't it it," he says, finally. "She was the only one in my room last night."

Although Harry's plan to distract Joseph turns out to be more brilliant and generous than I could have imagined I am still surprised at how well the old gardener takes to convalescence and life in the hotel. As July slides into August and the days grow even hotter and drier, I suspect that Joseph will be prowling the gardens on his crutches to make sure his flowers—especially his prized rosebushes—are getting enough water. Instead I find him comfortably ensconced in the Sleepy Hollow Suite, surrounded by an admiring coterie of art students and absorbed in planning the new conservatory

Harry has proposed. In addition to the students from The Art School who have come up to complete their garden follies for the contest, Harry has invited architecture students from Cooper Union and initiated another contest for the design of the new conservatory. Joseph has been appointed the ultimate judge.

At first I think the avid and loquacious students will get on Joseph's nerves, but I find him eagerly answering questions about his design inspiration for the *chuppas* he's built over the years. I watch while they show their sketches to Joseph, who then freely expounds on his ideas for the structures. He offers criticism and suggestions on their design projects and even asks them about their backgrounds and plans for the future. He seems especially fond of Natalie Baehr and spends hours going over her jewelry designs. I've never seen him so talkative.

When I think about it, it makes sense. Before he'd been forced to leave, Joseph had been an art student at a prestigious academy in Vienna. I once asked him why, after he survived the concentration camps, he didn't return to painting. He answered gruffly that he'd had to go to work, but a few weeks later, while we were putting in a border of blue salvia around the roses, he sat back on his heels and sweeping his hand toward the gardens said, "Isn't this better than a dead canvas," and, plucking a rose from a bush, "doesn't this smell better than turpentine?"

All these years the garden has been his canvas, and now he's finally being recognized for the artist he is. If I find his transformation unsettling, well, maybe that's just my problem. Maybe I'm just a little jealous. Even Sophie is less rattled by the change than I am.

"Maybe he just needed a little breathing space from his daily chores to get back to what really mattered to him," she tells me when I finally track her down to ask what she thinks about Joseph's new role. She's become, I only now notice, harder to find. For years she's filled in for all the odd jobs at the understaffed hotel, but now that Harry's hired a full staff and installed a new computer system her bookkeeping responsibilities apparently leave her with time to spare. Today I've found her on the back porch of the servants' wing, sitting in a rocking chair with an unopened notebook in her lap, watching the sun set over the Catskills. She looks away from the darkening horizon just long enough to study my face. "Is there a problem?" she asks me. "Do you think the garden is being neglected?"

If she'd asked only the first question, perhaps I would confide some of my misgivings. But then I notice her eyes move away from me, back to the light shifting over the distant ridges, and her hands stroking the cover of the book in her lap—a sketchpad, I notice, not an accounting ledger. I answer her second question instead. "No," I tell her, getting up to leave. "Everything is being taken care of."

I certainly can't complain about Joseph's replacements—Ian and Clarissa, a young couple, recently graduated from Cornell. And I'm happy to see Aidan released from manual drudgery and promoted to special-events coordinator. True, his new responsibilities require that we learn to spend ten minutes alone together without falling into bed. Aidan surprises me, though, with a level of seriousness I've never seen before. He's determined to make the Arts Festival a success. He's even stopped making fun of Sir Harry.

"So all you needed was to be dubbed yourself and you abandon all plans for the serf uprising," I tease him one afternoon while we're going over the guest lists in the library. We're sitting on the couch at the back of the room and I can't help but remember the night of Gordon del Sarto's lecture. I already searched the cushions for my lost master key but when I couldn't find it I made a duplicate from Paloma's and gave it up for lost.

"Aye, I've joined the oppressor. This is what comes of the sleeping with the upper class."

I slip my foot out of my loafer and run my toes up under his pant leg. "I see. You've used me to claw your way up to special-events coordinator. Next you'll be after my job."

"Maybe when you've gotten one of those six-figure contracts for your book you won't want it anymore. You'll leave me up here with no one but Joseph for company."

"Don't forget Joseph's new bevy of art students. Maybe Natalie will keep you company."

It's farther than I meant to go and we both know it. After glancing toward the courtyard (I notice that lately he's become the more cautious one) he slides closer to me on the couch and leans his leg against mine.

"I told you I just asked for her number that night." He shifts his weight and my skirt rides up a little. A draft of cool, damp air from the fountain in the courtyard wafts in and makes me shiver. "But I never used it."

I sigh, a little bit because we've had this conversation half a dozen times already, a little bit because it will be hours before we can really be alone. "Forget it, Aidan, I didn't mean anything by it. Besides," I say, wriggling my knee against his, "I think I'm more jealous of how much time she's spending with Joseph."

I see his brow furrow and can feel his leg tense against mine. "Jesus," I say, more irritably than I mean to, "it was a joke, Aidan."

"I know. It's not that, although I do wonder why it's so vital to you that you prove you're not jealous of me. Is it because you mean us to have the sort of 'unconventional' relationship that you and Jack have . . ."

"That was Jack's choice as much as mine, because he's an artist . . ."

"And I'm just a working stiff . . ." He stops and we both hear, above the murmur of water from the fountain, voices.

"You know that's not what I meant," I hiss, shifting a few inches away from him. "Jack didn't want more from me. He kept me at arm's length."

"And if he didn't keep you at arm's length? If he suddenly wanted more?"

The voices have come closer and I recognize them as belonging to the Eden sisters. I lean forward and draw Aidan's clipboard nearer so the Eden sisters will think we're busy and leave us alone. "It doesn't matter, Aidan, I would tell him it's too late. I told you that I'll talk to him as soon as his residency is over in September." I wave to the Eden sisters and to the stacks of folders on the table to indicate that Aidan and I are busy. Minerva returns the wave and starts toward us, but Alice pulls her back and steers her into the adjoining Gold Parlor. I turn back to Aidan, edging myself closer to him, but he's moved a good foot away from me and dumped a pile of folders between us.

"I can't have this conversation with him when he calls me from the pay phone at the artists' colony. And I can't tell him in a letter. Jack is too visual. I owe him an explanation in person."

"Well, you'll get your chance soon enough," he says, flipping open the top folder, which contains the registration form we've sent out to artists' groups. "He sent in his registration card for the Arts Festival a week ago. I was wondering when you were going to get around to letting me know."

It's no use after that trying to explain to Aidan that I didn't know about Jack's plans. I can hardly believe it myself. The last time I spoke to Jack he said he felt his work was going so well he was afraid to disrupt the flow by leaving for a weekend. It had been hard not to let on how relieved I was—not only because I could put off telling him about Aidan and avoid the possibility of their meeting, but also because it confirmed everything I've come to feel about the relationship.

It's the kind of explanation, though, I've always been leery of: *I knew all along something was wrong, but I didn't admit it until I found myself falling in love with someone new.* How convenient. So what if I can see now what a halfway, stinting sort of love I've had with Jack all these years, how he's used—okay, we've both used—the excuse of art to keep our distances? If it was really over, couldn't I have known that without sleeping with a twenty-nine-year-old? What if the situation were reversed? What if he told me he'd realized our relationship was over because he'd started sleeping with some younger woman? Maybe, it suddenly occurs to me, that is what he's coming here to tell me.

The wave of physical pain I have at that thought belies everything I've been trying to convince myself of about Jack. It's far worse than any jealousy I've had over Aidan and Natalie Baehr.

Although I know that the art colony has strict rules against calls between nine A.M. and four P.M. I decide to call anyway. Only not from the hotel. The fact that Jack has to talk to me from a pay phone is only half the reason I haven't wanted to tell him about Aidan over the phone—it's also because I know from experience how easy it is to listen in on calls at the hotel.

I stop by the desk to tell Ramon that I've got to drive to the printer in Poughkeepsie because there's a last-minute change in the program for the

Arts Festival. I tell him I'll be back by dinner and ask him to proofread the menu for me. I take the keys for the old Volvo—replaced this summer by a fleet of purple mini vans sporting the Crown Hotels logo—from the office and wave at Janine as she listens intently to her headset.

The Volvo feels as if it's soaked up all the heat of the summer and the upholstery is as cracked as the dirt path leading down to the parking lot, but still I feel like a teenager in her dad's convertible. I roll down the windows to breathe in the piney air. Instead I smell hot tar and dust. The pines on the edge of the road have a seared look, their needles glinting copper in the relentless sun. Something else bothers me as I drive down the mountain, but I can't put my finger on it until I get to the bottom. I stop the car at the new sign for the hotel, switch off the engine and listen. All I hear is the rustle of dry pine needles, a sound like brooms sweeping a wooden floor. I can't hear the creek.

I start up the car again and head toward the river. There's a pay phone at the Agway but now that I'm driving away from the hotel the motion feels too good to stop. The river is widening in my windshield, growing from the thin pencil line I see from the hotel into a wide expanse of thirst-quenching blue. The bridge and the hills on the other side—a view I've stared at all summer long—bulk and take on substance. It's like I've been living in a two-dimensional drawing all these weeks and now I've stepped off the page into real life.

Ascending the arc of the bridge I have a sudden urge to follow the river all the way back to the city. No wonder I've always avoided working at the hotel. My suspicions that it was a trap have been borne out.

Across the bridge, I turn south on Route 9, not really thinking through how far I plan to go—just enjoying the sensation of traveling. I wonder if this is how my mother felt that night Joseph drove her across the river to take the train to the city, that she was finally casting off the burden of the hotel—of me and my father—to start a new life.

I think of the scene in her book when the selkies shed their skins at the place in the river where the water turns from salt to fresh. The Hudson is tidal up until Rip Van Winkle, which is where you used to have to change trains to continue north and where my mother saw that woman throw herself under a train. I've always thought that the selkie story meant for her the transformation that occurred to her when she left the city and came to the hotel, but when the selkie sheds her skin the thing she becomes isn't her true self either. She always longs to return to the sea, to slip into her old skin. The selkies in my mother's book can't go back because of some lost necklace—the net of tears. What if, for my mother, the net of tears wasn't a lost thing, but a lost person without whose love she was not her true self?

What if running away with Peter Kron meant returning to her true self?

I've been driving so lost in thought I haven't kept track of where I am. I notice that the river has widened and when I see a sign for the Rip Van Winkle Correctional Facility I can hardly believe how far I've come. I remember the reason for my trip: to call Jack and find out why he's coming, but I still don't know what to tell him about Aidan. I wonder how my mother could have been so sure when she left us that she was leaving for the right person.

I see a diner on the right—a vintage chrome Airstream that looks just the place from which to call Jack—and pull over. True to my expectations, it's got a real phone booth with a worn wooden seat and a door that closes and switches on an overhead light. I dial the number, charging the call to my credit card, and prepare to do battle with the Cerberus of the colony—the receptionist.

"Yes, I know the hours between nine and four are reserved for 'creative output,'" I tell her, "but this is an emergency."

"Well, then, I'll send someone to his studio," she replies in a clipped voice that clearly says *philistine* and *enemy of the arts*. I think of all the writing I've failed to do this summer and wonder if I'd work better in such guarded isolation. I'd probably end up crocheting a doily for my laptop and watching squirrels all day long.

I wait for fifteen minutes. I imagine Jack wrenched away from a moment of creative inspiration, wiping his paint-smeared hands on his jeans, and trudging through the woods to find out what emergency has befallen me. How am I supposed to tell him that the emergency is that I'm sleeping with a younger man but I'm still racked with jealousy at the idea that he may also be having an affair?

When I hear his voice come on the line all I can think of is how much I've missed him.

"What's happened, Iris? Are you all right?"

"I saw your registration form for the Arts Festival and I didn't know what to make of it. Why didn't you tell me you were coming?"

He lets out an exasperated sigh and I think he's going to yell at me for pulling him away from his work.

"I asked that man at the desk if you'd see it and he said he didn't think so because there was a new special-events coordinator, so I spoke with him and specifically asked him not to let you see it. I wanted it to be a surprise."

"You spoke with Aidan?" What had Aidan said? *I was wondering when you would get around to letting me know.* But he'd known all along that Jack meant to surprise me.

"Was that his name? I thought he understood that I wanted to surprise you."

"But why? Did you have something important to tell me?"

"Oh, Iris, I don't know. I've just been feeling bad about how this summer has worked out."

"I thought the painting was going well."

"It's not that. I've missed you and I've realized how grudging I've been with my time. I thought if I surprised you by coming to the hotel for a whole week it would make up a little for how I've neglected you. To tell you the truth, I've been a little worried."

"Worried about what?" I ask, trying not to sound as guilty and nervous as I feel.

"That I've lost you. That you won't come back to the city in the fall."

"Why wouldn't I come back?"

"Because you'll want to stay on at the hotel. I know how much it's always meant to you, so I wanted to tell you—damn, Iris, this isn't how I meant to tell you—that if you want to stay at the hotel I'd come too."

"You mean you'd consider living up here?"

"Why not? I think I've had enough of the city. We could find a little house near the hotel, maybe with a barn I could use as a studio. You've said often enough that real estate is cheap up there."

"Jack, I don't know what to say. This is all so sudden."

"Don't say anything right now. I've got to go anyway—the receptionist is glaring at me from the other office. We'll talk about it when I'm up there. It's still okay, isn't it? I mean, you don't mind me coming?"

What can I say? Jack and I have been together for ten years. I owe him more than a summary dismissal from a diner pay phone. And if he's really ready for us to live together, am I ready to say good-bye?

"Of course I don't mind you coming. I think there's a lot we have to talk about." That's the best I can do, the only hint I give him that everything's not right. It leaves a bad taste in my mouth that the diner's stale coffee and greasy eggs and homefries only make worse. Still, I stay for an extra cup of coffee, dreading the return trip and facing Aidan. At the cashier I dawdle over the postcards and souvenir mugs—thick, cream-colored ones with a blue drawing of the Acropolis—and even buy a postcard because it's occurred to me that this might be the diner where Ramon used to work. Just south of Peekskill on Route 9, he always said. Besides, now I'll have something to show for this long, fruitless trip. Then, finally, because I can't put it off any longer, I leave and head north.

I make one more stop before going back to the hotel. Thinking about the section in my mother's book when the selkies shed their skins has reminded me of the woman my mother saw die at the Rip Van Winkle station. I haven't had a chance to follow up on it since I've been up here. It didn't seem as important when I'd hoped I would find my mother's lost manuscript, but now that the summer is almost over I have to face the possibility I'll never find it—or even that Hedda was wrong and there was no third book. In that case, I'll need another approach if I still plan to write a book about my mother. Aside from the unsubstantiated possibility that my mother was having an affair, the only solid piece of information I've gleaned all summer is that my mother saw a girl named Rose McGlynn die on the train tracks the day she left the city. Maybe if I can find out more about Rose McGlynn I can figure out why she was important enough that my mother named her fantasy world after her.

I don't really think the *Poughkeepsie Journal* will tell me much more than the *New York Times*, but there's always a chance that the story would have drawn more local attention up here. The receptionist at the newspaper office directs me to the microfiche room where back issues of the paper are stored. I take out the loop for 1949 and scroll toward June 22, operating the machine much more confidently than back in May. When I find the story I see that it's much longer than the *Times* version. I copy it and then, because there is no Rose Reading Room to repair to, read it under the flickering fluorescent lights.

"Tragedy at Rip Van Winkle—Woman Visiting Inmate at Prison Killed in Train Accident," the headline reads. I blink at the small, blurred type. The *Times* article hadn't said anything about the girl visiting an inmate at the prison. According to the unnamed "friend" in that article (whom I suspect is my mother), Rose McGlynn had been traveling north from the city to look for hotel work.

"The last person to see Rose McGlynn of Brooklyn, NY, was her brother John McGlynn, an inmate of Rip Van Winkle Prison. Just minutes after visiting her brother, who is serving a twenty-year sentence for grand theft, Rose McGlynn threw herself beneath the wheels of the train that would have taken her home, leaving behind on the platform a worn carpet bag and a multitude of unanswered questions. Perhaps she couldn't face the trip home alone."

If the story wasn't so sad I would laugh at the florid prose. Plus the *Times* said she was killed by the northbound train, not the southbound one. Who knows how much else this reporter—Elspeth McCrory, I see by the byline—got wrong. Still, she couldn't have completely made up the part about the brother in prison.

"The demise of this wild Irish Rose—" Oh, come on, Elspeth! "—was the culmination of a life full of tragedy, much of which was revealed during her brother's trial when Rose McGlynn herself related the sad story of their childhood in a special plea for leniency in her brother's behalf." Elspeth McCrory went on to summarize the details of that "life full of tragedy." The McGlynn children lost their mother when Rose was seventeen and John was fourteen, the eldest of three brothers. Their father, unable to care for the younger children, gave the boys over into state care—to St. Christopher's Home for Boys in downtown Brooklyn. One of the boys had died there; the other two had, one after another, fallen into a life of petty crime. Rose McGlynn, who had gone to live with relatives in Coney Island, was a familiar sight in the Brooklyn courthouses where she'd plead for leniency on behalf of one brother or another. (How, I wondered, had Elspeth McCrory gotten all this background story just one day after the train accident?) She was particularly attached to John, and so one could imagine her grief when he was caught and convicted for robbing the hotel safe where Rose worked.

I read this last part over again. According to Hedda, my mother had worked at the Crown Hotel. It made sense that the friend she traveled north with had worked at the same hotel. And as it turns out, she did.

Elspeth McCrory had gone on to breathlessly describe the "Crown Jewel Heist" of over two million dollars' worth of precious gems kept in the Crown Hotel safe as well as several costly items stolen from guest rooms. Some of the most valuable items belonged to the famous poet—and sister-in-law of the hotel's owner—Vera Nix. Vera Nix's testimony in the trial had been instrumental in convicting Mr. McGlynn.

And then I realize how Elspeth McCrory got all the inside dope on Rose McGlynn so quickly. The story of the hotel robbery must have been covered in all the papers. She just stole the background info and stuck it into her story. Pretty crafty, Elspeth, but how much of it was true?

I'd give anything right now for an hour in a library—or a computer with access to LexisNexis—but looking at my watch I see it's after five. The microfiche librarian is loudly packing up her purse and glaring at me resentfully. I'm not sure how late the Poughkeepsie library stays open, but I am sure that if I don't get back to the hotel by dinner my absence will be noted. Besides, why go to the library when I have a firsthand source? Harry should be able to tell me all I want to know about the Crown jewel heist.

Chapter Twenty-one

THE NET OF TEARS

*Where the river turns from salt to fresh the selkie sheds her skin.
It is here that the conqueror has his prison. Our men are here—
fathers, sons, brothers, sweethearts—behind the high walls. The
river runs beneath the stone walls and it's possible to slip between
the bars and swim to the pool of tears where the men come to see
one last glimpse of their women. It's dangerous, though, because
the salt tide from the sea comes and goes here and if a selkie is
caught inside the prison when the tide flows back she will drown.*

I took the chance, though, to see Naoise one last time.

*He was waiting by the pool, bent over the water, so that
when I surfaced I came through his reflection. For a moment he
must have thought he was still looking at himself, then he smiled,
and then he frowned.*

"You shouldn't have come here, Deirdre, it's not safe."

*"When did you ever care about safe," I said, laughing at
him, but then, seeing how his back was bowed over as if by some
unbearable weight I relented and held his hand. "You didn't think
about safe when you stole Connachar's jewels."*

*"Shh." He touched a finger to his lips and looked behind him
into the shadows. When he turned I saw the scars between his
shoulder blades where the knife had severed his wings.*

"I did it for us—to release us from this prison—besides, they weren't his to begin with. He stole them from others."

I sighed and was frightened to hear the sound echo off the walls of the dungeon. It multiplied, as if the walls had absorbed all the sadness they had ever seen and were sighing back. But then I saw the other forms in the water—my sisters—come to see their men one last time, and I realized the sighs came from them.

"A lot of good it did. He has his jewels again and you are here."

He bent all the way down to the water then, as if to press his lips to the river and drink, but instead he whispered in my ear.

"Not all. I saved the best. The net of tears—the net that must be broken to free us. I hid it . . ."

But as he spoke I felt a tug at my legs and a chill, like ice, moving through the water. The tide was retreating. If I didn't leave now I would be trapped here. Perhaps it wouldn't be so bad, to stay here with Naoise, better than living on dry land without him. I felt the river coaxing me to stay . . . to drown.

"Go," Naoise said, "you must go," and he leaned forward and pushed me away, whispering one last word in my ear. I could see through the water his back turned to me. I could see the long scars where his wings had been and, frightened, I kicked off from the slimy rock and dived deep. My tears drowned in the river, their salt flowing back to the sea. I didn't care then if I ever found the grate and made it out into the light and onto the land. I went deeper and deeper until my hands scraped something hard—the bars— and then other hands were pulling me through.

I opened my eyes and what I saw, there beneath the river, frightened me. My sisters, the selkies, were struggling in the ebb tide; long blue tentacles of salt water pulling at them, flaying their skin. I watched as the skin of one selkie was shredded into long strips and something white and raw kicked free and swam upstream. But another one was ripped in half by the struggle and her poor mutilated body sank to the bottom of the river.

I didn't have the leisure, though, to pity my sisters, because soon I was caught in the same struggle. No one had told me it would feel like this—to shed one's skin. And worse than the sharp salt fingers digging into my skin was the awful cold of the freshwater river waiting to claim me. A cold born of the glaciers to the north. It would be better, I thought, to die here and be eaten by fish, than to live in that cold. And as I saw others around me sink to the bottom I knew they had given in to that wish.

But then I remembered what Naoise had told me at the end. He had told me where to find the net of tears. How could I take that knowledge to the bottom of the river?

So I struggled against the tide and kicked free into the ice-cold water and blinding sunlight. I barely had strength left to crawl up onto the riverbank. Naked. Alone. My sisters—the few who had survived—had come up on the opposite riverbank. I was alone in a world of mud and ice and for a long time I lay there wishing I had died beneath the river.

When I get back to the hotel from Poughkeepsie I learn that Harry's gone down to the city to arrange for several paintings to be sent up on loan for the Arts Festival. I'm disappointed that I'm not able to ask about the Crown jewel theft, but truthfully, I'm so busy with preparations for the festival that I'd have little time to talk to him. I barely have time to talk to Aidan and then I notice he's avoiding me anyway, which puts me in an awkward position since he's the events coordinator. So when, on the morning before the first day of the festival, Ramon tells me that Mr. Kron has returned and left several Hudson River School landscapes behind the desk to be stored in the safe—which, Ramon tells me, is too small—I turn to Joseph to help me figure out where to store them.

It's early enough that his coterie of art students hasn't joined him yet. He's sitting at a window in his suite, his injured foot propped up on a footstool, surrounded by the faded mural of Ichabod Crane's flight from the specter of the Headless Horseman. Like the mural in the Half Moon Suite, this one also incorporates the view of the Catskill Mountains into the narrative. The bridge that Ichabod Crane must cross to safety seems to span the distant mountains, and its arch is echoed by a small ornamental bridge in the rose garden. Joseph, seated on the far side of the bridge, appears to be right in the path of the fiery missile of the horseman's head.

I sit on the edge of the footstool and, because I still can't get used to having a conversation face-to-face with him instead of working side by side in the flower bed, I find myself looking out the window as we talk. It's an appealing view—not as spectacular as the east side of the hotel with its panoramic sweep of the Hudson Valley, but beautiful in a quieter way. The sun hasn't reached this side of the ridge yet. Scraps of mist still cling to the ground; the grass is glazed with a light dew that will burn off soon enough. The garden is full of the quick darting shapes of birds hunting for food. The only guests I see are the Eden sisters sitting quietly in Brier Rose. Minerva has a pair of binoculars, but Alice is sitting with her eyes closed, as if meditating.

"The garden looks beautiful," I tell Joseph.

He shakes his head. "The ground is bone dry. I've asked Clarissa and Ian to stop watering the annuals and concentrate on the roses and other perennials. It won't look as pretty in a few weeks, but the season is almost over and at least the roses will survive to next year."

There's something melancholy in the way he says *at least the roses will survive.* As if he didn't expect to be around to see them. I wonder if this forced leisure has made him feel expendable and he has already mentally removed himself from the scene, just as he's apportioning water to the longer-living plants and pruning back the deadwood.

I can't think of any better way to tell him how much I still need him than to do what I've come to do anyway: ask for his advice. I tell him that the paintings that have just arrived won't fit in the hotel safe.

"The safe wouldn't be the best place for them at any rate; too many people have access to it. I can't tell you how many hotel safe robberies I've heard of over the years . . ."

"Do you remember the Crown Hotel robbery back in the forties?" I ask, remembering the article I read in Poughkeepsie.

Joseph turns abruptly away from the window and stares at me. "Who told you about that? Was it Mr. Kron?"

It would be easy to nod my head, but I can't lie to Joseph. "I looked up the newspaper for the day my mother first came here. A woman named Rose McGlynn died at the Rip Van Winkle train station. She was visiting her brother who'd been sent to prison for robbing the Crown Hotel."

Joseph's face looks suddenly chalky, washed of color. I lean forward and touch his hand, which rests on the arm of his chair. His fingers feel cold as earth.

"Is that how you heard about the robbery," I ask him. "Did my mother tell you about Rose McGlynn? Was my mother somehow involved in the robbery?"

Joseph pulls his hand away as if my touch had stung him. "Can you really imagine that your mother would involve herself in something like that, Iris?"

"Well, I think it's likely she knew Rose McGlynn. They were traveling together on the same train, they'd both worked at the Crown, and they both came from Brooklyn. If it was really Rose McGlynn's brother who committed the robbery . . ." I stop because Joseph looks stricken, but also because of what has occurred to me. "Rose McGlynn's brother was named John. That's how my mother was registered at the Dreamland Hotel. Mr. and Mrs. John McGlynn. John McGlynn could have been the lost lover whom she ran away with."

"No," Joseph says, "John McGlynn wasn't your mother's lover. Your mother would never betray your father like that." Joseph swings his injured foot off the footstool so abruptly that the heavy plaster cast smacks into my thigh. I cry out, less from the physical pain—which is considerable—than from the sting of Joseph's anger. But then I'm angry too.

"I'm tired of everyone telling me my mother was a saint. She died in a hotel room registered as another man's wife. She was leaving my father and she was leaving me. If it had anything to do with that robbery I want to know."

Joseph has struggled to his feet and is reaching for his crutches, which lean against the wall behind me. I grab his arm to steady him—and stop him long enough to answer my questions.

"Does it occur to you, Iris, that these might be dangerous questions to ask? That someone might get hurt." He lays his large hand over mine—I think to remove it from his arm, but instead he draws my hand closer to him and holds it against his chest. Through the worn cloth of his shirt I can hear the faint pulse of his heart. "I promise you that your mother wasn't having an affair with John McGlynn. She never meant to leave you or your father." He squeezes my hand a little harder. "*Shayna maidela*," he says, "I drove your mother across the river that night and I know she meant to come back. She went to settle something . . . to see someone . . . but I can't tell you who. Not now. It's not my secret to tell. Can you trust me enough to wait just a little?"

I look into Joseph's brown eyes, eyes so scored with wrinkles it's like looking into two wells sunk deep in parched ground. There's never been anyone I've trusted more. Besides, I have an inkling suddenly of what he knows and why he can't tell me. I remember the argument he had with Phoebe the night she went out onto the ledge and I feel sure it was something to do with my mother and Peter Kron.

"Do you promise you'll tell me when you can?"

"If you promise me you'll be careful."

I nod, meekly, like when I was little and he made me promise not to trample over his flower beds.

"Good," he says, releasing my hand and reaching behind me for his crutches. "Now let me show you where to keep those paintings."

We don't have to go far. There are two closets in the Sleepy Hollow Suite, one in the hall that joins the living area to the bedroom (which is the one Phoebe complained had loose floorboards) and one on the other side of the living area—which, I notice for the first time, has a double lock and a deadbolt on its metal door. Joseph takes out a heavy ring of keys from his pocket and unlocks it.

"Every once in a while we'd have a guest who wanted a secure storage area for valuables, so your father had three suites outfitted with locked closets and made sure he kept the keys. We don't usually open them for guests unless they specifically request it. It's perfect for storing those paintings."

"But we'll have to go in and out of your suite every time we need a painting. They're for different lectures so we'll be bothering you all week. Maybe we can use one of the other suites that has a locked closet."

"The other ones are taken—unless you want to use the one in Mr. Kron's suite, but I don't fancy you traipsing in and out of his room." Joseph looks up from his keys and holds my gaze for a moment before looking away. I wonder if he shares Phoebe's idea that I'm romantically involved with Harry. "Use this one, Iris. You've got the key to the outside door, so you don't need to bother me to get in. I can close the connecting door between the bedroom and the living area and there's an outside door from the bedroom I can use. I'll make sure no one goes in there who's not supposed to. At least I'll be doing something."

When I get back downstairs Aidan is in the office looking at the paintings.

"They're beautiful, aren't they?" I ask him. "Did you see the one of the hotel?"

"This one here? It looks more like a Greek temple. And it makes these hummocky little hills around here look like the Swiss Alps. I'd say these river school painters were prone to a bit of exaggeration."

"It was the whole romantic notion of the sublime," I say, happy that Aidan's even talking to me. "They were exalting the American landscape."

"Well," Aidan says, leaning the painting back against the wall, "of course I'm not an art expert like your fellow Jack, but even I know these are worth too much to be lying around the front office."

I decide to ignore the reference to Jack. "There's a locked closet in Joseph's suite we can use for them and any other valuable artifacts that won't fit in the safe. I was going to bring them up now . . ."

"Why didn't you ask me? Do you not trust me with them?"

"Honestly, I was afraid you'd think the job was too menial for you . . ." I say before I can help myself. At least it's the truth—I have been squeamish of asking him to do anything this last week—but I didn't mean it to sound as if he'd been shirking his share of the work.

Aidan glares at me for a moment, but then drops his head and rubs the back of his neck. "This ain't going to work, love," he says so softly I have to move closer to hear him. Over his shoulder I see Ramon at the desk, but he's busy checking in a guest. "Maybe I should just leave."

I touch the tips of my fingers to his elbow. "But this job is too good an opportunity for you to waste."

"Is that the only reason you want me to stay?" When Aidan looks up at me I'm alarmed at the expression in his eyes—he looks like a trapped animal. Maybe he really does want to leave.

"You know it isn't . . . it's just everything is so complicated right now. Can you trust me enough to wait just a little?"

The words sound familiar as I say them and then it occurs to me that I've repeated what Joseph asked of me not more than half an hour ago. At the desk the guest who is checking in drums his fingers while waiting for Ramon to run his credit card. Beyond him the lobby is empty and quiet in the bright sunlight streaming in from the terrace. A faint breeze stirs the sheer curtains at the French windows and the hems of the newly upholstered couches. I have a sense of the whole hotel perched on the ridge waiting, like a ship at anchor before it launches into the sea. Aidan beside me seems equally poised for flight.

Aidan touches the back of his hand to my face. "I'll wait for you, Iris," he says, "for as long as I can."

When I've made sure the paintings are safely stored I go into the breakfast room to find Harry. He's talking into a cell phone, but he motions me to sit and signals to a waiter to fill my coffee cup, all the while conducting a conversation mostly composed of large figures and obscure code.

"Offer long, above, fifty thousand shares BONZ, Bob Oscar Nancy Zebra nine spot sixty-nine. For the day."

After a minute I realize he's placing a stock order.

As soon as he folds the phone shut he turns his whole attention to me. "You're looking lovely this morning, Iris. That outfit reminds me of Coco Chanel."

I laugh and feel lighter than I have all morning. Of the two men I've spoken to so far, Harry is the first to notice what I'm wearing today—a boxy green linen suit and several long ropes of fake pearls—and the first to make me laugh.

"It belonged to my mother, but it's hardly Chanel. She had a knack for copying whatever was in vogue and as for these"—I twirl the fake pearls around my finger—"guests were always leaving their costume jewelry behind. There are boxes of this stuff up in the attic."

Harry lifts an eyebrow and reaches across the coffee cups to finger one of the pearls. "Yes," he says, "fake. But are you sure all of it is? Maybe I should have a look at those boxes."

"Well, if any of it was real surely the owners would have come looking for it a long time ago."

"You'd be amazed at how careless some people can be, but then I always thought jewelry belongs on those best suited for it. You, for instance, ought to have the real thing."

"Oh," I say, feeling the heat rise to my face, "I'd just worry about it getting stolen—which brings me to what I wanted to talk to you about . . ."

"There hasn't been anything stolen?" he asks, his expression instantly growing serious.

"Oh, no, of course not. I only wanted to talk to you about the security for the Arts Festival—for the paintings you brought up this morning."

"The Hudson River School landscapes? I thought I left instructions for them to go into the safe."

"Yes, but they were too large," I say, surprised he wouldn't have thought of this. Certainly he's seen the safe. "Joseph suggested we use the locked closet in his suite."

"An excellent idea. Have they been moved there?"

"Aidan Barry has seen to it already."

I think I see a shadow pass over his face and once again I wonder how much Harry knows about Aidan's background.

"Well, I'm glad they'll be close to Joseph. I'm sure he won't let anything happen to them. Nothing can damage a hotel's reputation more quickly than a robbery."

"We've never had anything worse than the odd missing piece of jewelry, which usually turned up after the guest blamed the poor maid. It would be awful to have a real robbery. Have any of your hotels ever been robbed?" The question is out before I remember my promise to Joseph. I wasn't even thinking of the Crown jewel theft—but of course now I am.

"One or two over the years, it's to be expected . . ." Harry's gaze has grown abstracted and drifts over the dining room, surveying the scene, no doubt to make sure everything is running smoothly. I should let the subject drop and keep my promise to Joseph, but then I'm fairly sure it's not Harry that Joseph's worried about, but Phoebe.

"Wasn't the Crown Hotel safe burglarized in the late forties? And some valuable jewelry stolen?"

Harry smiles, purses his lips, then smiles again, like a man at a wine tasting swishing some Cabernet around in his mouth.

"Yes, that's so. It was in 1949. Most of the jewels that were stolen belonged to my family estate. My brother, Peter, and his wife, Vera, were staying in the hotel and Vera liked to wear the family jewelry. There were pieces dating back to the Habsburgs—ancestors of ours. I strongly urged my brother to keep the jewels in a bank vault, but Peter was reckless and my sister-in-law was extremely stubborn—not unlike her daughter—and she insisted on wearing them in the most inappropriate of settings. Bohemian gatherings in the Village and jazz clubs in Harlem. She'd even brag about how much they were worth. It was almost as if she were begging someone to take them from her."

I recall Phoebe mentioning that all her mother's jewelry had gone back to the family estate after her death. *All that ancestral crap*, she called it. It didn't sound as if her mother was so disdainful of it—or maybe she was and that's why she wore it so carelessly.

"And then they were taken," I say, because Harry seems to have lost the thread of his story. "Were they ever recovered?"

"Yes. The thief was apprehended a few months later—the jewels were in his motel room. We were most fortunate."

"You don't make it sound like a fortunate occurrence."

Harry nods his head and touches his forefinger just below his right eye, tugging at the loose skin there. "You see much, Iris. No. The jewels were returned, but the damage was done. Something came unhinged in Peter and Vera after that. Maybe it was how Peter treated her. My brother was not perhaps suited for married life. He was never very stable after the war. Maybe it was the experience of being in a POW camp; he could never bear to be confined after that and he seemed to feel that the world owed him some sort of recompense for what he suffered. He repaid the Countess Oriana Val d'Este, who hid him in her villa at great personal risk to herself, by emptying her wine cellar and stealing some of her jewelry—he claimed later that she'd given him the jewelry to aid him in fleeing the country, but she told me otherwise when I met her a few years later at the Hotel Charlotte in Nice. Perhaps the Crown robbery brought up those unpleasant memories—or perhaps he blamed Vera for her carelessness with the jewels. Their marriage became a shambles after that—he had affairs; she became a morphine addict. She and Peter lived another twenty years but I've often thought she would have done them both a favor by driving their car off a cliff sooner. Their life together must have been a living hell."

It's a harsh assessment, but is it really any worse than Phoebe's depiction of her parents' marriage and the wedding band that she personally engraved with barbed wire and thorns?

"That's the thing about theft—it's a violation with repercussions beyond the loss of material goods."

There's an anger behind Harry's words I've rarely heard before from him. I notice the waiter at the next table look up from pouring coffee; even the omelet chef has turned, saucepan in hand, alert to the possibility of an angry boss.

"The thief must have served a long prison sentence," I say in an almost placating tone, as if I'd been the one to anger him.

Harry shrugs. "Twenty years. Yes, I made sure of that. But he wasn't the one who really hurt me. It was his sister who worked for me—a young woman I'd taken under my wing and hoped to advance. She started out working the information desk, but she'd been promoted to assistant manager. Quite an accomplishment for a woman in those days. I've always considered myself ahead of the times when it came to advancing women. It was her brother who robbed the safe. Of course, there was only one logical conclusion to draw."

"You think she gave him the combination?"

Harry widens his eyes and looks out the window. I'm startled to realize he's close to tears. After a minute he looks back at me, his composure regained, his voice cool. "I believed so, but I told the police that she didn't know the combination."

"But why not . . . if you thought she betrayed you . . ."

The right side of his mouth curls up in a sad little smile and he sighs.

"Oh," I say, guessing what he might be embarrassed about, "you were involved with her."

"I'm afraid so. Always a mistake becoming romantically entangled with an employee. I'm sure you'll be wiser than me in that respect, Iris. I couldn't bear the embarrassment of what would come out at the trial if she were implicated along with her brother. But then, the guilt must have been too much for her. Oh, I don't say because of what she did to me, but for how her brother ended up. The poor girl killed herself in the most awful way. She was decapitated by a train."

I don't have to feign shock at Harry's words because even though I know that Rose McGlynn died under a train at the Rip Van Winkle station, no one said anything about decapitation. I know I must look shaken. What I imagined—as soon as Harry said the words—was how horrible it must have been for my mother to witness that death. I think of all the people whom that tragedy struck—John McGlynn, Harry, his brother Peter, Vera Nix—and of how my mother's life became inevitably entangled in their lives. Had one of them—John McGlynn or Peter Kron—come back into her life all those years later?

"Iris, did you hear my question?"

"I'm sorry, Harry, I was thinking about that poor girl. What a horrible way to die. What did you ask?"

"I asked how you came to hear about the jewel theft. I wasn't aware that it was common knowledge."

In a newspaper article I looked up in Poughkeepsie while I was supposed to be at the printers, are the words that run through my head. The words that come out, though, are, "Joseph told me about it. We were talking about hotel security and he mentioned it as a case where the hotel safe wasn't the most secure location."

Harry smiles. I'm relieved to see the sadness his story has brought lift. "He's quite on the ball, our Joseph. I believe his talents have been wasted on gardening all these years. We really must make better use of him."

Chapter Twenty-two

THE NET OF TEARS

*I lay in the mud a long time, staring up at the cliffs rising above.
When I'd come up the river a mist had lain on the water but now
that mist had risen and traveled up into the mountains. The hills
closest to me were green and covered with dense forest. The next
layer of mountains was blue but I knew they too were covered with
the never-ending trees that stood like sentinels guarding the river.
Above the blue was a layer of pearl, like a silk slip dropped over a
rumpled bed. Something white glinted in its folds—like a diamond
earring caught on the cloth—and that's what finally drew me to
my feet—to see what it was.*

*My legs felt like two knives thrust into my hip sockets; the
mud sucked at my feet. I had shed my skin but still felt trapped in
a body not my own. But I stood there trying to read the horizon
until the colors began to change in the distance. What I thought
at first were clouds were more mountains. They went on forever!
How many steps would I have to take on this dry land before the
river would take me back? What I thought at first was a diamond
earring—and then a mirage—was a white palace, its columns rising from the sea of trees like a ship cresting the waves. That's where
I had to go. The Palace of Two Moons. That's where Naoise had
hidden the net of tears.*

"Rising above the grand river, enfolded in the misty hills of legend, the hotel that stands behind you has been more than a gathering spot for artists and art lovers for over a century and a half—it has been the inspiration for art, the cradle of romantic genius."

The guests, arranged in a semicircle of chairs, shade their eyes with their festival programs while Harry gives the opening talk of the Arts Festival. He stands in the middle of the Half Moon gazebo, which has been festooned with purple and cream crepe-paper streamers. Behind him the sky is clear all the way to New Hampshire—a radiant backdrop. The only problem is that because his back is to the strong morning sun his expression is unclear—he's little more than a dark silhouette against the breathtaking view.

"We all know that this region gave rise to the first American school of landscape painting. The river you see below us lent its name to that movement—the Hudson River School of painting—examples of which you will see and hear discussed during this week. What you might not know is the role the hotel behind you played in the genesis of our first homegrown artistic movement."

Some of the guests crane their heads around to peer back at the hotel. Since I'm standing under the colonnade—perched between lobby and terrace to watch for late arrivals—I'm caught in their gaze. I feel I should flourish my hands to present the hotel to them, but I can see it's not necessary. I can't see what they see since I'm under the colonnade, but I know what the hotel looks like on a clear morning with the eastern sun bathing its white facade, striking the Corinthian columns into pillars of flame.

Harry is explaining that what American scenery lacked to make it a fitting subject for landscape painting was romantic association. I lose a little of what he says every time I lean into the shadowy cool of the lobby to check the front entrance. Most of the conference attendees have arrived except for the one I'm waiting for—Jack, who should have been here an hour ago.

". . . what today might be exalted as unspoiled wilderness was considered woefully lacking in the vestiges of antiquity, which is why this building, with its classical columns, became such a popular subject for nineteenth-century painting . . ."

I notice that a woman in the back row is glaring at me and realize it's because I'm picking the peeling paint off the column I'm leaning against. Defiling this vestige of antiquity. I push myself off the column and take a turn around the lobby. Harry's speech, which should make me feel proud of the hotel, is depressing me. I don't want to think of the Hotel Equinox as a vestige of antiquity or a picturesque subject for landscape painting. It's my home. It's where I grew up. When I peer into the dark recesses of the Sunset Lounge, deserted at this hour, I can catch for just the briefest of moments a glimpse of my mother leaning against the bar, the curve of her hip against the padded leather banquette, a reflection of her dark hair and pale face in the silvered mirror above the liquor bottles. The smoky shadows still hold the faintest whiff of her perfume and my father's cigars.

Out there on the terrace Harry is appropriating the hotel for a larger role in a history less personal. Staking its claim for art. It makes me feel petulant—the way I felt when my mother was busy writing and I wasn't supposed to bother her.

I walk out the front entrance and stand on the flagstone walk, following with my eyes the line of the circular drive until it disappears into the trees. Jack could be driving up through the woods already and I wouldn't know it. The view on this side of the hotel is closed off by the thick forest of pine and oak, so dense it cuts off sound as well. I stare at the trees where the drive disappears from view as if willing them to disgorge Jack from their hold and notice that the oaks have started to change color already. Flares of red and orange, like sparks of flame, tremble in the early-morning breeze. The melancholy that has been licking at my heels all morning washes over me. Summer is almost over and I haven't gotten anywhere with my book. I'm no closer to understanding my mother than I was at the beginning of the season—if anything she seems to have taken a step deeper into the shadows. The one thing that seemed truly good about this summer is gone. Aidan hasn't talked to me all week and now Jack—the reason for our quarrel—hasn't shown up.

Even this sadness is wearily familiar—the same end-of-season malaise I felt every year when the summer, which had seemed to stretch out into infinity, was suddenly over. All the things that I meant to do with the long vacation left undone. Time catching me unaware as if the turning of the earth came as a big surprise.

I notice that Joseph's cane is leaning against the arch of Brier Rose. I take a step forward and see that he's sitting on the bench inside staring at the edge of the woods just as I was. I wonder if he's feeling the same end-of-summer melancholy that I am and if it's worse when you're as old as Joseph, or maybe that sense of time catching up with you is with you all the time because coming to the end of your life is like coming to the end of summer: all your plans and dreams left undone.

I start walking toward the gazebo, but then I see Joseph's not alone. At first I think he must be with Clarissa, the new gardener, but then the woman sitting across from him leans forward and I see it's Phoebe Nix. I'm so taken aback that I stop on the path. Perhaps I should interrupt them, though, in case Phoebe is grilling Joseph about what he knows about her father and my mother's involvement, but then I hear an odd, unfamiliar sound coming from the gazebo. Joseph laughing. I think I've only heard him laugh once or twice in my whole life. It makes me feel like the intruder—the stranger here.

A rush of wind, gathering itself up from the slope of the mountain through acres of trees, sweeps through the garden bringing that first edge of autumn coolness. I head back through the lobby, shivering, out onto the sun-warmed terrace where Harry is finishing up.

"The Hotel Equinox is well named," he says, bringing a hand up to his darkened face to wipe the sweat away. Out here on the terrace it is, thank God, still summer. "Because it is here that the ideals of the romantic period meet in balance. Sublimity in the expanse of the view—" Harry lifts his right arm to indicate the valley and the wide sky behind him. "—picturesqueness in its classical lines and romantic associations." He raises his left arm—not as high, I notice—to take in the hotel. He pauses for a moment, holding both arms out so that he looks like a giant blackbird perched on the edge of the ridge. "It is the ideal setting for a coming together of artistic ideas—for the airing of conflicts no matter how at odds some of those ideas might seem to be. My hope for this Arts Festival is that forces of opposition will join hands here." Harry sweeps his arms together and interlaces his fingers. "And I hope that at least a few of you will go away with some romantic associations of your own."

The audience applauds. It's my signal to head for the dining room to make sure the waiters are ready with pitchers of orange juice and that the trays of baked goods are uncovered. As I head along the colonnade, though, I bump into Aidan coming out of the dining room.

"I've got it," he says, tilting his chin inside where I can see a flurry of white jackets moving back and forth across the room and smell the freshly brewed coffee. "I could tell Harry was winding down when he started flapping his arms around. A bloke his age can't keep those gymnastics up for long."

I laugh, mostly because it's the longest sentence Aidan's spoken to me since we discussed where the paintings should be stored. "I want to thank you for taking on so much this week," I say, moving into the shade of one of the columns. "I never would have pulled all this together without you."

"Well, if not for you I'd still be sweating it out in that printing shop on Varick Street instead of here basking in the cradle of romantic genius."

"Pretty silly, huh?"

"Oh, I don't know." Aidan leans against the wall and I do too. "A lot of what he said made sense to me, especially that part about romantic associations." He turns his head to look at me and his hand, which is lying against the wall, grazes my arm. "It's not just us—although, yeah, that's a big piece of it—but it's also this place. It has a special feel to it, like it's standing outside time like . . . what's the name of that little Scottish town in the movie? You know the one that comes and goes every hundred years?"

"Brigadoon?"

"Yeah. Maybe it's because of all the people who've come and gone here. You can still sort of feel them moving in and out of the rooms, all the parties and the families. I can see why you've never truly settled down after growing up here. Every other place must seem a disappointment to you."

"No, that's not it . . ." I start to say, but Aidan's gaze has lifted from mine and strayed over my shoulder. The sun has reached this sheltered piece of the terrace and it strikes Aidan's face like the flat side of a blade.

"Well, maybe that will change for you now, Iris. Someone seems pretty happy to see you."

I turn to look and there's Jack striding through the stripes of sun and shade cast by the columns. I turn back to Aidan, but he's already gone, which is just as well because Jack practically lifts me off my feet embracing me.

"You're late," I say when he puts me down. "You missed Mr. Kron's speech."

"Frankly I've heard enough gibberish about art this summer to last a lifetime. Wait until you hear what I found on the way over here . . . is that coffee I smell?"

The guests are filing into the dining room now and queuing up at the coffee urns. Harry is waving me over to a group of curators but I pretend not to see him. I'm not ready to introduce Jack around yet.

"We'll slip into the kitchen and nab a thermos," I say, steering Jack inside. "We can take it up to your room."

"My room? Aren't I staying in your room?"

"Well, when you registered for the conference without telling me, you were assigned a room. Besides, don't you remember how hot it is up in the attic?" I'm able to say this without looking at him because I'm rooting in the shelves for a thermos. I find one that's missing its top and fill it from the coffeemaker. I pour some milk into a pitcher and hand it to Jack, running smack into the confused look on his face. "Is that all your luggage," I say, pointing at the duffel bag hanging from his shoulder.

"The rest is in the car. What's up, Iris? Are you really that mad because I was late? I saw a FOR SALE sign just off Route Thirty-two and I had to check it out. It would be perfect for us. A two-hundred-year-old farmhouse with a barn I could paint in . . ."

Jack must see the wild terror in my eyes because he stops. A two-hundred-year-old farmhouse for us to share. Six months ago it would have sounded like a dream come true, but now it seems like one of those abandoned projects of summer—an idea whose time is past.

"Let's go upstairs and get you settled," I say, handing Jack a basket of rolls. "And we'll talk."

We're heading to the elevator when I see that Hedda is in it.

"Do you mind taking the stairs?" I ask.

Jake shakes his head and he starts toward the main stairs. "No, let's take the back staircase," I tell him, "if I run into any of these conference people I'll get stuck running a million errands for them."

"What about that new guy, your special-events coordinator?"

"What about him?"

"Isn't he supposed to do all that?"

"Yes, but you can't tell a guest that." The enclosed stairway is hot and airless. The open thermos I'm carrying sloshes hot coffee on my wrist. We stop talking after the second floor and concentrate on conserving our breath.

"I put you on the fifth floor so you'd be close to my room," I say when we reach the top.

"Well, that's a relief, Iris. From the way you're acting I suppose I should be glad you didn't put me in the basement."

I wait until we're in the room to answer him. "What do you expect, Jack? I barely hear from you all summer and then you make plans to come here without even telling me. For the last ten years I haven't even been allowed to talk about living together and now you've got a house all picked out for us. How fast am I supposed to switch gears?"

Jack shrugs his duffel bag off his shoulder and lifts his hands up, palms out. "I thought the way we were suited you. Are you saying it's too late?"

I turn away from him because I don't have an answer, but also because the room is stifling. I wrench open a window and look out, my hands flat against the window ledge. I couldn't get Jack a valley view so he's facing the garden and the woods. The trees seems to stretch out endlessly and I can see, in among the burnt umber of the pines, flashes of red and yellow. Once again, the sight of the changing leaves makes me feel that I've run out of time, but more than that, those acres of pines remind me of the time I've spent with Aidan under their boughs. That fleeting panic I'd felt before is not only for time slipping away but for Aidan.

Jack has come up behind me and touches my arm. As I noticed downstairs, his touch leaves me cold. "I'm seeing someone else," I say, turning around to face him. "Or, well, I was. I don't know if we still are. I was going to tell you."

Jack steps back from me and sinks down onto the edge of the bed. "This is information I would have appreciated having before driving across two states to come here."

"I'm sorry," I say. I look around the room. I notice that there's a basket of fruit and a bottle of wine cooling in the ice bucket on the bureau. Courtesy of Ramon and Paloma, no doubt. There's even a vase of freshly cut roses on the night table. I walk over to smell them and then sit down on the bed next to Jack. I touch his hand and I'm relieved when he doesn't pull it away. "You've got to admit, though, they're two skinny states."

When I leave Jack's room I take the main stairs down. Curiously, I don't feel as bad as I should. I've probably ruined both relationships, but I feel lighter than I did this morning. Maybe it's the relief of having told Jack about Aidan. Maybe that end-of-summer melancholy just means it's time to let go of the things you didn't get around to doing.

On the second floor I notice that the door to Joseph's suite is open and that Aidan is standing in the middle of the room holding a painting up to the light coming through the window. I come into the room and stand next to him and admire the painting: a dawn sky without boundaries of horizon, colossal clouds tinged pink and orange expanding into limitless distance. I steal a glance at Aidan and see in his eyes an expression of longing that makes me ache to have him look at me like that—only what he seems to be longing for is to dive into the fathomless blue sky of the painting.

"Are you taking that to the Gold Parlor for the afternoon lecture?" I ask.

"No, I thought I'd hop in the old Volvo and take it down to Soho to see what I could get for it," he says, rolling his eyes at me.

"Aidan," I say, lowering my voice to a whisper, "do you think it's really such a good idea to make those kinds of jokes?"

"You mean considering my disreputable past? No, I suppose not, but don't think I'm the only one tallying up the value of these overgrown post-cards. One of the curators just told me that a painting by this same guy sold for half a million at auction last month. I don't see why they couldn't have just made do with slides. At least they'd be lighter." He shifts the heavy frame in his hands so that the sky skews sideways.

"I think Mr. Kron wanted to give the Arts Festival greater credibility . . ."

"I think he's showing off his connections in the art world . . . anyway, if there's nothing more, I'd better get this down to the Gold Parlor."

I want to tell Aidan that things aren't going well with Jack—that we might not end up together after this week—but that seems too much like stringing him along. Still, I hold him there, trying to think of something to say that will end this chilliness between us—that had seemed to be thawing earlier on the terrace before Jack showed up.

"Jack's staying on the fifth floor," I say lamely, maybe so he'll at least know that Jack's not staying in my room.

"Yes, I know, Iris. Did he like his roses? Joseph asked me especially to cut them for him."

"Oh, God, Aidan, I'm sorry . . ."

I move toward him to touch his arm, but he turns away from me, toward the hall door, and freezes. I look that way and see that Phoebe Nix is standing in the doorway watching us. She's wearing one of those straight, shapeless dresses she favors—this one the color and texture of overcooked oatmeal—and backless snakeskin mules that slap on the carpet as she steps into the room. She pauses for a moment in front of the open door to the closet and turns to Aidan.

"There you are," she says, "we're waiting for that painting in the Gold Parlor. So this is where the paintings are stored . . . I didn't realize this door led to a closet."

She steps toward the closet, but Aidan steps in between her and the open door. "Sorry, Miss Nix, Mr. Kron specifically requested that no one but me and Joseph have access to the paintings."

Leaning the sky painting against the wall, he closes and locks the closet door.

Phoebe shrugs. "That's fine with me . . . as long as you deliver the paintings promptly. You'd better go on down with that one . . . if Miss Greenfeder is done with you, that is." Phoebe smiles slyly on that last part and I can't help but think she chose her words purposefully.

"Aye," Aidan says, giving me one last look, "I think Miss Greenfeder's done with me." He leaves the room without looking at me.

"I want to speak with you later, Aidan," I say to his back, wishing the words sounded less like an employer's reprimand and more like a lover's apology. I'd follow him but Phoebe has planted herself in front of me, arms wrapped around her thin waist, tapping the back of her shoe against her bare heel until Aidan is out of earshot.

"Can I help you with something, Phoebe?"

"My uncle says you were asking him questions about the Crown jewel theft. I wanted to know if you plan to write about that in your book."

I glance at the hall to the bedroom and wonder if Joseph's still outside in the garden or in there where he could hear our conversation. Maybe it doesn't matter. Maybe he already knows I've broken my promise not to ask questions about the robbery.

"Joseph's in the garden," Phoebe, as if reading my thoughts, says. "I didn't tell him that you'd talked to Harry, if that's what you're worried about. I think the less said about that particular piece of history the better. It doesn't have anything to do with your mother's story. I don't see why you're bothering with it."

"I think it might," I say. "My mother traveled up here with a friend who worked at the Crown—it was her brother who robbed the safe—"

"Yes, the McGlynns. I know all about them. A couple of two-bit thieves. The brother had the nerve to say at the trial that my mother offered him money to steal her own jewelry. Of course no one believed him, but the press had a field day anyway—they said that at the very least my mother had flaunted the Kron family jewels in a way that invited the crime. They made up stories about my mother using drugs because, of course, that's what female writers do. My mother was only twenty-one years old at the time, but the press persisted in calling her 'childless' as if only a depraved, addict sex fiend would prefer writing to baking cookies and having babies. When my mother finally decided to have a child, she was criticized for having one so late."

"Phoebe, I think it's awful your mother was treated that way, but maybe my mother was affected by that robbery as well—it must have meant something to her for her to name her fictional world after the McGlynns. And then she was registered as John McGlynn's wife when she died—maybe she just used the name because she didn't want anyone to recognize her or maybe she was actually meeting him there."

"Is that what Joseph told you—that your mother went to the Dreamland Hotel to meet John McGlynn? Somehow I doubt he's told you anything— he's not exactly the most talkative guy in the world." There's a mocking edge to her voice that irritates me. I should, of course, tell her that it's none of her business what Joseph did or didn't tell me, but her assumption—correct in this case—that he wouldn't confide in me rankles.

"Joseph may be reluctant to blab about my mother, but she is my mother, and I think if I really wanted to know something he would tell me—eventually."

Although she has held herself very still throughout her speech a blue vein pulses at her temple and little half moons of perspiration have darkened the armholes of her shift. She spins the engraved wedding band around and around her thumb.

"You mean he hasn't told you anything yet, but you think he will. Maybe you should leave well enough alone. There could be some things you might not like to see printed about your mother."

I shake my head. "No. I'm not interested in presenting my mother as a saint or as some icon of suppressed creativity or a victim of patriarchy or anything other than what she really was."

Phoebe smiles. "Aren't you? Haven't you lived your whole life based on what you thought you knew about your mother's story? No marriage. No children. You've stayed away from the hotel until now. You've avoided everything you thought killed her—just like I've avoided everything that I thought killed my mother. Well, what if the story turned out to be different? What would you think about the choices you've made then?"

I suppose she thinks she's found the perfect threat. Honestly, I can see

the truth in what she is saying, but having just come from ruining two romances in one day I can't imagine that there are too many other bad
choices left to regret.

"I guess we all have to live with the consequences of our choices,"
I say.

She doesn't say anything right away. She looks away from me, out the
window toward the distant view of mountains. The light falls on her face,
on her fine, colorless hair that shimmers like water, and on her translucent
skin. She's so thin that the light seems to eat away at her body. I remind
myself that she never really knew her mother, and so her need to protect
her image of her mother might be greater than mine, but just when I'm
softening toward her—after all, I'm defending my right to write a book I've
all but given up on—she turns back to me.

"I don't think you'll feel that way," she says, "when you see what those
consequences are." Then she walks out of the room, slowly, the slap of
leather against flesh audible long after she has gone.

Chapter Twenty-three

THE NET OF TEARS

And so I took one step, and then another, toward the Palace of Two Moons, every step burning the soles of my feet—the skin there new and raw—so unsteady on my new legs I had to touch the tree trunks on either side of me for balance. At first the trees frightened me, they seemed to close in around me, closer with every step I took into the forest—but then I could hear them whispering to me. Their shade cooled me, their pollen drifted down over me and clothed my nakedness. Looking up at the sunlight slanting down between their boughs was like being at the bottom of the ocean looking up toward the stars. The wind that moved their branches was like the currents we follow at ebb tide.

I saw why Naoise thought he had come home. This forest was like the sea beneath our Tirra Glynn, where we lived before the serpent's pearl was broken into a million shards. I remembered then what had happened to Connachar, how the slivers of pearl had worked their way beneath his skin and gathered around his heart. Looking down I saw the green silt breeding on my skin, spinning itself into silk.

By the time I walked out of the woods I was clothed in an emerald gown, light as the wind that moves through the trees, green as the sea.

The Arts Festival is not only a resounding success, it is also a godsend to me, keeping me far too busy to deal with Jack or Aidan. Jack too is soon swept up in the lectures, seminars, and cocktail parties. Although he said he was tired of talking about art I spy him in small groups making those large sweeping gestures—as if he were painting the air—that I know he makes when he's talking about his work. I also spy a smaller gesture—the exchange of business cards with gallery owners and art critics and public television art show hosts—that bodes well for Jack's career. I'm glad that he'll get something out of this week.

Jack's not the only one moved by the talk of art. One evening in the middle of the week I go over to the staff dormitory in the North Wing to discuss an accounting discrepancy with Sophie. When I get to her apartment door, though, I'm arrested by an unfamiliar smell in the corridor. I pause at her door, which is partially ajar. A radio is playing softly—I recognize the Albany NPR station by its classical program and the static blurring its edges—but I can hear a faint rasp, which for a second I fear is my aunt gasping for breath. Then I recognize the smell: turpentine. I move back a step to see through the three inches of open door—with as much caution as if I had come across a wild pheasant in the woods—and watch as my aunt spreads color across an overcast sky above dark mountains. She's painting a rainstorm over the mountains behind the hotel. The rasping noise is the sound her brush makes dragging the rain down from the sky. For each stroke she steps toward the canvas and then steps back to look at what she's done. She looks like a young girl practicing a dance step with an invisible partner. I back away quietly; the accounting discrepancy can wait.

On the second to last day of the festival, Joseph judges the Folly contest, awarding Gretchen Lu and Mark Silverstein first prize for their collaborative entry—a gazebo called "Wing." Joseph has discarded his crutches for the event. He stands in the arch of Brier Rose, ramrod straight, addressing the little group of art students who have formed a half ring around him. The other conference attendees, the curators, gallery owners, and critics, stand in an outer ring, but it's really the art students he speaks to.

"When I first came here the world I came from had been destroyed, but for a Jew this was nothing new. The Talmud tells us that in the beginning the light of the world was held in beautiful vessels—" Joseph cups his hands in front of his chest as if holding an invisible volleyball. "—but greed and evil shattered the vessels—" Joseph reaches his arms out to the half circle, his fingers splaying as if releasing a handful of confetti, but his hands are empty. "—into a million pieces. It's our job to find these pieces and put the vessels back together. *Tikkun olam*. Healing the world. However you find to do it—planting a flower, teaching a child, painting a picture, or carving out a little house and bench for a tired old man to sit in—" Here Joseph signals for Aidan to draw the white sheet away from the new gazebo. "—you are putting a piece of the world back together again, creating a vessel to hold the light of the world."

We all look then toward the new gazebo—the new *chuppa*. The roof, made of overlapping cedar shakes carved to look like feathers, undulates over a single long bench. On either end of the bench stand carved swans, their long necks curving up to form armrests. The whole thing looks like it's poised to take flight.

Harry Kron, who's been standing on the edge of the crowd, comes forward to present Gretchen and Mark with their award money. The crowd shifts away from Brier Rose toward Wing and I notice that Joseph is slumping against the arch. I go over to him, but Natalie Baehr gets there first and helps him to sit down on the bench. I'm alarmed at how white his face is.

"I think we'd better get you upstairs," I say to Joseph. "It's so hot out here."

"I'd like to sit in the garden a while longer," he says, "but don't worry, *shayna maidela*, I know you have your hands full with the big party tonight. Natalie will take care of me and there's that nice Italian boy who'll help me back up to my room."

I turn and see Gordon del Sarto coming across the lawn. I know he's doing his big lecture tonight so I'm surprised he's not in the library fussing with his slides. He steps into the gazebo and sits down on the bench across from Joseph, next to Natalie.

"Did you bring it?" Natalie asks as soon as he sits down.

Gordon takes a green flannel pouch out of the pocket of his seersucker jacket. "The buyer at Barney's was loath to part with it. I had to promise you'd make another one for her."

"Barney's?" I repeat. I'm confused enough by the fact that Gordon and Natalie seem to know each other.

Gordon nods. "I had some dealings with the jewelry buyer there during our last auction. When Joseph told me about Natalie's work I knew she'd be interested and she was. She's commissioned a line from Natalie, but the real surprise came when I saw . . ." Gordon stops because Natalie is nudging him in the ribs.

"You're ruining the surprise," she says, taking the flannel pouch out of Gordon's hands. She hands it to me. "Here, I wanted you to have this, Professor Greenfeder. None of this would have happened if I hadn't read your story."

I tip the soft pouch over and a cascade of bright stones falls into my hand like water falling into a pool. Even though I know it's only made of glass and copper wire, I feel as if I've been given a Tiffany tiara.

"Oh, Natalie," I say, holding the strands up in the light so that the cut glass sends rainbows spinning around the gazebo. "You've given me my mother's necklace!"

I head up to my room soon after to change for Gordon's lecture. I have to dress now for the ball afterward since I won't have time in between. On the way up I pause on the second-floor landing to look at the large window that overlooks the terrace. Harry has ordered the chandelier that hangs above the window to be lowered into its center so that it will be visible from the terrace. It's part of an array of lighting effects for tonight, including floodlights to light up the hotel's facade and fireworks for after dinner. This particular chandelier was never electrified and my mother was always too afraid of fire to use it, but Harry has had it refurbished with candles. Paloma Rivera and two other maids have been cleaning the cut-glass pieces in vinegar since early morning. Each crystal drop shines in the last bit of sunlight. I can't wait to see what it looks like all lit up from the terrace tonight.

In my room I take a long bath. I use the new lilac-scented bath gel that arrived this week—along with tiny lavender bottles of shampoo and body lotion—all stamped in gold with the Crown Hotels logo. Then I stand in front of my closet in one of the new oversized bath towels with its Crown monogram, wondering what to wear. I've worn almost every dress my mother owned this summer, some so often that they no longer smell of cedar, but of my perfume and, if I press my face into the cloth, Aidan. I flick through them, the linen suits and chiffon cocktail dresses, the A-line shifts and cotton piqué sundresses, their delicate fabrics whispering against one another, their shapes belling out with air as I push their hangers along the rod, so that each one seems briefly animate, briefly embodied with my mother's form. My mother balanced on the edge of a chair in the lounge as she told a guest she'd given up writing, my mother's silhouette half glimpsed inside a gazebo with a man whose features I can't make out, my mother walking the halls with outstretched hands, fingertips patting the walls for hidden sparks, fingertips tapping against the walls as if she were typing on the plaster. It's all I've been able to remember of my mother from that last summer and I fear, now that this summer is coming to an end, all that I'll ever know of her.

I come to the last dress in the closet, still sealed in its cloth dress bag embossed with the name of the store where it was bought. Bergdorf Goodman, Fifth Avenue, New York. Pretty fancy for my mother, I think while unbuttoning the muslin bag; she usually bought knockoffs or had a dressmaker run up cheap copies of dresses she marked in the fashion magazines. When I push my hand inside the bag the dress inside slides off its hanger and slithers to the floor, a puddle of green silk around my ankles. I pick it up gingerly by its sheer chiffon straps and look for a zipper, which turns out to be cleverly concealed along a side seam.

At first when I slip the dress over my head I think it's not going to fit. It seems smaller than my mother's other dresses and for a moment while I'm trapped inside the narrow column of silk, breathing in its sweet perfume—

not my mother's perfume, I notice—I feel panicky, but then the fabric slides down over my hips, swooshes sideways across my thighs, and flares out over my ankles. I turn to look in the mirror and see myself transformed. The green satin, cut on the bias, skims over every curve like water hugging a rock. A green chiffon swag drapes from the shoulders and pools at the small of my back. Twisting my hand around to the back I can feel that small weights have been sewn into the fabric to make it drape like this. The only thing wrong is the neckline, which is so low that my throat looks bare and exposed. Then I remember Natalie's present. Noticing that I'm running late, I quickly pin my hair up and then fasten the necklace around my throat. It's perfect, glittering but light, the green glass teardrop the exact same shade as the dress.

I walk down the stairs—a dress like this deserves a long, slow entrance—savoring the swoosh of silk against my legs and the vaporish figure reflected in the darkened windowpanes that accompanies me. As I approach the second-floor landing the figure melts into a blaze of candlelight from the chandelier. Gordon del Sarto, just coming out of Joseph's suite with a small painting tucked under his arm, looks up at me and gasps.

"Iris, you look absolutely stunning. What an amazing dress. Who made it?"

I shrug my shoulders, which makes the little weights in the chiffon swag shiver against my back. "I have no idea. It was my mother's."

"May I?" Gordon asks, turning me around before I can answer and dipping his fingers down the back of my dress. I hardly have time to feel shocked or embarrassed. "Just as I thought," he says, tucking the tag back under the chiffon swag. "Balenciaga. I saw one like it at the Met's costume institute last year. This is very valuable, you know."

"Really? I can't imagine how my mother came by it . . ." Then I realize that the dress must have been left behind by a guest, like the fake pearls my mother always wore, and knowing that makes the satin feel suddenly oily against my skin. "Maybe I shouldn't wear it then . . . I mean, if it's really a museum piece . . ."

"Don't be ridiculous," someone says from behind me. I turn and see that it's Aidan. He must have been right behind me on the stairs. I hardly recognize him in his tuxedo and I remember now that Harry had suggested at the last staff meeting that he rent one for this event. "What's the use of a dress like that if it can't be worn by a beautiful woman?"

"Exactly," Gordon agrees, "it suits you. And Natalie's necklace is perfect for it. And you can't take that off because of the surprise."

I give Gordon a puzzled look.

"You'll see at my lecture, which we'll be late for if we don't go down now. Shall we?" Gordon offers me his arm. I turn to Aidan to see if he wants to escort me downstairs, but he's got both hands in the pockets of his tux.

"You go ahead," he says, "there's something I've got to take care of."

When we enter the library I still have my hand on Gordon's arm and I see Phoebe's eyes widen at the sight of us. Oh well, I think, she certainly went out of her way to tell me she and Gordon weren't dating. Harry also seems startled to see Gordon and me together and I remember that Phoebe told me that her uncle was under the impression that she and Gordon were involved. Does he think now that I'm stealing his niece's boyfriend? He certainly seems a little cooler to me. I'd expected that Harry, of all people, would comment on my dress, but he doesn't. He asks me if I've checked on whether the fireworks have been set up on the ledge below the terrace. When I admit I haven't, he looks annoyed and excuses himself to take care of it.

I think to follow him, but then Jack comes in talking to Natalie Baehr, and they both simultaneously wolf-whistle at my dress. Gretchen Lu and Mark Silverstein follow and they also make a fuss over me. By the time everyone finishes complimenting me I feel more self-conscious than flattered and it's time for the lecture to begin. I take a seat near the open French doors, hoping to catch a breeze from the courtyard. It's a stifling night and I'm beginning to sweat under the heavy silk.

"Our story begins not in the war-torn Europe of six decades ago, but nearly six centuries in the past, in quattrocento Italy . . ."

I remember that the last time I heard this introduction I was glad I'd have enough time to get upstairs to Harry's suite to "borrow" the registration book. Now six centuries seem a lot to get through before dinner.

Gordon covers the fifteenth-century background—the guilds, the rich merchants, increased interest in fashion and jewelry—and then calls for the first slide, Botticelli's *Allegory of Spring*. As soon as the lights go out I feel something brush against the back of my neck. I flinch, imagining that a bat has blundered into the room, but then I realize it's Hedda Wolfe, in the row behind me, smoothing the chiffon swag hanging down my back.

"Nice dress," she says.

I sigh, tired of the damned dress. No wonder I don't remember my mother wearing it. It's the kind of dress that wears you.

In my irritation, I've lost the thread of Gordon's lecture. He's describing the headdress popular in the fifteenth century, the *ferronière*. Instead of the stiff crowns worn in the fourteenth century, the *ferronière* was a loose band, usually of pearls but sometimes mixed with other gems, that held the hair back and draped over the forehead. He shows us a slide of a Filippo Lippi Madonna who wears a single rope of pearls on her forehead. The pearls and the Madonna's skin are equally translucent.

Her image fades into the screen, replaced by a portrait of a noblewoman by an artist whose name I miss. She's wearing a lavish pearl headpiece, pearl earrings, and ropes of pearls at her neck. Even her dress is studded with pearls.

"The *ferronière* was often part of the bride's parure. Pearls were seen as the perfect adornment not only for the Virgin Mary but also for brides, because they represented purity and chastity. A pearl *ferronière* might be handed down as part of a bride's dowry, traveling, therefore, from mother to daughter. Such a gift was given to Catalina della Rosa, the only daughter of wealthy Venetian nobles in the late fifteenth century."

The richly adorned noblewoman disappears and the thin, stern face of a child takes her place. She isn't wearing any jewelry.

"This is Catalina at age ten. Although the child of one of the richest men in Venice she had already, at this age, pledged herself in secret to the convent of Santa Maria Stella Maris. Unfortunately for Catalina, her parents had other plans for her."

Gordon goes on to show us portraits of Catalina's father, her mother, and the Venetian gentleman she was betrothed to at age fourteen. I'm so caught up in the plight of poor Catalina—who studied Latin, Greek, and Hebrew in secret and wore a hair shirt under her silk dresses to mortify the flesh—that I don't at first notice Phoebe standing outside the French doors hissing my name. I try to ignore her, but she just gets louder. Afraid she'll ruin Gordon's lecture, I get up and step into the courtyard.

"That's my mother's dress," Phoebe says as soon as I'm outside. "I want to know where the hell you got it."

I'm about to hotly deny Phoebe's allegation when I remember that it had occurred to me earlier that the dress could have been left behind by a guest. Vera Nix did stay here. Still, Phoebe's tone annoys me. She's speaking to me as if I were a maid caught wearing her mistress's clothes.

"What makes you think that? You could hardly remember it; you were an infant when she died."

Even in the dimly lit courtyard I can see Phoebe's face turn red. I hadn't meant to offend her—after all, it's not her fault that her mother died when she was still a baby—but I realize that when Phoebe speaks about her mother she manages to create the impression that she knew her. Maybe she feels as if she did, having worked so closely with her journals, and the reminder that she really didn't know her mother diminishes her role as her biographer. I'm beginning to see how seriously Phoebe takes that role and I'm also beginning to wonder if I want to become as obsessed with my mother as Phoebe is with hers.

"There's a picture of her wearing it at The Stork Club," Phoebe tells me, resting a hand at her throat protectively, almost as if she's feeling for the pearls a woman would wear with such a dress, only her neck is bare. "And it's described in a society column. I believe it's a Dior."

"Well, this dress is a Balenciaga," I tell her, "but I'd be happy to discuss the dress's provenance after Gordon's lecture . . ." I use the term *provenance* to make her see how silly the whole issue is, but I've forgotten how humorless she is.

"It's not the only thing your mother stole from my mother," she says, "which I believe you'll see when you find your mother's third book . . ."

"I'm beginning to think there isn't a lost manuscript," I tell her.

"Maybe you just haven't looked hard enough because you're afraid of what you might find."

I sigh, exasperated by the argument. "Phoebe, if you're so sure there is a manuscript, why don't you look for it. I'd grant you free run of the place but you've already given it to yourself."

Phoebe's eyes widen and for a moment I'm afraid I've gone too far, that she'll ruin Gordon's lecture with a scene, but she turns without a word and leaves the courtyard. Apparently she has no intention of sitting through Gordon's lecture.

Back in the library I try to pick up the thread of Gordon's narrative, but he seems to have strayed from the story of Catalina della Rosa. Instead he is discussing a seventeenth-century painting depicting *The Marriage of the Sea*—a Venetian festival celebrating Venice's conquest of Dalmatia and subsequent maritime dominance. I lean back, thinking that perhaps I can get Hedda to tell me what happened to Catalina. Was she forced to give up her Latin and Greek to marry the Venetian nobleman? But Hedda's chair is empty.

Before I can scan the room to see where she moved, the sound of Catalina's name draws my attention back to Gordon.

"Catalina's marriage was to be celebrated at this festival. Here I usually show the bridal portrait of Catalina in her full parure, but tonight I will beg of you your patience and forbearance. I have a little surprise planned."

Gordon tugs on the right end of his bow tie and the right side of his mouth lifts in a half smile as if it were connected to his neck apparel. I notice that he exchanges a quick look with Natalie, who is seated in the front row, beaming proudly at Gordon. Perhaps this is why Phoebe is in such a state—she's jealous of Natalie, not my dress.

"Catalina's marriage ceremony was to take place directly after the nuptials between Venice and the sea, the culmination of which occurred when the reigning doge tossed an elaborate wedding ring into the waters off the Lido, reciting as he did the formula '*Desponsesumus te, mare, in signum veri perpetuique dominii.*' Which translates to 'We wed you sea, in the sign of our true and perpetual dominance.'"

"Imagine," Gordon says, pausing to look up at his audience, "the crowd's surprise when the young bride, Catalina della Rosa, rose from her place of honor beside the doge and, tearing her costly *ferronière* from her hair, tossed the pearls and diamonds into the sea, uttering in flawless Latin '*Spondeo me, Domine, in signum tui veri perpetuique dominii.*' A slight variation from the original formula, which means 'I pledge myself, Lord, as a sign of your true and eternal dominion.' And then—" Gordon pauses again, laying his hands flat on top of the lectern and leaning forward. "—she threw herself into the sea."

A rustle moves through the audience, like wind moving through trees, as we all imagine the young girl, so desperate to avoid an arranged marriage, drowning herself. I can almost picture the heavy silks dragging Catalina down to the bottom of the sea, and I find myself tugging at the tight seams of my dress and brushing the chiffon swag off my back where it clings to my hot skin. There's something too, almost familiar about the story, something about that image of pearls sinking under the water . . .

"Much to Catalina's disappointment, however, she didn't drown. She was fished out of the water rather ignominiously and packed off to the family palace where she suffered no more than a bad head cold. The fact that their daughter would rather drown than marry the man they had chosen for her failed to impress the della Rosas. Plans for her marriage continued apace until a remarkable incident—a miracle, many believed—occurred. On the day Catalina's marriage was to take place the pearl *ferronière* washed up at the convent of Santa Maria Stella Maris—the very convent Catalina had pledged herself to in secret. When the mother superior of the convent told Catalina's parents of this miracle Catalina was finally granted her wish. She was able to enter the order of Benedictine nuns, where she lived out her life in scholarly pursuits, the details of which would require more time than we have tonight.

"Instead, let us turn back to the pearl *ferronière*, whose miraculous reappearance saved Catalina from a loveless marriage. What became of it? Because it was considered the agent of miraculous intervention, the della Rosas gave the *ferronière* to the Convent of Santa Maria Stella Maris, where it was placed on the brow of a statue of the Virgin Mary. Now, you might think it odd to adorn a statue of the Virgin Mary with such an elaborate piece of jewelry, but remember, the use of the *ferronière* as an adornment for the Madonna was not without precedent."

Here Gordon flips backward in his slide collection to the Lippi Madonna.

"Of course the della Rosa *ferronière* was more elaborate than this one. It had diamonds, as well as pearls, and a large emerald tear-shaped briolette, but these features were readily absorbed into the iconography of Mary. And remember, this convent was dedicated to Mary Stella Maris—Mary, Star of the Sea—a metaphor for the Virgin going back to the thirteenth century. What better adornment for a statue of Mary Stella Maris than pearls, which come from the sea, and a sea-green emerald, bright as a star? Unfortunately the statue was destroyed during the war, but we do have a fifteenth-century painting by an unknown artist that we believe was inspired by the statue, depicting the della Rosa *ferronière*."

Gordon has to flip through several slides to get to the picture. Of all the paintings he's shown tonight this one is probably the least remarkable as a work of art. It looks like half a dozen portraits of Mary you might see on devotional cards, the colors cartoonish, the figure of the Madonna somewhat lumpish, the composition awkward. She's sitting on a rock in front of a vista of sea and sky, looking for all the world as if she's on a picnic at the beach. What takes my breath away, though, is the ornament in her hair. A net of pearls and diamonds holds back her hair and drapes over her forehead, ending in a tear-shaped emerald.

"As you can see, not only is the face of Mary copied from Catalina's portrait, the *ferronière* is the same one worn by Catalina della Rosa in her bridal portrait."

The portrait of Mary shifts to the right side of the screen and on the left side appears the portrait of Catalina della Rosa in her bridal parure, her green eyes set off by the enormous emerald briolette resting in the middle of her forehead.

"And the same," Gordon says, signaling for Natalie to turn on the lights, "as the necklace worn by our gracious hotel manager, Miss Iris Greenfeder."

As the lights go on the audience turns toward me.

"Perhaps if you'd stand up . . ." Gordon is saying, but I'm already up and approaching the screen where the two images have grown paler in the light.

"Remarkable, isn't it?" Gordon asks me. "Natalie noticed it first when I was showing her the slides for the show."

"Is that the original della Rosa *ferronière?*" a woman in the audience asks.

I turn around and find myself the focus of the room's attention.

"No, not at all," Gordon explains. "The original della Rosa *ferronière* remained in the convent of Santa Maria Stella Maris until the outbreak of the Second World War. We think the abbot hid the necklace in the catacombs below the church to keep it from the Nazis, but unfortunately the church was bombed in the last days of the war and the necklace was not found in the rubble. The abbot had been killed by sniper fire only hours before the church was destroyed. Most authorities believe it was destroyed, but there is another theory that the *ferronière* was removed from the church and hidden in a villa south of Venice that belonged to a descendant of the della Rosa family. I'm in the process of researching that possibility . . ."

"Where'd you get that necklace, Miss Greenfeder," one of the restitution claims lawyers asks me in a rather challenging tone of voice. It's the second time tonight I've been accused of wearing stolen property. Fortunately Natalie Baehr comes to my rescue.

"It's only glass and paste," she says, standing and turning to address the crowd. "I copied it from a description in a story that Professor Greenfeder's mother wrote."

"Well, then," the lawyer asks, "where did your mother see the necklace—if it's been missing since the war?"

I turn to Gordon for help. I can see that his "little surprise" isn't going as he had anticipated, but he maintains a calm I wouldn't have thought him capable of. "We don't know," he says, "but I imagine she saw a copy of the Stella Maris Mary, which is widely copied and hung in churches dedicated to Mary, Star of the Sea."

"Yes," I say, the pieces finally coming together, "there's a St. Mary Star of the Sea in Brooklyn. My mother had me christened there because that's where she was christened."

"There we are!" Gordon says to me, and then, turning, addresses the room. "We've solved at least one mystery of provenance tonight. The provenance of an image." Gordon lays his hand on my elbow and with his other hand motions for me to return to my seat. I feel like the volunteer in a magic show dismissed from the stage. I sit down, too dazed to follow the rest of Gordon's lecture.

When the lecture is over I follow the rest of the guests out to the terrace, which has been set up for predinner cocktails. I should be checking to make sure everything is running smoothly in the kitchen and dining room, and that Harry's plans for the fireworks are in place, but instead I take a glass of champagne from the bar and sit down in Half Moon. I sit in the semicircle that faces the hotel and look up at the glowing facade. It looks like a fairy-tale palace tonight, illuminated by the floodlights Harry had installed just last week. The chandelier on the second-floor landing is ablaze with candlelight, each crystal drop glittering like a tear.

I notice Jack standing on the edge of a group, looking at me, and pat the seat next to mine to invite him over.

"I wasn't sure if I'd make your boyfriend jealous," he says, sitting down next to me.

"For one thing, I don't think he's my boyfriend anymore, and for another, I haven't seen him around."

I see Jack struggling with the urge to ask more questions but, to his credit, he changes the subject. "You must be excited about Gordon's discovery. Another clue to your mother's life and art."

I take a sip of champagne and look up at the second-floor window. A few guests are standing on the landing, no doubt admiring the chandelier. "It made me feel like an idiot," I say. "All these years I've been tracing the influence of fairy tales and Irish folk legends on her work and I never thought to look at the church. A Catholic girl from Brooklyn! I've never even been to that church, St. Mary Star of the Sea, except for when I was three."

"Well, you'll go now. I bet that portrait is there and something about Catalina della Rosa—who knows, maybe they've got a piece of her in a box . . . a whattayacallit . . ."

"A reliquary," I say. "That's what this whole project of mine is beginning to feel like. A grab bag of relics of my mother. A bag of bones. Do you know, Phoebe Nix warned me not to write something that might show her mother in an unfavorable light? Then, tonight, she accused me of wearing her mother's dress." I don't tell Jack that the dress might actually have belonged to Vera Nix.

"She sounds like a nut job."

"Exactly. Look at what a lifetime of living in her mother's shadow has done to her. I don't want to end up like her."

"Then maybe you should get away from here. Why don't we go back to the city, Iris." I feel Jack's hand on mine. I know it's the moment I should turn to him—he's giving me a chance to repair the rupture between us—but instead I find my eyes glued to the tableau unfolding on the second-floor landing. The knot of guests has dispersed, replaced by a lone figure—a slim woman in a plain, straight dress. It's hard to tell from here, with the chandelier candlelight between us, but I think it's Phoebe Nix.

"Damn, Jack, look, I think that's Phoebe outside Joseph's door. She's been pestering him all week to get him to tell her more about her mother when she was up here. I bet she's going to ask him if he remembers her wearing this dress."

The door to Joseph's suite opens, but I can't see who's there. The lights must be off in the living area. Phoebe goes into the room for a moment but comes out quickly, closes the door behind her and walks away, toward the elevators. A few minutes later I see another figure coming from the direction of the elevators—not Phoebe, though; a man.

"Isn't that your friend?" Jack says. At some point Jack's hand lifted off mine. I didn't notice until now.

"Yes, that's Aidan. He's probably returning a painting to the locked closet." I notice, though, that Aidan isn't carrying anything. He pauses outside Joseph's door and then lets himself in, leaving the door open. Then he disappears into the dark room.

I turn away from the brightly lit window and see that Jack has been watching me all along. "You didn't answer my question, Iris. About coming back to the city with me."

Over Jack's shoulder I see the dark valley and the lights along the river. Little specks of light—like fireflies—spangle the air above the river too and for a moment I think the fireworks display that Harry has planned for tonight has already started, but then I blink and the lights go away. They were only the afterimage of the chandelier candles I'd been staring at. I look back at Jack to give my answer, but before I can a sharp crack rends the still night air.

"It must be the fireworks," I say, looking back over the valley.

Jack shakes his head. "It came from the hotel."

I turn so quickly that the chiffon swag on my dress catches on the rough wood of the bench and I hear something tear. A figure on the second-floor landing is walking, no, stumbling, toward the window. For a moment he's caught in the light of a hundred candles and then the light seems to explode around him. I think it's the chandelier falling, but it's the reflection of the chandelier in the window splintering into a million shards as the man on the landing falls through the glass.

I'm standing before I remember getting up and kneeling beside the man who is splayed out on the terrace before I realize I've even started moving. Splinters of glass dig into my knees and the palm of my left hand, which I use to steady myself as I use my right hand to gingerly feel for a pulse, but I don't need the silence of his flesh to tell me that Joseph is dead.

PART III

The Selkie's Daughter

Chapter Twenty-four

A week after Joseph died I took the train back to the city. I was surprised to see that the trees along the Palisades were still green. It felt like years since I had glimpsed the first hints of autumn color in the woods behind the hotel and for a moment I imagined that I had somehow fallen asleep and missed the turning of the year only to awaken in a new spring. If only I could go back to this past spring, I thought, back to the night Aidan showed up on my doorstep, back to the train ride when I promised to help get him the job at the hotel. But there would be no going back. Joseph was dead and Aidan was gone, wanted for his murder.

When we finally got into Joseph's suite—I was reluctant to leave Joseph on the terrace even though it was clear that nothing could be done for him and it took some time before Harry was able to get up from the ledge where he had been checking the fireworks preparations—it was empty. The Hudson River School paintings were gone, although the lock on the closet showed no signs of forced entry. There were some signs of struggle in the living area: a broken lamp, an overturned chair, one of Joseph's crutches lying on the floor, a splotch of fresh blood on the carpet near where the crutch lay. Even before the DNA tests confirmed that the blood belonged to Aidan (cross-matched with samples from his prison record), the detective from Kingston had already established a fairly convincing scenario for what had happened in Joseph's suite.

It was not my evidence alone that placed Aidan in the suite minutes before the gunshot was heard. When questioned, Phoebe admitted—somewhat reluctantly, I noticed—that she had passed him in the hall after she left Joseph's suite. "He told me that he was making a last check on the paintings as per Harry's orders."

Harry denied that he had sent Aidan on any such mission. "In fact, I hadn't seen the boy all evening and I was annoyed that he wasn't downstairs supervising such an important event."

Of course, no one knew exactly what had happened once Aidan entered the suite. I told Detective March twice that it was too dark inside the room to see anything from where I was on the terrace. When he asked the question a third time Jack interrupted and told the detective that he'd been sitting right next to me on the terrace and what I said was true: you could see the hallway on the second-floor landing because it was lit by the chandelier, but the lights must have been off in Joseph's suite and you couldn't see into it from where we were seated.

"But at least you were facing the window when the gun was fired?" Detective March asked Jack. "While Ms. Greenfeder was . . ."

"I was looking out over the valley," I said. "I thought the sound was the beginning of the fireworks display, but then Jack said it came from the hotel . . ."

"Can you tell us if you saw Joseph Krupah leave the room before or after the gun was fired?" Detective March asked Jack.

"I'm not sure, but I think he was in the doorway, or maybe a foot or two into the hall, when I heard the sound. He was limping and I thought, *What's he doing out without his crutches?* and then when I heard the sound he fell forward, toward the window, and then he fell through it."

The gun was found two days later, caught in some brush on the ledge below the terrace—as if someone had tried to throw it off the side of the mountain but hadn't thrown it far enough. It was Harry Kron's gun—reported to the police as stolen a month earlier—and it had been wiped clean of fingerprints.

"Would Mr. Barry have had access to your suite the night your gun was stolen?" Detective March asked Harry when the gun was found. He'd asked Harry and me to meet with him in the Sleepy Hollow Suite, which had been cordoned off as a crime scene since the night of the murder. I hadn't been in the suite since that night and I'd expected to feel uneasy because of the blood on the carpet or the remains of fingerprinting powder that still lingered on the furniture and woodwork, but what upset me most was sitting in the same seat by the window where I had sat only a week before talking to Joseph, under the specter of the Headless Horseman whose fiery severed head seemed to leer at me from the painted wall. Now Detective March sat in the wing-backed chair where Joseph had sat, Harry sat in the matching chair on the other side of the window, and I was perched on the footstool in between the two.

"I leave it to my manager to decide who has a master key," Harry said, deferring the question to me.

"He shouldn't have had one that night," I said, "because Mr. Kron hadn't promoted him to special-events coordinator yet . . . he was just working in the garden . . ."

"And you don't generally give out master keys to the gardening staff?" Detective March asked me with barely disguised disdain. I was convinced he had taken a dislike to me the minute I confessed that I'd looked away from the window at the crucial moment and that aversion was strengthened when I explained that I had knowingly hired an ex-convict to work in the hotel.

"No, but all the maids have master keys . . ."

I saw Detective March write something in his notebook and guessed that it was a note to question all the maids as to whether or not they had given their master keys to anyone that night. I knew that Paloma would probably lie for me and deny giving me her key that night, but I guessed that she would lie badly and that the lie would cost her. I'd seen too many maids called into my father's office after a guest had reported some valuable item stolen from his or her room. I'd seen them come out, their faces bleached with fear and guilt, even the ones who were exonerated hours later when the watch or billfold showed up in the guest's own pocket.

"I lost my key that night," I told the detective, meeting his eyes as he looked up from his notebook, not out of bravery but because it was easier to face his antipathy than the look of disappointment in Harry's face. "I think I lost it in the library where Gordon del Sarto was giving his lecture that night."

"I believe Mr. Barry helped set up the slides for that," Harry said.

"So Mr. Barry might have found the key and let himself into Mr. Kron's suite . . ."

"But why? I mean, I know how much Aidan wanted to avoid going back to prison. He wrote a beautiful essay about it . . ." The look on Detective March's face stops me from further praising Aidan's eloquent rendition of Tam Lin.

"That's very nice, Ms. Greenfeder. I'm glad to know my tax dollars are going toward teaching prisoners to express themselves. Tell me, do you know why Mr. Barry was in prison?"

"He told me he was in a car with his cousin that turned out to be stolen and to have stolen guns in the trunk. He said he didn't know about the guns, but he did know his cousin was involved in raising money for the IRA."

Detective March made a choking sound in the back of his throat, which I supposed was his version of a laugh. "Uh-huh. Did he mention that when the car was pulled over he ran?"

"No, but . . ."

"And that the officer who pursued him was hit by another vehicle and died?"

I shook my head no.

"Sort of impulsive, your friend Aidan Barry. Flighty, you might say."

I remembered the look in Aidan's eyes when he asked me if he should leave. The sense I'd had of him poised for flight. Maybe he thought the paintings were his chance for a new life. At least that's what Detective March thought.

"This is what I figure happened," he told Harry and me. "Aidan Barry probably didn't have any definite plans when he stole Mr. Kron's gun but guys like him like to have a gun in reserve, just in case. When you so conveniently presented him with a key he naturally used it to check out his boss's room and when he came across the gun he took it for a rainy day—excuse the cliché, Ms. Greenfeder, English never was my best subject, unlike our Mr. Barry. I remember you English teachers hate clichés, but in this case I can't think of a better way of putting it, can you?"

I shook my head no. Great, I thought, on top of being a poor witness and having an irresponsible hiring policy, I had apparently offended Detective March by being an English teacher. No doubt I was paying for some martinet grammar-queen he'd had in the eighth grade.

"So he waits around to see what'll turn up at this nice hotel of yours." Detective March waved his hand toward the view of the rose garden as if to illustrate what a "nice" hotel it really was, only the garden was not looking its best. True to Joseph's last orders, the limited water supply had been allocated only to the perennials. The annual borders were dying and the grass was beginning to brown. The whole garden seemed to have gone into mourning for the dead gardener.

"You know I probably shouldn't admit this, being an officer of the law, but I used to sneak in here during the summers and swim at your lake. A lot of the local kids did it. I thought this place looked like Paradise. But I bet it didn't look as good to Mr. Barry as those paintings did. How much did you say they're worth, Mr. Kron?"

"Well, of course it always depends on the market. American landscapes have enjoyed a resurgence of interest lately . . ."

"A ballpark figure, Mr. Kron."

"Several million at least, I'd say four and a half million altogether at auction, but of course, on the black market it's hard to say."

"Well, a couple of million anyway. And your Mr. Barry is not unconnected." When he said *your Mr. Barry* he looked directly at me. "That story about gun smuggling wasn't a total fabrication—he does have some ties to the IRA, which as you may or may not know has been linked to art theft rings before."

"Ah yes," Harry interrupted, "I believe there's a theory that the Isabella Stewart Gardner robbery was engineered by the IRA . . ."

"So when he sees all these expensive paintings," Detective March went on, ignoring Harry, "—and we know from a Mr. Ramsey of the Cornell Gallery that Aidan Barry discussed with him the monetary value of one of the paintings—he decides that maybe hotel work's not quite the line for him after all. Maybe retiring to the Cayman Islands is more up his alley. I think about it myself some days, especially when another winter's bearing down—it gets awfully cold up here, as I'm sure you remember from your childhood, Ms. Greenfeder."

The detective paused so I could nod and when he still didn't say anything I wondered if I was supposed to reminisce with him about record-setting snows and blizzards of our youth. Or maybe I was supposed to break down and confess that the thought of spending another winter up here at this lonely hotel drove me to engineer an art heist with Aidan and I was only waiting to make my getaway to the Caribbean. I didn't say anything and, finally, Detective March continued with his imagined scenario.

"And look how easy it is." Now he gestured in the direction of the closet, which had been closed and locked. "A couple of million dollars' worth of art in a closet, guarded by an old crippled gardener. Let's give Mr. Barry some credit. He probably didn't figure that the old gardener would give him any trouble. He probably figured he'd be asleep. All he'd have to do is let himself into the suite—" Detective March got up and went to the front door of the suite, miming Aidan coming into the room. "—which he'd been doing all week, open the closet—" The detective took a key out of his pocket and opened the closet door, which swung into the wing of Harry's chair. "—which he also had a key for, and pack up the paintings and slip out of town. Probably had a friend with a car waiting down the road a bit. Unfortunately, Mr. Krupah wasn't asleep. Your niece told us that, Mr. Kron. She'd visited Mr. Krupah to ask him a question a few minutes before she passed Aidan Barry in the hall. I didn't quite get what the question was about. Something to do with a stolen dress?"

I sighed and prepared myself to explain the dress incident to Detective Marsh, but he held up a hand to stop me. "No matter. Miss Nix bent my ear about that dress for half an hour yesterday. I believe she would like me to shelve this murder investigation to find out who stole her mother's dress fifty years ago. All I care about is that five minutes before Aidan Barry let himself into this suite, Joseph Krupah was in the living room talking to Miss Nix about her mother's dress. Miss Nix said that he told her he was going to bed, but it would have taken him a few minutes to get down the hall between the living room and his bedroom, so when Mr. Barry let himself in Mr. Krupah was still in the hallway. Ms. Greenfeder, you be Mr. Krupah."

Detective March signaled for me to follow him across the living room and into the hallway that led to the suite's bedroom. He partially closed the door and left me there. I heard him ask Harry to "be Mr. Barry." I heard a door close and then Detective March whispering something to Harry that I couldn't catch. Then I heard a click and something creaked.

"Did you hear the door open, Ms. Greenfeder?" I told him I had. "Now come in."

I entered the living area and saw Harry standing at the closet door, his back to me. For a moment I didn't see the detective, but then I saw him standing between the closet door and the wing-backed chair, craning his head around to see the scene he'd set up. "As you can see, the minute Mr. Krupah entered the living room he'd see what Mr. Barry was up to. He knew that the paintings were locked in for the night, that Mr. Barry had no business coming back for them. I bet he always had his suspicions about Mr. Barry and it rubbed him the wrong way to see this punk stealing the paintings. I guess he was a pretty loyal employee, this Joseph." Detective March paused for Harry and me to concur. Harry, his back still turned to me, murmured something, but I couldn't open my mouth. *Loyal employee*. Is that how I'd sum up what Joseph had meant to the hotel and my family for the last fifty years?

"I think Joseph Krupah tried to avert the robbery. Not a very smart thing to do, but you've got to admire the old guy. He hits Mr. Barry over the head with his crutch—" Detective March came out from behind the door and raised his arm over Harry's unsuspecting head, bringing it down within an inch of his bald crown. "He must have given him a pretty good crack given the amount of blood on the carpet." We all looked down—Harry turning from the open closet—to look at the dark spot on the carpet.

"Thinking that Mr. Barry was unconscious, Mr. Krupah headed for the door to go for help." Detective March crossed the room and opened the door to the hallway. I could see the boarded-up window on the landing and a guest walking toward the elevators. "Only Mr. Barry regained consciousness when Joseph was still in the doorway and, thinking to stop the witness to his crime, he took out his gun and fired. Remarkably, the impact of the bullet didn't knock him down immediately. He was still on his feet, still trying to get away—" Detective March lunged into the hall, with Harry and me following at his heels, startling the Eden sisters who had been ascending the stairs. Detective March bowed to them and went on with his story, on the landing, with the Eden sisters hovering—no doubt eavesdropping— in the hallway. "—but unfortunately, he ran straight for the landing and lost his balance there. That's when he fell through the window. Aidan Barry gathered up his paintings, went down the back staircase—by that time the commotion on the terrace had brought all the guests and staff out of the kitchen and dining room—and left by the west side of the hotel where he probably had an accomplice waiting for him. We figure they headed to Canada on the back roads. We alerted the Canadian border patrol before morning but unfortunately our friends to the north aren't always as vigilant as we could hope."

I pictured Aidan driving north, the sun coming up over the Adirondack Mountains. It reminded me of another sunrise.

"How'd he carry them?"

"I beg your pardon?"

Detective March was already walking away from the window, his performance completed.

"The paintings. There were six of them, including a huge skyscape of dawn that Aidan could barely carry by itself. How did he get all six of those paintings down the stairs by himself?"

"That's a good question, Ms. Greenfeder. Maybe he had help—it would be worth noting whether any of your staff or management has any sudden influx in wealth over the next year. We'll keep an eye on that. In the meantime, perhaps we should do another search of the hotel and grounds in case

Mr. Barry stashed any of the paintings in the hopes of returning for them. I'm afraid it will cause some disruption to your guests . . ."

"I'm closing the hotel this weekend," Harry said, "so feel free to look to your heart's content. In fact, the staff and I will help you."

"Closing the hotel?" I repeated. It was the first I'd heard of it. I looked down the hall to see if the Eden sisters were still listening in but to my relief they had vanished. I knew they were planning to stay through the fall.

"I'm sorry, Iris, I'd meant to tell you, but Detective March has kept me so busy these last few days. Don't look so stricken; I don't mean to close it for good. I'd planned to get an early start on renovations and this unfortunate tragedy has simply accelerated my plans. We had only a handful of bookings for September—no groups, nobody very important—and there's sure to be a pall over the hotel because of the tragedy. We'll use the time to refurbish—we'll strip the woodwork, redo the floors, paint, and tear up all the old drapes and carpets. When we reopen next May you won't recognize the place. And although I know you won't believe me now, even this sadness over Joseph will have passed. After all, he wasn't a young man. Of course I know how distraught you are now. Why don't you take some time off? Go back to the city. I don't need you for the renovations—although of course you'll be kept on salary through the winter . . ."

I know I should appreciate Harry's generosity, but it's one of the things that nags at me all the way down the Hudson, the idea of being on the hotel's payroll while I'm leaving it to be gutted by the renovators. I'm not sure whom I think I'm letting down—Joseph, who's beyond my help, Aunt Sophie, who's already gone to Florida to join the Mandelbaums, or the hotel itself. It looked, in my last glimpse of it from the train station, so insubstantial and improbable, a white temple perched on a cliff above the Hudson, that I already feel as if it's a place I made up and that when I try to find my way back it will have been swallowed up by the forest, folded back into the mountains.

Certainly, when I climb the ramp up into Grand Central and run into the crush of northbound commuters, the stale smell of the city summer rising off them, it's hard to believe such a place of grace and coolness exists. Crossing the main hall I remember that when my mother embarked on her first journey north she said that the hotel seemed as distant to her as the constellations in the teal-vaulted ceiling. Did she feel, when she came back that last time, as I do now: as if returned from a trip to the moon?

By the time I've made it to the taxi queue outside I'm drenched in sweat and gasping in the fetid air. I try to shift the suitcase to my left hand, but my hand's still bandaged from the glass cuts I got on the terrace kneeling beside Joseph. I can feel too that the bandages on my knees have come loose, and that my jeans are rubbing against the scabs. When I finally sink gratefully into the torn upholstery of an un-air-conditioned cab I can see a moist dark crescent below each knee where the blood has spread. I roll down the window and watch the city passing by. The sepulchral white marble of the main library, the plane trees in Bryant Park, their leaves limp and rusty, the fruit and vegetable stands in Hell's Kitchen, the Red Branch Pub on Ninth where I stood with Aidan that night we walked back from the station together. When I realize I'm scanning the faces of the pedestrians for him I close the window, despite the heat, lean back in my seat, and concentrate on the meter for the rest of the trip.

After I pay the cab, I stand for a minute on the corner, looking across West Street to the river, gathering my strength for the five flights of stairs up to my apartment. Or, I admit, gathering myself to face the emptiness that waits for me in the little tower room I've loved so much all these years. I've never come home with such a sense of disappointment before. With each flight of stairs I find myself more and more reluctant to face that empty room. I've always returned to it as to a cloister, a place of quiet where I could finally turn away from the distractions of the world and write. This was the world I'd made for myself, an empty tower room with a view of the river, a place where what happened to my mother would never happen to me. I'd never have to flee the distractions of husband and child because I'd never have those things. What had Phoebe said? *Haven't you lived your whole life based on what you thought you knew about your mother's story? No marriage. No children . . . You've avoided everything you thought killed her.*

When I open the door, though, I'm greeted by light and air. The suffocating cell I've been dreading is instead open to the sky and river. I'm so relieved by how welcoming it looks that it takes me a minute to realize why it's not so lonely. It's because I'm not alone. Stretched out below the open windows on my couch, his forearm flung over his eyes to block out the late-afternoon light, is Aidan, fast asleep.

Chapter Twenty-five

I could back out, go downstairs, and call the police. I have plenty of time to think about it, standing there in the doorway, watching Aidan sleep. Long enough for the sun to lower toward the New Jersey skyline across the river. I have plenty of reasons too, which I list to myself as the light on Aidan's face and arm changes from gold to red. The red calls to mind the blood on the terrace after they moved Joseph's body and the splotch of blood on the carpet in Joseph's suite. I notice a bandage on Aidan's fore- head, black sutures creeping under the edges of the white gauze. So this isn't the first place he came to; he's had other help. What, then, is he do- ing here?

That's what finally makes me decide to close the door and sit down at my desk. If, as Detective March insisted, Aidan is so well connected, he'd have no reason to be here. Although I'm already schooling myself against believing everything he says—remember the DNA tests, I think, remember you saw him go into Joseph's room—I still want to hear his story.

He sleeps so long, though, that I grow impatient—and hungry. I meant to go to the Korean grocer on the corner once I dropped my bags off, but I'm afraid that if I leave he'll be gone when I get back. When I check the refrigerator I find eggs and milk with current expiration dates and a box of McCann's Irish Oatmeal double sealed in plastic bags on the counter. I find this last detail hopelessly endearing—he's a man on the run, but still he's careful not to attract bugs. I notice too that the few dishes he's used have been washed and left to dry on the drying rack, the dishcloth folded neatly on the counter.

It's the smell of cooking food that finally wakes him. I'm facing the stove, my back to the couch, when I hear him speak.

"I suppose it's a positive sign you've not called the police," he says, "or is that a last meal you're cooking me?"

I bring over the plates of eggs and toast and two mugs of tea—strong with milk and sugar the way he takes it. I usually have mine plain, but I remember from Barbara Pym's novels that sweet tea's supposed to be the thing for shock and I'm expecting to hear at least a few surprises when Aidan starts talking. At least, I'm hoping that what he says will surprise me. The alternative is that I already know the whole story from Detective March.

He makes room for me on the couch, but I pull my desk chair over instead. He rakes his hair back from his forehead and I can see how far the sutures go back along his scalp.

"Joseph gave you quite a knock," I say, sipping my tea and pretending when I wince that it's from the heat of the liquid.

"Is that how the police figure it?" he asks. "That Joseph did this?" He points to his forehead and then shakes his head. "Joseph didn't hit me."

"Then who did?"

"I don't know. All I know is that it was the same person who shot Joseph."

I take another sip of tea. "I saw you from the terrace," I tell him. "I saw you go into Joseph's room and then five minutes later we heard a gunshot and Jack said he saw Joseph run out the door and then fall through the window."

Aidan nods. I notice he hasn't touched his food. He's lost weight in the week since I've seen him, and grown pale again. He's gotten that same hollow look he had when he was in prison. "Jack said," he repeats. "Why am I not surprised?"

"Jack would have no reason to lie about what he saw. I'd already told him it was over between him and me." It's only half a lie. It's what I'd been about to tell Jack when the gun was fired and it is what I told him the next day.

"No, he wasn't lying," Aidan says. "I imagine that's what it looked like from where you two were sitting and I doubt I'll be able to convince you otherwise. Do you want me to tell you my story, or are you content with the police's version?"

"I'll try to keep an open mind," I say.

Aidan leans forward on the couch and I think for a moment that he's reaching for my hand, but he's only reaching for his cup of tea. He folds his hands around the mug, as if to keep his hands warm, or maybe just to keep his hands busy, because he holds the cup while he tells me his story without ever taking a sip from it.

"As soon as I went into the suite, I knew something was wrong. The room was dark and the wall switch didn't work. I tried a lamp on the coffee table and it didn't work either."

"The lights were still out when Harry and I went into the suite, but they were working. We turned them on."

"I've thought about that. Someone could have thrown the circuit breaker for the second floor. Most of the guests were at the party so no one would have noticed. I thought about going for a flashlight, but there was enough light coming through the windows—remember Harry had put in all those floodlights in the garden—to check the paintings."

"They were all there?"

"I think so. I was counting them—just to make sure—when someone hit me from behind and I fell down onto the floor."

"So how do you know it wasn't Joseph who hit you if you didn't see who it was?"

"Because the minute I hit the carpet I saw the door to the bedroom open and Joseph came in—no mistaking him with that limp. He saw me on the carpet, but instead of coming toward me he headed for the door. It scared me because I figured whatever—or whoever—he saw behind me had scared him. I tried to turn over to get a look behind me, but someone stepped on the back of my head. Hard. Right where I'd been hit already. I think I started blacking out. I remember, though, a block of light and some-one standing in it—bloody thought I was heading down the tunnel of light toward my final reward—but then something exploded and the figure in the light looked like he was flying toward the window. I think I did black out for a minute then, because when I came to the pressure on my head was gone and I was alone in the room. Alone in a room where a couple of million dollars' worth of paintings had just been stolen and a gun had gone off—I could smell it. It didn't take too much imagination to see the picture that was taking shape. I ran. Took off down the back staircase and went through the servants' wing—out the side and down through the woods. I got down to the Agway at the foot of the mountain and called some friends in the city to come pick me up—by morning the story was out and I knew Joseph was dead. I was sorry, Iris, I couldn't be with you. I know how he loved you."

He comes to a stop—winded from just the memory of all that running. I feel breathless too. All the light has seeped out of the sky outside and I can smell the river—a dank, low-tide smell. The uneaten eggs on both our plates have grown cold. I get up and take the plates to the sink.

"I don't blame you for not believing me," he says. "I didn't really expect you to, but I wanted to tell you. I had to tell you."

I turn around, lifting my hands, palms up, like some statue of impartial justice. "Why would someone else shoot Joseph? If you didn't kill him, who did?"

"Whoever hit me over the head and took the paintings. When I fell the sound woke Joseph and he came running in."

It's a plausible theory, and I would like more than anything to take it at face value, but I can't. "But why were you there in the first place? Harry said he didn't ask you to check on the paintings . . ."

"Well, no, he didn't ask me directly, that harebrained niece of his did."

"Phoebe?"

"Yes. I met her in the hall on my way down to the party. Did she fail to mention that to the police?"

"No, she said she saw you, and that you told her Harry had asked you to check on the paintings."

Aidan stares into his cup as if trying to read the tea leaves through the cold, murky liquid and then he shakes his head.

"You know, I had a feeling she was lying. Something about the way she insisted I turn right around and go back to the suite. When I was unlocking the door I noticed she was still standing in the hall as if checking to make sure I was following her orders."

I sit down on the couch beside Aidan and, closing my eyes, picture the second-floor hallway. It was one of my favorite places to play as a child because the landing there was wider and the chandelier was so beautiful to look at . . . and something else . . . because if I waited long enough I might see my mother there.

"Where was she standing?" I ask Aidan.

"What? I told you, in the hall . . ."

"*Where* in the hall. Down by the elevators?"

"No, closer. At the next door, I think."

"The door to the suite's bedroom?" I ask.

Aidan looks up from his tea. "You're thinking Phoebe let herself into the bedroom side of the suite, waited for me to open the closet door, and hit me over the head? But why?"

"Because she wanted something out of the locked closet. Remember when she came into the suite and was surprised that there was a closet on that side of the suite?"

Aidan nods and I notice that a little color has come back into his pale skin. "She spent the rest of that week dogging my steps," he says. "I thought she was just being a noodge—" I smile at the Yiddish expression—one I'm sure Aidan picked up from my aunt. "—but maybe she was waiting for a chance to get into that closet. Do you think it was the paintings she was after?"

"No, I think it was my mother's third book. I think she looked for it the first time she stayed in the suite—that's why those drawers were broken and the floorboards in the hall closet were loosened."

"But what would give her the idea that it was in the suite in the first place?"

"Her parents stayed in the suite right below it—Sunnyside." I close my eyes again to picture the landing outside the Sleepy Hollow Suite and I see the image from my dream: a door vibrating to the sound of typing. That's why I liked to play in that hallway—my mother must have used that suite to type and I got used to hanging outside for a glimpse of her. "Maybe Vera Nix heard my mother typing in there and mentioned it in her journals and it gave Phoebe the idea that the last manuscript was hidden there . . ." I stop midsentence and groan.

"What is it?"

"The first line of the selkie story—*in a land between the sun and the moon*—the Sleepy Hollow Suite is above Sunnyside and one floor below Half Moon. It's between the sun and the moon. I can't believe Phoebe figured that out and I didn't."

"But why would Phoebe want *your* mother's book so much?"

"Well, if Vera Nix was afraid there was something in the book that she didn't want known, Phoebe might also want to protect her mother's secret. After all, Phoebe's based her whole career on presenting her mother in a certain light."

"But what could Vera Nix have done that was that bad?"

I notice that Aidan and I have switched roles—that he's become the interrogator and I've become the apologist—trying to make a case for his own innocence. And if I can't? In the silence that follows I imagine Aidan making his next plan. Where will he go from here? I already know I don't have the heart to turn him in, but I also know that I can't help him. I hope for his sake that Detective March was right and that he is well connected. I don't think I could bear the thought of him being back in prison—or worse. I remember Elspeth McCrory's lurid headline that I'd read in the *Poughkeepsie Journal*: "Woman Visiting Inmate at Prison Killed in Train Accident." I think I have an idea now of how Rose McGlynn must have felt.

"What did you say?"

I hadn't realized I'd spoken out loud. "I'm sorry, I was just remembering this horrible story about a woman who killed herself after visiting her brother in prison."

"Thanks for that cheerful thought. I don't expect you to kill yourself, Iris, but it'd be nice if you baked a cake once in a while. Maybe I could take your class again . . ."

"Aidan, wait a minute. There is something that her mother might have done that would be pretty bad. Phoebe mentioned it herself—only to deny it. She said that when John McGlynn—that's the fellow whose sister killed herself—was on trial he claimed that Vera Nix paid him to steal her own jewelry so they could split the money from selling it. No one believed him, but what if it was true?"

"It wouldn't be the first time some rich person paid for her valuables to be stolen so she could collect on the insurance and split the profits with the thief. If this Vera Nix was hard up for cash . . ."

"Phoebe said the press made up stories about her using drugs, but Harry said she did have a drug problem. If the stories weren't made up . . ."

"She might have been supporting a habit. She might have owed money to people who didn't take kindly to having their loans reneged on. But if no one believed that John McGlynn fellow at his trial why would Phoebe worry about it coming out now?"

"My mother worked at the Crown Hotel where the jewelry was stolen from. She knew Rose and John McGlynn. She was traveling with Rose the day she threw herself under that train."

Aidan sits up a little straighter and leans toward me, so close I can see the dark smudges under his eyes and feel his breath on my face. "So if your mother knew that Vera Nix set up John McGlynn she might have written about it in her last book."

"Still, it's only a fantasy book. There is this whole story about a piece of jewelry being stolen, and I suppose it could have been based on the Crown jewel robbery—and there is this woman in a green dress like the dress I wore that Phoebe claimed belonged to her mother. Maybe the woman in the story is Vera Nix and we find out in Book Three—*The Selkie's Daughter*—that she was behind the robbery, but still it's a fantasy novel. Who is going to put all that together now?"

"But that summer Phoebe's mother came to stay at the hotel. What if your mother confronted Vera Nix with what she knew then?"

"It still would have been my mother's word against hers."

"Maybe your mother had some way of proving that Vera Nix was involved in the robbery. Who knows—she was a maid at that hotel—maybe she found a letter Vera Nix wrote. Think, Iris, what happened to your mother after that summer?"

"You know what happened, Aidan. She died in a hotel fire with another man."

"You told me they didn't find the remains of the man in the room where she died. What if she wasn't meeting a man? What if she was meeting Vera Nix to hand over whatever proof she had?"

Aidan touches the side of my face and it's only then I realize how hot my skin is. I feel like I'm burning up. As if the fire that had consumed my mother is consuming me. "Are you saying you think Vera Nix murdered my mother?" It comes out as a whisper, as if I'm afraid the words might ignite in the open air.

"I'm saying it's a possibility that Phoebe Nix thinks she did. And she thought Joseph knew where your mother was going that night and who she was going to see . . . what's wrong?"

Now instead of feeling hot, I feel cold, as if I had jumped into icy water to douse the fire under my skin. "That day she came into the suite—remember, when you were moving the sky painting? Well, after you went out she asked me if Joseph had told me who my mother was going to see the night she died. I didn't tell her he had, but I let her think that he would tell me if I really wanted to know. And then at the lecture that night I practically dared her to find the manuscript. If she did kill Joseph, it's my fault, Aidan, it wasn't just that he was standing between her and the manuscript—I made her see him as a threat."

"We still don't know that's what happened, and even if it did, you couldn't have known that she was crazy enough about her mother's reputation to kill to preserve it." He still has his hand against my face. I bow my head so that my forehead rests in the palm of his hand, his flesh cool against my brow. He slides his arm around my shoulders and pulls me closer to him on the couch.

"I should have known," I murmur into his neck. "I, of all people, know what it means to be obsessed by a mother who died young. I'm as bad as she is—pursuing my mother's story until the pursuit got Joseph killed and you wanted for murder—but I can't stop now. I have to figure out exactly what happened at the Crown in 1949 that could have made someone kill my mother at the Dreamland Hotel in 1973. I think, then, we'll know who killed Joseph."

"It sounds like a lot of work," he says, stroking the hair away from my face. "Do you want me to go now?"

I look into his eyes and see that restless look I've seen there before, the sense that he's ready to flee. I move closer and wrap my arms around him, running my hands down his shoulder blades, feeling a vibration under the skin that makes me want to hold him tighter to keep him from flying out of my grasp. It takes me a few minutes to realize that the trembling I felt beneath his skin is coming from me.

Chapter Twenty-six

Aidan leaves before dawn. He doesn't tell me where he's going, but he gives me a phone number where I can leave a message for him and directions to a spot in Inwood Park where he'll meet me at noon the day after I call.

"It's like Tam Lin in the story—telling Margaret to meet him at the well. I should bring some holy water and dirt from Joseph's garden . . ." My voice trails off, Joseph's name falling like a shadow between us. He gets up to get dressed, looking out the window where the light is gathering above the river. Then he sits down beside me on the bed and runs his hand in one fluid stroke down the length of my body, from forehead to toes. "If you haven't made that call in one week I'll not expect to hear from you and I'll understand. No hard feelings, Iris."

"I'll make the call, Aidan, as soon as I've found out something."

After he's gone I stay in bed waiting until it's late enough to call the librarian at John Jay College. When I taught there last year I brought my class to the library for a tour of its criminology archives and I'd had a long chat with the librarian about Scandinavian fairy tales.

"Sure," Charles Baum tells me, "always happy to help ex-faculty in their research. I'll leave a pass for you at the desk. If you need any help finding the right case just give a holler."

On my way up to John Jay I stop at the dry cleaner and tailor's on Eighth Avenue where Mr. Nagamora works. He's not at his sewing machine by the window and I panic for a moment at the thought that something has happened to him over the summer. After all, he's not a young man. When I ask the girl at the counter, though, she disappears into the racks of hanging garment bags and a few seconds later the thin plastic bags rustle and Mr. Nagamora surfaces from behind them. His face, the moment before he recognizes me, is as smooth as a stone, but then he smiles, revealing a thousand small wrinkles.

"Professor Greenfeder," he says, bowing ceremoniously, "my family will want to meet you." The counter girl reappears, as well as an older woman and a small boy, all disgorged by the rippling plastic bags like bobbins popping up on a still lake, all bowing when introduced to me. The old woman, whom I took at first to be his wife, is his sister, the young woman and boy his niece and grandnephew. Mr. Nagamora takes something out of the pocket of his cardigan—even in the subtropical humidity of the dry cleaner's he wears the same woolen cardigan—and begins to unfold it. I'm reminded of Joseph unfolding his handkerchief to wipe the sweat off his brow, but it turns out to be several sheets of white paper, which he unfolds and holds up to display the large A on top. It's Mr. Nagamora's retelling of "The Crane Wife." I remember how I hesitated over that A and for once in my life I'm glad of something I did impulsively.

Finally, when our audience has slipped back into the recesses of the shop I take out the bundle of green silk from my canvas book bag and lay it on the counter between us.

"Ah," he says, stroking the fabric gently, reminding me, of all things, of how Aidan touched me before he left this morning. "Beautiful silk." He folds back the waistband and looks at the label, nodding at the designer's name. Then he runs his fingers along the seams, as if the stitches were Braille. "Very fine work," he says. "This belonged to your mother?"

"Yes," I agree, because it's easier than going into the dubious history of the dress, "but I wore it and it got torn." He's come to the rip in the swag and the cuts made by the glass when I knelt beside Joseph. He rolls something between his fingertips and then holds up a tiny splinter of glass balanced between the tips of his fingernails.

"There was an accident," I say, embarrassed to hear my voice quiver over the last word. Mr. Nagamora holds up his hand to stop me from going on. It's the same imperious gesture he used when I tried to interrupt his story, which I'd guessed at the time was an echo of his father—his father, the silk weaver. I notice then what has struck me about Mr. Nagamora since I came in. He carries himself differently than he used to in class. All the slump has gone out of him. I feel sure it's not the A I gave him, though; it's telling his father's story. He's still telling it.

"I can fix," he tells me, and for a moment I forget we're talking about the dress.

I nod. "Thank you, Mr. Nagamora."

He pats the silk cloth, but I feel as if he's patting my hand. Then he writes up a ticket and tells me my mother's dress will be ready Thursday next.

For the rest of my walk up to John Jay I think about Mr. Nagamora's altered demeanor—the way telling his father's story has transformed him. I think too of my other students whose lives have changed since the spring: Mrs. Rivera, who has stayed up at the hotel with Ramon to help in the renovations, Gretchen Lu, who told me she planned to use the prize money from the Folly contest to travel for a year visiting textile mills in different countries (Mark said he planned to use the money as a down payment for a co-op in Hoboken), and Natalie Baehr who's sold her jewelry to Barney's. Even Aidan seems to be living out some version of the story he told last spring— caught in a limbo where my belief in him, my ability to see past the guises of enchantment, can save him or not. So many changes to come out of one little writing assignment! And what about my life? What chain of events did I set off when I sent my mother's selkie story to Phoebe Nix?

By the time I've arrived at the entrance to John Jay I feel like I've been walking one of those labyrinths set up in cloisters for meditation— that I'm following a path set out by unseen hands. There's nothing calming in following this path, though; I feel dizzy.

Charles Baum has left a pass for me at the security desk as he promised. Of all the colleges I've taught at—except for the prison, of course— John Jay maintains the highest level of security. I suppose it's inherent in the culture of an institution that's the leading criminal justice college in the country—most of the New York City police officers who go to college go here. It also has one of the best criminology libraries in the city, which is why I'm here today.

I take the escalators down to the lobby, past a row of flags that makes me feel like I'm entering the UN, and glass cases featuring a display on *The Irish in New York City Police History*, to the security desk at the entrance to the library. Then I go back up to the first floor (the library is self-contained within the building and can only be entered from the lobby) to find a free computer with access to LexisNexis.

When I took my class to the library Charles Baum had explained how to use LexisNexis to look up a specific court case. Unfortunately, I spent more time monitoring my students' attention level than paying attention myself. I flail about for a bit and then notice a printed flyer that describes in detail how to look up case law in LexisNexis. I click on Legal Research, then State Case Law, and then program a search for "John McGlynn" and "Crown Hotel" and then hold my breath. I vaguely recall that the case will only appear if it had been appealed and I don't remember Elspeth McCrory of the *Poughkeepsie Journal* saying anything about an appeal.

As it turns out, John McGlynn had a fairly compelling reason to appeal. Through the maze of legal terms in the Disposition and Headnotes, I glean that his appeal was based on the premise that the testimony of one of the main witnesses at his trial was considered tainted because she had previously proven incapable of identifying the accused in a lineup and she had changed her testimony several times during the course of the trial.

I scroll through the Syllabus, which summarizes the main points of the appeal, to the Opinion that elaborates on the circumstances of the trial. On the night of August 21, 1948, the night clerk at the Crown Hotel was asked to open the safe so that Vera Nix, who occupied the penthouse suite and was the sister-in-law of the hotel's owner, could retrieve a diamond necklace that she had placed in the safe earlier that evening. At that time the clerk discovered that the safe was completely empty. Miss Nix told the police that when she had put the necklace in the safe at eight-thirty that evening—"just before going out to a party at the Plaza"—the defendant, John McGlynn, had been "hanging around the front desk flirting with one of the maids."

"I'd seen him before, you couldn't miss him because he's a very handsome young man—in a wild Heathcliff-on-the-moors sort of way—and quite popular with the young Irish girls who worked at the hotel. I believe his sister worked at the hotel. Well, I noticed that when I passed him to go into the office to put my necklace in the safe he was looking at my necklace."

Based on this flimsy evidence, the police had gone in search of John McGlynn at his residence in Coney Island but were told by his landlady that he had vacated his rooms that morning—"even though he was paid up for the next week"—and left town without giving a forwarding address. This was enough, apparently, to convince the police that they had their thief. A week later John McGlynn was found at a motel near Saratoga Springs, New York. He'd been spotted placing a bet at the nearby racetrack. The police followed him back to his motel room where they found the jewelry that had been stolen from the Crown safe.

The fact that John McGlynn had been caught with stolen property in his possession had been enough to convict him. His appeal was based on additional evidence that came to light after his conviction. Apparently, six months before the safe robbery Vera Nix had reported some jewelry missing from her room. At that time she had told the police that she had surprised a maid "entertaining a young man" in the living room of her suite and she suspected that the maid had worked in collusion with the young man to steal her jewelry. She'd said that she thought that the man was the brother of the hotel's assistant manager and that the maid, "according to that little tag they all wear," was Katherine Morrissey.

I've been scrolling through the lines quickly, but when I see my mother's name I pause the cursor and lean back in my chair. I try to picture my mother, in a maid's uniform, caught with a young man in a guest's room. When I try to picture John McGlynn—handsome in a "wild Heathcliff-on-the-moors sort of way"—I see Aidan. The black hair and dark-lashed blue-green eyes, the pale skin that tinges pink in the open air. But I can't see my mother. I just can't imagine her caught in a compromising position, jumping to her feet and straightening her uniform—I can't imagine her in a uniform at all—and blushing and curtseying in front of the grand lady, Vera Nix. Maybe it's just because no one likes to think of their mother in a sexual context, but I think it has more to do with my mother's dignity, the way she held herself.

What I do remember, though, is that whenever a maid was accused of stealing something by a guest my mother would insist that my father keep the guest in his office while she went up to the guest's room to conduct her own search. Often she would discover the "stolen item" in the carpet or caught in the blankets, or lying carelessly beneath a book on the night table. Once, when a society dowager from Boston named Caroline Minton had the audacity to suggest that the maid must have given her garnet brooch back to my mother so that she could place it back in the room, my mother had silently left the office and ordered the bellhop to have Mrs. Minton's luggage removed from her suite and have her car brought up from the parking lot and packed. The hotel bill had been discharged and Mrs. Minton had been asked to seek other accommodations should she ever find herself in the region again. I can't imagine the woman who coolly ousted Mrs. Minton from the Hotel Equinox cowering in front of Vera Nix. Maybe I just don't want to. I have to admit that if my mother had been falsely accused by Vera Nix of stealing, it might explain why she was so vigilant in defending her own employees against similar fraudulent charges.

I go back to the screen to see what had come of this earlier accusation and feel vindicated by the outcome. When Vera Nix had been asked to identify the maid she'd caught in flagrante delicto in a police lineup she'd picked the wrong woman. She was given three opportunities to pick Katherine Morrissey from a lineup and failed every time. The charges had been dropped. When this incident came to light after John McGlynn's conviction it was considered sufficient cause to bring Mrs. Nix's testimony at his trial into question. Apparently, Vera Nix had a poor memory for faces—or at least the faces of the many maids, bellhops, valets, hairdressers, manicurists, secretaries, and waiters who attended to her regularly at the Crown Hotel. Although she claimed that John McGlynn's good looks made him memorable, she was unable to correctly pick him out from recent photographs. The picture she identified as John McGlynn turned out to be of the screen star Laurence Olivier, who had played Heathcliff in 1939.

So maybe it wasn't my mother caught with her boyfriend in the Nix's suite. Maybe it was some other unfortunate Irish girl—or maybe Vera Nix made up the whole thing. But why? She named my mother. She might not have known what my mother looked like, but she knew her name. She must have wanted to get her in trouble.

I stare at the blinking cursor on the screen in front of me until I notice that a vein above my right eye is pulsing to the same rhythm. The only thing that occurs to me is that if Vera Nix had been told by someone that her husband was having an affair with a maid by the name of Katherine Morrissey she might fabricate the whole episode to get the girl fired. And why not throw in a boyfriend at the same time to show her husband that he wasn't the only light in his girlfriend's life?

The remainder of the case file doesn't tell me much. Although Vera Nix's testimony was dismissed there was still sufficient evidence—possession of stolen property, fleeing the crime scene, prior history of small thefts—to uphold John McGlynn's conviction. I print out the case file and head back into the periodical stacks to look up the newspaper coverage of the trial.

Under "Crown Hotel Robbery" I find seven references in the *New York Times*, four in the *Herald Tribune*, and twelve in the *Daily News*. I also find that I'm getting hungry. I check my watch and see that it's after noon. I didn't have any breakfast—not having the heart to scramble eggs again after the uneaten eggs that I'd made for Aidan and myself the night before— and I'd been too anxious to get to the library to stop on the way. I don't want to stop now either. Beyond the dull, buzzing pain in my right eye and the haze of fatigue and hunger, a picture is beginning to slowly take shape in my mind. It's just too much of a coincidence that it was Vera Nix whose testimony first directed the police to John McGlynn and that she had tried to implicate him and my mother in a theft even before the safe robbery.

Clearly, Vera Nix had some vendetta against my mother—whether justifiably or not, she must have believed that my mother was having an affair with her husband.

Operating the microfiche viewer doesn't help my headache. Scanning through the old newsprint, the words blur into a gray slurry as the film unfurls. It reminds me of the story of Little Sambo—before Little Sambo got p.c.'d out of print—when the tigers race around and around in a circle and turn into butter. I skim through the earliest articles about the robbery and trial because they don't tell me anything new. It's only when I get to the appeal that I stop to read more closely. Once Vera Nix's testimony was discredited, there were several unflattering articles about her. There's a column on the society page of the *Tribune* criticizing Vera Nix for wearing the Kron family pearls to a coffeehouse in Greenwich Village and a particularly cruel cartoon of her in evening dress, dripping with jewels, reading a copy of *The Daily Worker* with her feet, in fur-tufted mules, resting on the back of a crouching, uniformed maid. I can see why Phoebe is bitter about how her mother was portrayed by the press, but honestly, what surprises me is that there isn't more. The last article that mentions Vera Nix pointedly denies the rumor that she had been accused in court of setting up the robbery. After that her name disappears from accounts of the trial.

The last article I look up is headlined "Sister Pleads for Leniency in Brother's Sentencing." I'd been hoping for a picture of Rose McGlynn, but instead there's a picture of John McGlynn in a uniform and peaked cap, leaning against a drum emblazoned with the words ST. CHRISTOPHER'S HOME BAND. I remember that Elspeth McCrory had mentioned in her article that Rose McGlynn's younger brothers had been handed over to the Catholic orphanage and surmise that Rose's plea for leniency featured this sad episode in her brother's history. I start to read it, but by now I'm so lightheaded I feel as if my brain, like Sambo's tigers, is turning into butter. I decide to copy this one and take it with me to the Greek diner across the street.

Passing back through the lobby, I find myself pausing over the black-and-white photographs of generations of young Irish police officers in the display case, perhaps because they remind me of that last picture of John McGlynn. It's funny, I think, how the Irish seem to be cropping up everywhere in my life just now. I've never thought much of my mother's Irish heritage—except for the selkie story she told me, she never made much of it herself. She didn't raise me as a Catholic (except for that one trip to Brooklyn to have me baptized), or speak of her relatives. Once she was gone it was easy, especially with a name like *Greenfeder*, to forget I had any Irish in me at all.

At the diner I order a BLT and iced tea and take out Rose McGlynn's plea for her brother, which the *Times* had transcribed verbatim.

"Our mother died when John was just fourteen," she told the court:

and as bad as it was for me, at least I was old enough to take care of myself. John and my two younger brothers, Allen and Arden, still needed a mother. My father was not able to care for them. He was that broke up about my mother's death that though he'd never taken a drop before the day she died he soon took to drinking. There'd been hard feelings between my mother's family and him so none of them would take on three young boys to raise. My father's sisters said they would have me, but not the younger ones. I wish now I'd thought of some way to keep them with me, but I could barely take care of myself. Still, I blame myself. It's a pitiful thing to have a family separated like we were.

I'll never forget the day we took them to St. Christopher's. Mind you, the Dominican sisters were kind and the monsignor himself came to speak to my father and me in the chapel. He said many a family had left their sons to St. Christopher's during the hard times when they could not care for them themselves. He said it was nothing to feel ashamed of, but when we left the boys there, in that great cold building without a soul who knew them, I felt as if we'd dropped them off the edge of a pier—like they do to kittens. My father would never look me in the eye from that day on and my brothers, well, I visited with them every Sunday. They looked well enough—they were probably eating better than they had at home—but there was always something missing in their eyes. And when it was time to leave, the younger ones, Allen and Arden, would cry and hang on to my legs. Not John, though. You could tell he tried to keep a brave face for the sake of the younger ones and it's that would break my heart even more. He was so young, but he'd grown into an old man in that place. He'd even developed a curve in his back, which the nuns said came from poor nutrition as a baby.

Then Arden died. He'd had polio as a baby and had never been strong and they said he died of pneumonia. I could tell John blamed himself for that. Now, I'm not saying St. Christopher's didn't do all they could for him, but when John got out it was like there was a piece of him missing. I tried to do what I could. I got him a job at the hotel—Mr. Kron, the owner, was very kind about hiring him—but now I wish I'd never gotten him the job. He'd had nothing for so long, he shouldn't have been around people who had so much. I don't know if he took Mrs. Nix's jewelry or not, but I know he'd never hurt anyone. Maybe the safe was left open and he couldn't help himself. Maybe Mrs. Nix said something to him about his selling the jewelry for her and he misunderstood. I don't know. But I do know that my brother's a good man, that he's been a good brother to me and to our two younger brothers, and that he's never had much luck. So I'm here to ask you respectfully to go easy on him, to remember he's a boy who lost his mother young and who deserves better than what this world's had to offer him so far.

Rose McGlynn made her appeal in May 1949 at her brother's retrial. The judge said in his sentencing that he'd considered the defendant's unfortunate family history, but that he didn't regard it as an excuse for criminal behavior. "Miss McGlynn herself is an argument against such excuses. She lost her mother at a tender age and had to leave her high school at St. Mary Star of the Sea before graduating, and yet she has, through perseverance and keeping to the straight and narrow, lifted herself out of poverty to a position of responsibility and trust at the Crown Hotel. If she could do it, why couldn't her brother?"

I imagine how bitter the judge's verdict must have been to Rose McGlynn. To have her success held up as proof of her brother's culpability must have been galling. No wonder she decided to leave the city. Then I remember too Harry's suggestion that Rose gave her brother the combination to the safe. If that were really true, her guilt must have been unbearable. No wonder she ended up throwing herself in front of a train after seeing her brother in prison that last time.

I read back over the newspaper story until I get to the judge's verdict—the spot where he talks about Rose McGlynn dropping out of her high school, St. Mary Star of the Sea. It's the same name as the church where I was baptized. My mother told me that she took me there because it was where she was baptized, but she'd never mentioned that it was also the name of a Catholic girls' school; it must be where she went to school, though, along with Rose McGlynn. Rose McGlynn and my mother must have been friends since they were children, which meant that my mother had known John McGlynn all those years as well. She must have watched the McGlynn family fall apart, the boys put in an orphanage, their sister vainly trying to keep them from sinking into a life of crime. The story is not only pitiable, it's familiar. I recognize it from my mother's fantasy world, which she called Tirra Glynn, and the story of Naoise who stole the net of tears from the evil king Connachar and was banished to a fortress on the banks of the drowned river. When Deirdre visits Naoise at the prison and she sees the other selkies shedding their skins in the river some of them are ripped apart by the current, just as Rose McGlynn's body was crushed by an oncoming train.

My mother must have felt like she was the sole survivor of some awful tempest. In the book Deirdre makes her way to the Palace of the Two Moons, clad in a green dress woven of the pollen that falls on her in the forest. My mother too made her way to the Hotel Equinox carrying her secrets . . . and what else?

I tap my finger on the name of the school. St. Mary Star of the Sea. The net of tears. I remember Gordon's slide lecture, the fifteenth-century portrait of the Virgin Mary, seated on a rock by the sea, crowned with a diamond-and-pearl wreath that looked just like the necklace described in my mother's books. What if the necklace—what had Gordon called it? A *ferronière*?—what if it had survived the war and somehow ended up in Vera

Nix's possession? I think back to Gordon's lecture and remember him mentioning the possibility that the *ferronière* had been hidden by a descendant of the della Rosas. I also remember that according to Harry, Peter Kron had hidden out in an Italian villa after escaping from a POW camp. If he stole the *ferronière* and let Vera wear it, it could have been one of the pieces John McGlynn stole. It must not have been with the recovered jewels—Gordon would know if it had been recovered—but maybe John McGlynn, knowing this piece was both especially valuable and that it wouldn't be listed in the police report, hid it someplace special. And then he told his sister, when she visited him in prison, where it was. Could she have told my mother before throwing herself under the train at Rip Van Winkle?

Those tigers in my brain are slowing down, showing their stripes now, like a carousel on its last revolution. I desperately want to call the number Aidan gave me to tell him what I've learned but I know it's not enough yet. Something's still missing. And the only place I can think of looking for it is in Brooklyn.

Chapter Twenty-seven

On my way to the subway I buy a five-boroughs map of New York City. Fortunately, it lists churches and I'm able to find St. Mary Star of the Sea on Court Street between Nelson and Luquer in the Carroll Gardens section of Brooklyn. I'm not all that familiar with Brooklyn, mostly because I hate taking subways. I usually tell people that I'm claustrophobic, but the truth is I hate going underground. I've even had trouble using some libraries—like the Beinecke at Yale—where the stacks are below ground.

Today, though, my phobia is happily placated by the whir of thoughts revolving inside my brain. Instead of tigers, now, I see Vera Nix in her siren's green dress, John McGlynn in his St. Christopher's band uniform, my mother and Peter Kron, and hovering outside this inner circle, Harry Kron. The one face that remains blurry is Rose McGlynn. I take out her plea to the court and reread the part in Rose McGlynn's story when she visited her brothers at St. Christopher's. *They looked well enough—they were probably eating better than they had at home—but there was always something missing in their eyes.* And then a little later, she'd said of John, *He was so young, but he'd grown into an old man in that place. He'd even developed a curve in his back, which the nuns said came from poor nutrition as a baby.*

Concentrating on the small faded print in the swaying train has made me nauseous. I close my eyes and find that a new figure has joined the carousel in my mind: a grotesque half man/half swan with cold black eyes. It's a creature from my mother's books, one of the men who turn into winged creatures. The transformation from man to beast, as my mother described it, is painful. Their emerging wings break their backs, and their eyes grow cold. I remember a single line from my mother's second book. *But when Naoise turned to me I saw in his eyes that the animal growing inside him had already taken over.*

I shiver despite the suffocating heat in the train. If my mother had known John and Rose McGlynn when they were growing up she would have seen this transformation. She not only saw John turn into a hardened criminal, she also saw his sister kill herself, saw her step off the platform, her worn suitcase left behind like a used skin, to be crushed by the oncoming train. Decapitated, Harry had said. No wonder my mother got on the northbound train and continued on her journey upstate, to the hotel where she and Rose had planned to look for work. There was nothing left for her back in the city but bad memories. The Hotel Equinox, and my father, must have seemed like an oasis of peace after the horror she had witnessed. But then something had happened, twenty-four years later in the summer of 1973, to reawaken those horrors.

I'm so deep in thought that I almost don't notice that the train has reached the Carroll Street station. I get out just before the door shuts and then take the stairs two at a time, breathless to get back up into the air. And back into the present. All morning I've felt the past tugging at my heels, a tide dragging me out to sea, and now I've washed up at the feet of St. Mary Star of the Sea, patron saint of seagoing sailors and shipwrecked castaways. The first thing I notice is that the church is nowhere near the sea. I check my five-boroughs map and see that the closest waterfront is the Red Hook docks. The second thing I notice is that the black iron gates in front of the church are chained and locked.

I look up and down a Court Street becalmed by the late-afternoon sun and then walk up to the corner. West on Luquer, deep shaded yards and plaster devotional statues guard the placid brownstones. The neighborhood feels quiet and private and, like the church, unwilling to give up its secrets. East on Luquer I find the church's rectory and a bell to ring. A small plaque below the bell reads, RING ONCE AND THEN PLEASE WAIT PATIENTLY. I ring once and wait, patiently at first but decreasingly so, for ten minutes. I pace back up to Court Street and notice a coffee shop called Le Trianon directly opposite the church. There are benches outside, shaded by a linden tree, where a couple in neoprene cycling gear sip iced tea while their giant rottweiler laps up water from a bowl chained to the bench. I head there.

Entering the café I feel like I've actually found the church, mostly because Michelangelo's God and Adam are lounging on a bed of clouds and blue sky painted on the ceiling. Everything else about Le Trianon is pretty— the hand-blown light fixtures, crafted to look like tightly furled lilies, the marble tables, and the selection of teas and pastries. Even the man behind the counter, short but muscular and bearing more than a passing resemblance to the painting of Adam on the ceiling, is handsome. I order an iced green tea and cinnamon scone and ask him if the church across the street is always locked up.

"Yeah, since some silver candlesticks were stolen from the altar a few years back. They're open for Mass at the crack of dawn and once again in the evening at eight-thirty."

"Damn," I say, "I came a ways to see it."

"Did you try ringing at the rectory door?"

"I rang once and waited patiently."

He laughs. "Those old ladies who work in the office are probably there but they don't like getting off their fannies. You could try again."

"Thanks," I say, taking my iced tea and scone. "By the way, why's it called St. Mary Star of the Sea? We don't seem to be anywhere near the sea."

He points toward the rear of the café to indicate, I gather, the neighborhood to the south and west of us. "A lot of this land was built up over the years. When the church was built a hundred fifty years ago the water came closer and there weren't so many buildings to block the view."

"Really? I didn't realize the church was that old. And has the neighborhood always been Italian?"

"My grandparents moved here just after the war," he says, "but they said there were still a lot of Irish then. Now we've got lawyers and stockbrokers willing to pay a couple thou a month for a studio apartment. You looking to move into the neighborhood?"

"Sounds like I couldn't afford it. Actually, I think my mother may have gone to school at St. Mary's. I was baptized at the church."

"No kidding. Well, look, considering you're from the old neighborhood, forget trying to raise those old bats in the rectory. Go over to the school and ask for Gloria. Tell her that her nephew Danny sent you and she'll get someone to show you the church. Plus, she's got all the records for the school going back to Moses."

"Thanks, that's really helpful. Oh, and by the way, I love the ceiling."

Danny rolls his eyes up to the painted heaven not eight feet above his head. "My brother Vincent, the artist. I'm just the baker. It's okay if you don't mind God hanging over your head all day."

I sit on the bench outside (the cyclers and rottweiler have gone) and watch dismissal from the school while sipping my tea and eating my scone (which is so light and flaky that I wonder who is really the artist in the family—Danny or Vincent?). Children file out the front door in orderly rows that split to the right or the left to mini buses waiting on Nelson and Luquer Streets. I watch mothers in clogs and long Indian skirts and mothers in suits and high heels and some fathers too in paint-splattered overalls or rumpled Brooks Brothers shirts—ties stuffed in shirt pockets—emerging hand in hand with their children. I don't know what I'd expected of my mother's old neighborhood, but it wasn't this pretty suburb, which seems too renovated and gentrified to still hold my mother's secrets. This is a neighborhood Jack and I could have moved to, I think. He could have found some studio space in the new, burgeoning artists' neighborhood, DUMBO (for Down Under the Manhattan Bridge Overpass), and we could have renovated a brownstone before the rents skyrocketed.

When the traffic out of the doors slows to a trickle I cross the street and go inside. The secretaries are still in the office, comforting a little boy whose mother is late for pickup while packing up their purses to go. I pick out the oldest-looking woman—who also bears more than a passing resemblance to Danny from Le Trianon Café—and ask if she's Gloria.

"I was talking to your nephew Danny across the street and he said you might be able to help me look up my mother's records. I think she went here in the late thirties, early forties. Also, I was kind of hoping to see the church . . ."

Gloria and one of the younger secretaries exchange a look. "Did you try the rectory?" the younger girl asks me.

"I rang once."

"Is Anthony still here, Tonisha?" Gloria asks. Tonisha nods, already hitting an intercom button on her phone.

"We'll get you into the church. If you want to look at the records you'll have to come down to the basement with me and find what you're looking for yourself. My back can't take stooping over those files." In fact when Gloria gets up I see she has a pronounced hump in her back and that she needs a cane to walk.

"If it's a real inconvenience . . ."

"Nah, do me good to get off my fanny. But it is cold down there . . ." She eyes my thin T-shirt and cotton skirt. "Here, take one of my sweaters." There are several sweaters hanging from a lopsided coatrack in the corner. The one she picks for me is a hideous shade of acid green trimmed in a muddy pink. When I pull it on the synthetic wool itches and smells vaguely of some kind of lotion. Calamine, I think as I follow Gloria down the basement stairs; the muddy pink trim is the exact color of calamine lotion and the green is the green of poison ivy. Still, I'm grateful for the sweater's warmth as we descend into the basement. If I thought the neighborhood at street level seemed too antiseptic to hold any traces of the past I should be comforted by the church basement, which looks, and smells, as old as the catacombs. The walls are hewn out of bedrock. The floor appears to be dirt.

Gloria pulls a string suspended from the ceiling and a naked bulb dimly illuminates the cavernous space.

"Wow, it's huge," I say, straining my eyes to see into the shadowy corners. I'm startled by what look like ghostly shapes in one recessed apse.

"It goes all the way under the church," Gloria tells me, and then, pointing to the ghostly throng in the shadows and crossing herself, says, "Those are the ousted saints. You know, the ones the Vatican decided weren't saints anymore. The church put their statues down here."

"How does a saint get ousted?" I ask, looking away from the hollow eyes of the marble and bronze figures, which seem to look out with all the piteous eloquence of dogs at the pound.

Gloria shrugs and pulls a wobbly office chair with torn upholstery and one missing caster over to a bank of file cabinets just opposite the niche of deposed saints. "The church decides they weren't real, like St. Christopher"—she fingers a medal at her throat, which I guess honors the defrocked saint—"or that their miracles weren't real, like Santa Catalina. What year did you say your mother went here?"

"Well, she was born in 1924 so she would have graduated around 1942."

Gloria pulls out a drawer and waves me to it. She rolls her chair back, takes a skein of wool out of her cardigan pocket, and begins to knit. I notice it's the same calamine pink as the trim of the one I'm wearing.

I crouch in front of the metal cabinet, wincing at the pain in my battered knees, and try to read the names that have been handwritten on white labels affixed to dark brown file folders. The folders are so tightly packed—without the benefit of hanging dividers—that every time I move one folder forward the sharp edge of the next folder slices into my cuticles. The spidery handwriting—I imagine a long-dead nun as ghostly and hollow-eyed as the statues whose gazes I feel boring into my bent and aching back—is almost impossible to read. Nor does this particular nun seem to have considered strict alphabetical order, like cleanliness, next to godliness.

"Do the Mc's come before or after the rest of the M's?" I ask, lifting my head up from the drawer.

Gloria looks up from her knitting needles which keep moving in her hands, "I have no idea, but if you want to see the church too you'll have to hurry up. Anthony takes his dinner break at four-thirty."

I go through all the M's but don't find Morrissey or McGlynn.

"What if she dropped out?" I ask. I realize that my mother never actually mentioned graduating, and I know that Rose McGlynn dropped out.

Gloria sighs and, letting the bundle of pink wool sag into her lap, touches her medal. I imagine she's asking St. Christopher to carry her out of the presence of fools and I also bet that Danny will get an earful tonight. She points a knitting needle in the direction of the deposed saints. "There are some boxes over there for the dropouts," she says. "I think they're grouped by decades."

It makes a sort of perverse sense that the dropouts would get to share eternity with the unpopular saints. I picture an afterlife with cliques like in high school, with women like my mother and Rose McGlynn floating in limbo—only I believe that the Catholic Church has also gotten rid of limbo—with the ex-saints. I kneel at the feet of a pasty-white saint and start thumbing through the 1940s for my mother and her friend.

I find them both, their files rubber banded together, a note folded and paper clipped to the top file. I unfasten the note, which retains a rusty impression of the paper clip, and read it first. "Dear Monsignor Ryan," she-of-the-spidery-handwriting has written,

Enclosed you will find the files of the two girls accused of stealing from the collection plate during last Sunday's Mass. As you will recall, we suspected Rose McGlynn immediately because of the recent disruption in her family and when questioned she did not deny her culpability. Later that afternoon, though, another student, Katherine Morrissey, came to my office and said that she was responsible for the theft. I noticed that both girls were wearing identical saints medals that I hadn't seen before. When I asked them, separately of course, where they got the medals they both became flustered and couldn't come up with a satisfactory explanation. (Both girls come from very poor families and the medals are gold and quite valuable.) I concluded that the girls stole the money and purchased the medals. I confess that I felt moved to pardon them when I realized that the money had been used to purchase a religious item, but then I noticed that the medals are of Santa Catalina, a local folk heroine whose beatification was recently revoked by the church. (I'm embarrassed to tell you that girls in this neighborhood pray to this so-called saint to find them husbands.) I was further disillusioned in the girls' characters when I was shown a picture of the girls (herein enclosed) cavorting at a local amusement park with a young man. You'll notice, if you look carefully and perhaps employ a magnifying glass, that the girls are wearing the medals in the picture. I assume they were purchased as part of their escapade. In light of their both confessing to the theft and this evidence of slatternly behavior, I must recommend expulsion from St. Mary Star of the Sea.

The letter is signed Sister Amelia Dolores, mother superior. It's disconcerting to read, twice in one day, of my mother being accused of petty theft. I'd rather believe that it was Rose McGlynn who stole the money, but then I remember finding the gold medal in my mother's jewelry box and my mother tearing it from my neck when she saw me wearing it. My father said she reacted like that because of how she felt about the Catholic Church, but now I wonder if the necklace had reminded her of this crime and its shameful aftermath.

When I fold the note and slide it back under its paper clip I notice that something is written on the back, on the half of the paper that had been facing the folder. This note is written in a different, larger and rounder, hand.

"Dear Monsignor, please note that the boy in the picture is only Rose McGlynn's younger brother, John McGlynn. I suspect that he is the one responsible for the collection plate theft and that the girls are protecting him." This addendum is signed Sister Agatha Dorothy.

I open the folder and the black-and-white photograph, turned yellow and brown with age, falls into my lap. They're leaning against a wooden railing in front of the ocean—John McGlynn, whom I recognize from his St. Christopher's picture, flanked by two pretty girls. At first glance the girls look like they could be sisters. They're both wearing tightly cinched skirts and lacy white blouses. Their hair is styled in the same swept-back pageboy, their lips painted an identical dark shade. I can just make out oval shapes at the girls' throats but it would take some magnifying glass to identify their necklaces as saints' medals. It doesn't take a magnifying glass, though, to pick out the differences between the two girls. My mother's hair curls buoyantly in the light breeze; her green eyes, fringed by dark lashes, are arresting even in a black-and-white picture. The other girl is a pale shadow; it's clear she's trying to imitate my mother, but her hair falls slackly to her shoulders, freckles mar her complexion, and she squints at the camera. It's not that she's not pretty, it's just that Rose McGlynn can't hold a candle to my mother.

I look over at Gloria but she's muttering over her knitting, having apparently dropped a stitch. I let the picture slide from my lap into the open book bag next to my feet. Then I quickly skim through the rest of the file, but there's nothing much to see here. Both girls got good grades. I notice that Sister Agatha Dorothy was their English teacher and that she'd given both girls A's in her class. It was Rose McGlynn, though, and not my mother, who had won the composition award their junior year. Even though there's not much of interest here, I find myself oddly reluctant to leave the two folders moldering at the feet of the reject saint, even when I notice that, fittingly, the plaque at the bottom of the statue identifies her as Santa Catalina, the "folk heroine" whose medals the girls had bought with the stolen collection plate money. Gloria is still ripping stitches out and unleashing a stream of Italian invectives at the unraveled mess of pink wool, so I slide the folders into my book bag along with the photograph, then straighten my aching back and tell Gloria I'm ready to see the church.

The church is beautiful; its soaring space a balm after the dank confines of the basement. The slim young man in ponytail and overalls—he introduces himself as Anthony Acevedo—flicks on the lights one by one as I walk down the center aisle, illuminating each section of the vaulted ceiling until I reach the main apse and the altar springs into light. Radiant stained-glass windows pierce the heavy stone walls, so that the figures in the window seem to float above the altar. In the center window, the Virgin Mary stands on a rock in a storm-tossed sea. What's disappointing is that except for her blue cloak her head is bare. There's no jeweled crown, no net of tears.

I turn to Anthony, who's come to stand beside me. "Thank you for showing me the church," I tell him, "it's really beautiful."

He nods, but then tilts his head at me and touches a finger to the skin below his right eye and tugs. "You were looking for something else," he says, "I can tell."

"I thought she'd have a crown," I say, trying not to sound like a petulant child, "I mean, I saw another painting of Mary Star of the Sea in which she's wearing a crown."

Anthony looks delighted. He leans forward and, even though we're alone in the huge church, whispers in my ear. "You're looking for Santa Catalina. Follow me."

"But I thought she was de-sainted," I say, following Anthony down the length of the nave, away from the altar. He turns into a small chapel near the front door. There's a bank of candles here, most burned down to nubs, some still sputtering from the previous night's Mass. Underneath the smell of melting wax there's another smell, something sweet, and then I notice that floating in the liquid wax are rose petals.

"The women who come to light candles bring the rose petals because of her name—Catalina della Rosa. Katherine of the Rose." Anthony points at the oil painting above the candles. A century and a half of candle smoke hasn't done it any good—I can barely make out the blue-cloaked figure in the painting.

"Isn't this a picture of Mary?" I ask, recognizing the traditional red-and-blue color scheme from my college art history classes.

"Yes, which is why it's still hanging in the church. But there's a legend that the model for the painting was actually Catalina della Rosa."

I move closer and recognize the painting from the slide Gordon showed—was it only a week ago?—at the end of his lecture, the portrait of Mary on the beach that was copied from the bridal portrait of Catalina della Rosa. I look up at her face, and there, half hidden by old varnish and smoke damage, is the emerald teardrop suspended from a crown of diamonds and pearls. My mother's net of tears. I reach into my book bag and take out the faded photograph of my mother and John and Rose McGlynn at the beach, their new golden medals gleaming on their throats. They all look so happy. It must have seemed like a perfect, innocent day. Was Sister Agatha Dorothy—I picture her as plump and round like her handwriting—

right when she guessed that John McGlynn had stolen the money? Did he steal the money and then take his sister and girlfriend for a day at the beach and the rides at Coney Island and then buy them the medals of their beloved saint? I'll probably never know, but I feel sure that the day—the beach, the medals—must have seemed like the beginning of the end to my mother once she was expelled from school and later when John was convicted of a more serious crime. No wonder she remembered the saint's headpiece as a net of tears.

Anthony touches my elbow gently. I expect him to be embarrassed by my tears, but instead he's guiding my hand to the metal box where the tapers are kept for lighting candles. I hold the slim piece of wood over one of the lit candles until it catches, but then hesitate before touching it to one of the unlit candles.

"What do the women who come here pray for?" I ask him, remembering Sister Amelia Dolores's letter. "To get married?"

"Not exactly," Anthony tells me. "According to my sister, they pray to Santa Catalina to protect them from marrying the wrong man."

Chapter Twenty-eight

Before I leave St. Mary Star of the Sea, Anthony gives me directions to St. Christopher's Home for Boys—now St. Christopher's Social Services. It's only a twenty-minute walk up Court Street and across Atlantic Avenue.

"Ask for Sister D'Aulnoy," he tells me, "and say Anthony at St. Mary's sent you."

Sister D'Aulnoy, I think walking up Court Street. At least she's only got one name, unlike Amelia Dolores and Agatha Dorothy. After a lifetime of having very little to do with nuns, now I'm besieged with them. My aunt Sophie told me one other story—other than my late baptismal—to sum up my mother's feelings about the Catholic Church. After I'd had my soul belatedly saved from limbo at age three my mother had tried sending me to a Catholic preschool in Kingston. One day she and Sophie had come to drop me off and I pitched a fit on the steps. "A full-scale tantrum," Sophie said, "something to do with your lunch box being the wrong one. Your mother was plenty mad at you herself, but then a nun stopped and told her what she would do if that were her child. 'Well,' your mother responded, 'maybe that's why God made me a mother and you a nun.' That was your last day in Catholic school."

The building I see across Atlantic Avenue is large and square and plain, six stories of yellow brick. The wall facing Atlantic Avenue has the blank look of a wall that was once hidden by a neighboring building that has since been torn down, a sort of surprised expression like a kid who's been caught daydreaming in class. To make up for it, St. Christopher's has painted its logo—a giant hand holding up a small, stylized infant—and an advertisement for its social services, all in a pale green that matches the architrave on the front of the building. Angels, carved in bas-relief from the same yellow stone, spread their wings just below the architrave.

It's an imposing building to approach and I find myself hoping, as I cross Atlantic, that Sister D'Aulnoy is more like Agatha Dorothy than Amelia Dolores. The person I find, after the security guard's phone call brings her to the front entrance, is a small, compact woman with short gray hair in civilian clothes that look like they've been ordered out of L. L. Bean or Land's End. Other than the small silver crucifix hanging from her neck and an enamel RC pin on her navy cardigan, there's no external sign that she's a nun.

She takes me to her office. We could be in any office building, except that at the end of the hallway glass doors open into a small chapel.

"Anthony Acevedo called and said you were researching a book about your mother," Sister D'Aulnoy says, seating herself behind a desk piled high with file folders.

"Yes, my mother grew up in this neighborhood and went to St. Mary Star of the Sea . . ."

Sister D'Aulnoy removes her half-moon glasses and lets them dangle from a bright orange cord around her neck where they soon become tangled with the silver crucifix. She folds her hands in her lap and sits back in her chair, waiting to hear my story. There's nothing at all in her demeanor to suggest impatience, but looking around me, at the stacks of folders, the brightly colored Post-it notes decorating every surface of her desk with messages like "Cookies!" and "Basketballs for Staten Island Home!," the pictures that line her walls of boys—young boys, black, Hispanic, white, boys in military uniforms and graduation caps and basketball jerseys—I know that Sister D'Aulnoy probably has at least half a dozen pressing demands on the time I'm about to take up. Which I suppose is a poor excuse for lying to a nun, but that's exactly what I proceed to do.

". . . and her brothers came here to St. Christopher's after their mother died." It's easy once I start. All I have to do is transpose my mother's story with her friend's. Besides, a little voice inside me pleads in self-justification, my mother made it her story. She took what happened to the McGlynns and turned it into a whole world—Tirra Glynn. Rose was her best friend; John, I feel sure, her childhood sweetheart. Their story caused her to flee the city in 1949 and their story brought her back to Brooklyn in 1973 where she died. It was because of them that I lost her, so in a way, they owe me a family allegiance.

"I believe one of my uncles, Arden McGlynn, died here and the other two, John and Allen, eventually ended up in prison. At least that's what the newspaper story said." I take out the photocopied story of Rose's plea to the court and hand it to Sister D'Aulnoy, but she gives it only a cursory glance and keeps her soft blue eyes on me.

"And your mother never spoke of them?"

"No . . . it must have been painful having her family broken up like that." As I say it, sitting in this cramped office which, for all I know, could be the very room where Rose saw her brothers when she came to visit, I realize for the first time how painful it must have been. Like me, Rose lost her mother when she was young, but unlike me she lost her whole world as well. Her father fell apart, her younger brothers were given over to strangers. In her plea to the judge she said she regretted not keeping them herself—but how could she have? She was only seventeen.

"I can understand that it must have been painful for your mother's family," Sister D'Aulnoy is saying, "but it wasn't unusual. When St. Christopher's was founded the boys who came here were orphans, often living on the streets, making a living—if you could call it that—as newsboys. But then, during the Depression, many families who couldn't feed their children turned to St. Christopher's to take care of the younger ones. Our records from that time are very spotty—children came and went sporadically—but I'd like to help you attain some sense of closure. What exactly do you want to know?"

"I'd like to know how old the younger brothers were and how Arden died and . . ." I pause, suddenly unsure of what I expected from coming here, and scan the faces on the wall. I notice that some of the photos aren't of boys, but of men in middle age standing in front of homes or businesses, with families, in front of Rotary Club daises. Alumni of St. Christopher's showing off their successful lives to their alma mater—orphans who've graduated into family men.

"I'd like to know if Allen or John is still alive. I mean, they could be, and they could still be in touch with you, right?"

Sister D'Aulnoy doesn't answer at first. I see her studying me and I'm afraid that she's somehow seen through my deception. If she doesn't believe these McGlynn boys are my uncles she's unlikely to provide me with any information of their whereabouts.

"I'd have to check the archives in the subbasement—" Another basement! My trip to Brooklyn is turning into a spelunking expedition, but then Sister D'Aulnoy must sense my reluctance, or else she wants to look at those files first by herself. "—I suggest you wait in the chapel. If I find anything I'll bring it to you there."

After the soaring space of St. Mary Star of the Sea this chapel seems low and plain. The stained-glass windows, deeply recessed into thick white plaster walls, let in only the murkiest trickle of greenish light. The ceiling is coffered into pale blue squares, which I suppose are painted to represent sky, but instead the effect is of standing under water.

"Did the chapel look like this in the forties?" I ask Sister D'Aulnoy.

"As our population became decreasingly Catholic the pews and altar were removed. But we've left the windows that depict St. Christopher carrying Christ across the river. They're more river than saint anyway. Here—" She motions me toward one of the chairs that stand against the walls. "—why don't you sit here while I go to find your uncles' files—" She touches her hand to my arm. "Many find it a place of peace."

She pads out of the chapel—silent on crepe-soled shoes—and I sit staring at the wall of stained-glass windows. The truth is I've never known quite what to do with myself in churches and synagogues, having had little practice or training. I'm never sure what to do with my hands or my eyes or my thoughts. I usually resort to art history lectures—ticking off vaults and naves and quatrefoil windows instead of stations of the cross—and today is no exception. I look at the stained-glass windows. Sister D'Aulnoy is right, there's more river than saint in them. Ranged along the long wall of the nave they depict a single episode: the giant St. Christopher carrying the child Christ across the river. At first the river is calm and shallow, but as St. Christopher begins his journey the waters become turbulent and deep. By the middle window the water is nearly over Christopher's head, his toes, pointed and arched like a dancer's, barely touch the river bottom, his neck strains to keep his head above water, and his right arm holds the Christ child just above the water's surface. Nor does the water recede in the next two windows. Instead, the river's current—swirls of blue and green glass—wraps around the giant's legs and arms like pieces of seaweed and even—I get up to get a closer look—snakes or eels biting into the saint's flesh. I've never seen this particular episode in Christ's life depicted quite like this, but it reminds me of something else: my mother's description of the selkies shedding their skin under the drowned river, in the place where the salt water meets fresh.

"They're unusual, aren't they?" I startle as if caught desecrating the holy water—or stealing from the collection plate as my mother had been accused of—but it's only Sister D'Aulnoy on her crepe-soled shoes crossing the chapel to stand beside me before the windows. "They were done at the turn of the century by a graduate of St. Christopher's. I think you can see the influence of art nouveau in the sinuous curves of the current and the way the water turns into various creatures. I've read in his letters to the monsignor that he wanted to show how St. Christopher carried the Christ child safely above the roiling river just as the home had borne him safely through the turmoil of his orphaned childhood."

I look at the last window, which depicts St. Christopher emerging from the water. The saint looks exhausted and battered by the deluge, not triumphant. The staff in his hand springs into luxuriant green foliage, which shelters him. It reminds me of my mother's book when the selkie Deirdre climbs out of the drowned river, flayed of her selkie skin, and walks through the forest, which clothes her in its foliage. And then I remember the stained-glass window at the Red Branch Pub of Naoise and his brothers—of course, they were named Allen and Arden!—carrying Deirdre across the water away from the evil king Connachar. The two stories must have become intertwined in my mother's mind. I feel sure my mother was thinking of these windows when she described Deirdre's transformation under the river, which suggests that she visited John McGlynn here.

"Would you like to see your uncles' files?"

I'm thrown for a moment by my forgotten lie. Not uncle, I think, my mother's sweetheart, the boy she left behind in a prison by the river.

"I'm surprised you found it so fast," I say to deflect Sister D'Aulnoy's probing glance—I imagine she's had years of experience detecting lies. "Down in the subbasement."

"It wasn't in the subbasement," she says, gently steering me back to the chairs across from the windows. "I thought the *McGlynn* name sounded familiar and then I remembered that one of our board directors had asked for the boys' files a few months ago. It was still on my desk."

"Who? . . ." I begin to ask the name of the director, but Sister D'Aulnoy is already fitting her glasses on to read something to me. I don't want to seem more interested in the board director than my "uncles," but I promise myself I'll get the name before I leave.

"I remembered it too because the nun who did their admittance papers wrote a full account of the family situation—a Sister Dominica—she was admirably thorough. Do you want to hear it?"

I nod, wishing Sister D'Aulnoy would give me the paper, but she seems determined to mediate between me and her predecessor.

"John McGlynn—that would be the father—came to St. Christopher's in March 1941 seeking shelter for his three sons because his wife, Deirdre—"

"Deirdre? His wife's name was Deirdre?"

Sister D'Aulnoy gives me a puzzled look over the half circles of her glasses. "Yes, Deirdre. That would be your grandmother's name. Didn't your mother tell you her own mother's name?"

I shake my head. The truth is, my mother never did tell me her mother's name—a fact that makes me blush with shame now. Seeing that, Sister D'Aulnoy lowers her eyes to the file and goes on.

"Because his wife, Deirdre, had recently died in childbirth. It was to have been Mrs. McGlynn's seventh child—" Anticipating my interruption, Sister D'Aulnoy holds up an admonishing hand. "—she'd lost the last two children she'd borne at home soon after childbirth and she'd been so anxious to deliver this one safely that she'd gone to the Hospital of the Holy Family. Unfortunately, Mr. McGlynn, perhaps out of the disorder in his mind resulting from grief and, I'm sorry to say, heavy drinking, blamed his wife's demise on the hospital. He thought the doctors had put the life of the baby before the life of his wife. He also believed that his wife's weakened condition was a result of having so many children—and he blamed the church for that."

"As if he had nothing to do with it." I actually clamp my hand over my mouth as soon as the words are out. No wonder my mother took me out of Catholic preschool. Nuns seem to bring out the worst in me. Surprisingly, though, Sister D'Aulnoy takes my comment in stride and, even more surprisingly, has more compassion for John McGlynn than I.

"He wouldn't have been the first—or the last—to blame the church for encouraging large families and prohibiting birth control. Poor woman. Imagine having seven children—and I see from the boys' birth certificates that she was only thirty-nine when she died! I'm afraid though that Sister Dominica had few words of compassion for him here. 'I warned him against impugning the church, especially in the presence of his young daughter who'd accompanied him, but he was too far gone in his grief to heed me and the girl, instead of thanking me, told me that her father wasn't saying anything she hadn't thought already. I'm afraid that since the girl is old enough to be on her own she's outside the realm of our help and we'll just have to do the best we can with the boys.' "

Sister D'Aulnoy falls silent even though I can see from the motion of her pale blue eyes behind her thick glasses that she's still reading to herself.

"Well? And what about the boys?"

"She gives a summary of their health, general physical appearance, and hygiene, all of which seems all right except for the youngest boy, Arden. He had a withered arm."

"A withered arm?"

"Yes, from an early bout with polio."

"Isn't he the one who died here?"

Sister D'Aulnoy shifts through the rest of the file and extracts an official-looking document. "He died a year after his admittance here. I imagine he was weakened from his childhood illness." Sister D'Aulnoy looks up from the file and I see a look I hadn't been expecting—apology.

"I want you to know that this isn't the only kind of story here at St. Christopher's. Many of the boys who've come here over the years have thrived, gone on to have careers and families . . ." I think of the picture-lined wall in her office. "I could show you some very inspiring letters from our graduates. Although the boys don't live here anymore—they're in group homes—many go to nearby colleges. I've suggested to the monsignor that the top floors of this building could be turned into a dormitory for those boys, but so far we haven't found the funding . . ." Her voice trails off. ". . . but none of that changes the fact that your uncles' experience here was not a happy one." I'm glad when she lowers her eyes back to the file. I'm not the one she should be apologizing to, but as far as I know there aren't any McGlynns left to listen to this story, so I do.

"The oldest boy, John, seems to have shown quite a bit of academic promise. The monsignor was recommending him for a scholarship to St. John's College, but after Arden's death his behavior deteriorated. When he reached eighteen he left St. Christopher's without graduating. There's a series of addresses given for him, most in Coney Island—I gather that's where his sister, Rose, had gone to live. He came back often to take Allen out for weekends, but . . ." Sister D'Aulnoy pauses over another letter, shaking her head. Several of the papers she's flipped through drift to the floor. I kneel to pick them up.

"On one of their excursions Allen and John were picked up for shoplifting in Flatbush. After that Allen wasn't allowed to leave the premises or have visitors."

"Not Ro—my mother either? That doesn't seem fair."

"Apparently your mother had been expelled from St. Mary Star of the Sea for stealing from the collection plate. The family was deemed a poor influence. It does seem a shame, though. There are several letters here from Rose asking to see Allen . . . I . . . I don't see copies of any response."

Sister D'Aulnoy takes off her glasses. I look up at her—I'm still kneeling, gathering the fallen papers, the marble floor cold on my injured knees—and see the tears in her eyes. She reaches for me and, to my horror, crouches down, puts her arm around my shoulders, and with her other hand clasps both my hands in hers. "Your poor mother," she says, "it must have broken her heart."

After that I try to get out of there as quickly as possible. I don't know what I'm more horrified by: the McGlynn family story or my own impersonation of a descendant. Sister D'Aulnoy promises me she'll look further into what happened to the boys and escorts me all the way down the long hall to the exit, still holding on to my hand as if I were a child. She points out the pictures along the wall showing the early founders of St. Christopher's, portraits of Dominican nuns who taught here, young men in service uniforms accepting medals, group shots of boys at picnics and basketball games and graduations. Then there are the photographs of well-dressed men and women at benefit banquets and charity balls. We're almost at the end of the hall when I see a familiar face. It's in a newspaper photograph that's been framed. The caption reads, "Chief Officers of the Board of Directors of St. Christopher's at the 1962 Annual Benefit Dinner." The group seated at a curved banquet, smiling for the camera, is of five men and one woman. I recognize one of the men as Peter Kron, but his isn't the face I've stopped for. It's Hedda Wolfe, seated next to Peter, one hand—I notice the fingers are slender and not yet gnarled by arthritis—resting on his arm.

"You said a board member had recently asked for the McGlynn file. Was it Hedda Wolfe?"

Sister D'Aulnoy looks as if she's going to tell me that the information is confidential and then she relents—in consideration, no doubt, of my tragic family history. "Yes, do you know Ms. Wolfe? She and Mr. Kron—not that one in the picture, but his brother—are two of our longest-serving board members."

"Um . . . I've heard of her. She's a famous literary agent." I wonder to myself how she knew about Rose McGlynn and her brothers and why she didn't tell me about my mother's connection to them. That feeling I'd had earlier in the day of following a labyrinth set out by someone else recurs, but this time instead of making me feel dizzy it enrages me.

Because she is still holding my hand I can't end my meeting with Sister D'Aulnoy by holding out a hand for a businesslike shake. She seems reluctant to see me go, one more McGlynn orphan let loose into the world by St. Christopher's, abandoned on the river's edge. I wish now that I could confess my lie—tell her that my mother was only John's childhood sweetheart, not his sister, that for all I know my mother still had a mother and father when she took off upstate—but when she pulls me into her soft arms, I don't resist. After all, I am an orphan now, as alone in the world as any of the boys who found their way to this door.

The traffic on Atlantic is a rude surprise after the quiet of the chapel. I'm nearly run over crossing back to Court Street. I turn once more to look at the building in the dying light and notice that one of the angels on the corner of the building has only one wing; the other wing has been broken off. I stare at it for a long time, thinking about Arden's withered arm, and the creatures in my mother's stories whose wings break through their spines, and also of the story that Gretchen Lu told me in the Greenmarket all those months ago, of a sister who tried to save her brothers by staying quiet and knitting them shirts of nettles, only she'd been unable to finish the arm on the last sweater and the youngest boy was left with a broken wing for an arm. Then I turn away and walk toward the subway to take me back to Manhattan.

Chapter Twenty-nine

It's dark when I emerge from the subway station on 14th Street and I feel as tired as if I had swum across the East River—as drenched too, from sweating in the un-air-conditioned train. My scraped knees, though, feel as if I had crawled here. I want, more than anything, to go home, take a cool shower, and order in Chinese food, but if I postpone to tomorrow this last visit it will be one more day before I can call Aidan. One more day he'll have to wait wondering if I'm ever going to call.

I walk west on 14th toward the meatpacking district. The trendy new boutiques and art galleries are closed now, but the stalls with their deliveries of freshly slaughtered meat are still open, the smell of blood mingling with the breeze off the river. I almost turn back, but then I see a light on in Hedda's loft and, sidestepping a jet of water from a meat vendor's hose, ring her bell. She lets me in right away, without asking for my name, as if she's been expecting me—or someone else.

Someone else, I would guess, from her low-cut silk sweater, a double strand of creamy pearls filling the wide neckline, and snug-fitting satin capris. If she's surprised to see me she does a good job covering it up; not that I can make out her expression too well since she's standing above me on the metal stairs, her face hidden in the shadows.

"Iris, finally! I've been trying you all day. Did you get my messages?"

"No, I've just come back from Brooklyn," I say, climbing the stairs. I hadn't noticed on my first—and only—visit here how the sound of footsteps on the metal stairs reverberates through the empty space of the warehouse's first floor.

"Brooklyn?" Hedda says when I've joined her on the landing. I notice that she's holding the door to her apartment partly closed behind her.

"Yes, to St. Christopher's Home for Boys. I believe you're familiar with it?"

One of her hands—the one not holding the door—flutters to her pearls, which click together in the echoing space, and then bats at her hair as if pushing back a wayward strand, but, as always, her hair is perfect, a glistening silver wing. "You'd better come in then," she says, holding the door open. "We should talk."

She takes me through the living room, past the spiral stairs leading to a second-story loft, and into the kitchen. Unlike the cold formality of the living area, this room is surprisingly cozy, filled with burnished copper pans and honey-colored cabinetry. She offers me a seat at a scarred oak refectory table and pulls a half-filled bottle of white wine from the refrigerator.

"No thanks," I say to her offer of a drink, as invitingly cool as the frosted green bottle looks. I need to keep my wits about me. "I'll have some water." As usual, the sight of Hedda struggling with as simple a chore as getting a glass and pouring water from a frosted pitcher disarms me, but I resist the impulse to feel sorry for her. *She's been lying to you,* I remind myself, *and her lies may well have gotten Joseph killed.*

She gives me my glass of water and pours herself a glass of wine, sets it down at the table, and sits across from me.

"So," she says. "St. Christopher's. You must have figured out your mother's connection to the McGlynns."

"No thanks to you. Did my mother tell you about Rose and John McGlynn?" She shakes her head, taking a sip of wine—a sip so diminutive I suspect it's to postpone answering. In all our conversations up to now I've been deferential, but she doesn't seem surprised or put off by my anger. In fact, a hint of a smile plays around the corners of her mouth.

"No, she never mentioned them. I imagine I was led to them in much the same way you were—through reading about the Crown jewel theft and trial. Of course I connected the name McGlynn to Tirra Glynn and to the name she was registered under when she died. Is that how you arrived at St. Christopher's?"

"Yes," I admit, "several months after you apparently. You could have saved me some time."

"It's not my job to save you time. I expect that part of your memoir will be the story of how you tracked down your mother's secrets. I hope you're keeping a careful journal . . ."

"This isn't about a memoir anymore, Hedda. Joseph is dead."

"I didn't tell you to hire an ex-convict to handle priceless paintings, Iris. I can't see what Joseph has to do with your research."

"Then why did you spend the summer interrogating him? And don't tell me you were after him for fertilizing tips."

Hedda takes a somewhat larger sip of wine, using both hands to steady the glass when she returns it to the tabletop. Then she sidles her chair over closer to me, her pearls clattering together like castanets with the awkward effort of her movement. "It was about another matter," she says in a quieter voice, "about someone else who had been a guest at the hotel."

"Peter Kron?"

She looks away from me or, rather, over my shoulder toward the stairs as if the man I'd just named was hidden upstairs in her boudoir. Only Peter Kron has been dead for nearly thirty years. When she looks back at me her eyes are shining, but whether with tears or anger I'm not sure.

"What makes you think Peter Kron is anything to me?"

"Well, the picture of you and him at the 1962 St. Christopher's benefit banquet for starters and—" I am going to say *and your reaction to hearing his name*, but the tears that have started coursing down her face have made that last part unnecessary.

I wait for her to gain control of herself—I'd make a lousy police interrogator—looking away as she uses the heels of her hands to wipe away the tears and succeeding in only smearing her mascara.

"It's true," she says finally. "I loved Peter Kron and he loved me. The first agency I worked for represented his wife, the great poet Vera Nix. He would call up looking for her because she had said she had a meeting with us, but of course she didn't. There are certain writers—not your mother, mind you—who think their artistic talent gives them the right to do whatever they please. It broke my heart to see what she put that poor man through. You could tell he wasn't strong—that he'd been through something bad in the war and that was probably why he hadn't the strength to leave her. My instructions when he called were to tell him that yes, Miss Nix was out to lunch with Mr. Lyle, but I'd misplaced the name of the restaurant they were dining at. As if I'd ever! Better for me to look like a stupid incompetent ninny than for Vera Nix to get caught with her knickers down." Hedda gets up to refill her wineglass. The pale greenish liquid sloshes into the glass and spills over the rim onto her gnarled fingers.

"So one day I decided to overstep the letter of my instructions just a bit. I said, 'Oh yes, Miss Nix and Mr. Lyle went out for lunch hours ago.' 'And I suppose you've misplaced the reservation again, Heddie,' he said. 'Well no, in fact I haven't, Mr. Kron, they're at the Plaza.' I knew once I said a hotel he'd go. So I did too. I waited for him in the Palm Court and when he came I told him everything—not just about the fictitious luncheons, but the stories I'd heard of what she really did when she went out of town on reading tours and things I'd heard her say about him. I told him I thought it was a crime the way she treated him and that he deserved much more. 'But do I deserve a girl like you, Heddie, with the courage to be honest?' I told him he did. We spent that weekend at the Plaza—I knew she was going out of town—and from then on whenever she was out of town we met there. This was in the midfifties, a few years before I started representing your mother, so you see, she had nothing to do with it."

"But you found out later from Peter that he'd known her at the Crown Hotel. Did he tell you they had had an affair?"

"Yes. He said he'd had a brief fling with her—of course I knew I hadn't been the first—and that Vera found out and accused her of stealing from her room to get her fired."

"That was in John McGlynn's retrial," I say. "Vera Nix accused my mother of stealing and then failed to identify her in a lineup."

"Of course. Someone told her that Peter was having an affair with a maid named Katherine Morrissey, the maid who probably was in and out of her suite twice a day, but she'd never bothered to look at her. For all her slumming around Harlem and the Village she didn't give a damn about the underclass. You see what a monster she was . . ."

"I don't doubt she was a monster—monster enough, perhaps, to still hold a grudge against my mother twenty years later when she ran into her at the Hotel Equinox, especially if she thought her husband was still having an affair with her."

"But we don't know that for sure. Joseph swears they weren't."

"That's what you were trying to find out from Joseph—and from me—whether Peter was still in love with my mother that summer."

Hedda reaches her hand across the table and lays her fingers over mine. They're damp from spilled wine and cold—not like Sister D'Aulnoy's warm hands. "I know you're probably wondering how it could possibly matter so many years after Peter's death. But he stopped seeing me that summer—he said because Vera had finally agreed to have a child—and I've always wondered if that was the real reason. There hasn't been anyone since who's meant as much to me as he did. I'd like to know that I meant as much to him."

"And what did you learn from Joseph?" I ask, taking my hand out from under hers.

"He didn't think they were having an affair. He said that when he saw Kay and Peter together they were arguing . . . and I think I know why. When Peter realized Kay Greenfeder was Katherine Morrissey he told me he wanted to see her because he believed that she'd left town with something of Vera's . . ."

"My mother wouldn't have stolen anything belonging to that woman."

"No, I agree, but Peter said it was something he had given her. I suspect he didn't tell her it belonged to his wife . . . in fact, he did it to me once. Gave me some earrings that later I saw on Vera in an old society page picture."

I'm about to say something about the character of a man who gives away his wife's jewelry to his mistresses, but I decide that maligning Peter Kron will be counterproductive at this point. Hedda's on her third glass of wine and I suspect that she's not a nice drunk. What I need now is a little more information, not a fight.

"Did Joseph say whether Peter Kron got what he was looking for from my mother?"

Hedda shakes her head, again setting those damned pearls rattling. "He said Peter left very abruptly in the middle of August, but he continued to call the hotel and ask to speak to Kay . . ."

"How did Joseph know that?"

"Janine, your telephone operator, told him."

"And did my mother speak with him?"

"At first, no, but then he left a particular message—a name, Joseph said, but Janine couldn't remember what name—and after that Kay took his next call. That was in the last week of September . . ."

"Just before she left for her conference in the city. She must have agreed to meet him at the Dreamland Hotel. He must have found a way to make her return whatever it was she had . . ." I look up and meet Hedda's pale gray eyes. Her tears are all gone now, her eyes clear—not even red from the effort of crying. Even her hair has remained unruffled.

"The net of tears. That necklace in Gordon's slide show that belonged to Catalina della Rosa. That's what my mother had that Peter wanted. And that's what you've wanted all along—not a memoir or my mother's lost manuscript. You thought that if I were up there looking for the manuscript I might find the necklace, but all the while you knew that there's no third book . . ."

"No, Iris, you're wrong there. Your mother did write a third book—she told me she did and Joseph says she was writing that whole last year. I thought if you found her last book it might explain what had happened—the way the selkie story and the winged men tell the story of the McGlynns and the Crown jewel theft and how she and Rose fled the city—"

"You thought it would tell you if she and Peter—he'd be the evil king Connachar, if I'm not mistaken—were in love again. You used me."

"No more than you would have used me to fulfill your ambitions of becoming an author. Please, Iris, you were willing to use your own mother to see your name on a dust jacket."

I open my mouth to protest, but then close it. She is, of course, right.

"Okay. Let's not blame each other. What I want to know now is who killed Joseph. You and I weren't the only ones hounding him with questions all summer. There was Phoebe too. What do you think she knew about my mother and her father?"

"She wasn't even born that summer."

"She had her mother's journals. She's been editing them . . ."

Hedda laughs. "She's been 'editing' those journals for ten years now. It's the joke of the publishing world—the rumor is that Vera Nix's journals contain the ravings of a drunken, insane woman. By the time Phoebe edits out all the drugs and other illegal or immoral activities there won't be enough to fill a comic book."

"What if one of the illegal activities Vera Nix wrote about was killing my mother?"

I'm expecting surprise, but instead I can instantly tell from the way Hedda's eyes flick back and forth nervously that this isn't a new idea. Still, she makes her voice scornful. "You think Vera Nix followed Peter to the Dreamland Hotel, surprised him there with Kay, and killed her? And then what? Set the hotel on fire?"

"Actually, I thought at first that she'd arranged to meet my mother there to get back something from her—some proof of her involvement in the Crown robbery, but I like your idea better. It explains the fire—Peter would have done that to cover up his wife's crime. Monster or not, she was pregnant with his child. And he'd know the hotel was a firetrap from his years of listening to his brother lecture on hotel fire prevention."

"I suppose it's possible . . ." Hedda says, looking away.

"You knew right away, didn't you? As soon as my mother died you knew it was Vera Nix who killed her. But you didn't tell the police because you still wanted to protect Peter. And when he and Vera died it was too late—everyone would have known you withheld information from the police."

"What good would it have done? Everyone involved was dead."

"Not everyone. My father and I would have known that she hadn't been running away with a lover."

"Your father never doubted Kay for a moment. As for you—I offered you the opportunity to find out the truth for yourself and look, you have. Would you have looked so hard if I hadn't agreed to represent your memoir? Would I have set you on this course if I was afraid of what you'd find?"

"You set me on this course without telling me that some people might be willing to kill to keep their secrets. Didn't you wonder what Phoebe would do if it came out that her mother killed my mother?"

"So you think Phoebe shot Joseph? Because he knew that Kay had gone to meet Peter that last night? It's possible, I suppose. I've always believed that Phoebe inherited Vera's mental instability, but why would she think that Joseph was finally going to tell someone who Kay went to see that night after keeping quiet for so many years?"

"Because you and I were both hounding him all summer . . . and because I may have given her the idea that Joseph was ready to tell me something," I admit reluctantly.

"Still, she would have to be really crazy to kill Joseph if he had no proof that Kay was going to meet Peter . . ."

"And if he did have proof—maybe a letter from Peter asking for the necklace—maybe the necklace itself—or my mother's last book, which told the whole story?"

"Why would she think the manuscript was in that room?"

"Because Vera Nix wrote in her journal that she heard my mother typing in the Sleepy Hollow Suite."

"So she went to Joseph's suite to look for the manuscript or the necklace—or to demand it from him at gunpoint—and then she shot him when he wouldn't give it to her and bonked your boyfriend over the head . . ."

"I think she planned to set Aidan up—she told him that he was supposed to check on the paintings one last time—" I notice Hedda's lifted eyebrow and realize I've just let her know that I've had contact with Aidan, but I go on nonetheless. I have a feeling she's the last person who's going to the police right now. "—she let herself in the bedroom door to the suite and waited until Aidan opened the closet to hit him over the head and then she shot Joseph when he tried to get help. As she'd planned to all along— so he could never tell anyone that my mother had been on her way to see Peter Kron the night that she died. I don't know if she found the manuscript or not but I'm pretty sure she didn't find the necklace."

Hedda runs her fingers over the pearls at her neck meditatively and now, instead of that annoying clacking, they make a sound like rain. "Why not? How do you know Phoebe didn't get the necklace?"

"Because I don't think it was in Joseph's suite. I'm not even sure Joseph knew where it was. But I think I do now."

Chapter Thirty

I n the end it wasn't anything Hedda said that led me to that final
revelation—the secret hiding place of the net of tears—it was her pearls.
The sound they kept making whenever she moved and they clicked together. It reminded me of my mother's pearls and the sound they made
when she leaned over me to kiss me good night and her pearls would fall
forward and click against one another. It's the sound I heard the night my
mother went away. I close my eyes and it's as real to me as if I were ten and
my mother was leaning over me—I can almost smell her perfume and feel
the soft collar of her coat . . . I open my eyes, as if to surprise my mother,
and for an instant I do see her—an afterimage of my last sight of her—in
her green coat with the fur collar buttoned to her throat. Any pearls she
was wearing would have lain under the coat. They couldn't have fallen forward and made the clicking sound I heard. Something else must have made
the sound and I believe now it was the stolen necklace—that my mother
took it out of her pocket and hid it in my bedroom. I close my eyes again
and hear her voice telling the selkie story, even though she wouldn't tell it
to me that last night. "In a time before the rivers were drowned by the sea,
in a land between the sun and the moon . . ."

Phoebe might have thought the lines referred to the Sleepy Hollow
Suite, between Half Moon and Sunnyside, but I've thought of another place
between the sun and the moon. On my four-poster bed where the old finials
had come loose Joseph had carved a sun and a moon. I think that my mother

decided at the last minute not to bring the net of tears with her—maybe she believed that she wouldn't be safe once Peter Kron had it—and that she hid it in the bedpost under the sun or the moon. She left it to me just as the selkie left her daughter a parting gift—a necklace woven out of sea spray and dew.

I've called the number Aidan gave me and I've checked the train schedules and my five-boroughs map for how to get from the Marble Hill stop on the Metro-North line to Inwood Park. There's nothing to do now but get some sleep for the long trip ahead of me tomorrow. I doubt I'll be able to sleep, but when I close my eyes I hear my mother's voice—the result of working so hard to conjure that last night with her—telling me the selkie story. I listen to it up to the part where the selkie's daughter brings her mother her skin and they both fall asleep wrapped in its warmth. I can almost feel her fingers in my hair, combing away the tangles, weaving her story.

In my dream I follow my mother into the sea. We swim together to the mouth of a great river and still the warm salt tide carries us as if we were riding in the palm of a giant's hand. It's only when I feel the cold fingers of the river's freshwater current that I am afraid. I try to catch my mother's hand—she is above me swimming between me and the river's surface where the sun shines through the water—but when I touch her the skin comes away in my hand. *But I thought I gave you back your true skin.* I can't speak the words because we're under the river but she turns to me as if she'd heard. She turns in a column of sunlight pouring through the water, turns like something unfurling in the sun's light, turns and keeps on turning, her face dark against the brilliant light, her skin falling away like a peel from an apple's core.

I awake drenched in sweat, parched and feverish. When I kick the sheets away from me I see bloodstains from the cuts on my knees that have opened up in the night. Even after I've taken a cool shower and drunk two tall glasses of water I feel hot and my throat feels sore. I take my temperature and find I've got a fever of 101. I take a couple of aspirin, rebandage my knees, and head out to Grand Central.

I've decided to take Metro-North not just because I've had enough of subways, but because I can get off at the Marble Hill stop, walk to Inwood Park, and then continue on the train up to the hotel. I'm not taking any luggage, save for my usual canvas book bag into which I've stowed my toiletries case, because I'm not sure yet if I want to let Aidan know that I'm going up to the hotel. He'll want to go with me and it's the last place on earth he should go.

I get off the Metro-North at the Marble Hill station and walk across the 225th Street Bridge, crossing the Harlem Ship Canal, which would be the border of Manhattan if not for the anomalous neighborhood of Marble Hill, which lies north of the canal. I pause on the steel bridge to look west at a large C painted on an outcropping of rock and a glimpse of the Hudson beyond the Henry Hudson Bridge. On a walking tour I took of the neighborhood several years ago I learned that the C was painted by the Columbia rowing team sometime in the 1930s and that the canal—which joins the Harlem River to the Hudson—was dug in 1917 in order to move iron to a munitions plant. Prior to the canal, the two rivers were connected only by Spuyten Duyvil Creek, which was sometimes more marshland than creek. When I enter Inwood Hill Park I see a reminder of that marshland—a tidal estuary, I read on one of the informative plaques set out by the Parks Department, rising and falling with the passage of the sea up the Hudson. A lone egret, slim and white, daintily picks its way along the shoreline. In the humid haze—and if you squint a bit to edit out the few skateboarders and picnickers on the grass—it's possible here to imagine Manhattan as it was when Dutch settlers first purchased it from the Algonquins. A swampy island—not even a proper island—embraced by three rivers and a creek at the mouth of the sea. In fact, the rock where Aidan has told me to meet him commemorates that sale—or at least its plaque commemorates the tulip tree, now cut down, under which the sale took place.

I'm early so I lean against the rock and watch some teenagers lounging on the grass—a group of girls in tank tops and shorts, passing a tube of suntan lotion around their circle, some boys in oversized canvas pants tossing a Frisbee back and forth—hitching their pants up over their slim hips after each throw—another boy with bleach-dyed spiky hair in the same uniform of oversized pants and black T-shirt lying on his side reading a book with a mermaid on the cover. He shuts the book, ambles toward me, and metamorphoses into Aidan. Aidan in disguise of bleached hair and sunglasses, managing to look about ten years younger than he really is.

"What gave me away?" he asks after kissing me. Two of the teenage girls lean toward each other and laugh. It was bad enough when I was a thirty-six-year-old dating a twenty-nine-year-old; now it looks like my tastes run to high school boys.

"The book," I say, plucking at the old paperback wedged under his arm. "It's my mother's. *The Net of Tears*—the second in the series. And the last. My father always hated this edition because of the mermaid."

"Yeah, I wondered about that, there aren't any mermaids in the whole damned book."

I smile, pleased at this evidence that he's read it. "Where'd you find it?"

"At a used-book store in Riverdale. I thought I might as well spend my holiday doing a bit of research." Aidan turns toward the lawn and notices the teenage girls looking at us. "Let's walk," he says, "I know a place that will give us a little more privacy."

The path Aidan leads me to is soon private enough, shaded by the tall canopy of trees and narrowed by the encroaching underbrush. In fact, after a little while, it doesn't look much like a path at all and we have to walk single file, Aidan in the lead.

"Are you sure you know where you're going?" I ask, batting at a swarm of tiny insects that have settled around my head.

"I grew up in this park," he says, turning his head slightly. At this angle, with the sunglasses and the dyed hair, it doesn't look like Aidan at all. An irrational cold tide of panic moves through me—or maybe not so irrational, I think. After all, I am following a wanted criminal into the underbrush of a city park where a body could be left to decay for years before anyone would ever come across it.

Aidan, unaware of my fears, is blithely rambling on about the park—about how it's supposed to be one of the oldest stands of uncut forest in New York State, how you can still find the ruins of millionaires' mansions in the woods and how the bones of a prehistoric mastodon were discovered at the turn of the century. He stops abruptly, turns on the narrow path, and wraps his arms around me. We're both so slick with sweat that his arms sliding against my arms and under my drenched T-shirt feel like a serpent coiling around my body; his mouth, hot and insistent at mine, seems to suck the breath right out of me, and I'm caught somewhere between struggling to the surface and wanting to sink deeper into the embrace.

When he takes his mouth away from mine he whispers into the hollow of my throat, "I didn't think I'd ever see you again."

I don't know what to say so I hold on to him tighter, the sweat binding us together until I can't tell where his skin ends and mine begins.

We cross a bridge that goes over the Metro-North tracks and come to a stretch of green grass and benches bordering the river. We sit at the northernmost bench where we can see all the way up to the Tappan Zee where the river is as wide as a sea. I tell Aidan everything I learned at John Jay and St. Mary Star of the Sea and St. Christopher's.

"No wonder your mother was inspired to name her world after that family—they had even worse luck than most Irish people I know. Reading this book of your mother's is like living every agony a people ever went through—the way the poor men's backs are split in two and the women's bodies are wrenched apart by the river. The wonder is she's writing for the most part about her friend's family, not her own."

"Well, Tirra Morrissey doesn't have quite the same ring as Tirra Glynn. I do think that the part about Deirdre's affair with Connachar came from her own history with Peter Kron, but I think Naoise is John McGlynn, that the imagery of the broken wings comes both from the carvings on St. Christopher's and what happened to Arden McGlynn's arm, and the selkie ripped apart in the river is Rose when she falls under the train. Remember, Rose was her best friend, and I'm sure she was in love with John. They were like her family."

I show him the picture of my mother with Rose and John at the beach in Coney Island and then I tell him about my conversation with Hedda.

"I don't doubt but that Phoebe would kill Joseph before letting him prove her mother a murderer, but there's one thing I don't quite get," Aidan says. "That necklace described in your mother's book—the one she calls the net of tears—you think Peter Kron stole it from Italy, gave it to his wife, and then John McGlynn stole it from her?"

"Yes. Remember, Gordon said that the *ferronière* may have been taken from the church and hidden in a villa by descendants of the della Rosas. Peter Kron hid out in a villa that belonged to some countess. After his first lecture I saw Gordon talking to Joseph. He thanked him for giving him a tip—Joseph said it had something to do with a countess he'd known after the war. Harry told me that he talked to the countess who shielded Peter after the war and that she was staying at the Hotel Charlotte in Nice. That's where Joseph worked after the war. I think Joseph was helping Gordon tie the theft of the *ferronière* to Peter Kron . . ."

"But you said Phoebe couldn't care less about her father."

"Yes, but his having the *ferronière* could tie Vera to the robbery . . . and to the murder of my mother."

Aidan nods and takes off his sunglasses and I notice that he has dark rings under his eyes. He looks unconvinced by my explanation—or maybe he's just too tired to follow it.

"I think we'll know more if I can find the necklace," I say. "Somehow I think my mother will have left some message with it to explain what happened. After all, that's why the selkie leaves her daughter the net of tears in the story—as a message of her love for her."

"I should go up there with you."

"You know you can't, Aidan. I won't be alone—Ramon's there."

"Maybe you should ask Jack to go with you."

"Aidan . . ."

"Really, Iris, I wouldn't be jealous. I'd rather know you're safe. Promise you'll go home now and ask Jack to go with you tomorrow."

"Okay," I tell him, looking over his shoulder at the broad expanse of river. "That's what I'll do. I can still leave a message at the same phone number when I've found out more?"

Aidan puts his sunglasses back on and nods. I wonder if he's trying to hide the scared, restless look that presages flight. I think of what Detective

March told me about how he bolted from the stolen car and caused a police officer to lose his life pursuing him.

"I'll find out something that will clear you," I say to Aidan. "Just stay here in the city where I can reach you. Promise?"

Instead of answering he hands me his copy of *The Net of Tears*. "Take this. I've finished it. Maybe you should reread it. It might give you some ideas about what happened to your mother."

"I will," I say, tucking it in my bag. "I forgot to bring anything to read on the train trip."

He stares at me but all I can see now is my own reflection in the mirrored lenses of his sunglasses.

"It's a good book," he says. "Why don't you take another look for the sequel when you're up at the hotel. I'd like to know how things turned out for the people of Tirra Glynn."

I'm glad that Aidan doesn't offer to walk me to the train station so that he can't see that I'm not taking the subway downtown. It's almost five by the time I pick up the Metro-North, and I'm so tired from our walk through the muggy woods that I sink into a seat without noticing that it's facing the rear of the train. I close my eyes against the glare off the river and half drowse. I remain aware, though, of the light shining through my closed eyelids and it becomes, in my fitful half-sleeping state, the sun shining through the water in my dreams last night. I see my mother silhouetted against the light, her face darkened, her body wavering and insubstantial.

I'm awakened by a nudge from a fellow passenger, a heavyset man leaning over me and breathing onion fumes into my face. "We have to de-train," he's saying. "Equipment failure. They're sending another train."

I stagger out onto the platform just before the train heads back south and look for a bench to sit on, but they're all taken up by disgruntled commuters who are dividing their time by looking down at their watches and then looking southward along the tracks. I find a wall to slump against and stare resentfully at the river and the sun setting over the hills in the west.

The view is familiar to me and after a minute I recognize the stop as Rip Van Winkle. Although I think the man with onion breath said *equipment failure* I have an eerie sense of déjà vu waiting at this stop for a replacement train. This is where my mother stood waiting for the tracks to be cleared of Rose McGlynn's body so she could continue on her way to the Hotel Equinox. I remember that when I was little she told me a version of the story—saying she waited at this stop to change trains (no mention of a friend's suicide) and thought about going back to the city. The possibility that she could have turned away from her destiny of meeting my father and having me always scared me, but now I find myself wondering how she could have possibly continued on her way after what happened here. I find myself considering crossing the bridge over the tracks and taking a southbound train back to the city—Aidan was probably right that I should get Jack to go with me—when I see the woman standing in front of me set down her suitcase and step toward the tracks. Without thinking I step forward, coming up alongside her discarded bag, and reach for her. Startled, she turns. I can't see her face because the setting sun's behind her back.

"Yes?" she says, puzzled. "Do I know you?"

I shake my head and step away from her suitcase. "I'm sorry. I thought you were someone else."

She smiles nervously and then points down the tracks. "Look," she says, "here's the replacement."

Chapter Thirty-one

There's no one to pick me up at the station—no Joseph, no Aidan—so I engage a cab to drive me across the river to the hotel.

"I thought the old Equinox had finally closed down," the cabdriver remarks as we cross the bridge.

"Only temporarily. For repairs."

"The word in town is it's closed for good."

"It will open again in the spring," I assure my driver.

But when we pull up to the front entrance, I'm not so sure myself. The hotel is completely dark. Even the outside lights are off.

"Doesn't look like anyone's home," the cabdriver observes laconically while taking my money.

"The desk clerk and one of the maids have been hired to stay the winter. The construction crew must have left for the night and switched off the electricity because of some repair—or maybe they cut a line accidentally . . ."

The cabdriver, uninterested in my speculations and seemingly unconcerned about leaving me alone here, shifts the taxi into drive.

"I may need a cab in the morning," I tell him.

He pauses long enough to hand me a card with the taxi company number on it and drives back around the circular drive, his taillights disappearing at the dark edge of the woods. When that light is gone I'm left in almost total darkness. I'd noticed that the moon, to my back as we crossed the river, is full, but it hasn't risen far enough to light this side of the hotel yet. Even without light, though, I can sense the desolation of the garden. The annual borders have withered into humpbacked clumps against the shaggy, untrimmed hedges; the rosebushes, thrusting out leggy shoots topped with dead blooms, sprawl against the trellises. Clearly the gardeners, Ian and Clarissa, have been let go even though I'd thought Harry planned to keep them on a few more weeks. A wind from the north sweeps through the garden, shaking loose a few leaves and making a dry sound as it moves through the withered vegetation. I shiver, wishing I'd thought to bring a sweater—it's so easy to forget it's colder up here—and go inside.

In the lobby, moonlight streams through the French doors from the east side of the hotel, pooling on the white dropcloths that cover the furniture and carpet. Two stepladders stand in the middle of the room. Large paint cans line the top of the front desk, which has also been draped in white cloth. The cans, on closer inspection, contain not only paint but various stains and cleaning fluids and a vast amount of polyurethane—about thirty six-gallon cans. A stack of receipts is weighted down by one of the cans, along with an inventory, in Ramon's handwriting, listing each item and what it's for. Another sheet of paper has fallen to the floor and when I stoop to pick it up a breeze steals into the room, rippling the sheets like a current moving over stones. I straighten up and walk over to the French doors where I find the one that's ajar—wedged open with another can of polyurethane. The painters must have done it for ventilation, but it was careless to leave it open with no one here. I close and lock it and then read the paper in my hands. It's a fax addressed to Ramon from Harry giving him the address of a plumbing supply store in Syracuse that carries the fixtures that are to be used for the new guest bathrooms. The fax is dated today and it instructs Ramon to make sure the fixtures are available for the plumbing contractors who are due to start work tomorrow. No wonder Ramon's not here—it's a good five-hour drive to Syracuse and the time on the fax reads three-ten P.M. He could never make the supply store before it closed. He and Paloma must have decided to drive there tonight, pick up the fixtures in the morning, and then come back. If I know Ramon he'll take the back roads through the Catskills and give Paloma a tour of all the old hotels where he appeared onstage, even the ones where his only performance involved singing with a tray of kreplach balanced on his shoulder.

I let myself into the office and check to see if the phones are still working—they are—and take a flashlight out of the supply closet. I consider for a moment calling the cab company and coming back in the morning, but I'm too anxious to see if I'm right about my mother's hiding place. Besides, I've been in the hotel many times during power failures; I imagine I could find my way up to the attic blindfolded.

The main staircase is amply lit by the windows on each landing. In fact, having the lights off allows for a view of the Hudson Valley and river under the moonlight unimpeded by ambient light. Walking up the stairs is like rising in a column of light pouring up from the river, and I feel as if I'm floating above the miniature world of the valley. Once, when I was four or five, my mother woke me in the middle of the night, wrapped me in her coat, and led me through the darkened halls to the fifth-floor landing. An ice storm had knocked out the power and glazed the valley in a crystal sheath. "Look," my mother said, "it's like being inside a snow globe."

When I get to the fifth floor now I stop at the window and look out at the valley, remembering the smoothness of my mother's hand on mine, the softness of the fur collar against my face. I had felt then that my mother created the spectacle for me with as little effort as it would take to tip a real snow globe over and set the miniature snow to falling. As I grew older I never doubted that she had the power to hold a world in the palm of her hand, the world she invented of fabulous creatures from a land under the sea, of women who could shed their skins and men who could fly. Now I wonder how much control she had over that other world. Maybe she had hoped to gain control by turning the demons of her youth into fantasy creatures, but instead the world she created welled up and flooded into the life she had made for herself here with me and my father.

When I turn into the fifth-floor hallway there is no light anymore from the windows. I switch my flashlight on and trail my fingers along the walls to guide my way to the attic stairs and up to my room. After a few steps I notice that my shoes are sticking to the floor; each step I take makes a faint sucking sound. I stop and take a deep breath, almost choking on the fumes. No wonder the workers left the French doors open downstairs—the floors have already been refinished with their first coat of polyurethane— the whole hotel reeks of it. Really they should have left more windows open for ventilation and I promise myself I'll do it before I leave. For now, though, there's nothing I can do about the damage my footprints do—I'll tell Ramon in the morning that this hallway will have to be redone. At least when I get to the attic stairs I find they haven't been refinished.

At my door I have to put the flashlight down to look through my bag for my room key. At first, when I can't find it, I curse to myself—I'll have to go all the way down to the desk again for a master key—but then I remember that I slipped it into a jewelry pouch in my toiletries case. I open the door, leaving the key in the lock, and set the flashlight on the top of my bureau, its beam directed toward my bed where it hits the chipped yellow paint of the sun finial. I'll try the sun first, I decide, but after I've lit a candle for more light.

Unscrewing the finial is harder than I thought it would be—Joseph must have glued it—and I'm beginning to think that if it's this hard it's unlikely my mother hid anything here when it comes loose. I shine the flashlight down into the hollow post. There's nothing there. When I lean over to put back the sun finial, which I'd left on the night table, I drop the flashlight behind the bed.

The flashlight is wedged between the headboard and the wall and I have to pull the bed forward—which sends the flashlight crashing to the floor. I'm reminded of my last clandestine effort—taking the 1973 registration book from Harry Kron's suite. At least now there's no one in the hotel to hear the racket I'm making.

I suppose it's thinking about the registration book that makes me do what I do next. When I've retrieved the flashlight from the floor I shine it on the back of the headboard and notice that the unfinished plywood on this side is crudely stapled to the sides of the headboard and one side is loose. I slide my hand in under the loose flap of wood and immediately feel the smooth leather edge of a bound book, which I manage to slide out from under the loose board. It's a registration book, but when I shine the flashlight on its spine there's no date. I open it and find that the pages have been cut out. In their place is a stack of typed manuscript pages held together by a rubber band. On the first page are printed the words: *The Selkie's Daughter: Memory of a Brooklyn Childhood*.

Sitting on the edge of the bed I remove the rubber band, turn to the first page, and read the first line, "In a time before the rivers were drowned by the sea, in a land between the sun and the moon . . ." and feel a wave of disappointment wash over me. It's only an early draft of the first Tirra Glynn book after all. Perhaps my mother hid it up here when she was still a maid . . . but then I read on and see that this is not a fantasy novel. After a few lines of the selkie story, which I notice now are enclosed in quotation marks, the narrator breaks in. "This was my favorite story when I was a child. My mother told it to me, as her mother told it to her, a long line of mothers going back to the little island where her family came from, Cloch Inis, Stone Island, which lies between Grian Inis, Sun Island, and Gealach Inis, Moon Island."

The land between the sun and the moon. I tear myself away from the book. There will be time to read later. It's hard to believe that after trying so long to tease my mother's secrets out of the web of her fantasy world the answers were here all the time—above my head as I lay sleeping—not coded in fairy tales or fantasy, but laid out in plain memoir.

I'm only the tiniest bit disappointed to realize that the existence of this book makes the one I'd planned to write unnecessary. My mother wrote her own story. She doesn't need me to do it for her.

I move the book aside and go to work on the moon finial, which pops off in my hand easily. Without bothering with the flashlight I stick my fingers down the hole and graze something soft as velvet. Dead mouse, I think with a shudder, but when I force myself to retrieve the little bundle I see it is velvet. A velvet jewelry pouch. I pour its contents into the palm of my hand, which I cup under the beam of the flashlight. It takes me a moment to realize what I've got and what it means and in the next moment I hear an odd sound coming from the floor below me—a sound like someone ripping heavy tape off a package—the sound footsteps make on wet polyurethane. I look back at what I have in my hands and know who it is that's coming and what I've got to do.

By the time Harry shows up at my door I'm sitting on the edge of the bed, which I've pushed back against the wall.

"My dear," Harry says, his hand on the doorknob, "I knew you would find it! I knew my faith in you would not go unrewarded." He slips the key out of the lock, pockets it, and removes a gun from the same pocket. Then he closes the door and approaches the bed.

"The *ferronière* and the manuscript. Well done! You won't mind if I have a look at the jewelry first—you see, I'm not such a big fan of science fiction."

I hand over the pouch, my eyes fastened on the gun in Harry's hand. "It's not a fantasy book," I say, "it's a memoir. My mother's life." Harry spills the contents of the pouch out into his hand and holds the string of jewels up in the beam of the flashlight. They glisten like a spill of water in the dark room.

"Lovely, isn't it? No one crafted gold like the quattrocento Italian goldsmiths. And it's not just the crude value of the stones—which is, I assure you, in the millions—but the history of the piece, the stories . . . why, your mother may have added value to it by including it in her novels. I'll consider it interest on a long loan."

"I suppose your brother Peter took it," I say, "and when you found out it was too late to give it back to the countess."

Harry laughs. "Peter? I'm afraid when I found him at the Countess Val d'Este's villa he was in such a stupor of fear and alcohol he wouldn't have been capable of distinguishing a fifteenth-century heirloom from a dime-store bauble. But the countess did mention to me that she believed the *ferronière* was still hidden in the church of Santa Maria Stella Maris. When my battalion entered the town—just hours after it had been retaken by the Allies—I went straight to the church. It had been hidden by the abbot but when I told him I was a Monuments officer and we needed to move all national artistic treasures to a safe location he showed me where he had hidden it. Unfortunately the abbot was struck by enemy fire—the town was crawling with snipers—and later, the church was bombed. So you see, if I hadn't taken it, it would have been lost forever."

I nod as if this explanation excused him of killing an abbot or any of the other crimes he's committed since to keep his theft a secret, but he's too enraptured by his recovered treasure to pay much attention. He doesn't care, I realize, what I think. If he did, he'd have gone along with my suggestion that Peter stole the jewels in the first place. He doesn't care because he doesn't intend to let me leave here. Knowing this is like taking the cold plunge into the pool below the falls—painful, but a relief of sorts after wading on the edge.

"You must have been very angry when John McGlynn stole it from you—after you went to so much trouble to get it."

"On the contrary, I hired John McGlynn to steal it for me. Peter—idiot that he was—had let Vera get a hold of it. My fault, I suppose, because I'd shown it to her. I might have gotten it back from her, but I wanted to get the rest of the Kron family jewels out of her hands as well. The stupid woman would have lost most of them eventually—so I figured why not kill two birds with one stone. The only problem was that when John left the jewels at the locale we had decided upon he neglected to leave the *ferronière*. He thought he could get away with keeping it . . ."

"Because he knew where it came from. Rose told him. She knew the story from St. Mary Star of the Sea. He thought that since you stole it, you wouldn't chase after him."

"Stupid boy. I had to have some friends with the police apprehend him—with the jewels he'd given back to me hidden in his hotel room—but by then he'd hidden the *ferronière*."

"Why didn't he tell the police you hired him to steal the jewels?"

"Who were they going to believe? A wealthy pillar of the community or a reform school dropout with a criminal record? I believe he tried it on his defense attorney and was smart enough to be talked out of trying it on a jury. I knew, though, that he wasn't smart—or patient—enough to wait twenty years to retrieve the *ferronière*. He would tell his sister."

"So you sent one of your men to the Rip Van Winkle train station to scare her into telling where it was." I picture the station as I passed through it today. The woman who stood in front of me who put down her suitcase and stepped forward toward the tracks. "Only he went a little overboard; he scared her so much she fell onto the tracks into the path of an approaching train."

Harry makes a disapproving tsking sound. "That's what comes of not attending to important business yourself. It gets bungled. By the way, how do you know I didn't go myself?"

"Because you would have realized the girl who fell under the train wasn't Rose McGlynn. It was Katherine Morrissey. Rose McGlynn—" I close my eyes and picture it again. The girl silhouetted against the sun setting over the river, turning and stepping back toward the tracks, the other girl stepping forward. "—my mother, was standing behind her. When she saw what had happened—when she knew what you were willing to do to get your property back—she picked up Katherine's bag and left her own on the platform so everyone would think the dead girl was Rose McGlynn and you wouldn't keep looking for her."

"Very good, Iris, you've got your mother's brain. Unfortunately you've also inherited her recklessness. Imagine her writing those books, telling the whole story as a fairy tale and describing the *ferronière* so precisely."

"You never read them, though; you didn't catch her that way."

"No. I have you to thank for that. The minute I saw you at the gallery I knew you were Rose's daughter." He touches the cold metal shaft of the revolver under my chin and uses it to tilt my face up toward him. It's the first time in my life I'm not glad to be told I look like my mother. I wonder if he plans to shoot me and then try to blame it on Aidan.

"But if you didn't know until this year, who killed my mother at the Dreamland Hotel?"

"Well, that's a very interesting story—too bad you won't get a chance to write it. I was in Europe that summer so I didn't know about it until I got back in the fall. I could tell something had happened to Peter because his slow, decorous decline into alcoholism, which had been going on for years, suddenly became a headlong plunge. I checked around a bit and heard about the fire at the Dreamland and finally pieced together that Vera had followed Peter there to catch him with some woman. When I found out the woman's maiden name was Katherine Morrissey I wasn't surprised, nor was I very interested. I'd known they'd had an affair years ago. It was careless of me, though, not to look into it further. My guess now is that Peter was trying to get the necklace from Kay—whom he recognized as Rose, of course—and that Vera mistook their 'business meeting' for a romantic tryst."

"So Vera shot my mother because she thought she was Katherine Morrissey." This hurts me more than anything else I've learned so far. That my mother's death was a mistake—a case of mistaken identity.

Harry reads my tears as fear for my own life. "I'm very sorry, Iris, that it has to end this way, and I wish I could think of any easier way to take care of you. Peter and Vera didn't realize how lucky they were that your mother's body was burned so completely that no bullet was found, but I can't depend on having the same luck."

As soon as he says the word *fire* I become aware of the smell on his clothes, the sickly sweet fumes of polyurethane.

"Aren't you worried that the fire will look suspicious?"

"An old hotel, careless workmen, all those cans of polyurethane left near a pilot light in the kitchen, every floor coated with the stuff . . . not only will it be easy to explain, it should be mercifully quick. The smoke will probably get you first." He moves so quickly I don't have time to react. The hand holding the gun swings back and then arcs down—a quick glint of cold metal that explodes into a white light inside my head, and then darkness.

Chapter Thirty-two

Now I'm the one floating on the surface looking down at my mother swimming below me. She is trying to tell me something, but when she opens her mouth no words come out, only bubbles that rise through the water and pop around my head—one, two soft explosions and then a series of sharper cracks like Morse code. My mother opens her mouth wide and one large bubble drifts slowly toward me, its thin skin shimmering like the plastic bags in Mr. Nagamora's dry-cleaning store. When it bursts the water around me convulses and knots itself into a hard muscle of current that flings me out of the water onto something hard. I reach for my mother, but instead feel only the hard-packed mud of the riverbank—which slowly, as I struggle to open my eyes, turns into the cold wood floor of my attic bedroom.

The explosions below me have stopped but I know what they were—thirty six-gallon cans of polyurethane set near an open flame. Peeling myself off the floor requires so much effort I wonder if I've been lacquered to the floor with polyurethane, but except for the tacky residue on my shoes, my clothes and skin feel dry. There's only a little dampness around my right temple where Harry struck me with the butt of his gun.

The memory of the gun does wonders to clear my mind. Although my flashlight is gone there's enough light coming in through the window to dimly illuminate the room—which means that the moon has risen far enough to light the west side of the hotel. How long have I been unconscious? Long enough for Harry to get downstairs, move the polyurethane cans into the kitchen and make sure they were close enough to a flame to explode. He'd wait to make sure they had caught fire before leaving.

I drag myself over to the window and using the edge of the windowsill pull myself up to look out. Six floors below me the garden and the drive leading away from the hotel are empty. The gazebos and flower beds, the narrow graveled paths and hedgerows look like a miniature landscape from here—a Christmas village set up in a shopfront window, lit by flickering red and orange bulbs . . . My mouth turns dry as I realize that the garden is lit up by the fire on the ground floor.

The door, when I try it, is locked. I stick my hand into my pants pocket, but it's empty. Did he search me and find the extra room key I hid there before he arrived at my door? Or could it have fallen out of my pocket when I fell? I dive to the floor by the bed, palms flat against the wood to feel for the key, willing myself to stay calm and search carefully, to ignore the sensation I have that the floor is already warm to the touch—that the flames are already licking at the ceiling of the room below me.

How long, how long becomes the chant in my head as I crawl over the floor. How long for the fire to rage through five floors and reach the attic? Will anyone see it from town and send help? But it would be too late—we always knew that up here—that's why my father installed a pump system from the lake. The pump system that Harry shut down at the beginning of the summer. Had this always been the plan? To burn the hotel down once he had what he wanted? I try to push the questions from my head for now. *Later,* I promise myself; there will be a later if only because I can't let him drive away from this, leaving the burned-out shell of the hotel like the hollow carapace an insect sheds.

I've searched every inch of floor around the bed and haven't found the key. I sit back on my heels and try to remember where I was on the bed when Harry hit me. I picture myself falling. Then I remember that often when I was little and I'd lost something—an earring, a bookmark—my mother would run her hand between the bed frame and the mattress and retrieve the lost item, flourishing it the way a magician pulls a coin from behind a child's ear. I stick my hand down between the mattress and the cold metal frame and find dust. But then, halfway down the frame, my fingers loop through a piece of string and when I pull it out I see it's the worn ribbon that my mother had threaded through the extra key. It must have caught on the metal railing as I fell to the floor—if it hadn't Harry might have heard it when it hit the floor.

I hold my breath when I turn the key in the lock—Harry might have blocked the door some other way—but the door swings open into the dark hallway. I take one look back and see that he's left the registration book on the bed. I guess he wasn't interested in my mother's story after all. I grab the book, stick it into my canvas bag—which I strap onto my back like a backpack—and leave before I can think about what else I'm leaving behind. Nothing that matters, I say to myself, touching my throat, and then covering my mouth with my hand when I smell the smoke. I dart back into the room and grab a towel from the bathroom, wet it, and use it to cover my mouth as I feel my way down the hall.

When I reach the fifth floor I can hear the fire below me—a rushing sound curiously like water. The only other thing I've ever heard like it is the falls after a heavy rain. Keeping one hand on the wall, one hand holding the damp towel over my mouth and nose, I start down the darkened hall. The back stairs, which lead down to the kitchen, might be safer because they're enclosed, but when I open that door a wave of smoke pours out, nearly overwhelming me. I close it quickly and crouch down on my knees, crawling with my shoulder to the wall until I can breathe easier. It makes sense, I realize, that if Harry started the fire in the kitchen the back stairs would fill with smoke first. I can only hope that the fire is still contained to this side—the north side—of the hotel and that the main stairs are still intact. As I head toward the stairs I listen to the rushing sound of the fire to see if I can tell if it becomes any fainter as I move south. Instead the sound seems to swell in my ears, a dull roar pulsing with the beat of my heart, taking the shape of human voices—horrible cries and moans, which I know are my own imaginings.

I stop and listen. I've come to the top of the main stairs and I can see from the window the terrace below lit up as though for a gala ball, only the shadows moving on the terrace aren't the shadows of guests dancing, they're the shadows of flames engulfing the hotel. The fire sounds like a multitude—

a great throng of people shouting. I have an image of all the guests who have ever stayed here over the hotel's long history—all their voices, let loose by the fire, crashing together—but then I hear one voice, clear and distinct above the rest, calling my name.

I take the towel away from my mouth and call back. "Aidan!"

I think I hear an answering call from the floor below so I start down the stairs, calling Aidan's name as I go. When I reach the fourth floor, though, the landing is empty. I stop and listen, but what I hear isn't a voice, it's the crashing of glass from below me accompanied by a scream.

"Aidan?" I call again. Had I imagined that it was him? Could it be Harry—somehow caught in his own inferno—and if it's Harry am I willing to risk my life to save him? Because if the crash is what I think it is—the landing windows exploding from the fire—I should head to the south stairs and try to get out that way.

"Aidan?" I call again when I reach the third-floor landing. Other than the splintered glass from the shattered window the landing is empty.

This time I hear my name. Not from below me, but from above. I'm sure then that I'm imagining the voice—that Aidan come to rescue me is no more real than my vision of my mother in the river.

I sink down to the floor, not so much to avoid the smoke that has thickened the air around me as because I am suddenly very tired. I wonder if this is how my mother felt when she left here to go meet Peter Kron at the Dreamland Hotel—a giving in to the inevitability of the fate she so narrowly avoided on the train tracks at Rip Van Winkle. Maybe, having stolen another woman's identity, she felt as if she had been living on borrowed time all along.

I touch my throat and the metal disc there feels cool. I unlatch the chain to look at it one more time—not the portrait of the saint but the engraved words on the back. TO ROSE, WITH LOVE, FROM HER BROTHER JOHN. This is what my mother left me in the bedpost—not the net of tears but the secret of her identity. The necklace Harry left with is Natalie Baehr's copy, which I had in my toiletries case. He's bound to realize it's fake once he sees it in good light. At least I've left one surprise for Harry. My mother must have taken the real one to her meeting with Peter Kron even though she would have known that he might kill her once he had it. I think I know why she went. Peter must have threatened to hurt her brother. That would have been the name that he left on the phone message that finally got her attention. She would have gone to bail him out—just as she'd stood up in court years earlier to plead his case.

I put the necklace back on—even if it doesn't answer all the questions it might at least raise some when I'm found—but keep my fingers on its cool metal. Catalina della Rosa, patron saint of single women. By flinging her bridal pearls into the Venetian canal she escaped an arranged marriage. How had Anthony Acevedo put it? Santa Catalina protected you from marrying the wrong man. My mother had fled the city and Harry Kron and found my father. She loved my father. I feel sure of it now. She didn't leave for another man but to help her brother—a child she was bound to protect before I was ever born, just as the selkie has to go back to her children under the sea.

When I hear my name again it sounds as if it's coming from the depths of the sea and when I open my eyes the smoke is so thick it's like looking through murky water. A light splits the dark and I see a figure above me. When he leans over me I see the hump on his back where the wings are struggling to break through the skin.

Yes, I think, touching the medal at my throat, Aidan's the right man.

"Come on, Iris, you've got to rouse yourself. Breathe into this." He gives me a wet handkerchief to hold against my mouth and, shifting his flashlight into his other hand, tries to lift me up. "We've got to go out the window," he says when I fail to rise up with him.

"That's easy for you to say, you've got wings."

Aidan laughs, but it turns into a cough. It occurs to me that winged angels don't cough. "I'd save your breath if that's the kind of nonsense you have to say. Come on." I get to my feet this time and Aidan steers me toward the stairs leading down to the second-floor landing, which are dark with smoke. I can hear the roar of the fire, like a beast crouching in wait for us.

"I thought we were going out the window," I say.

"The second-floor window," he says, nudging me forward. "Unless you really can sprout wings like the men in your mother's book. I grabbed some sheets to tie together to make a rope, but it won't be long enough to reach the ground from the third floor." Aidan keeps talking as we descend the stairs, to calm me, I guess, as if I am a nervous horse that has to be blinkered to be led out of a burning barn. "Aren't you wondering how I knew you were here?" He doesn't wait for me to respond before answering his own question. "I knew you were planning to come up here when you said you'd forgotten your book for the train—it meant you planned on taking a longer ride than just back downtown. Then I followed you to the station in Marble Hill and saw you get the Metro-North. I took the next train. I hitched a ride across the river, but he was only going as far as the turnoff to the hotel, so I had to hike all the way up the mountain. Harry's car passed me on the way down—I hid on the side of the road—and it half scared me to death. I thought he must have killed you already. As soon as I got to the garden I saw the fire in the kitchen. I stopped in the office just long enough to call the police in Kingston and give them Harry's license plate number. It should be interesting to the police when they pull him over, reeking of polyurethane, fleeing the scene of his own hotel on fire."

We've reached the second-floor landing and he kicks out the plywood boards covering the window. I hear them crack against the flagstone terrace. I can't help but remember Joseph's body broken on those stones. "He's the one who killed Joseph," I say turning to Aidan. "It's not enough that he's caught for trying to kill me and destroying the hotel."

"Well, then let's get out of here, so we can tell the police our story." Aidan drags me down in front of the window, takes off his backpack— which is what I took to be his incipient wings—and pulls out a bundle of sheets. "Guess where I got these?" he asks me as he starts knotting the sheets together.

I shake my head and look down the stairs toward the lobby. The flames have climbed the carpet runner and are licking at the wooden banister on the landing. While I watch, they shoot up the wall opposite the window, drawn by the airwell of the stairs. I see the ceiling around the chandelier blacken and bubble.

"All the sheets had been stripped from the beds—damned efficient staff you've got here, Miss Greenfeder . . . " Aidan is tying the end of the sheets to a radiator next to the window and tugging at it to test the knot. "But I remembered a couple of sheets we stashed in the dumbwaiter on the third floor." Aidan looks up from tightening all the knots along the rope he's made. "Remember that day, Iris?"

I nod at him and see his eyes widen. At the same moment I feel a searing pain hit my back, as if I had been lashed with acid. Aidan grabs me and throws me to the floor, using the weight of his body to smother the flames. Then he puts my hands around the sheet-rope and pushes me out the window.

"Just hold on," he says. I'm out in the cold air looking up at him, his head and shoulders dark against the bright flames behind him.

I'm the one who's supposed to hold on to you, I try to say, but the roar of the flames drowns out my words as the fire bursts through the window.

Chapter Thirty-three

One of the many dangers—along with massive infection and kidney failure—a burn victim faces is dehydration. Which is why the water used to scrub away the dead skin is a saline solution. I could smell the salt in the shower room before the treatment would start. There were other smells but I tried to focus on the smell of salt. The morphine would be kicking in—the good nurses knew how to time the dosage to carry you through the course of the treatment—and I'd close my eyes and try to think of the ocean. It was as good a technique for dealing with the pain as any, but I've wondered since if it hasn't ruined the ocean for me.

I had first-degree burns on 10 percent of my body. When the canvas bag—which held my mother's memoir—caught fire, Aidan knocked it off my back. My burns extended in two long strips down my shoulder blades—on either side of where the registration book lay against my back. The book, which was lost in the fire, and Aidan's quick reflexes, protected most of the skin on my back.

Aidan wasn't so lucky.

When the fire swept through the window he was already kneeling on the ledge, his hands grasping the sheet-rope. The flames caught the back of his shirt and he must have jumped because I saw his legs kick out just above my head and his body twist in the air, a cape of flame lofting above him. Somehow he managed to hold on to the rope. I climbed down as quickly as I could; he followed. Halfway down the pain must have been too much for him and he let go. I tried to break his fall, but when he landed against me I fell backward onto the terrace. The back of his head hit the stone—not as hard as if I hadn't broken his fall at all, but hard enough to knock him unconscious. Or maybe it was the pain from his burns that made him pass out. I smothered the fire on his back with the sheets we'd used to climb down, but I could see that the fire had burned down to the bone.

By then I could hear the sirens from the other side of the hotel heading up the mountain. I pulled Aidan out to the edge of the ridge—as far as I could get him from the burning hotel—and ran around to the front to get help. Two firemen came back with me to carry him around the hotel and load him into the ambulance. I left with him. I don't remember looking back at the hotel or even thinking about it. The last I saw of the Hotel Equinox was a few hours later from the medevac helicopter that took Aidan and me to the Manhattan University Hospital Burn Center.

The sun was climbing up the eastern side of the ridge, but when it got to the ledge a wall of smoke stood where the hotel used to be. Beyond the smoke lay the Catskills and from where I lay in the helicopter it looked like another ridge had been added to the line of mountains—a cliff hewn of mottled gray marble shot through with flame-red quartz. As I watched I saw the wall of smoke was moving, lifting off the base of the ridge and drifting east to the river, and I thought of the story of Henry Hudson's ship the *Half Moon*, floating above the Catskills. As my first shot of morphine took me under I imagined that ghost ship sailing down the river below me, heading out to sea.

The first person I saw when I woke up in the hospital was Aunt Sophie. I couldn't figure out how she'd gotten there from Florida so quickly until I learned that I'd been unconscious for thirty-eight hours. She told me Aidan's condition was stable, but he hadn't regained consciousness yet. He had suffered third-degree burns over 30 percent of his body. Over the next few weeks I learned a great deal about burn degrees and body percentages. The question it boiled down to—no pun intended, although that's mild compared to some of the ones I heard in the burn unit—was how much of your skin can you give up without losing it all.

The nurses told me it was probably a blessing that he was unconscious and during my own treatments I agreed. The fire hadn't touched his face or the front of his body, so he looked peaceful—like he was sleeping. He was Tam Lin who falls asleep in the woods and is taken away by fairies. Soon he'd come riding past the well and I'd pull him down from his enchanted steed and throw a circle of earth and holy water around him. I'd hold on no matter what shape he took.

At first I didn't want to see any visitors but Aunt Sophie and Aidan's mother, Eveline, a tiny woman aged beyond her years by cigarettes, who sat silent as a stone by Aidan's bed with a rosary in her hands. I wanted time to stop while Aidan was sleeping the way everyone in the castle goes to sleep while Sleeping Beauty is under her spell. I didn't want to know the end of the story until he was back in it. But then Sophie started carrying little bits and pieces of what my visitors had to tell her and I started passing them on to Aidan—like bread crumbs dropped in a path to lead him out of the forest.

"They caught Harry on the Thruway," I told him. "Not only was he covered in polyurethane, he had three of the Hudson River School paintings in his trunk. And the fake *ferronière* in his pocket. He's been arrested for arson and attempted murder—of me—and for Joseph's murder. The warrant for your arrest has been revoked."

"I think I saw his eyelid flutter a little bit," Eveline confided to me. "I'm sure he likes the sound of your voice."

I thought it amazing that Eveline Barry didn't blame me for her son's condition. I would have. She seemed to accept this colossal bad luck with a grim determination to sit it out every day until Fiona, her sister, came and took her home, stopping on their way at St. Patrick's to light candles for "both of you." I thought Eveline was probably making up the bit about his eyelid fluttering, but I decided on that day to see whoever came to visit me who could tell me a piece of the story that I could pass on to Aidan. That would be my circle of earth and holy water.

I hadn't quite bargained on Phoebe Nix as my first visitor. Even though I knew she didn't kill Joseph I couldn't pretend to like her since learning that her mother had killed my mother. Especially when she told me she suspected it all along.

"In her journals she wrote obsessively about Kay Morrissey. She couldn't believe some little maid that Peter'd had an affair with had turned into a writer. That's what drove her wild. When she stayed at the hotel she could hear your mother typing in the room above hers, and it drove her crazy— she was convinced that she was writing about the affair."

"So that's why you hid in Joseph's room that night—you thought my mother's manuscript was in the locked storage closet with the paintings. You told Aidan that Harry wanted him to check the paintings so he would unlock the closet . . . but then how did you expect to get into the closet?"

Phoebe lifts her shoulders a centimeter or two—which passes as a shrug for her. "I thought I'd startle him by coming into the room unexpectedly and . . . I don't know . . . just sort of convince him to let me look in the closet. . . ."

I stare at her and she looks away. It's impossible for me to believe that she would come up with such a lame plan . . . but then I realize that what she'd really meant to do was *seduce* Aidan into letting her into the closet.

"Can you believe the nerve of that woman?" I complain later to a comatose Aidan. "Like she'd have had a chance with you! And then she told me that after the Dreamland Hotel fire her mother wasn't able to write at all. Like I'm suppose to say 'Gee, I'm sorry that killing my mother gave your mother writer's block.'"

Aidan's composure strikes me as reproachful so I go on. "She did apologize for trying to tell me what I could and couldn't write. *That was very unprofessional*, she said and then she told me she was prepared for whatever I might write in my memoir. I didn't mention that I've given up on the idea of writing it." To Aidan's continued silence I add, "I know, my mother's book burned up in the fire, so I guess I still could write the memoir, but I've been thinking that maybe my mother wrote her own memoir so I wouldn't have to. I know it sounds kind of crazy—and I'll never know for sure—but I think that's why she called it *The Selkie's Daughter*. The mother in the selkie story wants her daughter to be free and I think that's what my mother wanted for me. She wouldn't want me to spend my life telling *her* story, she'd want me to tell my own."

My next visitor is Hedda. She comes to me like a penitent seeking absolution. She had no idea that Harry was trying to get the necklace back and that he had killed Joseph. If she had, she would have told me he was upstairs in her apartment the night I came to see her—which is how he knew I was on my way up to the hotel to find the necklace.

"He reminded me of Peter," she tells me in a hushed voice more suitable for the confessional than the busy dayroom of the burn unit. "That's why I was drawn to him this summer." Hedda lays her hand over mine. She's had an operation on her hands since I saw her last and the gauze bandages remind me of the gauze they use to rub the dead skin off Aidan's back. I take my hand away. Maybe when Aidan wakes up I'll find it in my heart to forgive her, but not now.

Jack comes several times—as do Ramon, Paloma, Natalie, and a few of my other students. Mr. Nagamora brings me a soup made from seaweed and miso, which he says will help my skin heal. He comes so often I finally realize that he's coming to see Sophie. In the last week of September he takes her to a concert at the 92nd Street Y and she takes him to an exhibit of Indonesian textiles at the Brooklyn Museum.

When Sister D'Aulnoy comes I ask her into Aidan's room, not because I expect a holy intervention but because I figure a nun in the room might get his attention. I start out by telling her I lied when I came to St. Christopher's, that I didn't know Rose McGlynn was my mother at that point or that John, Arden, and Allen were my uncles.

"But you see, it turned out you weren't lying. Sometimes God leads us to the truth when we think we've strayed farthest from it."

I look at Aidan, still in the tangle of tubes that feed him and take the poison from his burns out of his body. His skin is paler now than it ever was when he was in prison. I remember something he said in that paper he turned in. *I think that sometimes when you get used to a bad thing—like being in prison or getting kidnapped by fairies—it's better to live with that bad thing than trying to change it. Because what if you get a chance to change things and you mess up? What if it's your last chance?*

"I would have preferred not to know the truth," I tell Sister D'Aulnoy, "if this is the price for it."

She follows my gaze down to Aidan's face. I expect a motivational speech, a sermon along the lines of *The truth shall make you free*, but instead she shakes her head sadly. "We don't get to choose what truths God reveals to us—but we do get to choose what we do with that truth—whom we share it with and how."

She takes a slip of folded paper—a bright pink Post-it note—out of her cardigan pocket and hands it to me. "I did a little research. Your uncle John died of a stroke in prison the year before his sentence was up. Allen, his younger brother, is still alive. St. Christopher's started getting donations from him about ten years ago from a Coney Island address. When I went to the address his landlady said he'd moved to an assisted living facility near the boardwalk. He's still there. He's seventy now and not in the best of health. I gather he lived a pretty hard life but gave up drinking about ten years ago and his landlady says he was a quiet and clean-living tenant."

For the entirety of this speech Sister D'Aulnoy holds the bright pink slip of paper out to me. Even when I notice her arm begin to quiver from the strain of holding it up I don't take it. "I think he could tell you some things about your mother." I look away from her and Aidan to the window where pigeons noisily crowd the thirtieth-floor ledge. "Maybe there are a few things you could tell him about his sister," she adds.

I sigh, an echo of the pigeons cooing outside the window, and take the slip from her, pocketing it without looking at it.

"I don't know if I want to leave him that long," I say, meaning Aidan. "Besides, I hate taking the subway."

The next day, while I'm playing a game of gin with Sophie, Mr. Naga-mora, and Aidan's aunt Fiona, Aidan opens his eyes. Sophie has just declared gin. Aidan looks over at us and remarks that he saw a movie once about some guys playing chess for another guy's soul but he'd have thought his soul was worth more than a game of cards. My cards flutter to the floor as I move to the bed and Sophie runs out to tell the nurse. Fiona goes to get Eveline from the cafeteria.

"I've been having this dream," he tells me, "about birds pecking at my back. Isn't there a Greek guy whose organs get eaten every day by some bird?"

"Prometheus—he was punished for stealing fire from the gods. The doctors say the worst of the treatments are over." It's only a half lie because what they told us just yesterday was that Aidan was about halfway healed. In a few weeks they hope to graft a new synthetic skin onto the bare patches on his back.

Fiona and Eveline come back then, followed by the doctor. By the time Aidan's been brought up to speed on his condition he's fallen back to sleep. Fiona and Eveline leave to go light some more candles at St. Patrick's. Before Mr. Nagamora leaves, Sophie says there's something he wants to tell me, but that I need to come back with them to the dry-cleaning store. I don't want to leave Aidan, but the nurse assures me he'll sleep for hours now.

"Go on," one of the nurses tells me, "he's out of the woods now."

Taking the crosstown bus with Sophie and Mr. Nagamora, I hum that phrase to myself. *He's out of the woods now.* My all-time favorite, I decide.

The dry-cleaning store is closed and the rest of Mr. Nagamora's family has gone home. Sophie leads the way through a tunnel of quivering plastic, batting the bags out of her way as if she'd spent her life running a dry cleaner's, to a back room facing on a little garden. I notice that the painting of the rainstorm over the mountains is hanging on the wall.

"I'll make some tea, Isao, while you show Iris."

"Show me what?" I ask.

"We didn't want to tell you while you were still worried about Aidan," Sophie calls from the kitchen—even while she's out of the room she's running the show. "Because we knew you couldn't focus. But now that your mind's a little easier—well, someone's got to tell the police."

"About what?" I ask Mr. Nagamora. "I've told the police everything I know."

Mr. Nagamora nods eagerly. "Yes," he says, "you had no way of knowing about this. Not your fault! Good thing, though, you bring the dress to me."

"What dress?" I ask, but then I notice it, hanging in its sheath of sheer plastic on the door behind Mr. Nagamora. "Don't tell me Phoebe Nix has been here trying to get her mother's dress back."

"I have a theory about that dress." Sophie, carrying a tray loaded with teapot, teacups, and a plate of rugelach, comes in from the kitchen. "Your mother had it with her when she came to the hotel—I saw it hanging in her closet and . . . well, you know me, I asked her where she came by such an expensive number. I could tell she was embarrassed. She said it belonged to a girlfriend. She said a man gave it to her, but she had to get rid of it because the man's wife had seen it on her and been furious because he had given the same dress to her. Imagine! Well, at the time I thought there wasn't a friend—that she was the one who'd been given the dress. But now I think that Peter Kron gave it to Katherine Morrissey—the real Katherine Morrissey—and your mother had it because she had her suitcase. I never saw your mother wear it. She must have thought it had brought her friend bad luck. But then I got to thinking about how she kept it all that time even though she never wore it and . . . well, show her what we found, Isao, I can't wait to see the expression on her face."

Mr. Nagamora unlocks a metal filing cabinet and takes out a small lacquered box decorated with a pattern of dancing cranes. He opens it and holds it out to me with both hands, his face creased into a thousand lines of delight. The silk weaver presenting his finest sail to the ship's captain. The box is full of jewels. Pearls, diamonds, and one emerald cut in the shape of a teardrop.

"Where? . . ." But of course I've already guessed. The weights that held down the swag on the green dress. My mother had sewn the net of tears into the green dress.

Two days later I take the subway to Coney Island.

"You have to go," Aidan tells me. "It must have been Allen who was in trouble with Peter Kron, because John McGlynn was already dead. Your mother went back to Brooklyn because Peter had something on him. We'll never know if you don't go see him—the old guy could die of a heart attack any day."

"I don't need to know any more," I say, half truthfully. "Look what's come of running after my mother's story."

Aidan takes my hand. "We've come of it," he says. "Besides, I want to know how it ends."

So I go. Back down into the subways, all the way to the end of the line. I follow the directions to Bel Mar—Gracious Living for Seniors by the Sea, which turns out to be a high-rise facing the boardwalk. Allen McGlynn meets me in the Buena Vista Social Room. I don't know what I'm expecting, but not this tiny bald man in a yellowish fisherman's cardigan and kelly-green golf shirt. Someone must have told him once that green brought out his eyes. It's the only bit of him where I can see my mother, but I fasten my eyes over his shoulder, at the strip of blue Atlantic just visible above the boardwalk outside the windows. I don't want to be swayed by family resemblance right now—at least not until I know what role he played in my mother's death.

"Sister D'Aulnoy says you might be able to shed some light on what happened to my mother in 1973," I say to a spot over his shoulder. An orderly in a white uniform opens the sliding glass doors, letting in the smell of the ocean. It brings me back to the treatment room at the burn unit— where Aidan probably is right now. "Did you see her that year?"

Allen runs a withered hand over his shiny pink scalp. "I learned from John that she was still alive just before he died. I think he felt bad leaving me all alone and I'd been telling him how I missed her sometimes worse than I missed our mother. I remembered her better . . ."

"So you went up to see her at the hotel?"

He nods and looks nervously around the room, smiling briefly at someone who waves at him and then squelching it. This isn't shaping up to be the family reunion he was expecting.

"I saw you too, from across the garden. Rose pointed you out to me. You probably think I went to ask her for money, but you'd be wrong. Not that I didn't need money. I had a sickness for gambling back then, along with a sickness for drink, which I've put behind me now by putting myself in the hands of a higher power—" I fidget just enough to let him know I'm not entirely comfortable with the twelve-step philosophy. It was one thing hearing about God from Sister D'Aulnoy, another thing hearing it from the man who may have lured my mother to her death. "—and I owed some money to half the loan sharks in Brooklyn. I never said a word to her about that though. I was just glad to see her. When I was little she told all us boys stories—the stories our mother told us before she died—"

"How'd she find out about the money you owed?"

"Mr. Peter Kron told her. He must've seen us together at the hotel and he tracked me down. He offered to buy up my chits—otherwise, he told her, some fellows from Red Hook were planning to break both my legs." He looks around the Buena Vista Social Room and lowers his voice. "Would you mind if we continued this conversation out on the boardwalk?"

I imagine that he'd rather not have his canasta buddies learn about his past, and it's on the tip of my tongue to say something like this, but then I look at him. This is my mother's brother, I remind myself, whom she loved enough to risk her own life. "Sure," I say, "I'd like to take a look at the ocean."

Out on the boardwalk the sun and ocean breeze nearly take my breath away. We walk a little way and stop at a sheltered bench facing the ocean. It's easier to listen to the rest of the story with both of us looking toward the sea.

"Rosie told me that Peter Kron wanted something she had—a piece of jewelry. I guessed it was part of the haul John had gotten from the Crown. She said she didn't care about giving it to him only she was afraid once he had it he might kill us both. I couldn't figure why he would, but she said it had something to do with where the necklace came from and Peter being scared his brother might find out he had it. She told me she would meet Peter at the Dreamland Hotel and make arrangements to give him the necklace, but that I should wait for her on the boardwalk instead of coming to the hotel in case something went wrong. I guess something did."

"Peter's wife followed him to the hotel and shot her," I tell him. "She thought they were having an affair."

He nods and stands up, turning his back to the sea. "I was here that night, waiting for her, when I saw the Dreamland Hotel on fire." He points to a space between two tall buildings. "That's where it was, between those two buildings."

I look at the place on earth where my mother died. I guess that's important—people plant crosses by the side of the road to mark where the car crashed; in Italy they lay flowers in the alley where the latest mob victim's body is found—but I don't feel anything of my mother's spirit residing in that sliver of air between the two buildings. I do feel it, though, in the man standing next to me, his face wet with tears now, his hand trembling as he passes it over his pale green eyes.

"I left the city then. Got on a train and took it clear across the country to Oregon. Spent the next twenty years traveling from town to town until I finally found my way back here to where I started. I should've come and told you, but I thought maybe it was better I stay away from you—that if Peter Kron's brother was still looking for the necklace I might draw his attention to you if I got in touch."

"Weren't you interested in knowing what happened to the necklace?"

He shakes his head and looks at me for the first time since we left the building. "No," he says. I know he's telling the truth. It's not the truth I was looking for, but as Sister D'Aulnoy says, you don't always get to choose your truth.

I wonder what he'd think of the plans being made for the necklace now. Gordon del Sarto, going on a tip from Joseph, had indeed located the Countess Oriana Val d'Este, and it's turned out that she has at least as much claim to the *ferronière* as the Catholic Church. The case could be in court for years. As an alternative, Hedda Wolfe and Sister D'Aulnoy have petitioned the church and the countess to allow the necklace to be auctioned off, the proceeds to benefit St. Christopher's. There's talk of a college scholarship and a dormitory—on the top floors of the old orphanage—for boys who have aged out of the system. I imagine Allen McGlynn would like the idea, but I decide not to mention it now. It will be months before the fate of the necklace is decided—time enough to tell him when it's certain.

"St. Christopher's had a kind of summer camp for the orphans here at the beach," Allen is telling me now. He sits back down on the bench and I notice how tired he looks. "Rose would come and take me and John out for the day. We'd eat ice cream and sit by the water and Rose told us all the old stories our mother used to tell us. She said that was our best way of remembering her. But then Rose stopped coming and I forgot the way the stories went."

He rubs the cuff of his shirtsleeve across his face and starts to get up, "Well, I guess that's all I can tell you. I hope it helps . . ."

I tug his shirtsleeve to make him sit back down.

"I can tell you one of her stories," I say, "if you want me to."

He looks so eager it embarrasses me. I look away, fixing my eyes on the blue horizon. "In a time before the rivers were drowned by the sea," I begin, "in a land between the sun and the moon . . ."

THE SEDUCTION OF WATER

A Reader's Guide

CAROL GOODMAN

The Bones of the Story

Tracing the genesis of a novel after you've written it can be a little like reconstructing a skeleton from millennia-old bones that have been scattered over great distances. I'm pretty sure, though, that this book started with the single image of a mother telling a bedtime story to her daughter. It was certainly a familiar image since, for the last ten or so years, I had ended each night by reading to my daughter for at least an hour. I chose, more often than not, fairy tales, both because she seemed to like them and because I have always loved them. Back in graduate school, I'd written a paper called "From Old Wives to Warrior Princesses" on the presence of fairy tales in contemporary fiction. I've always admired writers such as Angela Carter, A. S. Byatt, Margaret Atwood, and Alice Hoffman who integrate elements of fairy tales into their fiction, and I'm a big fan of Marina Warner's study of fairy tales, *From the Beast to the Blonde*. Ultimately, though, the image of a mother telling stories to her daughter had a more intimate source: the stories my mother told me.

Instead of fairy tales, my mother brought me up on stories of her Irish-Catholic childhood in Depression-era Brooklyn, and moving to Coney Island as a young woman on the eve of World War II. In many ways these stories were as exotic and remote to me as fairy tales. Ice was delivered to their cold-water flat in Bay Ridge by a horse-drawn cart, and oatmeal was cooked on a wood-burning stove. To a child growing up in a prefab development in suburban Pennsylvania, my mother's descriptions of prewar

Brooklyn sounded as quaint as Hansel and Gretel's cottage. There was that same sense of cheerful and thrifty poverty. Dinner was sometimes bread and hot milk with sugar because that was all they had, but still her father prepared it as if it were a delicacy. Although they were poor, they never took charity and were proud and grateful when my grandfather got a job digging ditches for the WPA. My mother had only one white shirt to wear with her Catholic school uniform, but her mother washed and bleached and starched and ironed it every day so that "it could have stood up on its own" and looked every bit as good as anyone else's.

My mother's stories were filled with characters as colorful as any fairy tale's. Her aunt Nanny was a burlesque dancer who dressed like a gypsy and was once arrested in New Haven for slapping a woman who turned out to be the police chief's girlfriend. When my mother and her parents went to the jail to bail her out, my mother was so horrified to see her beloved, beautiful aunt in a crude cell with an exposed toilet that she burst into tears. The police chief bent down and said to my mother that he would let her aunt out if the little girl "sang a little song and danced a little dance." My mother always stressed at this point in the story—no matter how many times I had heard it—that she was a painfully shy child and nothing could have been more frightening to her than to perform in front of a strange adult. But she did. And her aunt Nanny was freed. Later we both conjectured that there must have been some exchange of money as well, but still, it was as good a Rapunzel story as I ever heard.

Like any genuine fairy tale, my mother's childhood was rife with darkness and tragedy. She had a younger brother—Martin, but everyone called him Pet because when he was born my mother jealously referred to him as the family "pet"—who died in childhood.

"What of?" I asked, horrified, but also peculiarly drawn. In my safe, post-vaccine, post-antibiotic 1960s world I'd never known a child to die. In my mother's world, her own baby brother had died.

"I was never sure," my mother told me at first, "but I overheard the doctors say it had something to do with his head."

Over years of telling this story, it eventually came out that my mother blamed herself for Pet's death because he had fallen while she was babysitting him (she was under ten when it happened—later, she gave this as a reason for never letting young children baby-sit), but in later years she guessed that the reference to his "head" might have had something to do with meningitis. Unfortunately, my mother never shared with her parents the fact that she held herself accountable for Pet's death. She thought they were generous and forgiving for never bringing it up or holding it against her.

I think it was only by telling Pet's story over and over again that my mother was finally able to let go of that guilt. At first the details of the story emerged as I grew old enough to understand them, but then they also grew as she understood them through the telling. My mother was making sense of her life by telling it to me. I can think of no better introduction to the writing process than witnessing that kind of storytelling, even though it was sometimes unsettling to hear what she had to say.

Listening to my mother's stories, I was entranced by the other world she had lived in, but I also suffered a peculiar sense of displacement. It's always a bit of a shock to realize that your parents have an existence outside their role as caretaker to you. It is that foreignness that makes the Selkie story so disturbing because it suggests the possibility that the mother can leave—which, in fact, she does. Nothing is more frightening to a child than a parent's disappearance (death itself seems like an abandonment to a child) and my mother had that experience as well.

Like the daughter in the Selkie story, my mother lost her own mother young; she was seventeen and her mother was only forty-one. She was with her in that tenement kitchen when she suddenly collapsed. A blood clot, left over from a childhood bout of rheumatic fever, had flown to her brain, killing her instantly. In the aftermath, my mother moved to Coney Island—only miles away from Bay Ridge, but a completely different world. For one thing, she had never met a Jewish person. One of her favorite stories is how she overheard a woman asking a deli owner for "sour cream" and laughed because she thought it was a joke. Coney Island in the forties was also filled with gangsters and heroin addicts. For a pretty, young girl on her own (my mother was and is quite beautiful—shopkeepers, once she stopped laughing at their sour cream, called her *shaineh maidel*, "pretty girl" in Yiddish), it would have been easy to fall in with the wrong crowd. Many beautiful young girls (according to my mother, Coney Island in the forties possessed an unusual percentage of beautiful girls) who were not so discriminating as my mother became prostitutes and drug addicts. These cautionary tales, which my mother favored as I entered my tumultuous adolescence, always ended with the pretty young girls losing their looks and their teeth. It was exciting to learn that my mother had known the legendary "Kiss-of-Death" girl (a Mafia girlfriend whose every boyfriend seemed to die prematurely), but also daunting to hear these teeth-loss stories as I headed out on a date. They sounded like an old-fashioned curse for bad behavior along the lines of the red-hot iron shoes Snow White's stepmother (in the original Grimm version) is forced to dance in until she dies.

Although I might have begun to suspect the instructive nature of some of my mother's tales, I knew even then that I was lucky that I got to keep hearing them and watch the ongoing process of my mother making sense of her life. What, I wondered, would it have been like if I only had the stories? That's Iris's situation in *The Seduction of Water*. All she has left of her mother is her stories, from which she must reconstruct her mother's life and begin to construct her own story. The stories are Iris's inheritance, her talisman.

There's a kind of fairy tale in which a young girl whose mother has died is protected by some charm or familiar animal representing the lost mother. In "Yeh-hsien," a Chinese version of Cinderella, the mother's spirit inhabits a magic carp, which befriends and comforts Yeh-hsien. When the evil stepmother kills the carp, its very bones continue to protect the girl. This somewhat gruesome device of protective bones also appears in the Grimms' "Aschenputtel," in which an orphan girl is literally sheltered by a hazel sapling that grows out of the mother's buried bones; and in the Scottish tale "Rashin Coatie," in which the dead mother inhabits a red calf and continues to watch over her daughter even after the calf is slaughtered.

Instead of bones, Iris's mother bequeaths to her stories. The Selkie story embraces the fear of losing a mother but also promises that a mother's love is an enduring legacy. The fantasy tales contain—encoded—Iris's mother's own childhood tale of loss and resurrection. Most importantly, she passes on to Iris the ability and willingness to reveal and explore herself through storytelling. It's what my mother gave to me through a lifetime of storytelling: the ability to make sense out of one's own life and, out of that sense, craft the best life. An inheritance every bit as valuable as good bones and a sound set of teeth.

Reading Group Questions
and Topics for Discussion

1. Discuss your favorite fairy tale from your childhood. How did you learn the story and what did you learn from it? What does it mean to you now?

2. The fairy tale assignment galvanized Iris's students and helped them find their own voices. Why do you think this assignment was successful on so many levels?

3. Did you ever have a school assignment that affected you in such a manner? Discuss why it reached you and what it taught you.

4. Both Iris and Phoebe are haunted by the early loss of their mothers. Discuss how these characters have been shaped by and have adapted to their losses and, more generally, how the death of a parent or a parental figure affects us all.

5. A schism exists in Iris's life: There's a *before* and *after* her mother's death. Do you have such a defining event in your life? Discuss the various life-changing events—births, deaths, and other rites of passage—that can result in such a before-and-after outlook.

6. Iris's mother's death is the defining event of her life when this novel begins. Did you think it was going to remain the defining event by the close of the novel?

7. Iris confesses that she is "still not comfortable being the giver of grades, the passer of judgment." Can you identify with her struggle? Why is it so difficult for Iris to pass judgment?

8. When Iris begins to investigate her mother's past, she comes to understand that her mother felt like an impostor in her new life at the Hotel Equinox. Why is this so? Discuss the many reasons why people might feel like impostors in their own lives.

9. Iris wonders whether Danny, the baker she meets in Brooklyn, or his brother Vincent, the painter, "is really the artist in the family." What do you think? How do you define an artist?

10. The financial and personal toll exacted in securing the time and space to create art is central to this novel. Discuss the hurdles that artists face. Do you think female artists still confront more obstacles than their male counterparts?

11. Have you ever suffered from writer's block or a comparable affliction in your own life? Did you resolve it? If so, how? If not, why not?

12. Thinking about her relationship with Jack, Iris speculated, "Lover and beloved. Didn't there always have to be one of each?" Do you agree?

13. Aidan believes that "there's more sorrow in not following your heart." What do you think?

14. The seven-year age difference between Aidan and Iris troubles Iris greatly. Do you think the pairing of older women and younger men—as opposed to the reverse—still carries a social stigma? Is this changing?

15. Aidan is not a career criminal, but he worries that that will be his fate once he is released from jail. Discuss the plight of the ex-convict in our society.

16. Iris's mother spent much of her life observing and recording the carelessness of the wealthy and how they could ignore and mistreat those who served their needs. Discuss the class tensions in this novel, from the plight of Iris's mother to Harry Kron's attitude toward his staff to Aidan's fears that he is not "good enough" for Iris.

17. Iris's unfinished dissertation is an analysis of her mother's very personal fiction; an analysis hobbled by the daughter's ignorance of the mother's past. Discuss the complex blend of mythical, religious, and personal influences in K. R. LaFleur's fantasy novels.

18. Do you think learning the full truth about her mother will set Iris free to live her own life on her own terms?

19. "She wouldn't want me to spend my life telling *her* story, she would want me to tell my own," Iris concludes at the close of the novel. Do you think Iris will write again? If so, what do you think she will write?

20. What do you think would have happened to Kay and her family if she had told her husband the whole truth about her past? Could the tragedies that followed have been averted?

21. Which characters are your favorites and why? Did you wish to hear more (or less) from certain characters in this novel?

22. Discuss the structure of this novel. Did you find the story-within-the-story format compelling?

23. Do you think that *The Seduction of Water* defies categorization in a single genre? How would you describe this novel to prospective readers?

FOR A SNEAK PEEK
AT CAROL GOODMAN'S
NEXT THRILLING NOVEL,

THE DROWNING TREE,

PLEASE TURN THE PAGE.

———

Coming in hardcover in July 2004

Published by Ballantine Books

Chapter One

I am late for Christine's lecture.

I almost didn't go. I wouldn't have gone if Christine hadn't especially asked me to come. The force of her preference was as irresistible now as it had been nearly twenty years ago, when of all the girls at Penrose College, she chose me to be her best friend. So even though I'd made a vow to avoid the campus during reunion—and had managed to do so, so far—I find myself on Sunday afternoon rushing through the lengthening shadows toward the library, just as I had on so many Sunday evenings during college, making a last dash to catch up on everything I'd avoided doing all weekend.

Usually it was Christine herself who had lured me away from my work in the first place, who had unearthed me from whatever hole I'd buried myself in. "The Middle Ages can wait," she'd say, "but the Sargent exhibit at the Whitney is ending this weekend." She was always reading about some art exhibit that was just about to close. Carried along by her enthusiasm, I'd follow her to the train station, trying to keep up with her fast stride, in the wake of her long blond hair that streamed out behind her like the wings of a dove quivering on a current of air.

As I open the heavy library door I almost catch a glimpse of that hair, shining in a swath of sun behind me, but of course it's an illusion. Christine is inside, standing at the podium, miraculously transformed into this older, more constrained woman—*a lecturer*—her long golden hair tamed into a sleek coil.

"This is where you'd find me," Christine is saying to the audience as I slide into a folding chair in the back of the crowded hall—even the second story galleries are packed with students sitting on the floor between the stacks—"after dinner Sunday nights, when the work I'd happily neglected all weekend finally caught up with me."

Rueful sighs stir the group seated beneath the stained glass window. Clearly, I'm not the only one who'd been reminded, walking toward the library through the late afternoon sunshine, of those last-minute penitential pilgrimages. And this is where I *would* find her, already at work on some paper due the next day, somehow arrived before me even though when we'd finally gotten back to the dorm from the city she'd claimed she was going to her room to sleep. While the escapades she'd led me on left me tired and bleary-eyed, they somehow left Christine refreshed and inspired. She would manage to write through the night and the paper she'd turn in on Monday morning would be the one the professors would hold up as the most original, the most brilliant.

"When I approached the table here below the window I always imagined that the Lady looked down at me askance," Christine continues. " 'Oh, so you've finally seen fit to join us,' I imagined her saying. I believe I endowed her with the voice of Miss Colclough, my sophomore Chaucer professor." Christine pauses for another ripple of knowing laughter. Miss Coldclaw, as we called her, was legendary for her withering comments and draconian teaching methods. "In fact, over the years, as I studied below her I endowed the Lady in the Window with many roles: muse, companion, judge. But of course these were my own projections. What we've come to consider today is who she really is, what she has to tell us—the class of 1987—about ourselves, and why it's so important that we save her from decay."

Christine turns slightly and tilts her head up, meeting the gaze of the figure in the glass as if she had been passing on the street and recognized a friend at a second-story window. Throughout the lecture she turns like this to address the Lady as if they were contemporaries—and truly, even though Christine is dressed in a spare, sleeveless black shift (Prada, I think), and the Lady is robed in a medieval gown of embroidered damascene (abraded ruby glass with silver stain), there is a kinship between the two women. There's something in the curve of their spines—Christine's when she leans back to look up at the window, the Lady as she arches her back away from her loom to look up from her labors—that echoes one another. They've got the same yellow hair, the Lady's by virtue of a medieval metallurgical process called silver stain, Christine's thanks to a colorist on the Upper East Side. The Lady's abundant Pre-Raphaelite locks, though, are loose, while Christine's long blond hair is twisted in a knot so heavy that when she bows her head back down to her notes her slender neck seems to pull against the strain. I realize, from that strain and from how thin she's gotten, what a toll this lecture has taken on her and instantly forgive her for not making time to see me these last six or seven months—the longest we've gone without seeing each other since college.

"No doubt we all heard the same story on the campus tour. The window was designed by Augustus Penrose, founder of the Rose Glass Works and Penrose College, in 1922, for the twentieth anniversary of the college's founding. It depicts Augustus's beloved wife, Eugenie. As we all know, Penrose College grew out of The Women's Craft League, which Eugenie had created for the wives and daughters of the men who worked in her husband's factory."

A *college born from a glorified sewing circle*, is how Christine put it once, a bit too loudly, at a freshman tea. But of course she doesn't say that to this assembly of women in their tailored linen skirts and pastel silk blouses, their Coach bags and sensible Ferragamo shoes. Penrose College may have originated from a socialist dream of aiding women from the under classes, but it soon became a bastion of East Coast wealth and privilege.

"But before we accept that the Lady in the Window is merely a celebration of the medieval craftswoman," Christine continues, "let's review the social and artistic background of Augustus Penrose. His family owned a glass works in England, Penrose and Sons, in Kelmscott, a small village on the Thames River near Oxford, which supplied medieval quality glass for stained glass designers, including William Morris, the Pre-Raphaelite artist who also happened to live in Kelmscott. Young Augustus was particularly influenced by the opinions of William Morris, who believed that integrity ought to be restored to the decorative arts. When Simon Garrett, a wealthy factory owner from the north, purchased Penrose and Sons, he encouraged young Augustus in his artistic pursuits—and so did Garrett's daughter, Eugenie, who fell in love with Augustus. As you know, the two married, and were sent by old Simon over to this country in the 1890s to found an American branch of the glass works. Augustus and Eugenie wanted to do more, though, than run a glass factory. Influenced by Morris's ideas, they were soon in the vanguard of the Arts and Crafts movement. . . ."

Now that Christine has moved onto the firmer ground of her expertise in art history, I let out a breath I hadn't known I was holding. I realize how nervous I am for her—how much I want this lecture to be a success for her—a comeback.

Back in college, Christine had a sort of glow about her, a radiant energy that drew people to her. We all believed she would go on to great things, even when she eschewed a Ph.D. in favor of a job at a New York gallery and freelance writing on the arts. We thought then that she'd write a brilliant book or at least marry one of the famous artists she was often seen with at gallery openings. By the tenth reunion, when none of these things had happened and she got so drunk that she passed out during the Farewell Brunch, that glow of promise began to fade. Her name disappeared from the class notes; when I ran into people from the college who had known her, they would ask after her with a solicitous edge of concern in their voices as if expecting to hear the worst. Sometimes, I suspected, *hoping* to hear the worst.

Many were surprised, then, when the programs for the fifteenth reunion arrived with the announcement that Christine would be delivering the lecture on the Lady window, which the class of 1987 had elected to restore as their class gift. I wasn't, though, because I'd seen Christine through rehab four years ago and urged her to apply for a Penrose Grant, which supported alumnae who wanted to switch careers ten to twenty years out of college (the "second-chance" grant, we often called it, a perfect prize for Christine, who always managed to pull her act together at the last minute and shine brilliantly) so that she could go back to graduate school. I even suggested she make the window the subject of her thesis, and when McKay Glaziers won the bid to do the restoration of the window—the first really big conservation project we've gotten since I convinced my father to expand into stained glass restoration—I suggested to the college that Christine deliver this lecture. So you couldn't really blame me for being nervous for her.

While Christine continues lecturing on the Pre-Raphaelites and Arts and Crafts Movement, I let my mind wander and my gaze shift to the window itself, brilliant now in the late afternoon sun. The upper half is dominated by a large rounded window—a window within a window that frames a green pool carpeted with water lilies and shaded by a weeping beech. The view of mountains in the distance is the same as the view we would see if the window were clear: the deeply wooded hills of the Hudson Highlands on the western bank, still forested because Augustus Penrose bought up all the land on that side of the river for his mansion, Astolat. When Astolat burned down in the 1930s, he and Eugenie moved back to Forest Hall, their house on this side of the river. All that's left of Astolat are the water gardens that Penrose designed, the centerpiece of which was a lily pool similar to the one depicted in the window.

While the landscape portion of the window echoes one of Tiffany's landscapes, the figure of the Lady is strictly medieval. Of course, as Christine is explaining now, the Pre-Raphaelites were in love with the Middle Ages, and in love with beautiful women with long, flowing hair and expressions of abandon. This one has just looked up from her work. As she arches her back you can feel the strain of the long hours she has spent bending over her loom. A flush of color—skillfully produced by *sanguine*, a hematite-based paint used since the sixteenth century to enhance flesh tones—rises from her low-cut bodice up her long neck to the plane of her high cheek bones. It makes you wonder what she's been dreaming of over her loom.

"What I always wondered," Christine is saying now, "is why she is looking away from the window and why she has such a rapturous expression on her face. Her expression suggests some kind of revelation. Who is this weaver supposed to be? Remember that Augustus rarely painted his beloved Eugenie just as *Eugenie*. As the Pre-Raphaelite painters he admired had before him, Augustus often chose to depict his model in the guise of a figure from literature."

Christine presses a button on the speaker's dais. A slide screen unrolls on the wall to the right of the window and fills with an image of a young girl bending over a lily pool, her cascading hair turning into heavy branches that trail into the water, a sheath of bark just beginning to creep up her slim legs. "In fact, the only other painting without a known mythological source is this one, *The Drowning Tree*, which seems to echo the tales of transformation Penrose was so fond of. He painted Eugenie as Daphne turning into a laurel as she flees from Apollo—" *The Drowning Tree* fades and is replaced with the more familiar image of the running girl sprouting leaves from her fingertips. "—and as the nymph Salmacis merging in her sacred pool with Hermaphrodite, and Halcyon turning into a kingfisher with her drowned husband. . . ."

Christine clicks through one picture after another, naming each mythological figure as the image appears and fades. She goes so quickly that the faces begin to blur together until we are left with the impression of one face—one woman appearing in many guises. Which is, of course, the impression Christine has been trying to create. They are all Eugenie— whether frightened as Daphne, lusting like Salmacis, or in the throes of shape-shifting like Halcyon. When the screen goes dark an image of that face, radiant, haloed by bright red-gold hair, seems to burn on the blank screen for just an instant, glowing like the face in the stained glass window.

"Who, then, is she, our lady in the window? Why, after all these tales of transformation, would Augustus choose to depict Eugenie as some anonymous weaver in his last known portrait of her? To answer that question I ask you to notice the 'window' at her back. Many people have assumed that the landscape in the window depicts a view of the Hudson Highlands where Penrose built his grand estate, Astolat. But if you look carefully at the arrangement of ridges in the landscape—" The flickering red arrow of Christine's laser pointer skims over the ridge lines in the window. "—and compare them to the arrangement of hills in the actual landscape—" A photograph of the view across the river appears on the slide screen. "—you will notice that the ridges are actually reversed. This is not a window—it's a mirror reflecting a window."

"And in what medieval story is a beautiful young maiden condemned to look at life only in its reflection? Why 'The Lady of Shalott' of course, Tennyson's version of an Arthurian legend. You probably remember it from Miss Ramsey's Nineteenth Century Lit class."

What I remember from Miss Ramsey's class was having to memorize Tennyson's endless ode to friendship, "In Memoriam." But as Christine outlines the story, "The Lady of Shalott" comes back to me: the enchanted maiden in her island tower, prohibited from looking directly at the world, weaving what she sees reflected in a mirror set opposite the window.

I look at the river landscape in the window and then at the scene unfolding in the Lady's loom. If this were the Lady of Shalott, they would be identical, but they are not. In fact the loom is blank. She seems to be weaving plain, unfigured cloth.

Still, Christine makes a good argument for identifying the Lady in the Window with the heroine of Tennyson's poem. The name Augustus Penrose gave his mansion—Astolat—is an alternate name for Shalott. The pose of our Lady is similar to that of several Pre-Raphaelite Ladies of Shalott, as Christine demonstrates through a series of slides. She even has an explanation for why the scenes in the window and on the loom don't match. According to Eugenie Penrose's design notebook, the original painted panes for those sections were cracked during firing and had to be replaced by plain colored glass in order for the window to be ready in time for the library's dedication.

I make a mental note to ask Christine for a copy of Eugenie's notebook—it might come in handy during the restoration—and turn my focus back from the slides to Christine.

"If we accept that the Lady in the Window is the Lady of Shalott, the next question you are probably asking yourself is why. Why choose a doomed medieval damsel as a subject for a window in a women's college?

When Vassar has a window depicting Elena Cornaro, the first woman Ph.D., why is it we have a maiden *literally* trapped in an ivory tower. What was Augustus Penrose thinking?"

"Eugenie Penrose left us only one clue in her notebook. Although more craftswoman than artist, Eugenie used her considerable skills as a draftswoman to turn Augustus's paintings into cartoons for stained glass. Under her own sketch of the window she has written: 'Here with her face doth memory sit.' It's a line from Dante Gabriel Rosetti—one of the Pre-Raphaelite painters much admired by Augustus Penrose. Why, though, would she say this about her own portrait? It suggests to me that the figure of the lady reminded Eugenie of someone else, and I believe that someone was her sister, Clare.

"Perhaps you didn't know that Eugenie had a sister; not many people do. She was her half sister, the child born out of wedlock when Eugenie's mother ran away from Simon Garrett, but taken back into the family when the mother died. Clare was eight years younger than Eugenie and had always been physically—and mentally—frail—"

The screen to the right of the window fills with a sepia image of two girls standing in front of a river beneath a large shaggy tree—a weeping beech, I think. I recognize the taller woman as Eugenie, but only because she's got the same severe hair-style that she wears in every picture I've ever seen of our illustrious founder. The other woman in the picture is almost identical to Eugenie except for her hair, which cascades loosely around her shoulders. Something about the photograph seems familiar. At first I think it's because it's the same setting as the one in the painting *The Drowning Tree*—the tree in the background the same weeping beech—but then I realize it's also because the contrast between the two women in the photograph, one prim and reserved, the other ethereal with her flowing hair, echoes the differences I've been noticing between the Christine I remember from college and the woman who's delivering the lecture. And yet, as Christine tells the story of how Clare came with Eugenie and Augustus when they left for America, and how by the time the threesome arrived in New York, Clare was suffering from some sort of delusional hysteria, I can see that she's enjoying the story's shock value—just as the old Christine would.

"She was sent," Christine concludes, "almost immediately upon her arrival in New York, to the Briarwood Insane Asylum, just a little upriver from here, where she lived out the rest of her life."

It might be my imagination, but it seems to me that Christine meets my eye for a moment when she names Briarwood. We both have a personal connection to the mental institution: She grew up just down the road from it and members of her family have worked there for generations. My connection is more recent: My ex-husband was institutionalized there fourteen years ago. I wonder if this is what she meant when she told me on the phone several weeks ago that she had discovered something while conducting her research that might have an impact on me. I'm more worried right now, though, about the impact that Christine's revelation will have on the audience. Eugenie Penrose has always been held up as an exemplary figure and role model—the college's secular saint.

"Imagine what it was like for Eugenie to know that her sister was a mental patient just up the river from here. Did she fear she might follow in Clare's footsteps? Or that her children would suffer from an inherited malady? Remember, the Victorians believed that madness was hereditary. . . ."

Christine bends her head down to look at her notes. Unlike her previous pauses, this one does not seem timed for effect. I see, for the briefest of moments, a look of confusion pass over her face. She's flipping through her note cards as if she'd realized that her lecture was running over and decided to skip something. It occurs to me, though, that she has another reason for skipping this part of her lecture.

"Let's go back to the poem," she resumes. "It's when the Lady of Shalott sees Lancelot in the mirror that she disobeys the rules of her enchantment and looks directly at the world, thus condemning herself to die. She is not content to die in the solitary confinement in which she's dwelled, however. She finds a boat and sets off on her death journey down the river so that by the time she has died she will have arrived in Camelot and the object of her affection, Lancelot, will witness what his love has wrought.

It's not a passive death. The Lady of Shalott is the woman scorned who secures her revenge through her own death. She is the woman left behind, watching her unfaithful lover disappear over the horizon, Dido staining the night sky with her own funeral pyre—a beacon of recrimination to Aeneas' departing fleet—or Madame Butterfly singing her last aria.

"It makes no sense to cast Eugenie in this role. It makes perfect sense, though, if we accept that the lady in the window is not Eugenie, but her sister, Clare, who looked enough like Eugenie that most people would think the portrait was of her. Only Eugenie and Augustus would know the truth."

Christine pauses to allow this idea to sink in. The silence in the library feels charged, but whether because the audience is appalled at the notion that the window depicts not our beloved founder but her crazy sister, or because they are impressed by Christine's scholarly sleuthing, I'm not sure. I've encountered this ambiguity in reaction to Christine before when, in classes or at parties, she would come out with statements so shocking and forthright that for a moment her audience would sway between embarrassment and admiration.

"If we see the figure in the window as Clare, Augustus's message becomes clear. The window depicts the moment that the Lady turns from her loom to look directly at Sir Lancelot—the moment when she disobeys the rules of her confinement, the moment that seals her fate. She is not content to dwell in the cloistered realm of women's work and she pays a heavy price for her rebellion. She is the artist, as Tennyson said, caught between reflection and reality—at the moment when love releases her from shadows into substance. I believe that Augustus imagined this figure as his sister-in-law finally released from the spell of madness, and that he designed the window as a tribute to her.

"I believe that Augustus Penrose was also thinking about the generations of young women who would sit beneath this window. And so we must ask what her message is to us. I believe that the Lady is the student waking up from the cloistered world of the academy into the demands of the real world. In other words, she is you and me."

I notice that the room has gone very still. There's no nervous ripple of laughter. The women lean forward in their seats, their pale clothes soaked in the bright colors from the window. Later, they might carp at Christine's unorthodox interpretation of the window, but for now she has their full attention.

"When I look back at my time here at Penrose it is as though I lived in a sealed tower, aloof from the world. Some might say we were too sheltered—that we dwelled in a world of shadows and that for many the strong sunlight of the real world was too much."

Christine raises a hand into a gold beam cast by the sun shining through the Lady's yellow hair and twirls her fingers around as if she were grasping the light. *How in the world,* I wonder, *could she have planned that?*

". . . that like the Lady of Shalott the journey away from here too quickly became a slow drift toward death." Christine unfurls her hand and it's as if she has released the golden light into the room—a dove set free by a master magician. She pauses, allowing the silence to swell. Although there is little doubt that she is talking about herself now, about her own disappointments and failures, I sense that everyone in this room understands what she is saying. For whom of us has life turned out the way we imagined it would when we left here?

"But I don't believe that Augustus Penrose wished us to be afraid of the journey—no matter where it might lead. He wanted us to be ready to look up from our books and away from the shadows—no matter where our awakening would lead us. I believe he conveyed his message in the way he painted the lady's face. Look at her—look at the flush of color that bathes her. It is the reflection of the sun striking her for the first time in her life. She might be bound for death, but in this moment, the moment in which she chooses life over shadow, she is more alive than she has ever been.

"Remember, too, that the window behind her is not a window but the mirror from which the Lady has turned away. In looking through the window she is looking at us, the women of Penrose College assembled here before her. We are her reflection, we are her future. She has broken the spell that enslaves us. It's up to us what we do with that freedom."

Christine has chosen the perfect moment for her conclusion. The glass in the river scene, which was lit up by the sun during the first part of her lecture, is now cool and shadowy. The light has moved through the Lady's yellow hair, down her face and bare throat, and settled into the bodice of her brocaded dress. Every woman here must remember the superstition— one of those silly campus legends women's colleges are famous for—that when the light shone through the lady's dress it was shining through her heart. If you were touched by that red stain you would die young. Christine, standing in front of the window as the setting sun hits the glass, is bathed in the ruby-red light.

About the Author

CAROL GOODMAN is the author of *The Lake of Dead Languages*. Her work has appeared in such journals as *The Greensboro Review*, *Literal Latté*, *The Midwest Quarterly*, and *Other Voices*. After graduating from Vassar College, where she majored in Latin, she taught Latin for several years in Austin, Texas. She then received an M.F.A. in fiction from the New School University. Goodman currently teaches writing in New York City and lives on Long Island.